FORSAKEN IN THE FOREST

A Sheriff Elven Hallie Mystery

DREW STRICKLAND

www.drewstricklandbooks.com

ISBN 978-1-964110-05-9 (hardcover)

ISBN 978-1-964110-06-6 (paperback)

Cover Design by Juan Padrón

For my dad,
thanks for being there to help shape me into the man I am today.
And also passing down the good looks ;)

JOIN MY READER'S LIST

Members of my Reader's List get free books and cool behind the scenes information to go along with them.

They're also always the first to hear about my new books and promotions going on.

To be a part of the Reader's List and get your free book, sign up at:

https://drewstricklandbooks.com/mail-list/

PROLOGUE

Colin Kennison's jaw radiated with heat. He'd just been sucker-punched by Lucas Stinger, the well-known bully around town. Of course, this didn't surprise Colin at all. It only bolstered his reason for being here in the first place.

He was going to teach Lucas a lesson.

Colin rubbed his jaw, having taken a series of steps backward after being hit.

"Hey, he wasn't ready!" Jeremy Smith shouted. He wore a puffy, off-white, down-filled parka that fit the temperature outside, but it made him look like a marshmallow.

They'd met in the forest, which was the usual spot for whenever a planned fight was established. Most of the time, Lucas would just smack kids around at school, or around the community when adults weren't present. But after so much bullying, Colin wanted to make sure there was a time and a place for this.

"Shut up and stay out of it," Lucas spat.

Jeremy quickly did as he was told. Colin didn't care, though. Nobody else had the balls to stand up to Lucas, so he understood the position of the other kids. Lucas was older than everyone else at thirteen years old. Colin was only eleven himself, but he'd shot up like a beanpole over the last year, according to his mother.

But Lucas was still a brute. Most people would have thought he was sixteen on first glance. His shoulders were wide, his arms were thick, and his weight was more than just an average heft. And as Colin could attest, when he threw a punch, it felt like getting hit with a sack of rocks.

But Colin had a plan. One that would stop Lucas from picking on the rest of them. Well, as long as it worked.

Over the last week, he'd convinced some of the other boys to join him in standing up to Lucas. They didn't have to do much of the heavy lifting; no, that was Colin's job. All they had to do was one little thing when Colin gave the signal.

Lucas would never even know what hit him.

It had to work. Because if it didn't, it would only send Lucas on a tear through the community, letting him know that he could get away with anything. He'd become unstoppable. And the rest of the boys would live in fear for as long as he was around.

That's why it *had* to work. And Colin would do everything in his power to make that happen. If the other boys chickened out, he'd still see it through to the end. Even if it meant getting his ass beat into a bloody pulp.

At the very least, nobody could say that Colin didn't have the stones to stand up to Lucas. And maybe Lucas would figure Colin was too much work to keep picking on.

But the other boys would be on their own.

"Come on, Colin!" Stan Miller shouted. "Hit him back!" Stan and Jeremy stood there, the only ones brave enough to say anything.

Lucas glared at them both, standing in front of the rest of the kids. All the others had been too afraid to join in with Colin's plan, but they sure as hell wouldn't have missed the chance to see someone stand up to Lucas. Or maybe they just wanted to see a fight. One ending in someone getting beat up, with no preference for who it was.

Colin stood tall, his chin still aching, but if he didn't steady himself, he knew that Lucas would have an opportunity to give him a good whooping. And then he wouldn't get the chance to enact his plan.

He walked to Lucas, fists up and ready to fight. Lucas sneered, then followed it with a laugh. "Oh, I'm so scared, *Cowwin,*" he said, using a baby voice on Colin's name to taunt him.

Colin gave no shits, though, and kept heading for Lucas, his eyes locked on the tubby brute. Lucas reared back, slow as molasses, then swung at Colin. This time, however, Colin saw it coming and ducked just in time. He popped up around Lucas's arm and took his shot. He landed one right to the side of Lucas's face around his eye socket.

The crowd gasped as Lucas tumbled to the side.

It was the first time anyone had ever hit Lucas back. Lucas held the side of his face, and Colin wondered if he even needed to go with his original plan. Maybe he could just beat the hell out of Lucas right now. After all, nobody had ever seen the kid take a hit before. Was that all it would take? One strategic blow to send Lucas spiraling so he'd lose the fight?

Or maybe Lucas would cry. Be the little bitch that he always accused the other kids of being when he picked on them or beat them up.

Lucas steadied himself and pulled his hand away from his face, studying his palm. There was a large gash along his eye socket, a little blood beginning to trickle down.

Instead of submitting, though, Lucas locked eyes with Colin. He bared his teeth, sucking air in through his teeth so it sounded like a whistle. Colin had never seen that kind of fire in anyone's eyes before.

So much for Lucas backing down after being hit. All it did was ignite something inside the older boy. Something Colin knew immediately would be far too much trouble to stand up to.

It was time for the plan.

"You fuckin' bitch," Lucas spat. "I'm gonna bury you for that."

Colin swallowed at the sight of Lucas charging toward him.

"Shit," he mumbled, not expecting Lucas to be so quick on his feet now.

"Colin, go!" someone shouted.

Colin wasn't sure if it was one of his pals he'd convinced to help him, or just a random kid in the crowd who came to watch the beat-down but got cold feet once it became too real. Whatever the case, Colin took their advice. He spun around and took off running deeper into the forest.

"You little bitch!" Lucas shouted as he chased Colin through the trees. "When I catch you, you're dead!"

Colin didn't doubt it, so he wouldn't be caught. He only had to make it to the other side of the hill. Then he knew that he had Lucas. As long as Trenton was still there and didn't back out of the deal. If that happened, well, then Colin was in for a very painful experience.

But Colin had faith that Trenton would still be there. He was his best friend and had never let him down. Plus, Jeremy and Stan had shown up to support Colin. That told Colin that he wasn't in this alone.

The ground was wet and covered in dead, soggy leaves. Colin's feet kept sloshing through them, but his legs never stopped pumping. He'd come out here enough that he knew to lift his feet high when he ran; otherwise, he risked his foot catching a gnarly tree root and planting himself face-first into the muck. With how angry Lucas was, he couldn't let that happen.

Though, he wished he could see Lucas from the others' point of view. That idiot was bound to trip once or twice, sending him into the mud beneath him. But nobody was on Lucas's ass to threaten him with a beating, so it didn't matter. And if anyone laughed at him for doing so, they risked Lucas's attention and anger directed toward themselves.

Colin stole a glance behind him, and sure enough, he saw Lucas in the distance. Leaves and mud stains covered the front of his shirt. Colin let a half-smile slip across his face, but he kept running. Lucas was still gaining on him. Anger was quite the motivator for him.

And then just ahead, Colin saw the exact spot he was looking for.

It was the top of the hill, but more of a ridge. It wasn't a steep drop like a cliff, but definitely nothing that anyone would want to fall down. There was a thick crop of trees just near the edge that had grown together to create a barrier.

Colin pushed harder, heading uphill, which was slowing him down. He could feel Lucas right on his heels, and Colin didn't dare take another glance or he would surely be caught. And he was so close right now.

He made the final climb and reached the top, running just past the tangle of trees now to his left.

"You stupid asshole," Lucas grunted, taking deep gasps of air from all the running. "Where'd you think you were gonna go?"

Colin turned around, shot a quick smile to the crop of trees, and locked eyes with Lucas. "I came here to teach you a lesson, you little bitch," Colin stated. "You're done bullying me. You're done bullying Jeremy and Stan and Trenton and everyone else in this community. Do you hear me?!" He was yelling now, his confidence high.

Lucas, however, did not seem to care. "That's a lot of talk for someone who's about to lose all his teeth." He was out of breath, but he didn't stop. He started to climb the hill, rage fueling him.

Colin wanted to talk some trash to Lucas, but he was too focused on making sure he didn't slip up and let Lucas get the upper hand. Everything hinged on the next couple of moments. He took a quick look behind him to the angle downhill just behind him, then back to Lucas.

"You ready?" Colin asked. Lucas was only a few feet away now.

Lucas smirked. "Me ready? You sure got your wires crossed on what's about to happen," he said, a stupid grin spreading across his dumb face.

"I wasn't talking to you," Colin said. "Do it, Trenton!"

Colin dove to the side so he didn't get caught in the line of fire.

Lucas spun around, and that's when he saw Trenton. He had

been hiding behind the tangle of trees, right at the edge. Lucas had never seen him, which was entirely the point.

All the kids standing by, watching the fight happen, were now at the bottom of the hill where he and Lucas had run from. They were all going to see it go down, which was what needed to happen. Lucas would get one-upped right in front of the whole community.

Colin watched as Trenton charged a few steps toward Lucas, a huge tree branch in his arms. It was so heavy that Colin was worried his friend wouldn't be able to lift it at first, but Trenton was fueled by the rage of being picked on endlessly over the years by the big brute in front of him. The branch dragged at first, but once Trenton let out a guttural growl that turned into a primal shout, he lifted it up from the ground and swung it at Lucas.

Lucas saw it coming, but he had no time to react.

The branch slammed into Lucas's chest, and his eyes went wide at the impact. Lucas stumbled backward one, two, three steps. It was on the fourth step that he slipped, his foot not finding any ground at all.

And then he went over the edge.

Colin knew he would be fine. He would just get roughed up... hopefully a lot.

Climbing to his feet, Colin rushed to the edge. Trenton did the same, and the rest of the kids ran up the hill, trying to join them so they, too, could see Lucas get his comeuppance.

Colin watched the bully tumble down, rolling and catching random twigs and stones as he went. It was steep, so Lucas wouldn't be able to stop, and soon enough, he'd come to the end. The rest of the kids caught up and peered over.

Everyone gasped when they saw Lucas, and then they erupted into laughter.

Colin's plan had worked, and they'd taken down the bully. He wasn't sure how Lucas would take it, but they all now knew that if they banded together, they could stop him. And now Lucas knew that they *would* stop him.

Eventually, Lucas's roll slowed down, and he finally came to a stop once he reached the bottom where the ground leveled off. He slid right into a pile of wet leaves and other mystery muck of the moist forest. Colin could practically smell it.

"Is he dead?" Trenton asked nervously.

At first, Colin's heart sank when he saw Lucas's still form, and he wondered if they'd gone too far. But when Lucas let out a long groan, he was put to ease.

The bully at the bottom of the hill tried to raise himself. Colin could see blood on his face, but no wound. He'd taken the beating that nature had dealt him, which was probably a lot softer than the one Lucas had planned to give Colin that day.

The kids continued to watch and laugh at Lucas's newfound misfortune.

Once Lucas got to his hands and knees, almost ready to climb to his feet, he froze where he was. Colin could see Lucas studying something carefully in the leaves. And then he fell over, scrambling to get away from whatever it was.

"Colin! Colin!" Lucas screamed, but his tone wasn't seeking revenge or retribution. No, it was filled with fear. He was screaming for help. "Colin, get me out of here!"

In Lucas's scramblings, erratic and sloppy, he'd kicked a mess of leaves away from what he was screaming about. He slid and fell back down, right on top of it again. His screams reached a new peak when he rolled on top of it and tried to get away, but instead, the thing somehow got caught on him, clinging to his wet clothing, and rolled with him.

But even from where Colin and the other kids stood, way up on the hill, it was obvious what Lucas was screaming about.

He'd fallen right on top of a body. That of a person, and not freshly dead. No, this body had been torn up. By animals or something worse.

Everyone saw it, and everyone screamed before running off, leaving Lucas to fend for himself.

Bear Colter grimaced as he looked down at the body half in the muck that had gathered at the bottom of the hill. It stank to high hell, but more from nature than the body itself. Stagnant water, mud, leaves, and other bacteria had gathered and been undisturbed until the boy had fallen into it.

The boy, Lucas, sat crying in the distance, holding an ice pack against his head with a blanket wrapped around his shoulders. He fought against the shivers from the water soaking into his clothing and the temperatures quickly dropping. They hadn't gotten so much as a word from him other than something about the whispers he'd heard through the trees.

The whispers... that was the problem with the community. They were mostly just things the kids spread around. That was under-standable, for kids to spread tales. But the adults? Some of them believed in the old legends. Bear didn't buy into that junk, but he'd be lying if there wasn't just a little part scratching at the back of his head, like the old buried memories of his youth were trying to convince him that those things were real. That *this* was real.

Cora McCreary comforted Lucas, rubbing his back after Bear had been alerted to the body. Bear was good at a lot of things, but comforting children wasn't on that list. A woman in her sixties was much better suited for that. Having no children of her own, Cora generally acted as the town mother. Bear was grateful for her being here now.

"That's Shayla Vaughn, ain't it?" Roy asked.

Bear looked at the man next to him wearing his red flannel jacket, which was his usual garb. It didn't matter what the weather was, Roy wore it. He had a smudge of dirt on his face from hiking out here with the rest of them.

Bear nodded. "Yup," he said. "Hard to tell with all the... well, you know, but I'm pretty sure it's her."

The body had been torn apart by animals, clearly. But other than being ripped up, all the main parts were there, so far as they could tell.

"How do you think Maybelle is gonna take it?" Roy asked.

Bear scoffed. "How the hell do you think an aunt is gonna take hearing that her niece was found murdered in the woods?"

"Murdered?" Roy echoed. "Killed, sure. But these are animals we're dealing with. Unless, of course, you buy into the superstitions."

Bear shook his head. "And how do you think she got out here in the first place? And what about the other girls who've gone missing along with her? Think a bear or a pack of wild boars took all three of them out? Doesn't add up."

Roy turned to Bear, and he knew immediately they were going to be at opposite ends of this thing. They generally were about a lot of things, but Bear still trusted Roy. He wanted the best for the community, just like himself.

Still, he was well in over his head on this one. And if he was right, then so was Roy.

"Bear, you down there?" a voice shouted from up the hill that Lucas had rolled down.

Both Roy and Bear looked up. "That you, Benson?" Bear asked.

"Yep, and I brought help," Benson said.

Bear watched two people walk around the edge and slowly make their way down, though not the same way Lucas had. They opted for the less intensive way, which looped around and down from the right.

"Benson? And who the hell is with him?" Roy asked. "Nobody else is gonna know better than us on this one." Roy gave it a minute, and then his face dropped into a scowl. "You didn't, did you?"

Bear shrugged. "We just found Lila's best friend torn up. His sister is still missing, so I had to give him something to do while we talked. Besides, a fresh set of eyes would help. This is above our pay grade."

Roy stepped into Bear's face so close, the apple moonshine on his breath stung Bear's nose. "We don't open up to outsiders. It's bad enough she's here in town. Now we gotta be bringing her into our affairs," he growled.

Roy spun around, but was immediately met by Benson, who looked like a lost puppy, along with the woman Roy referred to as *an outsider*.

Roy ignored Benson and stepped in front of the woman. "What the hell do you think you're doing here?"

"From what it looks like, doing what you can't," Madds answered, standing her ground. "Now, let me see the girl."

CHAPTER ONE

THE AIR IN THE ROOM WAS TENSE AS ELVEN HELD HIS GUN, THE barrel pointed in the direction of the bathroom, right where Madds stood. He was still trying to process everything. He was still feeling a slight buzz from the alcohol he'd just drank at Martin's bar, having left to let Zane and the others celebrate his win, and Elven's loss.

But that wasn't on Elven's mind anymore.

That buzz was quickly fading, now though. No matter the amount of booze that was pumping through his veins, he was sobering up real quick. Being ambushed by the woman he had fallen for, only to be stabbed in the back, metaphorically, and shot in the gut, literally, before she ran off so that he thought he'd never see her again, and now breaking into his motel room, had a way of doing that.

His head was spinning at the sight. Or maybe he wasn't as sober as he thought he was. Either way, Madds was here, and she was asking for his help.

"So are you gonna lower the gun, or are you gonna shoot me?" Madds asked. She sounded like she was trying to be lighthearted with it, but her words held a clear tinge of worry. Part of him didn't want her to worry about anything like that from him, but the other part wanted her to stew in it. His emotions were all over the place, and he couldn't pick a lane.

But Elven had to admire the audacity. And, possibly, the arrogance.

"I haven't decided yet," he finally said. He clearly wasn't going to shoot her unprompted, but he wasn't going to take the risk right now. So he kept holding the gun.

Madds sighed, her shoulders slumping as she did. "To be clear, it was an accident when I shot you, you know that, right? I was spiraling at the time and was angry with Hollis for everything. And then you just—"

"Madds, I was there," Elven said. "I don't need a play-by-play of how it went down."

"I wouldn't be here if I didn't think it was my only option."

"I'm not sure if that's a good thing, Madds," he said. "Don't feel guilty for what you did? Don't want to make amends? Just want to be on the run the rest of your life? You're far from the person I ever thought you were."

Madds winced, and again, part of him enjoyed it. But he couldn't help but remember the person he believed her to be, and that hurt him.

"You don't have to tell me what a shit person I am. I already know that," she said. "Even so, I know you're the man I believe you to be. I just hope that the pain I put you through isn't going to blind you from being that person still."

Elven wasn't sure what to say to that. He studied her face. Her cheeks were more gaunt, her hair was shorter, and her flannel shirt was a far cry from her usual style. He immediately wondered where she'd been hiding out, because he knew it wasn't anywhere in town.

"I searched everywhere for you once I got out of the hospital," he finally said.

"I can tell," she said, motioning over his shoulder with her chin. He still had the pictures and places plastered all over the wall. He had been about to pull them all down, giving up the search and letting go of Madds, before she came right back into his life. "But you looked everywhere in town. You never checked the hills."

"That's where you've been?" he asked.

She nodded. "A place called Old Knuckle. It's—"

"I know the gist of the area," he said. "I'm surprised they didn't run you out of there. They don't generally react well to strangers hanging out. Not sure how you managed that."

"At one point, Hollis had done—"

"I don't really care," Elven cut her off. It was true. However she'd found herself there, and somehow been accepted, didn't matter. She was here now. The people in Old Knuckle weren't his problem.

"That's fine, but it's also why I'm here," she said. "Like I said, I need your help. Some girls have gone missing, and now one of them has turned up dead."

"That sounds like a job for the sheriff. And like you said, I ain't him anymore," Elven said.

"That's the point," she said, taking a step toward Elven, seeming to no longer care about the gun. He knew he wasn't going to shoot her, and so did she. But he still held it up as he listened. "Nobody there will trust someone with a badge."

"Oh, so now I'm supposed to go all vigilante up in the hills? Just because I don't hold a badge anymore doesn't mean I don't still abide by the law."

"You did it once before," she shot back. "In Monacan."

Elven bit his lip for a moment. "That was different," he admitted, remembering how Madds had been in trouble. It was the start of their romantic relationship, but Elven didn't know at the time that it was also the beginning of his heartbreak.

"Elven, I can't do this alone," she said. "Most of these people don't even think that the girl was murdered. They think it was a wild animal."

"Maybe it was," Elven said.

Madds shook her head. "It isn't. But not everyone will believe me."

"And they'll believe me?"

"I've got a few people in my corner. Some who are desperate enough to allow the help of an outsider like me, and like you."

"If they are working with you, then why seek me out?"

"Because I'm at a dead end," she said. "You're better at this than I am."

Elven couldn't help but let out a small laugh. "I don't know about that."

"What happened to the cocky, borderline arrogant Elven Hallie that I know?"

"He had a mole on his team who he got close to, and was subsequently stabbed in the back by her," he said.

That shut Madds right up. She looked like she was sucking on a lemon, the way her mouth puckered inward. But it wasn't enough to keep her that way.

"I'm sorry, Elven," she said. "I really am. But I'm here, practically begging for you to help me on this."

Elven watched her closely, knowing she meant every word she said. But he also meant what he said. He still wanted to uphold the law. He may have bent rules in the past, maybe even broken some, but this was different.

"Okay," Elven said. "Put your hands out so I can search you."

Madds rolled her eyes. "I'm not armed, but whatever it takes." She put her arms out.

Elven went to her and gave her a quick pat down, careful not to take any deep breaths and be reminded of how things used to be. He didn't want his judgment to be any more clouded than it already was. Once he was satisfied, he put his gun back in the holster.

Madds smiled at the sight. "Good, now can—"

"You're under citizen's arrest," Elven said, grabbing her arms and pulling them behind her back.

"What?" Madds demanded. "Elven you can't be serious. These girls—"

"Will get the help they need when I tell Zane Rhodes, the new sheriff, what is going on," Elven said. He pulled out a set of cuffs that he'd kept from the station and slapped them on her wrists. Only the badge was the requirement to hand over, after all.

"Elven, you're making a mistake," she said.

"Yeah, well, it wouldn't be the first one," he said. "Let's go."

He opened up the door and followed Madds out of the motel room.

CHAPTER TWO

"I came to you because I trusted you," Madds spat, not trying to hide her anger.

Elven closed the door behind him, not bothering to lock it. He didn't want to turn around and risk her taking off. She had a history of running, after all.

"Yeah, well, I guess you know how it feels now," he said. He kept a hand on her shoulder and guided her forward gently. The air was cold and crisp, but he'd warm up once they made it into his truck.

Madds growled out of frustration. But Elven knew she had no other play at this point, so she could vent all she wanted.

It was only two steps out of the door before Elven felt the familiar shape of a barrel pressed against the back of his head. He froze in his steps.

"Let her go," a voice said from behind him. Elven didn't recognize the voice, but it was a male and possibly younger. Maybe early twenties at most.

Elven didn't let go of Madds. "I don't know who—"

The barrel shifted, but it was followed by the hammer being pulled back. "I said, let her go," the voice said.

"Benson, just put the gun down and get out of here," Madds pleaded.

"You know I ain't gonna do that," Benson said. "You said this asshole was gonna help, but it doesn't look like that's happening."

Elven chanced a move and slowly turned his head so he could see who this *Benson* was holding the gun against his head. Elven was right, he was young. He had curly brown hair that covered his forehead and acne on his face. Early twenties seemed too old. Elven figured he was eighteen, if he was even an adult.

Benson shoved the gun harder at Elven's head. "I said—"

"Son, I don't know what this is, but you don't want to do this," Elven said, trying to reason with the kid.

"I know, but here we are, so let her go."

"Can't do that," Elven said defiantly.

"Elven, just listen to him," Madds said. He could hear the desperation in her voice matching that of Benson's.

"Mister, this bullet ain't meant for you, but if you don't let her go, it will be yours," Benson said. "She's the only one right now that's been doing anything to help me. So I trust her when she tells me that you're my best bet to find my sister. So if you're trying to take away my only hope of finding her, then you're just another roadblock to deal with. Now, let her go."

Elven lifted his hand from Madds's shoulder and held it in the air. "Alright, you got it," Elven said. He believed Benson and wasn't going to push the issue.

"Now uncuff her," he said.

Elven sighed, moving his hand down.

"Slowly. You go for that gun on your hip, and it'll be the last thing you do."

"I don't doubt it," Elven said, slowly moving his hand to his pocket and pulling out the key to the handcuffs. He unlocked the cuffs and took them off Madds's wrists. She took a few steps away from Elven, rubbing at her wrists.

"Now, show me your hands," Benson said.

Elven lifted them both, his elbows bent and palms forward. He slowly turned around to stand face to face with Benson.

"Elven, I'm sorry," Madds said.

Elven shot her a look that said more than words would, but suffice it to say, he wasn't thrilled. "Alright, Benson, what's the plan now?" Elven asked.

"Now the three of us are gonna get into my truck and head to Old Knuckle," Benson said. "I ain't gonna hurt you. I just want your help to find my sister. But if you need some inspiration to do it, then I'll hold this gun on you the whole way."

Elven sized Benson up. He believed the kid when he said he didn't want to hurt him, but he also believed that he'd do whatever it took to get what he needed, which also meant shooting Elven right here in front of his motel room. But this kid was scared and desperate, not some criminal mastermind.

It wasn't worth fighting the kid and risking a stray bullet. Elven didn't want to hurt the kid any more than the kid wanted to hurt Elven.

"Might as well see where this goes," Elven said, giving Madds one more incredulous look before heading down the steps toward the beat-up pickup truck Benson guided him to.

CHAPTER THREE

ELVEN APPROACHED THE PASSENGER SIDE OF THE OLD, BEAT-UP Ford Bronco, as instructed by Benson. He would have been more impressed with the vehicle if it had been taken care of better. There were dings all over, and the letters stating the make had all fallen off except for the F. Still, he knew it would fetch a pretty penny to the right buyer in whatever condition it was. But being that the kid was from Old Knuckle, Elven was sure he had no idea what he was actually sitting on.

"Get in," Benson said.

"I need to make a phone call first," Elven said.

Benson scoffed. "Like hell you do. I may be young, but I ain't no idiot."

"The jury's still out on that one," Elven shot back. "But you're gonna let me make that call, or I won't get in."

Benson shook the gun in Elven's face for added effect. "You know what happens if you don't," he threatened.

Elven said, motioning his eyes down to the gun still in his holster. "For being such a mastermind here, you must have missed kidnapping 101 where they tell you to take their weapon," he said. "So now, if you don't let me make this call, I'll draw on you, and one of us will surely regret it. Whether that's me or you depends on how likely you are to pull that trigger on a man who did nothing to you."

Benson swallowed hard, and Elven could tell that the kid knew he was in way over his head at this point. Benson's hand shook, and Elven knew all he had to do was grab it, shove it, and twist. He'd have the gun out of Benson's hand before the boy could do anything; he wouldn't even need to fire his own weapon.

Elven slowly let his hand drift down to his own revolver. Benson wasn't even going to see it coming. All Elven had to do was—

Elven was shoved against the car and felt a hand against his side, pulling the revolver off his hip. In his intense focus on the kid, Elven hadn't seen Madds walk around the Bronco and come up behind him. She shoved her hand into his pocket, yanking his phone from it.

"Guess we're past the wining and dining part of this?" Elven asked, trying to cover up his bruised ego from letting her get the drop on him.

She pulled away and held the gun in her hand, but not by the grip. She was not trying to come off as threatening. "Now, you boys can stop comparing dicks? I'll let you make the call, Elven, but no sheriff, no Tank, no Johnny, no Meredith."

"Fine," he said. "I need to call my mom, anyway."

"He ain't making a call," Benson insisted.

Madds scrunched her brow, and Elven could tell nobody was happy about whatever this little arrangement was. Finally, he decided to let them off the hook. "Yeti is at my mother's house. If I don't come pick him up this morning, she's gonna be asking a lot of questions."

"Victoria is watching Yeti?" Madds asked in disbelief.

"Yes, she is," Elven said, getting defensive. "If you weren't busy stabbing all your friends in the back, you'd know that she has actually been very helpful over the last couple of months."

Madds didn't respond to the dig. Instead, she looked to Benson. "You don't want that kind of heat," she warned the boy. "Elven's mother will have everyone out here looking for him. And I do mean everyone."

"Mothers," Elven said with a shrug.

"Wouldn't know," Benson replied. "My sister took care of me."

Elven pursed his lips, understanding now how much was on the line for the kid. "What do you say, then?"

"Fine," Benson said. "But we'll do it on the road. That way, you're less likely to try something."

Elven wasn't going to argue that point. He just wanted to make sure that Yeti was taken care of, and that his mother didn't get too worried.

"Now get in." Benson motioned to the vehicle with his gun.

Elven opened the Bronco door, its hinges creaking loudly, and climbed in. It only had two doors, but there was no roof covering the back of the vehicle, so instead of Benson needing to fold the seat down and climb behind Elven, he just hopped over the side and plopped into the back seat. Madds took the driver's seat. Elven doubted she would have agreed to hold a gun on him.

"Cuff yourself to the door with both hands," Benson said.

"Are you kidding me?" Elven groaned.

Benson shoved the gun toward Elven. "Do I look like I'm kidding you?"

Elven sighed. "How am I gonna make my call?"

"If you're cuffed, I won't have to hold the gun anymore, and I can hold the phone to your ear," Benson said. "Now who's the idiot?"

He seemed to be pretty proud of that one, and Elven couldn't argue with it.

Elven did as he was told, cuffing himself to the inner door handle. When he was done, he held his hands open to show he'd complied. That seemed to be good enough for Benson to put his gun away. Madds held the phone to Elven's face to unlock it and handed it to Benson.

She fired up the vehicle and took the highway, letting Benson find Victoria's contact information. He seemed to do alright, because he was putting the phone against Elven's ear soon enough.

"Elven?" Victoria asked, her voice groggy like he'd just woken her up. That's when he remembered that it was the middle of the night, and not everyone was being ambushed or kidnapped right now. "Is everything alright?"

"Yeah," he said, letting out a sigh. "Sorry for calling so late, Mom."

"It's okay," she said. "My Ambien hasn't hit yet."

"You gonna remember this?"

"Not if you don't hurry."

"Right. Something came up, and I need you to watch Yeti a little longer," he said.

Madds jerked the wheel, making a turn quickly. She clearly wasn't worried about being caught for speeding. Zane was too busy celebrating, so that risk was almost zero to begin with.

The wind picked up from the speed, and Elven shivered. Benson didn't seem bothered by it at all.

"Are you driving?" Victoria asked.

"Yeah," he lied. "So can you do that for me?"

"I mean, I wasn't expecting this," she said, "but I think I can manage. You're just really putting me out here."

But Elven could hear the smile on her face. She was glad to be watching the dog, but he let her have the moment.

"I really appreciate this," he said. "I know Yeti is in good hands."

"Of course he is," she said. "I did raise you, and look at how that worked out."

Elven smiled.

"So, what's the big emergency you have to help with?"

Another win for Victoria and her observational skills. "I didn't say I was helping—"

"I know that tone, and I know the type of man you are. Go ahead and keep your secrets, though," she said. "But Elven, you know you're not the sheriff anymore, right? You don't need to be picking up and running off to help with whatever is going on."

"This one I didn't really have a choice with," he said. "But thanks, Mom. I love—"

The phone cut out and beeped, letting him know that the call had been dropped. He pulled his head away and saw there was no service.

"Hit the dead zone," Benson said.

"Guess we're all squared away," Elven said, knowing that where they were headed, there wouldn't be any more chances for phone calls.

CHAPTER FOUR

THE DRIVE OUT OF DUPRAY AND UP DEEPER INTO THE HILLS HAD been quiet. Benson must have been feeling a bit chillier because he sat with his arms wrapped around his body in the back seat. But he never voiced a complaint or even let out a shiver.

Elven, on the other hand, was far colder than he'd like to admit. If he knew they were going to be on this expedition when he left the motel room, he might have thought to put something a little warmer on. On top of that, he didn't know there would be no top to the vehicle. Not his ideal choice in the middle of winter. The only thing that was saving them right now was the fact that it hadn't snowed yet. Of course, he tried to keep those thoughts out of his mind so as not to jinx himself.

At one point, the wind had picked up so much that Madds finally had enough and put her hair in a bun so it didn't fly around her face. Elven caught himself watching her as she did so, but quickly shoved any emotion, or whatever he was feeling, out of his head. It was becoming far easier to replace any sentiment he felt for her with anger. It kept him safe, and it kept him clear.

The road had changed from paved to gravel, then gravel to dirt, then dirt to overgrown, and finally to what looked like hardly anything other than some tire tracks through the forest. He didn't make it out to Old Knuckle much. Well, really, *ever*. But that's the way everyone liked it. The townsfolk, if anyone could call them that, kept out of the main areas of Dupray for the most part. And Dupray kept out of their business.

There was an understanding, but there was also a bias. The people in the hills didn't like outsiders coming through, and everyone knew it. It was more than just being met with side eyes and rude attitudes. It could get dangerous for people to come through when they weren't wanted. Every town had its secrets, and Old Knuckle was no different. The difference was, Old Knuckle was the type of town that seemed to do anything to prevent those secrets from getting out.

Eventually, they came to a point in the road that tapered so narrow, Elven thought the side view mirrors would hit the trees and break right off. But Madds slowed the drive to a creep and managed to make it through without a scratch. That's when the first building on the trail showed up. It was a small shack of a building with an American flag out front, and a sign that read "US POST OFFICE."

And that's where the road ended. There were no other parts of the town in sight.

"You live here?" Elven asked Madds, lifting an eyebrow.

Madds drove around the side of the shack, where a small clearing through the trees broke open, revealing far more vehicles than the solo shack would suggest. She found an empty spot and put the vehicle in park. "Not here," she said.

"Can't take vehicles the rest of the way," Benson added before climbing over the side of the Bronco and landing on the ground. "Come on."

Elven opened the door, but didn't step out. Instead, he just held his hands open while leaning so the door could open further. "Wish I could, but seems I'm a little stuck," he said sarcastically. He still wasn't happy about his current kidnapping situation.

"Oh, right," Benson said.

Madds came around the side of the Bronco and unlocked the cuffs, letting Elven rub his wrists where they now felt exposed. "I am sorry about this," Madds said.

"But it's not keeping you from doing it," Elven retorted, not caring how *sorry* she said she was.

"This way," Benson commanded, waving for them to join him.

Elven didn't feel inspired to comply, which Benson must have sensed. The kid pulled the gun and waved it around as if everyone had forgotten he had it.

"I ain't keen on making a hike uphill in this weather," Elven said.

"Good thing you won't have to, then," Benson said. "The ATVs are right up here."

Elven groaned. "I ain't letting you cuff me to one of those things. We end up flipping it in those woods, and I'm as good as dead."

"He's not wrong," Madds pointed out.

Benson nodded, his lips a thin line while he considered what to do. "Okay, then you drive while he holds on," Benson said to Madds. "You said he won't hurt you, right? And if he tries something, I'll be right behind. See? We have solutions."

He smiled and motioned to keep walking to the other side of the post office building.

Elven did as he was asked—or maybe it was told at this point. And right around the other side was where he saw a couple of ATVs sitting. Elven wondered how many times the vehicles in the parking lot, if this patch of earth could be called that, had been used. Or if they just sat, rusting away. Not a ton of people came down to Dupray proper from the villages in the hills.

Madds hopped on the faded green 4-wheeler while Benson took the blue one. Madds patted the seat behind her. Elven hesitated, but finally got in behind her. He tried to keep his distance, but once he had to wrap his arms around her and squeeze tight, it was a little hard to do that. He caught the scent of her hair briefly as she shook her head, whipping a few loose strands just under his nose.

The moment was short-lived, though, as she fired up the vehicle and took off without a word. Her scent quickly rushed away as the wind picked up from their ride. Something Elven was grateful for. He gave a quick glance behind him and saw Benson right there, goggles over his eyes and a grin on his face. Elven didn't see the gun in the kid's hand, but at this point, getting off this ATV would be far more dangerous than it was worth. And even then, he'd still have to deal with the gun.

For now, he was stuck on this ride to Old Knuckle. What happened then, well, that was anyone's guess at this point. But if they thought he was going to just go along with this plan the whole time, they had another thing coming. Elven would just have to wait for the right moment.

After a brief ride through the trees on a well-worn path, the actual town came into view. It wasn't much to look at. In fact, it was only a few trailers they passed by. The first ones looked old and outdated. Elven spotted a porch that needed some work, with an elderly man sitting out front. In front of the trailer, a pair of head-stones told him that this man's family was buried right there on the property. It didn't surprise Elven—he'd seen it plenty of times in various small areas in the hills—but it wasn't anything he would see in Dupray on the regular.

There were a number of different trailers and even some old RVs that looked to have been here before he was even born. The tires weren't just flat, but completely rotted away. They must have had a way to get them up here when the community was formed. Back then, the roads more than likely weren't as overgrown as they were now.

At some point, it seemed they had reached the center of town. At least, he figured it was from the cluster of buildings and the amount of people who gathered there. But even though it might have been the most populated spot of Old Knuckle, it made downtown Dupray look like New York City.

Madds found an empty area to park the ATV, alongside what looked like the largest building he'd seen in Old Knuckle so far. It was nothing to write home about, that was for sure, but it was wide enough that it looked like it could hold a decent amount of people. Maybe that was where the people here held any sort of meeting or town hall.

Benson pulled up next to her, and they both turned off the engines at the same time. Elven climbed off, ready to get on two feet and get some distance from Madds.

"So this is where you've been living?" Elven asked.

Madds nodded. "More or less."

"And I thought Dupray was a big adjustment for you."

When Elven turned around, he saw that a lot of the town had come to see what the hubbub was about, even though it was so early in the morning, the sun barely a haze over the horizon. All eyes were on them, and they didn't look too happy. He had a feeling that it was because of his presence more than anyone else's.

It was clear that while Madds and Benson wanted his help, nobody else in town did.

CHAPTER FIVE

BENSON LED THEM TO A SMALL, SINGLE-WIDE TRAILER THAT WAS littered with junk out front. He navigated a path through the rubble like he'd done it a thousand times before. Just at the base of the steps, Elven could see two tombstones at the edge of the property, though there was no fence line to tell him for sure. He didn't get a good look, but if this was Benson's place, he wondered if those graves belonged to his parents.

Benson held the screen door open for both Madds and Elven. It smacked and rattled against the frame once everyone was inside. Benson didn't bother to close the main door. Upon entering, Elven figured that was so he could air out the place.

From Elven's vantage point, he could see just about the entire place in one twirl. He'd been in many trailers in his time in Dupray, but he wasn't quite sure what to consider this one. Was it a case of depression? Was it a hoarder in the making? Or was Benson just that focused on other things to notice the mess?

Open boxes of cereal littered the counter along with the bowls that housed Benson's morning breakfast, and quite possibly, yesterday's lunch and dinner, too. Cleanup hadn't been big on Benson's priorities, apparently. The rest of the trailer matched the small kitchen Elven had just walked into. A couch sat in the living room with piles of clothes all over. The couch itself looked worse for the wear. Stains from various spills could be spotted between the various laundry piles. What made Elven laugh—on the inside, of course—was the huge bottle of bleach on top of the coffee table in the center of the room. He doubted if it had ever been opened or used.

To the left of the door was the small hallway leading to the bedroom and the bathroom. The small accordion door was half-closed, but Elven could see just enough to tell him that the mess wasn't any better in the bedroom. In fact, it might be worse from what little he could gather. He was surprised the place wasn't teeming with bugs or rodents, though maybe they were just out of sight.

When Elven gave Benson a look, it was clear that the kid didn't notice the filth at all. Maybe this was just the way of life in Old Knuckle, but it was surely sad. Elven felt sorry for the kid. After all, his parents weren't around. Actually, he had said his sister raised him. Elven was just making assumptions about what had actually happened to the kid's parents.

Madds, however, picked up on what Elven was feeling and gave him a nudge. Elven met her eyes, and she motioned toward the small dining table that looked like it had come straight from the '70s, with its vinyl chairs and yellowing hue. She kicked a chair out for him to sit down. He gave it a quick once-over, making sure he wasn't about to sit on some mystery splotch. He wasn't generally a germaphobe, but this setting was far worse than he was used to.

"Show him the pictures," Benson said.

Elven studied the boy as he tensed up, ready to share whatever information he had. Elven kept an eye on that gun, wondering when the right time would be to grab it from him. He still wasn't interested in staying in his current predicament.

Madds pulled out a folder and placed it on the table. She flipped it open to show the image of a young woman. She was dead, dirty, and looked like she'd been through it. At first glance to him, it looked like an animal did it.

"This is Shayla Perkins," Madds said. "She was found a couple weeks ago in the woods."

"She was also one of Lila's best friends," Benson added, leaning into the table like he was hyper-fixated on the conversation.

"Lila is Benson's sister," Madds clarified. "I've tried digging everywhere I can think of, but nobody knows anything."

"And you want me to—" Elven began.

"I want you to find my sister and kill whoever did this to Shayla," Benson said.

Madds sighed. "I want you to see what I'm missing," she said. "I'm hitting a wall, and nobody else here has any ideas."

"And then what happens when I figure it out? You'll just let me go?" Elven asked.

"You have my word," Benson said.

Elven studied the picture for a moment, but it wasn't very long. He saw the teeth marks on the girl's body, the ones that didn't look anything like a person's. And he saw the chunks of flesh that had been pulled from her. Other than that, there were no bullet holes or knife wounds that he could see in the pictures he'd been given.

"Alright. Then, in my professional opinion, it looks like an animal attacked her and killed her," Elven said. "I'm sorry." He stood up from the table, the chair skidding across the linoleum. "Now, should I take one of those ATVs on my own, or you wanna give me a lift?"

Benson grit his teeth, and Elven watched his face go red. He looked to Madds like he expected her to do something. "You said he could solve this," Benson said to her.

"And I just did," Elven said. "Now, you gave me your word that—"

Benson stood up, his gun still gripped in his hand. He raised it up toward Elven. "I said when you find—"

But this time, Elven wasn't having it. He smacked the kid's wrist with one hand and grabbed the gun with the other. Benson struggled, but Elven popped him in the nose once, which caused the kid to release the gun. Elven spun it around and pointed it right at Benson's face.

"Madds, give me my gun," Elven said, staring down Benson, who now held his nose. Blood trickled down over his lips.

"Elven, you aren't going to shoot him," she said. "You're not that man."

He turned to Madds, moving the gun from Benson to her. "Give me my gun." He didn't want to make any more threats. She was right, for the most part, but he wasn't sure he could trust his answer when it came to what he'd do with her. He was still an emotional wreck.

"Elven, I—"

"Mister, you move one inch, and I won't hesitate to put you down right here and now," someone said from outside.

Elven chanced a glance to the side where he could see through the screen door. A large man held a rifle in front of his long beard.

"I mean it," the man said. "You stop pointing that gun at the lady, and don't put it back on Benson, either."

Elven sneered at Madds. "And all this is supposed to make me want to help you?" he asked, but he didn't drop the gun.

"Mister—"

"I heard you," Elven said. "I'm just debating if I want to do it or not."

Elven could hear the rifle rack for added emphasis. "I ain't messing around."

"And neither am I."

"Bear!" Madds shouted. "It's alright, I've got this under control."

"Sure don't look like it!" Bear, the man behind the gun, shouted back.

Madds looked panicked, her eyes shooting left to right like she was trying to figure out what to say to defuse the situation. Benson didn't add much, still holding his nose, but now looking at Elven with pleading eyes.

"Elven, please," Madds said. "I need your help on this one. And I also don't want to see you shot right in front of me in Benson's kitchen!" Her voice was ragged, like she truly meant what she said.

"Wouldn't be the first time," Elven snapped. "Only this time, you're not behind the trigger."

Madds slumped her shoulders. "Fine," she said. "You win. I shot you. I'm a shitty person. I fucked you over, and I deserve all the snarky comments and hatred you can give me. Now, will you just put the gun down?"

Elven shook his head. "That's not what I want, Madds."

She nodded. "Okay, then," she said. "How about this? You give me one full day of looking into this case. If by the end of the day, you still think this was an animal attack and nothing more, you can leave."

"Like hell he can," Benson hissed, his voice sounding more nasally from whatever swelling had already occurred.

Madds glared at Benson. "Keeping him hostage here when he doesn't want to help isn't going to do any good." She turned back to Elven. "And if you do that for me, then I'll go with you back to Dupray."

"Back?" Elven asked.

"So that you can take me to the sheriff," she said. "But if you do see something at the end of the day that tells you this girl was murdered, then you stay and help catch whoever is responsible."

Elven thought a moment, then shot another glance at the man called Bear through the screen door. Madds's deal was a whole lot better than being shot in this filthy kitchen. Finally, he nodded.

"Alright," he said. "But if I do stay because I find something—and that's a big *if*—after everything's all said and done, you still come back with me so I can take you in."

Madds hesitated. He wasn't sure she would agree to it. But he had to admit, if she did, it meant she truly believed this was a case worth looking into.

Finally, she nodded. "Deal," she said.

Elven had her at her word, so one way or another, Madds was

coming back to Dupray and facing her crimes. Of course, that was if her word was worth much of anything at this point. But one thing he did think it was worth, though, was the risk.

Elven lowered the gun and placed it on the table.

CHAPTER SIX

Bear Colter was a large man, which was fitting, considering his name. Unless, of course, it was because he was as hairy as he was large. Still, Elven had a feeling that it wasn't his real name but a nickname. Bear reminded him of Tank in that manner. But Tank was far more clean-cut and rigid, mostly due to his military background. Bear didn't seem that type. He seemed more like he'd learned his life skills from living in the woods.

The four of them sat at the table, Madds having cleared a new space for Bear. He looked comical, sitting there. His size made the small table look like the kiddie table at Thanksgiving. He wore suspenders over his worn, gray shirt. If there was ever a definition of "mountain man," Bear Colter fit it to a T.

Bear stared down Elven for a good minute before finally accepting that he wasn't going to shoot anyone. Elven could tell that the man had a soft spot for Benson, and he wasn't too happy about the bloody nose Elven had dealt the kid. Benson didn't seem too pleased about it, either, but now that Madds had made the deal, the two men seemed to accept Elven's presence.

Though, of course, not exactly with open arms.

"I don't know how you thought this would go, but what am I going to tell everyone else in the community?" Bear asked, mostly looking to Benson for an answer.

"I figured you could smooth it over, like you did with Madds," Benson said, having pulled his hands away from his face. His nose was red and already starting to bruise from the purple hue the edges were taking. He'd cleaned the blood up with a tissue that he'd left sitting at the edge of the table. Elven wondered how long it would take for him to throw it out, or if throwing it out was even an option.

"You think Madds being here is *smoothed out?*" Bear asked, shaking his head in disbelief. "Hell, most of these people are pissed at me for bringing her in on this whole thing. Now what am I gonna tell them I'm doing, walking around with the goddammed sheriff?"

"Former sheriff," Elven corrected.

Bear growled. "It don't matter. What once was will always be."

"Doesn't seem to bother you that Madds here used to be a deputy, and before that, a police officer," Elven said, giving a side glance to Madds, who looked suddenly uncomfortable.

Bear stared at Madds for a moment before he shook his head and looked back to Elven. "We have to make allowances where we can," he said.

"But the former sheriff is where you draw the line?" Elven asked.

Bear slowly shook his head. "Being a Hallie is where I draw the line," he said. "And for you, that might be a good thing. Your name alone is bound to get you shot in a place like Old Knuckle."

Elven sighed. It was all coming back to him being a Hallie. He was never going to be able to outlive that one, was he?

"Guess I can't argue that one," Elven said. "I'll just see myself out, then."

"Elven, sit," Madds said, slamming her hand on the table. She turned to Bear. "You need his help. I can't figure this out on my own, and none of the people in your community have an eye like Elven."

Bear crossed his arms. "That's if this is even a case to be figured out," he said. "All we're doing is pissin' a whole bunch of people off, digging in places nobody wants us to dig."

"And why don't they want you to dig?" Elven asked.

Bear sneered. "Not because of these girls," he said. "But they all like to keep to themselves. So as far as I can tell, we're just stirring up a bunch of shit that should stay where it's at."

"But you don't truly believe that, do you?" Elven asked. He saw something in Bear. If the man allowed Madds to be here and look into things, he must really think there's a case here.

Bear turned his chin up, but didn't say a word. Madds sighed. "You told me that Hollis Starcher used to come through here, is that right?" she asked.

Bear groaned, still not talking, but his attention was triggered at the mention of Hollis.

"Fine, don't say anything," Madds said. "Your loyalty to the man is something to admire."

"I ain't got any loyalty to that man, you hear me?" Bear barked, slamming his fist on the table. Madds had clearly struck a nerve. "Tore this place up, running drugs through here. He caused a lot of heartache for some of the families here. Ain't never been the same since."

"How so?" Elven asked.

Bear glanced his way, debating on telling him, but he relented. "He paid a few people, not just to keep quiet, but to cook for him. Yeah, we got a few dollars running through here, and at first, some people benefited.

"But what he didn't tell them was how dangerous it was," he continued. "Three of them boys did something wrong, and their trailer blew up right in the middle of the day. Took out their neighbor's place, leaving Missus Richardson without a grandson because he was playing right next to the door." Bear was tough, but the story was triggering something in him because his face was turning red. Not from anger, from sadness. "You ever seen a kid burned up, still moving 'cause he wasn't dead yet? That shit fucks with a man." He pointed to his head when he said it.

"What happened after that?" Elven asked. "With Hollis, I mean."

"He came back, trying to get some new people here to work for him. Nobody in their right mind wanted to, but there were a couple of nibbles. Roy Leven and I put that shit to bed before it could take off and start again," he said. "Hollis was none too happy with us, but we told him to stay the hell out of Old Knuckle."

"And I bet that went over well," Elven quipped.

"He sent some people up here," Bear said. "People died, but in the end, we agreed to stay out of his business if he wanted to find any nearby communities around here, as long as he kept his paws off the good people in Old Knuckle."

Elven nodded. "I'm sorry to hear about all that."

"I heard he made some deals with some folk, taking over that old cabin that Bohannon owned. If you can call it a cabin—that thing was a glorified shack. But those people didn't seem bothered by him being there after Bohannon passed," Bear said. "I may have agreed to it, trying to save this community, but Hollis can burn in hell for doing what he did here."

"Well, it ain't hell, but I can tell you that he ain't as comfortable as he used to be," Elven said. "He's sitting in prison right now, awaiting his trial. One that is a sure thing."

Elven made sure not to mention anything about Madds and her relationship with Hollis. He figured she didn't say anything about it when they took her in, and if he brought it up, he couldn't be sure that Bear wouldn't turn around and take his frustration out on her right now.

Bear eyed him up and down, his brows scrunched together as he did. Elven wasn't sure if he was trying to figure out if he was lying or confused by the statement in general. But finally, he gave a nod. "Good," he said. "I'm surprised you were able to touch him. He keeps a tight leash on his people, and an even tighter lid on his operation."

"Don't I know it," Elven said. "But he's where he belongs now."

"Then maybe what Madds says about you isn't all wrong," Bear admitted.

Elven lifted an eyebrow. "Depends on what she's saying."

Bear shrugged. "She's been trying to tell me that a Hallie is actually good for something. Not trying to milk the people for everything they're worth, but instead trying to make things better for them. And that you've done a lot of good, and are better at investigating than anyone else she's met."

Elven glanced at Madds, who didn't look his way. He cracked a small smile. "Is that so?"

"She also says you can be one arrogant son of a bitch," Bear added.

Elven let out a short cackle, and it was Madds's turn to crack a smile.

"But I say if you put Hollis behind bars, then maybe you got some right to be here." Bear sighed and leaned back like he was debating his next move. "If Benson's in, and you're willing to come in and fix this mess, then who am I to say no?"

Benson nodded. "I want to do whatever it takes to find my sister," he said. "If it means working with Elven Hallie, then so be it."

CHAPTER SEVEN

With the crime having been a few weeks back and Shayla Perkins's body already being buried, Elven figured it was best to start with speaking to the girl's family first. Madds had already done a lot of interviewing and other investigating before he'd gotten here, but it was time for a fresh set of eyes and ears. Madds was a very capable cop, but he couldn't assume she hadn't overlooked something.

If she disagreed, well, she wouldn't be asking Elven for help now, would she?

Besides, Elven was brand-new in town, so he needed to get the lay of everything and everyone. Investigating and using evidence was one thing, but gut instincts were another. That's where Elven excelled.

Bear led the way on his ATV as Benson followed close behind, riding his own. Elven rode on the back of Madds's like before, but this time there was no threat of a gun to make him do so. He just didn't have his own vehicle. Now that his mind was on the actual task at hand, however, he didn't mind riding with Madds.

In some ways, it reminded him of better times when he was a sheriff and she was a deputy with no romantic ties between the two.

Just two officers trying to do good for the community. Of course, that had all been a lie, but at the time, Elven didn't know that.

They zipped through the narrow pathways away from the center of town. He now fully understood why people in Old Knuckle didn't use cars and trucks to get around, because other than the main drag, which was still very tight to get through with a truck, there was no way they could drive regular vehicles to the homes. It was just far easier to get by with one of these smaller ATVs.

Eventually, Bear and Benson both slowed to a crawl, taking a look at the ground ahead. There were some branches that might make their passage difficult, but Benson pointed to the right, and they turned down the path, picking up speed again. The cold air slapped against Elven's face as he and Madds followed behind, trying to keep up with the other two. For a tight-knit community, everything still seemed so spread apart.

Once Madds and Elven finally caught up to them, Benson and Bear were already dismounting off of their rides in front of a trailer. There was a small sign on the door that read "PERKINS." The home was tucked in the trees, but the area was very well-kept. The only things out front were a couple of 4-wheelers they owned, and a couple of dog bowls on the small porch in front of a doggie door cut into the wall.

Benson turned to Elven. "This is Shayla Perkins's place."

"Considering we were headed here, and other clues," Elven said, lifting his eyes to the sign, "I put it together." He didn't bother smiling. He was still a little salty after having a gun pointed at him for so long.

Elven headed past Benson, but Bear stepped in his way. "Take it easy on the kid," he said. "I'm not saying how he approached bringing you here is right, but he's dealing with a lot. Maybe bring out the kid gloves a little more with him."

"Same can be said for me," Elven said, his eyes shooting toward Madds for a brief second. "So maybe I need some of that *kid-glove* treatment. What do you think?"

Bear nodded. "Well, considering you're a grown-ass man, I'd say you need to suck it up," he said. "Besides, I ain't asking you. I'm telling you."

Elven continued to look up at Bear, who was more intimidating than Elven had originally given him credit for. He'd dealt with bigger and scarier men plenty before. But he had to admit, nobody had called him on his bull before in a way that he didn't have much of a retort for. Elven respected people from all over, but he may have misjudged Bear at first glance.

He ran his tongue along the inside of his bottom lip. "I'd say you have a point," Elven said. "I can do that."

"Then you and I might just get along through this thing," Bear said, holding out a hand. Elven shook it firmly.

"Don't get your hopes up. I still don't know if a crime happened," Elven said.

"Come on, I'll make the introduction," Bear said. "I radioed ahead, making sure that Maybelle was home. Sometimes she's out picking wild herbs, and who knows when she'll be back. Said she'll wait 'til after we're done talking, so I don't want to keep her waiting."

Bear headed to the trailer and up the steps to the porch. Benson followed behind.

Madds bumped her shoulder into Elven on her way, but stopped to meet his gaze. "Don't know if I've met anyone other than Meredith who could call you on your bullshit," Madds said with a playful smile.

A little pull on his heartstring made him start to crack his own grin, but he quickly shoved it away when he caught himself.

"The less we talk, the more time I have to decide if there's anything worth investigating," was all Elven said.

CHAPTER EIGHT

Maybelle Perkins was far older than Elven had expected, but he was under the impression that she was Shayla's aunt, so more her mother's age. As it turned out, she was actually Shayla's great-aunt. Shayla's father lived like a drifter who had come in and out of town various times in the past, but eventually never came back, shortly after Shayla was born. Shayla's mother had expected him to stay and take on responsibilities that any father should shoulder, but he had other ideas.

They'd mostly lost contact with the man, but Maybelle said he was a truck driver, which explained his continued coming and going. She said he had died at some point, but far after he'd left them. She caught wind of it while scanning the various frequencies, hearing of some man being stabbed by a lot lizard for being too rough. This was a decade after he'd disappeared from Old Knuckle for good.

When pressed as to why she thought he was Shayla's father, she shrugged and offered a knowing smile. "Something in the wind just felt like it was him," she said. "Not to mention, the chatter mentioned a scar on his chin that matched Shayla's father's."

Nobody pushed for more information. If they had, they would have come up completely empty because Maybelle had said everything she'd known about the man.

Shayla's mother and Maybelle's niece, however, had stayed in Old Knuckle until the day she died. And that day came when she flipped her ATV and went head over handlebars right into a tree. The ATV had continued rolling on and finished the job the tree had started. That was when Shayla was fourteen years old. Since then, she'd lived with Maybelle, the only remaining member of her family left alive in town.

Maybelle wore a knit hat, her hair down around her ears. While fetching the foursome of visitors some hot tea, she mentioned the hat was gifted to her from her friend Cora, the town seamstress, who had knitted it for her last winter. She sat down on a rocking chair while sipping her own tea, giving a pained smile like she had been thinking of the winter a year back. One when her great-niece was still alive.

"I know that Madds here has already asked a bunch of questions," Elven said. "But—"

"Oh, just go ahead and ask 'em. I don't mind repeating myself. I could talk about Shayla all day long if you let me," Maybelle said. "I'm old and understand how life works. Pain is what it is, but I work through it fine like anyone else."

Elven felt his lip tick upward in a smile, admiring the woman's strength. "Fair enough," he said. "Do you have opinions on what happened to her?"

Maybelle let out a long breath, her lips flapping as she did. "I thought you were gonna ask me about Shayla, not about my speculation as to what happened. Isn't that your job?"

Elven shrugged. "Seems most people think it's an animal attack," he said. "But some think otherwise. Figured if you have an opinion on it, then I could dig into the whys and go from there. But if you'd rather—"

"Oh, no," she said. "I don't mind. Just trying to understand for myself." She adjusted herself in her chair as she gave thought. "To be honest, I'm not sure."

"And why's that?" Elven asked.

"Because she wasn't stupid enough to be in the middle of the woods alone to be caught by something out there to take her down," she said. "And because I don't believe she was alone."

"You think she was with Lila and Sadie?" Benson asked, his voice picking up.

Elven turned around, narrowing his eyes at the kid. Then he glanced to Bear, who picked up on it and gave Elven a nod. Bear leaned over to whisper something to Benson, who looked down.

"Sorry, didn't mean to interrupt," Benson mumbled.

"He ain't wrong," Maybelle said. "Those three girls did everything together. Besties, or whatever they call it these days. I can't keep up with all that talk. I been through too many generations now."

"So you think all three girls were together when they went missing?" Elven asked.

Maybelle gave a firm nod. "Sure do," she said. "Makes the most sense, too, don't it? Now, the question is why and where they went missing."

"Alright, so what do you think?"

"The only way that it woulda been an animal is if the three of them wanted to skip town and Shayla got cold feet," she said. "Maybe the three of them got so far, and she came wandering back, but they didn't come with her. Though, even that don't seem likely, considering how good those girls were with each other."

"And why would they be skipping town?" Elven asked.

Maybelle swayed her head, holding her palms up. "Whispers," she said. "Those girls had dreams of grandeur. Well, maybe not grandeur, but bigger than Old Knuckle. They talked about what they'd do when they got out of town. Most girls their age do, but most of us wake up and realize that this is home. And ain't nothing out there for us."

"Do you think they were gonna wake up and think that?" Elven asked. "Or do you think they really were trying to leave?"

Maybelle sighed. "I don't know. Coulda been all talk, maybe just dreamin'. Shayla didn't seem the type to leave, but Sadie and Lila? Those two girls may have had it in them to do it."

"Lila wouldn't leave," Benson said, shoving himself into the conversation again, this time unapologetically. "She wouldn't have left without saying anything to me. And if she did, she sure as shit wouldn't have let Shayla come back on her own without making sure she was safe doing so."

"I'm sorry, honey," Maybelle said. "I ain't saying she did or didn't, I'm just—"

"Well, she didn't," Benson said, standing up. "That's what I'm saying." His fists were clenched at his side so tight that his knuckles had gone white.

Bear wrapped his arm around the kid's shoulders. "Come on," Bear said. "Let's take a break. We can come back in a minute."

Benson clenched his teeth a few times, his jaw pulsating as he did. Finally, he turned around and let Bear walk him out. A rush of cold air swept in as the door opened, then closed abruptly.

Maybelle shook her head. "Lila was a good girl, and that Benson ain't a bad kid. He's just had it rough, and now with his sister missing, I know he's struggling." She looked at Elven. "So you think that you can find those girls?"

Elven sighed. He wasn't even sure there was anything about this case, but with two other girls missing, maybe there was. But like Maybelle said, could they just have left town thinking that anything was better than living in Old Knuckle?

"I'm not sure," he admitted. "Right now, I'm just focusing on what might have happened to Shayla first."

Maybelle nodded. "Well, since you're asking me, is it possible she was attacked by an animal? Sure, anything is possible. Just like them rumors about the woods and what lurks out there might be possible, but it ain't probable. The things that had to take place for an animal to attack her and kill her would be making a lot of allowances. And I just think all of that happening to create this situation would have to be a ton of coincidences. And coincidences like that, I just don't believe in."

Elven nodded. "So you're saying you think she was attacked, but not by an animal?"

"That's exactly what I'm saying," she said.

"I'm gonna ask you another question, and I'm sure you know where I'm going with it," Elven said.

Maybelle nodded, showing Elven that she was already ahead of it.

"You have any ideas of who might do that to her?"

This time, Maybelle considered the question for a long time. "That's one question that I don't got a theory about," she said. "If I did, it would mean I don't trust this town. I don't trust my neighbors. And I gotta say, if I start looking at what I consider my community, my family, like that, then I'm not sure how I can keep pushing on here. You get what I'm saying?" Her eyes looked red, like she was holding back tears. It was clear that she didn't want to speculate, but at the same time, she'd already been doing it.

"I do," Elven said. "Thank you for your time."

The door opened again. This time, Benson looked a lot cooler in temperament. "I apologize for how I was acting," the young man said, wringing his hands in front of him. "I'm just worried about my sister."

"Oh, honey, you got nothing to apologize for," Maybelle said. "I pray every night that she turns up safe and sound, along with Sadie, too."

"If we figure anything out, we'll let you know," Madds said, standing with Elven. They ushered themselves to the door, but Maybelle stopped them before they left.

"Oh, honey, did they ever find Shayla's things?" Maybelle asked.

Madds turned. "I thought they had given you all the belongings that were found with her?" she asked. She turned to Bear, who nodded in agreement.

"I got some, but they didn't give me her little doll," she said. "She wouldn't go anywhere without it, though I searched everywhere in the house once you found her. Wasn't here, so she had to have it. She was always futzing with it. A little plastic doll with hair that could be styled up all wild-like."

"We searched the area, but we'll scour again," Bear said. "You got a picture of it?"

Maybelle nodded. She pulled out a framed picture of Shayla holding the little doll just as she'd described. It was a Troll doll, but Elven didn't feel the need to explain that to Maybelle.

"It would be nice to have, if you could find it," Maybelle said.

"I remember seeing Shayla with it whenever she was with Lila," Benson added. "When I was little, I wanted to play with it. But she wouldn't let anyone else hold it, so I didn't push the issue."

"That was her security blanket," Maybelle said.

"We'll do our best," Madds added.

The four of them exited onto Maybelle's porch, Elven closing the door gently behind him.

"Troll doll?" Elven asked.

"It wasn't with her things," Madds explained. "Now, you think—"

"Animals could drag a body, and the elements could hide a small toy like that," Elven cut in. "It doesn't mean anything other than you didn't find it." He wasn't going to give in just yet about something more sinister happening to the girl. There was no evidence that suggested otherwise. Just a nice old woman who had a feeling. That wasn't enough for him.

They all left the woman's porch and headed to the ATVs. Before firing them up, Bear looked to Elven. "Sadie's parents' house isn't too far from here if you wanna speak to them next."

"How far is it where you found Shayla?" Elven asked, now curious.

"It's pretty far from here," he said. "We can hit that after we talk—"

Elven shook his head. "Let's go check the scene first. Maybe we can find that doll, and see if there's anything else that may have been missed. I know it's early enough, but I'd like to keep daylight on our side while there."

Bear nodded, then fired up the engine. "Alright, then let's get to it."

CHAPTER NINE

Aﬔﬓ some driving out to the middle of nowhere, which was funny considering Old Knuckle was already in the middle of nowhere, they dismounted from their ATVs. Elven began to survey the scene, but Bear stopped him.

"This ain't the scene," he said. "It's just that the trees are too tight, and there's too many drop-offs for it to be safe to ride through here. We go on foot from here. It ain't too far now."

Bear led the four of them over the moist leaves and dirt. It had been a mild winter so far, with the snowfall not coming yet, but Elven knew it was only a matter of time. Right now, he was grateful that it had only been rain and cold weather. Once the snowfall was here, any investigation would have to wait until after it melted.

Maybe that would have been better for him, though, and he wouldn't have been kidnapped until the spring. He smiled, thinking of how ridiculous this entire situation was. But he was a man of his word, so he'd spend the day looking into it. There would be no short-cuts on this one just because he wanted to get out of here.

Benson kept up speed with Bear, which was fine with Elven. As much as he was furious with Madds, she was also the one he knew best. Even after lying to him about who she was, working with Hollis, stabbing him in the back by muddying his investigations, and making Elven bend his rules when it came to his job, she was still the only one he might be able to lean on while he was up here.

Of course, he hoped that wasn't going to be for long. But for the moment, she was all he had.

"You've been here a while, right?" Elven asked her.

Madds nodded. "Yeah, about as long as I've been gone, anyway. Why?"

"Did you know this girl before she ended up dead?" Elven asked.

"A little," she said. "I mean, I wasn't spending a lot of time with her, but most people here I've met in passing. She was nice to me whenever I was around."

"And how about the other missing girls? Lila and Sadie."

"Same thing for Sadie," Madds said. "I didn't know her well, but she was nice, too. But Lila, I knew a little better than the others."

Elven slowed his walk some, just to make sure that they were out of earshot from the others. Both Bear and Benson didn't seem to notice. "Think they could have just left?" Elven asked.

Madds shrugged. It wasn't that she didn't know, but that it was a possibility. "Lila is a nice girl, but she had things she wanted to do. The things that someone wasn't going to find in Old Knuckle. Shit, Elven, they probably wouldn't have even been found in Dupray. I think she wanted out, that's for sure. I think that's why those girls were nice to me, because they liked me for being an outsider, for being from somewhere they'd never been and only dreamt of. The suburbs of Arizona aren't what I'd call a big city, but to those girls? It was bigger than they'd ever known. I think their brains would explode if they ever went to someplace like New York or Chicago."

Elven smiled. "It's a big change, that's for sure."

"The real question that you should be asking, though, is whether or not Lila would leave Benson here to get out of Old Knuckle," Madds added.

"And what do you think the answer to that is?" Elven asked.

She shook her head. "I truly don't believe so," she said. "He's a good kid. A little green, a little uneducated, but means well. She ended up having to take care of him while she was a teenager, and he's just a few years younger. So not too far off in age, but still, those responsibilities are a lot. She may not be his mother or have the full-on emotions of one, but she still cared for him and did her best. I think she loved him too much to bail like that. If anything, she would have brought him with her."

Elven looked ahead as the two men in front of him started an uphill climb. He and Madds joined in as they hit the bottom of the hill.

"Do you think Benson would leave Old Knuckle? Even if his sister asked him?" Elven asked.

Madds sighed. "He seems to like it here," she said. "It's what he knows, and he's content with it. I don't know if he'd leave."

"I know you like the kid," Elven said. "But maybe that's the question we should really be asking, then."

CHAPTER TEN

The air was colder once they'd climbed down the side of the hill and into the small valley where Shayla's body had been found. Elven had heard the story about the kids fighting and the boy falling right on top of the girl. It sounded like that kid was going to need some sort of therapy, but Elven knew he would never see any of it here.

Then again, because he was a bully, maybe it was the universe's way of teaching the kid a lesson. Elven wasn't one to overly speculate on something like that, though.

He was too focused on the real reason he was there.

He took a deep breath, the cold air stinging the back of his throat as he did. He let out a series of coughs as if he'd just inhaled a foreign object. There was a difference up here in these hills. The air was fresher, not tainted by the factories and mines of the past. Not many people were around to combat Mother Nature like in the towns. Even with driving ATVs around, the pollution was so little. Coupled with the fact that it was higher in elevation, Elven's body wasn't used to this type of clean air.

He rubbed his arms, reminded of his lack of a heavy coat. He would just have to tough it out for the time being until he headed back home at the end of the night. Assuming they found nothing that told him that foul play had occurred, of course.

And right now, nothing was telling him that it had occurred, because he was staring at a whole lot of nothing with the scene in front of him.

It had been weeks, so there wasn't much to make of it. Bear pointed out where the body had been found, at the base of the steep decline. Dead leaves littered the area, along with branches, rocks, and other things that would be seen in the middle of the forest. It was a little muddy, but that was also to be expected.

"There's nothing here that is helpful to support your case," Elven said. "I'm sorry, but I just don't see it."

"Just keep looking around," Madds said. "At the very least, maybe we can find the doll for Maybelle."

Elven agreed, hoping to at least give the old woman some sort of closure on the matter. It wasn't much, but that was something he could do.

"We searched in this area here," Bear said, making a circle in the air like he was pointing to some invisible line. Elven wasn't sure exactly where it began and ended, but it didn't seem too far outside of where Elven could see through the trees. "We need to expand the search to outside of there. Just don't wander too far. I want us to still be within shouting distance for safety. I'm also assuming everyone is armed?"

Elven nodded in agreement. He could see that even though Bear was not law enforcement, the people in the town looked to him as their makeshift sheriff. Or maybe their leader. He wasn't sure what they would call it, but one way or another, Bear had seated himself in a place to take care of the others when they couldn't. It was a big job, but it was something Elven could respect.

Elven went to the right of Bear and the left of Madds. Benson was on the opposite end. The four of them fanned out, continuing to walk in a straight line from where they stood around where the body had been found. Eventually, Elven walked so far that when he looked to his sides, he could no longer see Madds or Bear.

The ground was a lot harder here, which made sense as the body's location had been at the bottom of a decline, so the water would pool and run off. Where Elven now stood was a little higher. Any water that found its way here would only roll off and down into the divot where he came from. The leaves, however, were still moist.

He would venture to guess that once the sun dipped below the horizon, the temperatures dropped below freezing. Another reason that the ground was so hard here. It would literally freeze at night and thaw in the day.

Elven still hadn't found anything that told him he was dealing with a crime. Nor did he find anything that even remotely looked like it belonged to Shayla. No doll, no purse, no shoes, no piece of clothing. Nothing. The only thing he was finding was a bunch of trees, a few chirping birds, and a few scurrying paws through dead leaves in the distance from some smaller animals frightened by the newcomers trampling through their territory.

Elven pushed on, hoping that something might change. There was a handful of bushes and some moss growing along the shady side of a large tree. He headed toward them, stepping around the bush, and saw something that caught his eye.

Just behind the bushes was a small divot in the earth. It wasn't very deep. In fact, it was pretty shallow. But it looked as if the top layer of dirt had been scraped off, and something, or someone, had tried to dig into the soil beneath it.

Elven studied it, wondering if it meant anything. There were no clothes around, or even blood, for that matter. But it had been a few weeks, so would any of that still be around now? Maybe yes, and maybe no.

He sighed, putting his hands on his hips as he looked around. Nothing in the near distance told him this meant anything, so far as he could tell. He looked back down and tried to measure the length of the divot. He paced the length, trying to decide whether it was body-length or not, and still wasn't sure. It was long, and if he were to make it stretch, he might say it was five feet. But he was trying to make it work, if he were being honest.

There were a few paw prints in the dirt, but as he thought before, it had been a while since the girl had been found dead. Still, something tugged at him in his gut, and that wasn't anything to ignore. Was this a burial site? Were the paw prints from an animal digging her up?

It was still far too shallow for that kind of thing.

A gust of wind came cutting through the trees with a *whoosh*. Elven felt the chill of it run straight through him and down his spine. But along with the wind came another noise. It sounded like a wind chime, or maybe some bottles clinking together. Whatever it was, it definitely wasn't anything natural.

He looked around, trying to figure it out, but couldn't. He squinted down, shielding his eyes as if it would help him see far, like he had a pair of makeshift binoculars. When he figured nothing was working, he let his hands fall to his sides and sighed, throwing his head back.

That's when he saw it. Or rather, them.

The tree where he stood was incredibly tall, but it was also large, its branches spanning wide. He hadn't seen it because he wasn't looking up, focused mostly on the area in front of him. But from those branches, what looked like hundreds of bottles dangled from strings.

And something else looked to be up there, too. He just couldn't get a good view of it because it was so far up there.

"I got something!" Elven shouted, hoping that the others could still hear him like Bear had instructed earlier.

Right on cue, Bear gave a holler to confirm. "Heading that way!"

"Coming!" Madds shouted.

"Gotcha!" Benson joined in.

At least they hadn't wandered too far, Elven thought. But Elven didn't want to wait for them. He wanted to work on his hunch before anyone could talk him out of it. He still didn't trust anyone in this town. Benson and Bear seemed like good people, but he'd been wrong about that kind of thing before. Elven was going to make sure not to fall for the same thing twice.

Finding a branch low enough that he could get leverage, Elven propped his foot up on the base of the tree. He climbed, taking the tree as it came, planting his foot where he could, and grabbing onto what he could. By the time Bear, Madds, and Benson showed up, Elven was halfway up the tree.

"Elven, what are you doing?" Madds shouted. "You're gonna get hurt."

"Doesn't this look a little suspicious to you?" Elven asked, still making his way up.

"Kids throw the bottles up there," Bear said. "It's been happening for ages. Hell, I think I threw a couple of those up there myself when I was nine. Ain't nothing else to do out here."

"I think there's something more to it," Elven said.

"Just don't fall and break your neck," Bear said. "I ain't dragging your ass all the way back to town."

Elven looked out, finding a spot in the tree where he could rest a moment. He was in line with what he had been looking at; he just had to reach it. He grabbed a branch, pulling himself forward, but he overestimated its sturdiness. The branch cracked, then snapped right off.

Elven stumbled forward.

"Elven!" Madds shouted.

Elven started to fall forward but put his arms up, just barely catching another branch with his hands. His feet were still in the divot of the tree, and he stared down at the ground, his stomach leading toward it first. He swallowed, pushing down with his hands until he backed up enough that he could stand up straight.

He laughed. "I'm alright," he said, his voice a little shakier than before. But he was whole, so that was something. He just needed to watch each branch before putting his full weight on them.

He studied each of them, trying to figure out the best path to head out to the limb where the thing that caught his eye was. It seemed sturdy enough, so he just had to climb two branches and then shimmy himself out so he could reach out and pull it up. He began the next climb, this time taking a little more time and effort to test the branches.

They held fine, and he continued on. Once he made it to the largest branch, he started to crawl outward. He could see it in front of him, and it was exactly what he thought. He reached out and hooked his finger around the string, looping it around and giving it a tug, pulling up the figure.

And then in his hand, he held a small Troll doll. It looked like the one in the picture that Maybelle had shown them, only a little more weathered from being exposed to the elements for what he assumed was a few weeks. But there was something else to the doll, too. An addition.

Whoever had strung it up had put something on its back. It was crude, made from twigs and leaves, and something else he couldn't put his finger on, but if Elven were to guess, he'd say it was meant to be wings.

He made his way back to the trunk and slid down, a much easier trip than climbing it. Once his feet were on solid ground, he held the doll up.

"Know any animals that would hang that up there?" Madds asked pointedly.

Elven shook his head, letting Madds feel validated. "Looks like we've got a killer on our hands," he said.

CHAPTER ELEVEN

THE OLD CABIN HAD BEEN IN HIS FAMILY FOR AT LEAST A hundred years. Of course, so many people around these parts had similar places dotted throughout the woods. He'd come across many of them over his years on this earth. And he was sure many people had come across his.

But in this area, if it didn't belong to you, the unwritten law was to keep walking if you see something. It was to respect the privacy of whoever used the cabin, sure, but it was also more than that. It was for self-preservation.

A lot of people had secrets they didn't want to get out, and he was no different.

Because he was the unofficial watcher of the woods. Even more than that, he was the Keeper of Angels. That's what he thought of himself as. In fact, it was more than just that. It was the title he'd been given.

Not many people knew it, but that was okay. Because he had a duty that was higher than himself. And it had been given to him by another great Keeper.

The cabin was small, but it was plenty more than he needed for the job. And it was more useful than any large, obscene place that he could imagine. What was best about the cabin was the solitude. It offered what he couldn't get anywhere else.

And that was peace.

The quiet was what he craved the most when he was doing his duties. There was a lot on his mind, and with too much chatter around him, too many vehicles buzzing by, he would be far too distracted. And when his thoughts were jumbled, that's when mistakes were made.

And he couldn't afford any mistakes during his work. He had to be sure of what he was doing. Otherwise, the wrong people could get hurt. And he wasn't a murderer. He was just a man, selected by God, to walk this path. He'd been given the green light to do whatever it took. He just couldn't take that for granted.

He walked through the cabin's small living room, if it could be called that. It was more like a main room. There was a cot along the wall for sleeping. A table in the center where he could eat. There was a makeshift kitchen, though there was no electricity, so no refrigeration. Nor was there running water, but that was okay. He made do with what he was given. There was, however, a wood-burning stove. He could cook with it, too. A blessing when it came to his work.

And then there was the basement. Just a few short feet from where he stood was a door, and behind that door, a set of stairs that winded down into the earth where the temperatures were much cooler. In the summer, it was for everyone's benefit. But the winter? Well, he wasn't going to complain about what he'd been given, but to say that it was uncomfortable might be an understatement. Still, the surrounding ground kept the space more insulated than the top floor, so it was better to be in the ground than out.

He walked to the door, let himself in, then down the stairs he went. His boots thudded against the wood floor and then on each step as he allowed himself to take a peek at what he had. The temperature shifted for the better as he went down, but he still needed the heavy coat. It was dark in the small hallway underneath the building, but he grabbed the lantern off the wall and quickly lit it, shining its light out in front of him.

That's where he could see the various doors leading into all the different rooms. There weren't many of them, only five. But it was more than enough for his work. Just like right now, he was only using two of the rooms for his purposes, and one for another. The other were sitting dormant, waiting for the chance to be used by another angel.

He hoped he didn't need to use them, but he took care of his tasks when he needed to. Sometimes he went years without having to keep angels, but other times, the work was plenty. And right now was one of those times.

He walked the short hallway, his ears tuned into the various noises that might come as he paced by the doors. To his right, there wasn't a peep. Someone must be resting. Or maybe someone was too frightened to make any noise.

Those were the good angels. The ones he didn't need to put too much effort into. The ones who would do as instructed, and his work would be much shorter. Longer was allowed, of course. But eventually, all angels had to go.

But to his left, he could hear the sniffles. She was afraid. But not in a way that made her frozen. In a way that made her cause problems. He knew she would beg and plead. To be let go. But they both knew that the time for that had long passed.

Because there was a reason she was in his charge. Only angels who deserved to be held by a keeper would find themselves here.

He rested his forehead against the door, listening to the sobs on the other side. He traced his hand over the wood, wishing he could make it all better for her. He didn't enjoy their fear or their punishment, but life wasn't just about doing what you wanted to do. It was about doing what was required. And hard work made for a good man.

He slid his hand down over the metal bar that locked the door. He lifted it up and latched it against the wall. Then he took a deep breath and pulled the door open.

He hung the lantern on the wall just inside the doorway and turned to face the angel on the floor, her legs under the blanket he had given her. After all, it was cold out, and he didn't want her to be miserable. That wasn't the point of being here. He wasn't trying to torture anyone.

As soon as he locked eyes with her, though, she didn't seem to mind the cold. Tears ran down her face as she backed up quickly, uncovering herself from the blanket. She was trying to stay as far away from him as she could, but she hit the wall and had nowhere else to go.

"Please," she said.

He knew it—she was a pleader. A beggar. One of the angels who would try to do anything other than her duties with the keeper.

"I won't tell anyone if you just let me go."

He watched her carefully. Her breathing, it was so sporadic and quick. Even through the dim light, he could see her pulse thumping at her neck. If it went any harder, he might think her vein would burst right there as she sat on the floor. And then her eyes. They never drifted from his own, but the tears just wouldn't stop.

"You and I both know that isn't true," he said. "But that's okay. I don't blame you. It's just in your nature. So young still."

"I-I-I just want to go home," she said. "Please don't do this. Don't touch me."

He smiled, slightly confused. "I don't know what you think is going to happen right now," he said. "But you're safe here."

"You're not gonna..." She didn't finish her sentence, instead just letting it linger in the cold air.

He closed his eyes and let out a long breath before opening them again. "Are you hungry?"

She shivered, clearly unsure of what to say. Finally, she gave a small nod. "Y-yes."

"Good. If you eat for me, then this will all be easy," he said.

He turned around, exiting through the door he'd come through, and locked it behind him. Maybe she wouldn't be as much trouble as he had originally thought. Another blessing that God had brought him.

He smiled, heading up to prepare the food. But inside, he still knew there was more work to be done. Work that was hard every time he had to do it. But it made him a better man when it was done.

CHAPTER TWELVE

Elven held onto Madds on the back of the ATV as she followed Bear and Benson along the pathway, heading back into town. At some point, he was going to want to drive, or get his own vehicle. He gave no cares that he was holding onto someone while they drove, and he sure had no issue with the fact that it was a woman. What he did have a problem with, however, was the fact that it was Madds.

Just being this close. Having his arms wrapped around her. And smelling her hair, feeling her warmth... well, it was messing with his head. It brought back far too many memories of when things were good, but with those memories also came the memories of how it all fell apart. Her betrayal, and his heart shattering. The last thing he needed was to be distracted like that while working a case.

Of course, he hadn't said he was staying. But if his word was worth anything to them, then they should assume that he was going to.

They'd spent far too much time out in the woods, and Elven was exhausted. He'd been up all night, and now all day. He'd fully sobered up a long time ago from his night out, which made it even worse. He much preferred to sleep that off instead of being awake for it. And now it was getting late again. The sun was coming down, and he wondered how much longer he would be able to keep his eyes open.

But there was still work to be done, and he didn't think he should wait until the morning to get to it. He wasn't trying to rush the investigation, but too much time had already passed since Shayla's body had been found. As far as he was concerned, there were still two girls missing, and the more time went on, the more likely it was that they were looking for graves.

In all honesty, that may be exactly what they should be looking for. Of course, he wasn't going to tell Benson that. He wasn't even sure if he should tell Bear that. It might be something he needed to keep to himself, or at the very least, wait until he and Madds had time alone to discuss.

They came to a fork in the road, one way leading to the heart of town, the other down a quickly darkening path where the trees cast long shadows from the setting sun. Bear and Benson had come to a full stop, waiting for Madds to catch up. The town wasn't too far from this location, from what Elven remembered when they passed through it before while on the way from Maybelle Perkins' house.

But when Madds and Elven reached the two men, they saw that they weren't alone. There were three other men on their own ATVs, waiting for them. It seemed like they were in a heated conversation with Bear about something. What gave Elven the most concern, however, were the guns at the ready from the two men behind the one who drove point.

In West Virginia, it was a common occurrence for people to have weapons. And even more common in heavily rural areas like Old Knuckle. That didn't surprise him. But he could read people fairly well by their body language, and he could see these men weren't just on a friendly drive through the trees.

No, in fact, it seemed like they'd come out to speak to them.

About what? Well, Elven was sure he was going to find out as soon as Madds cut her engine.

And just as he thought, his intuition hadn't let him down. He hadn't heard much over the rumble, but it was clear as day once she throttled down. Thankfully, she didn't fully cut the engine. Elven figured she'd picked up on it, too, and it was better not to shut it off in case they needed a quick getaway.

Madds gave Elven a glance, keeping a little distance between them and the rest of the men. "Be ready to bolt if we need to," she said, confirming his thoughts.

"This something that happens often?" Elven asked, keeping his voice low.

"That guy right there, the one running point with the stupid mustache," she said. "That's Roy Leven. He's not a fan of me being here. I'm not too familiar with the other two, but I think it's safe to say that they feel the same way."

Elven nodded. "Has anything escalated further than words while you've been here?"

Madds shrugged. "I mean, if you're asking if anyone's pulled the trigger, then no. But knowing your charming personality, I'm sure we'll see it soon enough," she said. He could hear the smile cross her lips.

Now that the engine was low, Elven could finally hear what they were saying. And Roy Leven seemed to have a lot to say on the matter.

"It was one thing to bring this outsider into our community," Roy said. "Taking up space when there's none to be had. She's trying to make friends everywhere she goes, but I don't get it. Ain't nobody wants to be up here unless they're hiding from something."

"He's not wrong about that one, is he?" Elven whispered to Madds.

She shook her head, but didn't say a word.

"You can make all the assumptions you want, Roy," Bear said, "but it doesn't make it true. Besides, most people in towns like Old

Knuckle want to stay away from most people for one reason or another. What makes her any less ideal to you?"

"I ain't gonna argue about her anymore on this," Roy said. "Your little pet can stay or go for all I care. But I heard the rumors in town, and looks like it's true." He pointed to Madds, but Elven was pretty sure the finger he pointed was aimed right at him. "Now you're bringing more people from the outside. And for what? You think they can help solve this issue we got? Hell, we can go solve it right now and shoot whatever animal killed that girl."

"It's more than that, Roy," Bear said.

"Yeah, she was murdered!" Benson yelled. "We found—"

"Is all this ruckus because of me?" Elven shouted, cutting Benson off before he could reveal that they'd found Shayla's doll hanging from the tree. No need to share that little bit of information with the whole town.

"Depends on who you are and what you're doing in my community," Roy said.

Elven hopped off the ATV and walked a few feet toward the other men. He slapped Benson on the back and squeezed his shoulder. It wasn't painful, just a firm hand like a father would give his son. Benson turned to Elven and saw the look he gave him. He wasn't sure if the kid figured it out, but Elven was trying to make it as clear as he could that Benson needed to keep his mouth shut.

"I'll take it from here," Elven whispered.

Benson gave a slight nod like he understood.

"And who might you be?" Roy asked, eyeing him up and down.

Elven saw the mustache from afar, but now he understood why Madds had called it stupid. It looked like a comb hanging over his lip.

Before answering, Elven took stock of the three men. Roy had a gun on his hip, but didn't seem interested in drawing it. The two behind him, however, had rifles in some makeshift holsters on their ATVs. They sat at an angle where they'd be able to grab the rifles and draw at a quicker rate while seated. He wasn't sure if that was something to be wary of or if they just liked to drive around, shooting at things for fun. Perhaps it was both.

"Elven Hallie," he said. "And I'm—"

"You gotta be shittin' me," Roy said through grit teeth, his voice no longer irritated. Now it was downright angry. "You brought the goddamned sheriff here?" He was glaring at Bear now.

"I'm sure word travels a bit slower up to Old Knuckle," Elven said, "but I ain't the sheriff any longer. And Bear didn't bring me anywhere. I came on my own volition."

It was a lie, but it was one Elven figured he could get by with. No need to put the focus on Benson or Madds at this point. Madds barely had any goodwill here, so far as he could tell, and it wouldn't be right for Benson to shoulder that kind of weight when he was just trying to do right by his sister.

Roy Leven glared down at Elven, but his hand never made it to his belt. "We don't want the sheriff, or former sheriff, around here."

"If I was still the sheriff, you'd have no right to say one way or another, now would you?"

Roy smiled. "Maybe so, but you just said it yourself. You don't hold that position now. So get out."

"Alright," Elven said. "I'll head out right now, and on my way down, I'll make sure to fill the new sheriff in on everything I've seen. The murder of the young girl, and the two other missing girls to boot. I'm sure, being the new guy on the block, he'll have something to prove about the whole thing. I'd like to see how that one pans out, don't you?"

"You sure are one cocky son of a bitch," Roy said. "I'm sure that gets you a lot where you're from. But here, it don't mean shit. You'll have to back those words up if you want to use them out here in Old Knuckle."

"I don't doubt it," Elven said. "So just try me, and I'll make sure to prove it."

He let his hand go down to his hip, placing his palm flat on his revolver just like he used to while he was the sheriff. It felt good to get back into the swing of things, even if he no longer had the legal power to back it up. "I'll let you see that I'm more than just words."

"Boys, we don't need to start anything," Bear said.

Roy smiled, raising a hand up. "It's alright, Bear. I want to see this *Elven Hallie* do more than just blow some hot air. I bet he likes to think of himself as some sort of cowboy hunting down Indians or the like. What is it, then?" he asked, looking at Elven. "So bored, you gotta meddle in others affairs? Or you like to feel powerful in other ways than just money?"

Elven sighed, but not audibly. He just seethed with his mouth closed. "Surprise, surprise. Judging me by who my family is."

"Don't get much clearer than that, in my opinion," Roy said.

"By your logic, then, your family must have been the type to look the other way when a crime happened," Elven said. "That, or maybe it's something else."

Something in Roy's eyes shifted dangerously, and Elven could tell he'd pushed the right button. Or maybe it was the wrong button. Whatever the case, he was about to get the reaction he was hoping for.

"You entitled motherfucker," Roy barked. He brought his hand down quickly to his gun.

But Elven was ready for it. He didn't intend on drawing on the man. He wasn't looking to kill anyone. Besides, the two men behind Roy would put him down before he could take them out. Elven was quick, but outdrawing three people at the same time was a skill he wasn't one hundred percent sure he possessed. Not that he would tell anyone that, of course.

Plus, how would that look if he could? The outsider that nobody wants there, former law enforcement and last name Hallie, comes to shoot three of their own dead? He wouldn't be long for this world after that one. Bear himself might just put one in his back for that.

Instead, Elven lunged at Roy and pulled him off his vehicle, flipping him in the air and throwing him down in the dirt, where he landed hard on his back. He stepped on his hand and put a foot against his throat, standing tall above him. The two men who had ridden behind Roy were already pulling their rifles from the janky holsters they'd made.

Elven fished for his own gun, maybe just a little too late. Flipping a man off his vehicle took a lot of work. Luckily, he wasn't alone in this.

"Hey!" Madds shouted, her gun already pulled out and aimed right past Elven and toward them. "Show me your hands!"

The two men glanced at each other, having just seen the situation they were currently in. They slowly raised their hands up, but they clearly weren't happy about it.

"Quite the entrance you're making already," Roy said, his voice strained from Elven's boot pressed firmly against his throat.

A gun went off, drawing everyone's attention. Bear sat on his ATV, his back straight, and his rifle pointed to the air. He did not look amused at the theatrics in front of him. "That's enough. Take your foot off him, keep your gun holstered, and let him up," Bear told Elven, then turned to Madds. "And you can put that pistol back where you pulled it from."

Madds's eyes shifted between Bear and Roy's men, still seated on their ATVs. "I don't like the way they're looking at me," Madds said, still not putting her gun away.

Bear lifted his eyes toward them. "The Morrison brothers? Shit, I don't know if I ever seen them hit anything in their life. They're harmless, ain't you boys?" Bear asked, smiling wide.

They both nodded, their hands still up. The bigger one spoke up. "We just came out to see what the commotion was. Roy asked us to back him up if he needed. He's the asshole who started the whole thing." He pointed at Elven.

"I was sitting right here when the whole damned thing happened, so you don't have to tell me," Bear said. He turned back to Elven and Roy. "Now, do I need to point this at you two, or are you gonna ease up?"

Elven lifted his foot off of Roy's throat, holding a hand out for him to take. Roy studied it cautiously, then finally relented as he slapped his hand into Elven's, letting Elven hoist him to his feet.

"Interesting to see the new company you decide to keep, Bear," Roy said. "I know we don't see eye to eye on everything, but this is a far cry from our normal grievances."

"I told you before, we're just trying to find these missing girls and who is responsible for Shayla Perkins's murder," Bear said.

Roy climbed back onto his ATV. "The four of you seem pretty sure of something, so why don't you fill me in? 'Cause from where the rest of us stand, it looks like she was attacked by a bear or something else."

"It's the something else that I'm thinking it was," Bear said.

"Then care to share why?" Roy asked, staring him down.

Bear seemed to understand Elven's reaction earlier and didn't say a word. Roy looked to the rest of them, but no one mentioned anything about the doll.

Finally, Bear spoke up. "Where are the other girls? If it was just one bear attack, then why no other bodies?"

Roy nodded. "Maybe they left town."

"Bullshit," Benson said. "Not Lila. Not without me."

That seemed to soften Roy up, and he let out a sigh, slumping his shoulders. "Look, we can sit here all day going back and forth like this and get nowhere."

"Agreed," Bear said.

"Just don't push this thing so far that you can't come back from it," Roy said pointedly. "You aligning yourself with these outsiders is one thing. But you go around accusing your neighbors and kin, well, that's a completely different thing."

Not waiting for anyone's reply, Roy fired up his ATV and spun around. He drove off back to town, his two friends in tow.

CHAPTER THIRTEEN

Elven was still exhausted, but after that tiff with Roy Leven and, as Bear called them, the Morrison brothers, his adrenaline had picked up. There was no way he could sleep right now, but he knew once he calmed down, he would be ready to. In fact, he knew that the fumes he was running on wouldn't last long, so when he did finally lay down, he would crash.

But until then, he figured it was better to use as much time as he had to push more into the case. So they headed straight to Sadie Vaughn's house.

Bear led them most of the way down the other fork, opposite the one Roy and his buddies had taken back to town. Bear was right—Sadie didn't live too far from where Maybelle Perkins and Shayla lived. Or at least, it was in the same general area; to say they were *close* might have been a stretch. It seemed unless someone lived in the center of the community, there was nothing "close" about Old Knuckle.

So few people, spread out over a large area in the twisting mountains. Yet, at the same time, it was a very tight-knit community. Just some of the charm that West Virginia offered, Elven supposed. He loved it here, even in the most rural of places. In some ways, he was jealous of these people. They were surrounded by those they trusted, along with the beauty of nature that the state provided.

Of course, that was also part of the problem. All it took was one bad apple to spoil the rest when it came to trusting someone. Elven knew that far too well.

Elven wasn't sure where they were going, but he saw a few landmarks that stood out, which told him the area that he had already been through. But for the most part, it was all just trees and trails to him. It would be far too easy to get lost here if he didn't try to learn the various twists and turns in the paths, along with the small differences in the area. It wasn't until they came upon a new house or trailer that Elven was confident they were in a different spot in Old Knuckle.

But when Bear slowed down and finally came to a stop, there were no residences in sight. Instead, he'd stopped at just a larger spot on the trail so that Benson could pull up beside him. Madds and Elven came up slowly behind, parking while Bear looked around at the surrounding area.

"What's up?" Madds asked. "Why are we stopping here? The Vaughns' place is right up ahead."

Bear turned around to face them. The look on his face told Elven he wasn't too happy about something. "You don't need to remind me where the Vaughns' place is," Bear said, and Elven knew where this was headed. "I've lived here my whole life. In fact, it's why we're stopping. Because I want to make sure that the four of us are all on the same page about something."

"And what might that something be?" Elven asked, irritated once more to be in this situation. He'd been dragged up here against his will, and now that he'd agreed to be here, he was being met with a whole lot of attitude from everyone here.

"Roy can be a downright—"

"Motherfucker," Madds completed.

Bear stared her down, his lips a thin line. "I wasn't going to go that far. More leaning toward 'piece of work,' but you got the point across."

"I think my way works better," Madds said.

"Either way," Bear said. "Roy still has this community's best interest at heart. He's not a bad man."

"I don't know that," Elven said.

"Well, I'm telling you that," Bear said, not backing down. Elven wondered how much of a problem this was going to be for him. "And he's not wrong about what he said. These people are my neighbors, friends, and kin. Looking into everyone here for murdering one of our own is gonna ruffle a lot of feathers."

"This line of work does that," Elven said. "Can't tiptoe around things just because someone is gonna be offended or take it the wrong way. Taking on the job of hunting down a criminal isn't gonna make a lot of friends when the suspect pool is your own backyard. It's to be expected."

"And what's not expected is to get into blows with every damn person we come across, is it?" Bear asked. "'Cause I only got so many bullets to waste before I decide to actually put one where it might be the most effective. You understand?"

Elven smirked. He respected the way Bear operated. "I just figured I ought to operate by prison rules," he said. "Take down the biggest one I can find. Assert dominance."

Bear snickered. "Then you'd have started the fight with me, not Roy."

"You might be the biggest in size, but you're far from the biggest idiot here," Elven clarified.

That made Bear crack, a boisterous laugh echoing out of him. "You got me there," he said. "I love Roy, about as much as another man can, but working with him is like walking the woods barefoot. It'll get you there, but you'll regret it the whole way through."

"I hear what you're getting at," Elven said. If Bear could give him a little, then Elven could give it back. "I'll ease up and not start things. But if anyone starts it with me, I won't hesitate to finish it."

"That's reasonable," Bear said. "I wouldn't expect any less."

Elven held a hand out. "Then we understand each other," he said.

Bear shook it, though Elven figured this wouldn't be the last time that he and Bear would have a moment like this. Old Knuckle was foreign to him, and so was the way he was gonna have to operate. He was gonna have to get used to stepping on toes and massaging them later.

"Does someone wanna tell me why we didn't just tell Roy we found Shayla's toy strung up in a tree above what we think was the spot she was buried at?" Benson asked. "That would have avoided the whole thing, wouldn't it?"

Bear sighed. "Because telling Roy would be giving up the only information we have that the killer knows. Isn't that right?"

Elven nodded. "And like I said, I don't know Roy."

"You think Roy might have something to do with it?" Benson asked, his eyes darting between Elven and Bear.

Elven shrugged. "Too early to tell for me, but Bear is the one who said he knows him," he said. "I'm curious about that myself."

Bear shook his head. "Roy ain't got nothing to do with it," he said. "But I don't know if he can keep his mouth shut about it. I sure as shit know those Morrison brothers like to gossip like schoolgirls."

"Fair enough," Elven said. "Thank you for keeping it under wraps."

"For now," Bear said. "But if the time comes that it is better to be spoken, then I'll speak it."

"I couldn't agree more," Elven said.

Bear looked back at the path for a moment, then turned to face Elven and Madds. "Like Madds said, the Vaughn residence is right around this bend. Can I trust you not to put your foot on any throats?

And you not to pull your damned gun on them?" He pointed to Madds.

"I'd love to promise you that, but I don't want to walk into a situation and have to break my word," Elven said. "But I'll use my discretion a little better."

Bear shook his head. "I guess that'll have to do."

CHAPTER FOURTEEN

THE SUN HAD JUST ABOUT FULLY SET BY THE TIME THEY PULLED up to Sadie Vaughn's home. It was another trailer, but not as rundown as Elven had seen throughout the rest of Old Knuckle. It was larger and raised, with a skirt around the base. There was a set of stairs that led to the door, but no porch at all, unless you considered the flat entry point to be a porch.

But there was a seating area on the ground, just to the left of the stairs. There were a bunch of flat stones and pavers laid out to create a nice patio. It looked to be well-maintained, even though it was clear that the job hadn't been done by a professional. There was a large grill, along with six Adirondack chairs that looked like they'd been made out of pallets. Some dingy cushions had been placed on each seat.

The place was homey and tucked in the trees, just like most of the other trailers that Elven had seen since entering the community. He could see two other trailers in the distance through the sparsely forested section behind the Vaughns' place. Some people did have neighbors close by in this town. That is, if the trailers were inhabited.

"Are the Vaughns expecting us, like Maybelle was?" Elven asked as he dismounted from the ATV.

Bear shook his head. "Didn't radio ahead, but at this time of the day, most everyone is home for supper," he said.

"And you think interrupting their dinner is appropriate?"

Bear shrugged. "If it were my kid who was missing, I wouldn't give a damn who interrupted my meal to tell me they were trying to find her. Hell, I'd invite them in to break bread with me. Wouldn't you?"

Elven nodded. "The way you put it, absolutely. But when it comes to the people in this town, I'm not sure you agree with everyone on that," he said. "You underestimate how much people seem to not like me."

Bear shook his head. "I think I estimate the right amount," he said. "If anything, I think I underestimated how little they care that it's me you're working with. Then again, Maybelle seemed more than willing to speak with you. I have a feeling the Vaughns will surprise you."

"Famous last words," Elven said with a shrug. At the end of the day, it was like he said. He wasn't there to make friends. He was there to find some missing girls and catch a killer. He just wanted to avoid making enemies every time he knocked on a door.

The door swung open before Bear could knock. In the doorway stood a man with a large beard. He wore overalls and a sweater. There was a jagged scar just under his eye that looked old, given how much it blended in with his natural skin tone, only slightly lighter than the rest.

"You all just gonna stand out here on my property gabbing away, or you gonna come tell me whatchoo want? Either way, I'd appreciate it if you kept your voices down," the man demanded.

Bear was bigger than the man, but it didn't seem to intimidate him any. Bear, however, held a hand up as an apology. "Ronnie, we didn't mean to bother you. Just had to talk it out before wanting to interrupt you in your home. Any chance we can come in and talk?"

Ronnie, the overall-wearing bearded man with the scar, took a deep breath and scanned the foursome standing on his property before turning back to Bear. "Depends on what you wanna talk about? You can just speak your peace here if you want. Otherwise, if it's gonna take a while, let's sit outside. Darlene is sleeping, and I don't wanna wake her."

"That's fair," Bear said. "Apologies for the disruption. I know she's had a rough go of it, so I don't want to cause her to stir."

Ronnie nodded, his stance softening some. "Don't make a thing of it," he said. "Come on."

He motioned to the Adirondack chairs on the makeshift patio, following Bear down the steps after closing the door softly behind him. Elven, Madds, and Benson joined the other two, sitting in a half-circle. Ronnie lit up a lantern he'd picked up, then hung it on the small black hook dug into the ground.

"Hope we're not out here much longer," Ronnie said. "Haven't wanted to light up the fire pit in some days."

"We don't want to cause too much of an intrusion," Bear said.

"Then better get to it," Ronnie said.

"We're here because of Sadie," Bear said, trying to cut through the fat, though Elven figured they'd already had plenty of that.

Ronnie pulled out a tin of Skoal, fiddling with the tobacco inside before tucking some in his bottom lip. He swayed back and forth as if he was trying to make the wooden pallet chair into a rocking chair. The four feet never left the ground, however.

"I had a feeling," he said. He took a long, hard look at Elven. "You're too pretty to be someone who might have stumbled upon her out here. And I ain't never seen you, either."

"No sir, I'm not from here," Elven said.

"No shit," Ronnie said. "So what're you doing in Old Knuckle, and what business do you have being with Bear while he's asking about my daughter?"

Bear cleared his throat. "That's what—"

"Bear, I mean no disrespect, but I'm asking the stranger," Ronnie said. "You come to my property asking about my missing daughter with folks I ain't never seen, or barely seen." His words hit Madds when she clearly wasn't expecting them. "It makes a man wonder what the hell is going on. And it makes him wonder why the hell his old friend didn't just come right out and spell it to begin with. Now then, who the fuck are you?"

"My name is Elven," Elven said, deciding to leave off his last name. However, he doubted it mattered. He knew his name wasn't the most common thing to hear. "And I'm here helping to look for your daughter."

Ronnie prodded at the lump of tobacco in his lip before spitting a string of brown-tinted saliva out to his right, hitting the ground with a wet slap. "That's all good and well, but what do you know about finding girls who skipped town?"

"Is that what you think happened?" Elven asked.

"Son, and I say this with the utmost respect, but I haven't the slightest fucking clue who you are," Ronnie said. "Why the hell should I tell you that?"

"I'm from Dupray," Elven said. "And I used to be the—"

"Goddammed fucking sheriff," Ronnie said with a grumble, like he'd just made the connection.

"The official title was just *sheriff*, but you're right," Elven said. He wondered if every single person he came across in Old Knuckle would have this very reaction. It was already getting old as it was. He either not explained who he was, but then why would they want some random person helping? Or he told them he used to be the sheriff, but of course, nobody wanted law enforcement around. It was a lose-lose situation to be in.

"Heard you lost," Ronnie said.

"That's why I said *used to be*," Elven said dryly.

Ronnie cracked a smile. "Smug sonabitch, ain't you?"

"Some would say," Elven said.

"But not you?"

Elven shook his head. "I'd put it as more confidence. Those people who think it's smug are just insecure."

"So tell me, former sheriff," Ronnie said, leaning in. "You think you can find where my daughter went?"

"Depends on what you think happened," Elven said. "You mentioned she ran off. Why's that?"

Ronnie looked around at the half-circle he was in. Two of them were familiar faces, while the other two were practically strangers, even though Madds had been there for a few months already. Elven got the feeling she hadn't made a ton of friends while here. In Old Knuckle, that seemed hard to do when everyone was so cautious to open up to anyone new.

"Because she was always talking about leaving this place," Ronnie said. He started to mimic a whining voice. *"There's no future here. Ain't no boys who I can date here. Old Knuckle is dying. I'll strip for money if that's what it takes to get out of here.* You know, all that sort of thing. Hell, practically every damn time we got on her case about something, she was throwing it in our faces." Ronnie paused, staring off into the woods. He shook his head for a moment. "I just didn't think she'd actually do it. Not without saying something to us before going."

"So you never thought she was serious, then?" Elven asked.

Ronnie shook his head. "Not until I heard her speaking to her friends about it," he said. "They thought they were sly, but these walls are damn near paper."

"Her friends?" Elven asked.

Ronnie pointed to Benson. "Lila and Maybelle's girl."

Benson immediately looked saddened to hear that.

"They were making plans," Ronnie continued. "And that's when I realized that I actually might have to let her go. But like I said, didn't think she'd just pick up and run off without saying nothing."

The door swung open, and a man stepped out on the stairs. He was young, around Benson's age, and he looked a lot like Ronnie, just without the beard or scar. "Who you out here with, Daddy?" he asked.

"Bear and Benson," Ronnie said, leaning back and looking up. "That new girl in town, and now this one." He motioned toward Elven. "Whole damn town's filling up with new faces." He turned back to Elven. "This is my son, Davin."

Davin gave them all a good look, his face twisting in disapproval. "The hell you all want?"

"They're here about Sadie," Ronnie said. "Says they're trying to find her. This one here is the *former* sheriff, and for some reason, he's taken a liking to what's going on up here."

"Ain't nothing going on that needs attention," Davin said, rushing down the steps. "Not sure when we all decided to tell anyone who asked our business, but this is some bullshit." He kicked Benson's chair. "You got some nerve bringing them around here. I know you ain't got a mama, but you know better than this."

Benson caught himself with his hand as his chair nearly tipped all the way on its side. He pushed so that the chair legs landed back on the pavers and stood up, clearly distraught at what Davin had said to him. "Davin, I'm just trying to find Lila. I know—"

"Time to cut the cord and let your sister go. She's her own person, and you should be your own man," Davin said. He stood for a moment, as if he was going to wait for Benson to say something, but then just shook his head and threw up his arms. "Whatever, just fuck off."

Davin stormed off into the dark.

"Davin!" Benson shouted. "Davin!"

Ronnie didn't seem bothered by the scene, instead opting to spit another load of brown saliva right on top of the puddle he was making. "He ain't coming back for a while," Ronnie said.

Benson growled, but instead of plopping back down, he took off after him. Elven wasn't sure if he should intervene or not, but Bear put a hand out as if telling Elven to stay. It was like they'd said—he was a stranger, so what did he know about whatever feud was happening right now?

"Should I go after him?" Madds asked, apparently missing Bear's gesture.

"They'll be fine," Ronnie said. "Boys being boys. Hell, makes me wonder if he's just mad he didn't get out when Sadie did."

"What if Shayla wasn't mauled by an animal?" Elven asked. "What if we could find evidence that said she was murdered?"

Ronnie cocked his head, lifting his eyebrows. "I don't like to play the *what-if* game, Sheriff," Ronnie said. Elven didn't feel the need to correct him on his current state of unemployment. "But I will tell you one thing—before you go floating rumors like that around here, you better be damn sure that it's the truth. I don't need my Darlene to be worrying about nothing other than her little girl making it to the city safe and sound, you hear me? She's damn near a wreck as it is. I don't know what that kind of thing would do to her."

Bear, Elven, and Madds exchanged a glance. It wasn't the right time to bring out their evidence. He didn't think Ronnie had anything to do with it. He seemed more like he just wanted to buy into the idea that his daughter had run off instead of something happening to her. He was protecting his family.

Of course, it was a lazy way to do it. He still had family in trouble. He just didn't want to admit it.

CHAPTER FIFTEEN

Benson chased after Davin in the darkness. The trail was easy to navigate; he'd done it a million times in his life. Davin and he hadn't hung out in some time, but when he was younger, Benson was over here almost every day playing with him, or Davin would be at Benson's house. Either way, they were always in each other's lives back then. The two had been damn near inseparable at one point in Benson's life.

Then his parents died, and everything went to shit.

Benson knew the truth about Davin's family. It wasn't all roses and sunshine. Ronnie seemed like a good father for the most part, but Benson had seen the cracks from time to time. He drank a little too much, he got angry a little too easily, and he overreacted on more than one occasion. But being popped in the mouth here and there was a lot different than full-on child abuse, and Benson knew it.

Darlene, however, had never been the greatest mother. She favored Sadie, that was for sure. And she never hit Davin, but because of the way she felt about Sadie, it meant that Davin never got the attention he deserved. On top of that, Darlene seemed to always be sleeping.

When Benson was a child, he never thought much of it. Just one of those funny quirks that other families had. Just like how his own mother would never make a sandwich with mayonnaise. Only mustard for her.

But as Benson got older, he realized that it wasn't just some family quirk. Darlene had a problem that wasn't being addressed. Even he could see that once he started hitting his teens. He was never sure what it was, but now he had a feeling. Those pill bottles around the house made it pretty obvious. He figured that was part of the reason Ronnie hadn't let them inside. Darlene taking a nap wasn't news to him.

Was she having trouble sleeping since Sadie had gone missing? Benson couldn't be sure. It was plausible, but he figured Ronnie was just covering for her. It was easier to do that than face the reality that was his life.

But that wasn't why he and Davin had parted ways, or whatever he'd call it. No, that might have been part of why they hung out so much. Davin didn't have the greatest mother figure in his life, so he'd used Benson's mother as a surrogate.

Benson's mother was amazing. Caring and nurturing. Benson knew what he had, and he wasn't jealous when his mother took an interest in Davin. Hell, he loved it. It meant that he and Davin could hang out all the time. He'd come over for dinner almost every night. He'd sometimes come by when Benson wasn't around, searching for that little bit of love that he was missing at home.

It was when Benson's parents died that Davin stopped coming by. He didn't blame him. It was hard. Too hard for him. And anytime they hung around each other, both of them were just sad. Eventually, they drifted apart.

Benson was angry about it, but he figured that was life. He was too sad to care. And by the time he was able to deal with his emotions, too much time had passed. Davin was a different person than the kid he used to play with.

But it didn't mean that Benson had to give up completely on

Davin. That's why he chased after him into the darkness right now. He wanted to talk, to make it right. And to make sure that his old friend was okay.

"Davin, wait up!" Benson said, picking up his own pace.

"Leave me alone, Benson," Davin said, but didn't stop.

Benson finally reached him and grabbed at his arm. "Davin, come on, man."

"Fuck off, Benson," Davin said, finally stopping to face him. "Why are you even here?"

"Cause I want to make sure my friend is okay."

"Friend? Jesus, man, we haven't been friends in years," Davin said. He looked confused, as if what Benson was saying was truly unreasonable.

In a way, it felt like he'd stabbed Benson right through the heart. "I know," he said. "But just because we don't hang anymore doesn't mean we can't still be—"

"What?" Davin asked. "Friends? You don't know shit about me anymore."

"I know you plenty," he said. "I know your mom isn't taking this well because she loved Sadie more than anything. I know she's probably sleeping off some pills right now. I know that you miss my mom. Maybe even more than I do."

Davin shook his head. "You're such a fucking idiot, you know that?" He threw his hands in the air and let them flop to his side.

"Am I wrong?"

"Spot-on work, Benson. You nailed all of it. But it don't mean shit 'cause life goes on," he said. "But you gotta be bringing in these outsiders to our business. Why are you digging into this?"

Benson furrowed his brow, now angry that Davin even had to ask that. "You know why," he said. "Because Lila wouldn't have up and left without telling me."

"Newsflash, asshole. Nobody wants to stay in Old Knuckle with their little brother as an anchor around their neck," he said. "You want to find your sister? Then leave this fucking town and go look for her. But get these fuckers out of our business." He shook his head. "The fucking sheriff? What the hell are you thinking?"

"Why do you say that?" Benson asked. "What do you think they're going to find here?"

"Nothing!" Davin yelled. "That's what. And I want to keep it that way!" He stepped into Benson's personal space, poking at his chest with his finger. "And if you knew what was good for you, then you'd do it, too."

"Well, maybe I don't know what's good for me," Benson said, his voice a growl. He was beyond pissed now. Nobody was going to tell him what to do when it came to his own family. "So why don't you fill me in."

Davin grinned his teeth, but it was a grimace more than anything else. "You go sniffing around too much where nobody wants ya, the only thing you're likely to find is a bullet. You got me?"

The threat was heard, but Benson still had no idea why Davin was acting this way. It seemed like this was about a lot more than just some outsiders coming through town, asking questions. It seemed like he had something real to hide. And it had Benson wondering what it could be.

"What are you hiding?" Benson finally asked.

"Stay out of my way, Benson," Davin said. "Get out of town, and take those assholes with you." He turned around and started walking into the darkness again.

"Davin," Benson said, grabbing him by the arm again, but this time, Davin spun around, swinging. He connected with the side of Benson's face, dropping him down on his ass.

Davin spat to the side. "Don't say I didn't warn you." And then he disappeared into the night, leaving Benson there holding onto his face as the throbbing came.

CHAPTER SIXTEEN

The conversation with Ronnie Vaughn had gone about how Elven figured it would. Hearing that Ronnie truly believed his daughter had left town, though, was a little bit of a surprise. Especially the fact that he didn't want to try to find her. The denial was strong in that man, and he was sure there was more than one reason for it. Elven wondered if digging into that would actually help his investigation, or if it was just a distraction and a waste of time.

What he was curious about, however, was what looked like a fresh shiner developing on Benson's face. But the kid didn't seem very forthcoming with the details on that one, so he decided to leave it be for now. Besides, the adrenaline had finally worn off, and Elven was ready to hit the sack. He was afraid he'd be delirious if he didn't get some rest soon. He didn't want to be completely useless tomorrow when he knew they'd be canvassing the town for information.

He didn't want to spend a whole day in bed. He wanted to get out of Old Knuckle sooner than later. He'd worn out his welcome as soon as he set foot in town.

The four of them regrouped a ways off of the Vaughn property.

They didn't want to disturb them any longer than they already had. Besides, the family seemed to have a lot of problems, and Elven wasn't certain that they were completely innocent. In both the two girls' disappearance and Shayla's murder? That was still up in the air. But there was something suspicious about the place; he just couldn't place it yet. So he didn't want to feed them any more information than they needed.

Once closer to the center of town, where there were some lights from the nearby buildings and houses, they all rounded up, debating what the next move would be. As far as Elven was concerned, he just needed to be pointed in the direction of his accommodations.

"Nothing more tonight," Elven said, letting out a long yawn. "I'll be useless in the morning if I don't get any sleep."

"That's fair," Bear said, nodding in agreement.

"Thank God," Madds said, stretching herself.

It seemed like everyone was ready to put their head on a pillow. Everyone except for Benson, that is. The kid seemed contemplative, which went against everything Elven had seen from him the whole day. Something had definitely happened out in the woods with Davin.

But also, Benson seemed to have a lot more energy than the rest right now. Was it because of the altercation? Or was it just because he was eighteen years old and used to staying out all night?

"I'm good to keep going," Benson said, confirming what Elven had just been thinking. "Don't you think we should keep trying to figure it out? Isn't that what they say? Letting a case get cold is bad, right?"

Elven looked at the kid with soft eyes. "Benson, I appreciate the spirit, but this case has been cold for some time. It's been far longer than forty-eight hours, hasn't it? It's been weeks."

"That don't mean anything," he said. "You're here now."

"And it seems like there isn't much we're finding yet," Elven said. "You got any ideas of what we should be doing tonight? 'Cause at this point, canvasing the entire forest is all I got, and between the four of us, I don't think that's gonna cover much ground."

Benson didn't seem too happy at this idea. "So you're saying it's pointless?"

Elven shook his head. "Nothing like that," he said. "I'm just saying that Madds and I need to discuss what's already been covered, get fresh eyes in the morning, and go from there. You've done good so far. I'm convinced this is something, and I gave my word that I'd stay to see it through."

Benson nodded, seeming to accept the answer for now. Elven could sense the frustration and disappointment in the kid, and he couldn't blame him one lick. His sister's friend was dead, and his sister was missing. Elven was surprised that the kid had gotten any sleep these past weeks.

"All good points," Bear said. "We'll meet up in the morning, then."

Bear was about to head out on the trail to wherever it was he called home, but Elven stopped him. "Which brings me to my next question," he said. "Where am I staying?"

"Ain't with me, unless you want a hammock and a couple of blankets," Bear said. "Might be a little chilly for ya."

"You can stay with me," Benson offered.

Elven remembered the state of the kid's trailer and immediately didn't like that idea. He'd be fighting off roaches and rodents all night. "Appreciate the offer, but—"

"Yeah, Ginny Tiller has an extra room in her place," Madds cut in. "That's where I'm staying. I'm sure she won't mind."

Bear nodded. "Probably your best bet," he said. "Besides, you won't find a better biscuit in town than Ginny's."

Benson seemed to agree with his puppy dog-like nod and wide eyes. Elven thought the kid was salivating just at the mention of biscuits.

"Come on, Benson," Bear said. "I'll see you home." He fired up the ATV and drove off.

Benson hesitated, turning to Elven. "Thank you," he said. "For helping and sticking around, I mean."

Elven gave a nod and watched the kid follow Bear. He just hoped that he could live up to the hope that he saw in the kid's eyes.

CHAPTER SEVENTEEN

Ginny Tiller's place was a lot larger than Elven had expected, and it wasn't a trailer like most of the other homes Elven had visited. It was a wooden cabin that looked about as old as Old Knuckle itself. It wasn't in the center of town, but at the opposite edge from where they'd entered Old Knuckle. It stood out from the forest, almost right in the center of the trail that led to it, causing the path to curve around at an awkward angle.

From what Elven could tell, it was about an hour's ride from where Maybelle Perkins lived. Elven was reminded of his original thought—that Old Knuckle was very spread apart for being such a small community. Then again, maybe it wasn't so much spread apart than the fact that the roads zigzagged all over the place, making it take a lot longer to get around.

Madds slowed down to a crawl as she approached the building. Most of the lights were out, save for one in what looked to be an upper-floor bedroom and the porch light. Other than that, darkness engulfed the entire area around the dwelling, making it feel like they were inside a dimly lit bubble.

Elven couldn't see a single other home, building, or light for as far as his eyes could reach. It seemed very peaceful and secluded, and at the same time, the sheriff inside him felt incredibly exposed. The last time he lived in a secluded cabin... well, all that was left of it now was a pile of ash.

Madds parked the ATV alongside another one next to a small shed tucked to the right of the cabin, slightly behind it. Elven was glad to finally get off the thing, missing the padded seats of his truck. His backside was going to have to get used to it if he didn't figure out this case sooner than later. He loved the outdoors as much as the next person, but there were some comforts that he'd come to love, too.

"A bit far out here, ain't it?" Elven asked.

"Ginny's about the only one who was willing to let me stay when I showed up," Madds said. "I don't know if I have the right to complain about where it's at."

"So she's at least aware of the situation with me, right? Me coming up here and asking for a place to stay was talked about?"

Madds stopped and smiled. "She knows I'm coming back. I figured we'd just iron things out once you were inside."

"This should be fun, then," Elven said sarcastically. "How many more times will I have to explain that being a former sheriff isn't a bad thing? And that I'm here to help? Oh, and don't forget I'm also an outsider."

Madds shoved Elven playfully. "In the few months I've been gone, don't tell me you lost that Elven Hallie charm you're known for."

"From what I hear, that charm is actually just being cocky," Elven said, matching her playfulness. It felt good to smile with her, but every time he did, it slowly slid from his face again.

He saw in her eyes that she felt the same way. "Come on, let's go talk to Ginny. She'll love you," Madds said. "Maybe she even has some dinner on the stove."

Elven's stomach growled in response. He hadn't thought of food, but he was suddenly reminded that he hadn't eaten all day. "Sounds great to me," Elven said, not caring what might even be on the stove.

"It's not too late, so she might still be awake. Depends on how far into her book she's gotten, but she might have fallen asleep reading. She tends to do that sometimes," Madds said.

She sounded like she'd bonded with the woman and had an appreciation for her. Just from that, Elven could tell Ginny Tiller was a good woman. You could tell a lot about what type of person someone was just by the way people loved them.

Madds went to the door and opened it right up, not needing a key to do so. Elven wasn't a fan of that, but he also understood that needing to lock the doors at night wasn't a top priority. Another tell as to how nobody thought there was any danger from one another up here. It was going to be an uphill battle to convince people there was a guilty party around here, and he wondered if he ought to just tell everyone about the doll.

That would be something to think about in the morning when his head was clear and his belly was full.

Ginny Tiller's cabin was hot. Almost immediately, Elven spotted a wood-burning stove radiating heat, cutting through the winter cold that desperately tried to invade the place. He pulled his light jacket off, not wanting to sweat.

"It's not as hot in the rooms, don't worry," Madds said, reading his mind and pulling her own coat off.

"Maddison," a woman called out from somewhere in the cabin. It was much bigger than Elven had thought when he pulled up, but somehow still felt cozy. "Is that you, dear?"

Elven looked at Madds, lifting an eyebrow. "Maddison? Didn't figure you liked that name."

Madds shook her head. "She's a nice old lady," she whispered. "I'm not gonna correct her. She probably thinks Madds is a strange name to call me."

Elven shrugged. "She's not far off on that one."

"Says the man named after a pointy-eared fantasy species," Madds shot back. "I'd like to see what she comes up with to call you."

Elven thought Madds might just stick her tongue out at him, but she managed to keep it civil enough.

A set of steps facing the entrance led up to a loft, where he assumed there was a bedroom. He spotted the old woman make her way down to them, her legs shaking at every step. He wondered how long she'd plan on continuing to live up there instead of down here. It didn't seem very practical, but he wasn't going to tell her that right now. For all he knew, going up and down those stairs every day was the only thing keeping her able.

"Hello, Ms. Tiller," Madds said.

"I told you, call me Ginny," she said. "Last names are far too formal for me." She finally made it to the bottom of the steps and paused as she saw that Madds wasn't alone. "Oh, looks like you brought some company." She reached down for her glasses that hung from a thin chain around her neck.

"This is my, uh, *friend* Elven," Madds said. "He's looking for a place to stay, and I was hoping that he could take one of your extra rooms."

Ginny waved a hand for them to get closer. "Come on in, I ain't gonna bite. Let me get a good look at you." They both walked further into the main room, and Ginny shook her head. "Oh my, it's chilly out there. Both of you look like two freshly smacked asses with those red cheeks. Come on, warm yourselves up. I'll go fetch you some supper off the stove. Have a seat right there." She pointed to the table to the right of the front door and next to a window before she disappeared through a door that led to the kitchen.

Elven pulled out a chair for Madds to sit, then pushed it in for her when she was settled. He then grabbed his own chair and plopped down. He smiled at her, lifting his eyebrows. "Interesting lady," he remarked.

Madds smiled. "She's not wrong, though," she teased. "You do kind of resemble an ass, smacked or not."

Elven snickered so hard, he almost snorted. "I think I'm so tired and hungry that everything is tickling me right now."

"And here I thought it was just my comedic personality," Madds replied with a smile.

Before Elven could say anything in response, Ginny came back through the doorway, holding two plates with small bowls on top. Steam lifted from the food, telling him it was gonna be fresh. When she got closer, his mouth started watering at the scent of it.

"Hope you like tater soup," she said. "There's a little chicken on the side with a biscuit." She placed the food in front of them, and Elven didn't think he'd seen a better-looking meal in his life.

"Thank you," Madds and Elven said in unison.

"Well, dig in," Ginny said. "I already ate, so I'll just yap at ya about the rules in the cabin if you're gonna stay here. What'd you say your name was again? Elliot?"

Elven waited a moment, trying to finish chewing before speaking. He covered his mouth with a hand, not wanting to be rude. "Elven," he finally answered.

She soured her face, still not understanding. "I don't know if you got a mumble, or if my ears just ain't hearing right," she said. "But I swore you said *Eleven*."

"Close enough," Madds said, stifling a laugh.

"Alright, then, Eleven. Ain't never heard of a number for a name, but I ain't your mama who named you," she said. "I start breakfast at six in the morning. It stays on the stove 'til I get sick of looking at it, usually nine. If you get some, then good. Dinner, same thing but night. I expect it to be quiet when it's dark, you got that?"

"Yes, ma'am," Elven said.

"Call me Ginny," she said, cutting through the nonsense.

"Alright, Ginny," he said, scooping more of the soup up into his mouth.

"People don't like newcomers coming through Old Knuckle, let alone staying here," Ginny said. "But I ain't like that. Maybe it's 'cause I'm on the outskirts where I see strangers from time to time, but mostly, it's because I know a good deal when I see one."

"Deal?" Elven asked.

"I ain't doing this out of the kindness of my heart," she said. "How else is an old woman supposed to get by? Maddison here didn't tell you?" She gave her a side eye with a wink.

Madds smiled. "I figured the blow would be softened once he had your cooking," she said, throwing her own wink.

"Smart woman," Ginny said.

Elven smiled. He didn't mind paying. In fact, he would have insisted at the end of all this. It wasn't like he was short on cash, and he was really glad that he still had his wallet on him when being taken on this journey to Old Knuckle.

"That's fair," he said. "I'm guessing cash is okay?"

"It's the only thing I trust," she said. "Until the government tries to take that away, too. Always meddling. Taxes, am I right?"

Elven had his mouth full and raised his hands, giving her a nod of acknowledgment that made her smile.

"Well, alright, then. You'll be down the hall on the left, across from Maddison," she said. "We can settle up whenever you're ready. You look like a trustworthy fella. And if she says you're good, then I believe it."

"Thank you," Elven said.

"I'll leave you to it," she said, heading back toward the stairs. Halfway up, she stopped and turned back to them. "Oh, I almost forgot. No hanky-panky!" She was practically wagging her finger at the both of them, like they were being scolded for something that hadn't even happened.

"Ma'am—er, Ginny," Elven said. "You got nothing to worry about there."

Madds chuckled softly to herself, shaking her head.

"Like hell I don't," Ginny retorted. "You can cut the sexual tension in the room with a knife." And with that, she went upstairs to her bedroom.

Elven looked at Madds, who only held her hands up like she wasn't going to take the blame.

CHAPTER EIGHTEEN

It had been a long, tiring day of work. Not that he was being paid for anything anymore. It might not be his job, but it was still work, nonetheless. Once his belly was full, he made his way to the hallway to get ready for bed.

The hallway was short and stubby, with just his room, Madds's room right across the hall, and a bathroom at the end. He figured he'd seen the entire cabin from the entryway, other than up in the loft where Ginny's bedroom was. He assumed there was also a private bathroom up there for her by the way the ceiling in the downstairs bathroom looked. There was a large brown splotch, like it had seen some water damage from whatever room was up there. It wasn't currently leaking, so she'd had it fixed at some point, but the aesthetics of the place apparently wasn't high on her priority list to attend to.

The shower was hot, which was a pleasant surprise to him. Most places up here were lucky to have running water. He didn't know if it was because the infrastructure had been damaged, or people just couldn't afford the bills to keep it running. It was probably somewhere in the middle, like most everything else in life.

His nighttime routine was far shorter than usual. He hadn't had the chance to pack any of his things, so he had to make do with what Ginny kept in stock. It was a far cry from the moisturizers and retinols that he kept at home. He hoped his skin wouldn't suffer too much while up here. Madds seemed like the type that would have more than just a bar of soap, so he could hit her up. Of course, that might open up another bag of worms, so maybe it was best to just put up with it.

He hated to admit it, but the playful banter with Madds had felt good earlier. But he didn't want to make a habit of it. Part of him was angry that he enjoyed it so much. He made a mental note to steer clear of any more of that.

He exited the bathroom, towel around his waist, but was stopped short as soon as he set foot outside the door. Steam followed him out, billowing down the hall past him and right into Madds's face. She stood there, waiting for her turn.

He immediately looked down, seeing she was less clothed than before. Nothing inappropriate, but she wasn't wearing the flannel look she had before. Just an undershirt and small shorts.

He gave a small, awkward nod, trying not to stare. "Sorry, didn't mean to take too long."

She shook her head. "It's alright," she said. "You deserve it. After all, we dragged you up here."

"Yeah. You did," he said dryly.

She stood there, her eyes shifting around the hallway like she was unsure what to say next. Eventually, she did. "Well, yeah, I did. Sorry about that."

He let the apology linger, not sure if there was anything to accept. Instead, he opted to talk about the case. "I was thinking now that I'm here and sold on joining in this investigation, we could go over your notes if you have them. I'm assuming you have some sort of list? Maybe your dead ends at the very least?"

She shook her head. "No, of course not. I mean, yes, I do have a list," she clarified. "I just figured talking to the families was the best thing to convince you to stay. I guess we got lucky that we found that doll when we did instead."

He nodded. "Agreed."

"Did you want to go over that list tonight, or..."

"I think tomorrow is for the best," he said. "I'm surprised my eyes are still open right now."

She smiled and gave an awkward laugh. "Yeah, I think I'll sleep well tonight," she said, then she went quiet for a moment, the silence between them thick. "Do you really think Benson had something to do with this whole thing?"

Elven shrugged. "Madds, I don't know anyone here. I'm not sure, but probably not. I just haven't ruled anyone out yet. As far as confidence, you're about the only person I can trust at this point, and that's saying a lot."

That seemed to cut deeper than Elven intended, but it also wasn't a lie. If Madds took the jab as hard as it looked, maybe there was good reason for it. Elven definitely thought so. He wasn't in the game of tit for tat, but perhaps it was justified.

"I guess so," she said.

Elven lifted his chin toward his room. "I'll let you by so I can get to bed."

"Oh, right," she said, pushing herself against the narrow hallway. Elven matched her but on the opposite side. They both scooted by, only inches away from each other as they did. She made it to the bathroom, and he made it to his room.

"Elven," she said, and he stood in the doorway, turning around to look at her. "Thanks for sticking around."

"I gave you my word," he said. "There's enough proof for me to be here on the case."

She nodded. "I know, but still. Thank you."

"I'm not just doing it for you," he pointed out. "I'm gonna hold you to your word, too."

She bit her bottom lip. "I will."

She took a deep breath. He watched her eyes as they crawled

everywhere around him and finally landed on the scar on his abdomen. The one that was caused by the bullet she had fired. She looked saddened at the sight. She let out a long sigh, knowing that she'd done that to him.

"I'm so—"

"Goodnight, Madds," he said, stepping into his room and closing the door before she could say anything else. It wasn't his job to make her feel better. And he wasn't ready to accept an apology. There was a lot more than a bullet hole she had to be sorry for, anyway.

CHAPTER NINETEEN

The night air was cold next to the window. She kept it cracked at night to let a cool breeze in, but sometimes it was too much and would catch just under the blankets, making her shiver awake. But if she closed it, she might get too hot and sweaty from the fire that burned in the stove. It was a balance that was never exact, but for the most part, it worked okay.

Tonight, though, was different.

She wasn't home, but instead in the middle of the woods. Not only that, but she was in the basement. Sometimes being there made it feel creepy. No matter how many times she was told that she was safe there, something about it never rang true. Maybe it was the work that he said he had to do, or maybe it was just not being in her usual bed. But either way, she was now wide awake in the middle of the night.

Walking around wasn't permitted. She knew that he'd be mad if he found out, but if she laid here all night, she'd never fall back to sleep. She felt the sudden urge to pee, too, so unless he'd locked her door, she needed to venture out of her room.

Sometimes he liked to do that, and she hoped that he hadn't

tonight. He kept her safe, but sometimes she didn't think it was fair that he thought she should hold it all night. If she wet her bed, then she'd never hear the end of it, and her backside would feel it for days after he brought his belt to it.

It wasn't fair, but like he'd told her so many times over, life wasn't always fair. It was the hard stuff that made us stronger.

She didn't understand that. After all, she was only nine years old. She could be told something over and over again, but she'd never experienced what it truly meant.

But because it came from *him*, the Angel Keeper, she knew it was the God's honest truth. She was his top angel, and he never made her feel any less than that. So why should she question him?

Still, peeing in the middle of the night seemed like something she should be able to do to avoid wetting the bed. It was the mature and responsible thing to do. And he was always telling her about his responsibilities, so this one was hers.

Her bare feet touched the wooden floor, the temperature shift sudden. Even though the air was warm, somehow the floor was always cold. It must have had something to do with being in the ground, but she couldn't know for sure.

She pulled her nightgown out from the covers, tucking it in her arms so that it didn't drag. It was three times too big for her, and she didn't want to get it dirty.

That was another thing that he would be angry about if it happened. There were so many rules she had to remember, but she was really good at that part. The remembering. It was just following them that she struggled with.

She went to the door, hoping that he had trusted her enough to keep it unlocked. Her hand wrapped around the handle and turned. That was the easy part. She pushed it, and much to her relief—and some surprise—the door swung open. He hadn't put the metal bar on the outside, so the door let her right out into the hallway.

She smiled wide, knowing she was doing something she wasn't supposed to. Sometimes it was fun to be a little bit naughty. She just had to make sure she got away with it, and then it would be her little secret.

She stepped into the hallway slowly, like she was testing the waters with a toe in first. When she wasn't yelled at, or didn't see the glow of the lantern growing closer, she put her whole self out into the hallway. She spread her arms out, tracing her fingers along the walls as she walked. It was freeing to be out and about in the cabin when everyone else was sleeping.

But as she got closer to the stairs, she knew she had to be extra quiet because they could be creaky. The wrong step would wake her keeper, and then she'd be in big trouble.

She got to one of the closed doors, placing her head against it, listening for anything. Sometimes there were noises from the other angels, the ones she was told hadn't done what they were supposed to. Not in the way that she was doing something she wasn't supposed to. Those were little white sins compared to the sins that they had committed.

She didn't fully understand that, but she pretended she did. She just nodded and smiled whenever he told her things like that. It seemed to make him happy, and then when he was happy, so was she.

The first door she tested, she didn't hear much of anything, just some long, deep breaths. She figured the angel inside was sleeping. She didn't want to disturb her, because if she did, she risked waking her up, and then she might scream—or worse. And if that happened, well, she was already in trouble just for being out of her room.

But when she reached the second room, she heard sniffling. There were some other deep sobs, and she knew the girl—the other angel—inside was awake. Not only awake, but crying. She didn't like it when people cried. It made her sad, and she hated being sad. She didn't want anyone to be sad.

She thought about what she should do, but she knew that if it were her crying, she'd want someone to come help her. Maybe rub her back and tell her it would be alright. She didn't have a mama of her own, but she knew that's what mamas were supposed to do.

Sometimes she missed hers—not that she ever knew her. But she knew that missing her mama was also normal, whether or not she'd ever met her. So she knew that the other angel probably was missing hers, too.

It was decided. She was going to help her.

The bar on the door was heavy, but she'd lifted them before when the keeper wasn't looking. She had mastered the trick when she was playing around one day, placing her body right underneath it and pushing up on the metal with all her muscles. It popped right up, scratching against the latch. She paused, hoping that she didn't make too much noise.

When she was satisfied that she didn't hear anyone coming down the stairs, she walked the metal bar to the side until it was propped up against the wall. She didn't hear the girl sniffling anymore, but she was probably just scared about who was outside her door. After all, nobody was supposed to be coming in at this hour.

She opened the door, poking her head inside. She saw the whites of the other angel's eyes in the darkness. She was still awake.

"Don't be sad," she said. "It's gonna be alright."

The other girl was much older than she was. She looked like a beautiful princess to her. She hoped that when she was older, she could look like her with her long brown hair and her wide blue eyes. Her skin was red around her eyes from crying, along with her nose, but it was still so clear and soft-looking.

"Wh-what's your name?" the older angel asked.

She smiled wide, stepping into the room. "I'm the top angel," she said. "But he sometimes calls me Auriel. He says it's my special angel name. He didn't tell me what yours was. Did he tell you your angel name yet?"

The woman on the floor studied Auriel a moment, her chin quivering. Finally, she nodded and swallowed. "My real name is—"

Auriel ran to her and placed her hand over her mouth. She shook her head. "I can keep a secret, but he says never to use our outside names in here," she said. "That's a golden rule that we can never break." She felt the tears run down her hand from the older angel. She smiled, stroking her back. "It's okay. It's gonna be okay."

This didn't seem to help much, just made the older angel cry even more. "D-Dina," she finally said. "That's what he said my name was."

"That's a beautiful name," Auriel said. "You have beautiful hair. It's so dark, like mysterious. Mine is just this plain light blond." She ran a hand through her hair to show Dina.

Dina stared at Auriel for a moment, her eyes searching for something. Auriel couldn't tell what it was, but it was almost like an empty stare. As if the woman in front of her had no idea what was going on. She was scared, and that was alright. Auriel felt scared all the time.

"Where are we?" Dina finally asked.

Auriel shifted around, unsure what to say. She wasn't really sure what to call this place. It wasn't really her home. No, that was further in town. This was a second place. A place where she slept and he did his keeper work.

"Someplace safe," was all Auriel said. That's what he always told her.

"I need to get out of here," Dina said. "Can you help me leave?"

Auriel pulled away and walked a few steps toward the door. What Dina had just said was something that the keeper would be very angry about if he heard. She looked to Dina and shook her head.

"That's another golden rule," she finally said. "Don't let him hear you say that, you hear?"

"What is going to happen to me?" Dina asked, this time crawling toward Auriel.

Before Auriel could answer, though, she heard the floor creak above her head. "Oh no," she said. "He's awake." She suddenly realized she never had the chance to pee and regretted stopping in with Dina. "I'm gonna be in big trouble if he finds me. Please don't tell him."

Auriel rushed to the door, opening it and turning to look at Dina.

"Wait," Dina said. "Don't leave me in here." She was whispering, but her voice was starting to get louder.

Auriel put a finger to her lips, her head now the only thing left inside. "Keep quiet," she said. "I'll come back to see you the next time he's asleep. Don't tell him I was here."

And then Auriel shut the door, pulling down the bar. Dina slammed against the door, but Auriel was already halfway down the hallway.

Auriel heard the footsteps above her get louder and faster. She quickly made it to her room and closed the door. But she could still hear Dina pounding on her own door. She frowned, knowing that wasn't going to be a good thing for her.

And just as she had feared, she heard the keeper walk into the hallway and open a door. That's when he started yelling, and just after that was when Dina started screaming.

CHAPTER TWENTY

Elven was up before the sun, which wasn't that great of a feat, considering it was winter. He felt like he'd slept far longer than his usual, but his body had definitely needed it. Pulling an all-nighter, getting abducted at gunpoint, being grilled by everyone in town, getting into a handful of physical altercations, and, of course, having his emotions all twisted up by finding Madds all in one day had a way of wearing a man out. All things considered, he felt like a new man once he was up and out of bed.

He could smell the breakfast that Ginny Tiller had made mention of the day before. And just as she'd promised, it was on the stove. It smelled delicious, and he hoped there was some protein along with sweets. It was gonna be a long day, and he needed some real fuel.

There wasn't a single clock in the building, so far as he could tell, and with it still being dark, it was hard for him to know what time it was. But from the way breakfast was still pretty darn warm, he figured it wasn't much later than six in the morning.

The house was also warm, from both the kitchen and the wood-burning stove in the living room. Elven spotted the bacon, eggs, and biscuits and gravy. It was a good spread. Much more than he'd ever expected when he first entered Old Knuckle. He knew there were no hotels, and after seeing Benson's place, he figured a pack of snack cakes was the best he could expect to eat in the near future.

After dishing up some food onto one of the plates that Ginny had stacked on the counter, he brought it to the table and sat down. Ginny made her way downstairs, dressed in a floral housecoat.

"I see you wake up earlier than your friend in there," she said.

Elven cut into the biscuits and gravy, shoveling a huge heap into his mouth. It was delicious. A far cry from anything healthy, but at this point, he wasn't concerned about that. Once he was back in Dupray, he could worry about his waistline and intake of trans fats. Right now, he could let himself enjoy the little bit of happiness he was finding in Old Knuckle.

"Yes, ma'am—I mean, Ginny," he said. "I'm assuming this is a normal thing?"

She grinned. "You mean Maddison sleeping in?" she asked, following it with a laugh. "I'm not sure if it's the weather, the setting, or if what they say is true about beauty sleep, 'cause I don't think I've ever seen her up before the sun since she came here."

He smiled, but his attention went to the door when a knock came. He gave Ginny a questioning look. He had no basis for worrying, but it just didn't seem normal for someone to come visit at this hour all the way out at the edge of civilization where they were now.

She waved him off, though, cool as a cucumber as she opened the door.

"Ginny," a familiar voice said. "I was hoping—"

"You get your ass in here before all the cold air comes in," Ginny said. "And don't go around asking—I set out a plate for you, too. Sit down, and I'll fetch it."

"Thank you, Ginny," he said.

Benson walked in with a big smile on his face. Once he hit the light, Elven could see what Ginny was getting at last night when he walked in. Benson's cheeks were lit up red from the cold, just like someone had slapped them. Of course, Elven wouldn't have quite described it quite like Ginny had, but then again, Ginny was a special kind of lady.

But more than that, right under his eye was the shiner that he'd come back with after speaking with Davin. It was a deep purple bruise now.

Benson sat beside Elven, who continued to eat greedily. Even after eating last night, Elven felt even hungrier this morning. That, or Ginny's cooking was some kind of sorcery because it was so delicious.

"Ginny's biscuits," Benson said. "They're something, ain't they?"

Elven nodded, finishing what was in his mouth. "You weren't lying about that," he said, wiping his mouth after.

Ginny came out, holding a plate of steaming food in one hand, a carafe of coffee in the other. She placed the food down and filled two of the four empty cups that sat on the table. Both Elven and Benson grabbed a cup. It wasn't Elven's preferred method of making coffee or brand, but he would take what he was given and be grateful. Ginny was doing far more for him than he could have expected once he heard he was staying here.

"You boys dig in and don't worry about clean-up," she said. "Leave 'em there, and I'll take care of it. I know you've got a lotta work ahead of you today."

She disappeared back upstairs, leaving them both to their food. Elven raised his eyebrows in her direction, curious. "Suppose word gets out fairly quick around here?" Elven asked.

Benson nodded. "Like wildfire sometimes."

Elven smiled. "Reminds me of home. Guess we're not too far off."

"Guess not," Benson said, his entire focus now on his plate in front of him.

Elven was glad that Ginny had left them alone, and that Madds wasn't here to intervene. It gave him some time to speak to Benson one on one. He seemed like a good kid—technically an adult, but Elven couldn't be too careful and needed to be sure. He took a big swig of his mug, thinking how he wanted to approach the conversation, then set it down.

"Tell me about Old Knuckle," he finally said.

Benson was mid-stab of his fork when the question came, and he hesitated. He opened his mouth, thinking, and finally shoved a bite inside. He didn't bother to finish eating it before answering.

"I mean, it's home," he shrugged. "Grew up here, have friends here."

"It's all you know?" Elven asked.

Benson nodded. "I've left Old Knuckle before, if that's what you're gettin' at. And not just that little trip down to Dupray to grab you, either."

"How about West Virginia?"

Benson shook his head that time. "Nope. My parents never took us anywhere like that," he said. "Mostly just the parks in the state. When I was eight, we made a road trip out to New River Gorge for a whole week. Even at that age, I knew how beautiful it was." There was a small smile on his face, like he was remembering a better time in his life.

"And how about your sister?" Elven asked.

"She was on that trip, too," Benson said.

"I mean, had she been elsewhere? Outside of West Virginia?"

Benson shook his head again. "The only time she could have that I wouldn't know about is before I was born, and she'd only have been like three years old. But I don't think she ever did."

"Think she ever wanted to?" Elven asked, trying to keep it light.

Benson weighed the idea for a moment. "I think everyone wants to at some point," he finally said. "But reality is a lot different than fantasy."

"Does that go for you, too?" Elven asked. "Did you dream of getting out?"

"Sure," he said. "Seeing big cities like New York. Or going somewhere like Hawaii and seeing the ocean. Maybe somehow we could have made a vacation there, but ain't like we could afford it. Even when my parents were alive, we couldn't do that."

"What about moving?" Elven asked. "Ever dream of that?"

Benson shook his head. "Old Knuckle is home. For better or worse, it's where I belong."

Elven hesitated for a moment, knowing that he was getting close to a line that might make Benson react emotionally. But he had to push, even just slightly.

"Did Lila feel the same way?" he asked.

Benson was a lot smarter than Elven had given him credit for. Because he picked up on the question's deeper meaning without hesitation. "What are you getting at?" Benson asked, putting his fork down.

"I'm just trying to ask if she had been talking about leaving," Elven said.

"And I told you she hadn't," Benson said. His tone was verging well past defensive and getting into offensive territory.

"That's not what both Maybelle Perkins and Ronnie Vaughn said," Elven said. "You heard it from both of them yourself."

Benson threw his fork against his plate. "What is your point, then? Lila didn't tell me everything? If that's the case, then I guess you got me there. Real great detective work," he said sarcastically. "I'm so glad I brought you up here."

Benson stood up to pull away from the table, but Elven stopped him. He stood and grabbed his arm, pulling him back so that he could be right up in his face to smell the coffee on his breath.

"I ain't gonna ask questions that everyone likes. That goes the same for you," Elven said. "The hard questions are necessary, which is exactly why you brought me up here."

"And instead of asking them to me, you should be asking everyone else," Benson said. "This is a waste of everyone's time. But most of all, Lila's."

Elven didn't let up. "The only waste of time happening is your stubbornness right now. I don't know you, so why should I trust you?

'Cause you say so? How about I apply that logic to everyone else in town? The sooner I get you out of the way, the sooner I get to the real killer and have one more person in town I know I can trust." He poked his chest with his finger. "What do you say?"

Benson bit his bottom lip, looking at Elven warily. "I've told you everything I know."

"You said you didn't want to leave Old Knuckle," Elven said. "That it's home to you."

"That's right," Benson said. "But part of it being home to me is my sister. If Lila ain't here, I don't got a whole lot, now do I? Look, I wouldn't want to leave Old Knuckle. Maybe Lila would have, maybe not. But I do know that if she wanted to, she would have told me and given me the choice to go with her."

"And what would you choose?" Elven asked.

Benson sighed. For the first time this morning, Elven saw the welling of tears in Benson's eyes. "I said without Lila, I've got nothing, didn't I? I'd have gone with her if that's really what she wanted."

Elven studied him a moment, his eyes wandering all over Benson's face as a tear dribbled down over Benson's bruise as it went down his cheek. "I'm sorry about your sister," Elven said. "And I'm sorry about the questions."

"You trust me now?" Benson asked.

Elven nodded, knowing he probably could have from the beginning of this whole thing. After all, everyone else had written the girls off as having run off. Benson could have just leaned into that if he was trying to get away with murder.

"Depends," Elven answered. "You gonna tell me how you ended up walking away with that bruise on your face?"

Benson sighed, but before he could speak, someone interrupted.

"Did I walk in on something here?" Madds asked, standing in the hallway, her eyes puffy from just waking up.

CHAPTER TWENTY-ONE

Benson was extremely hesitant to fill in Madds and Elven on what had gone down between him and Davin. He explained how they used to be friends, but that friendship had faded until it fell apart into the almost nothing of a relationship that it was currently. But after a few questions and prodding, Elven realized Benson was just trying to protect his friend who'd had a very rough situation growing up.

Elven could see that Benson had a good heart, which made this case even worse. They would have to press the people he called friends and family for information, and eventually cross a few lines to find out what they needed. And at the end of it all, Elven knew that someone in this town was going to be found responsible for the death of Shayla, and whatever had happened to Lila and Sadie.

He hoped for everyone's sake that the girls would be found alive, but with how long it had been, well, the odds were stacked against them. Elven wasn't going to say that to Benson, though.

Right now, he was just focused on the next step in the case instead of what they may, or may not, find.

Learning about Davin, however, did pique Elven's interest.

Benson may think there was nothing other than some old beef between them, but Elven thought his behavior was a little strange. Sure, times were tough, and emotions were high, considering Sadie was also missing, but Benson wasn't making threats. He was doing whatever it took to find her. Even if it meant breaking the rules and bringing in some outsiders to help.

Elven couldn't understand the unwillingness to work with a stranger if it meant finding one's family members alive. He could never understand that type of pride, and honestly, he hoped that it never found him or anyone he cared about.

Once they waited for Madds to finish getting ready, which didn't take as long as the men had thought it would, they were on their way to the center of Old Knuckle. Benson led the way, though, at this point, it seemed like Madds knew her way around the community fairly well. But Benson said he wanted to make sure they didn't run into any trouble on the way, so Madds welcomed the escort. Apparently, she'd caught some trouble before when traveling alone through the trails. It was nothing she couldn't handle herself, of course, but it was still an obstacle they didn't want.

Though, Elven was sure that Benson's presence alone wasn't going to be much of a deterrence. After all, yesterday, they'd had Bear with them and still ran into issues with Roy Leven and the Morrison brothers.

But now that Elven had filed Benson away as a trustworthy person, he was glad. The more they could do that in the community, the better and faster they'd get at finding the other girls. Only three hundred or so more people, Elven thought.

It was cold and still dark out when the three of them set out to the center of town, but by the time they reached it, the sun was already poking its head over the horizon. The trip was long, and Elven wondered if they were setting themselves back by being so far outside the main group of people. Then again, how was it really any different than where he lived in Dupray? Or at least, where he lived before it was torched to the ground?

Maybe it was better this way, so he didn't have to deal with people not liking his presence in Old Knuckle. Out of sight, out of mind. That sort of thing.

Just when he was thinking that, he and Madds were suddenly in sight. He could feel the whispers of the people rummaging about. It was a total shift in the mood, almost immediately.

There weren't a ton of people around, but there were enough. He didn't recognize them, so either they hadn't seen him, or they hadn't heard. Or maybe it was both, and he was just oblivious to who they were because they hadn't made an impression like Roy Leven had.

They pulled up to the main building, or what Elven assumed was the main building, like they did yesterday. The three of them dismounted from their ATVs, and Elven looked around at the area as the sun started to brighten it up.

"Bear said he'd be here," Benson said. "Said he wanted to take you both to see something."

"Where is he?" Madds asked.

Benson shrugged. "Said to sit tight if he wasn't here."

A woman approached, looking unsure, like Elven was a wild animal that she didn't know if she should engage or not. She had blond hair and a small, hook-shaped scar next to her nose. She looked to be in her late fifties.

"Benson," she finally said, turning her attention away from Elven to the kid. She switched from unsure to a smile real quick once she met Benson's eyes.

"Hey, Cora," he said. "How's everything going? How's your pop doing these days?"

Cora shrugged. "You know, about the same as always."

He nodded. "That's not a bad thing, though. Means he's still here."

Cora smiled warmly. "Ain't that the truth. Thanks for the perspective." She bit her lip. "Any news? You know, about Lila?"

Benson shook his head. "No, but we're getting somewhere. You know Madds, but this is her friend Elven."

Cora studied Elven curiously, but she didn't offer a handshake or greeting. "I see," she said. "And that would be Elven Hallie?"

Elven nodded. "Yes, ma'am," he said. He held his hand out, not intending to wait for a better greeting.

She took it hesitantly, but quickly pulled back, turning to Benson. "Benson, can I talk to you? In private?"

Elven sighed. "If this has anything to do with me, then you might as well say it to my face," he said, having had enough.

She pursed her lips, cautious about what she should say next. "Alright, then," she said. "I was gonna ask what in the hell he is thinking bringing you up here."

Elven looked around, seeing a few people starting to gather behind Cora at the sound of her raised voice. There were maybe ten total people around to listen.

Bear rolled in on his ATV, just in time for the theatrics about to take place.

"I'm gonna have to answer this a thousand times over, ain't I?" Elven asked, though it wasn't a question he was looking for an answer to. "Tell you what, you wait right here. I'm gonna figure this out, and we'll chat about it. Does that sound good?"

"What's going on?" Bear asked.

"We're going to have a little town meeting," Elven said.

CHAPTER TWENTY-TWO

ELVEN WAS DETERMINED TO BRING THIS WHOLE *OUTSIDERS* thing to a head right here and right now. He'd had a word with Bear and Benson, who knew what to do. Bear had an air horn and jumped on his ATV, riding a tight circle around the paths near the town center. Elven could hear the horn loud and clear, so he assumed the others on the outskirts could hear it, too.

Elven didn't want to have the same conversation a thousand times over. It was going to be an even bigger waste of time than riding around for a bit and waiting an hour for everyone who cared enough to show up, then make a big show of it all for another hour. So that's why they set out to get everyone and anyone who had any interest in these new people to come in and have a chat.

They waited a bit after Bear returned. After they roused what felt like a good grip of people, Elven figured they were ready. Elven didn't know if he should have them all go sit down inside the large building or if doing it outside was the best option.

When Bear stood in the clearing, Elven figured that was where the town hall was gonna be. They hadn't gotten the whole town, but it looked like forty or so people had come out to join them. It might have been the biggest gathering Old Knuckle had ever had, for all Elven knew. Most people in small towns, while tight-knit, still liked to keep to themselves. It was why they lived where they did, for the most part.

When it seemed like everyone was done revving their ATVs or making their way into the clearing, Bear leaned toward Elven. "I sure hope you know what the hell you're doing," Bear muttered.

"And I sure hope I've got your support in this," Elven said. "Like right now."

Bear smiled. "Already told you that you do. Just don't make me regret it."

"No promises," Elven replied with a wink.

"What is this about?" someone shouted.

By the look on everyone's faces, Elven knew he better cough up some answers quick as to why he roused them all.

"Yeah, why'd you make all that ruckus, Bear?" another person asked.

Bear held his hands up. "Everyone, I wanted to get ahead of this so we didn't keep running into the same problem over and over again."

"Well, get on with it, then!"

"You all have seen Madds around town," Bear started. "I know it's been a bit of an adjustment. We don't usually get new faces around here. But you've all taken to her, well, I guess better than expected for Old Knuckle."

That got a few chuckles from the group. A good sign. But there were some grim faces that Elven could see, telling him that not everyone liked the new girl in town. If they didn't like her, then they surely wouldn't like him.

"Well, now we got an even newer face," Bear continued, and Elven could sense the hesitation in his voice. They exchanged a glance, and Elven gave him a nod. "His name is Elven." Another pause and a clearing of his throat. "Elven Hallie."

There was a loud, long drawn-out groan from the crowd. About half the crowd looked plenty fired up.

"Why you bringing a Hallie around here?" someone shouted. "This is the end of Old Knuckle as we know it!"

Others joined in, and Elven could only imagine the pitchforks they were thinking of pulling out. He had to get ahead of this before it got out of hand.

Was rounding people up going to bite him in the backside? Did he just get them all together to form a mob to run him out of town?

"Alright, alright," Bear said, motioning with his hands in the air placatingly. "Let's give him a chance to speak, and then you can raise your concerns. I felt the same as you until I heard what he had to say." The shouts quieted down for a moment, and Bear looked to Elven. "Better step up before they step on it again," he muttered.

Elven shook Bear's hand, hoping that everyone could see the exchange, and stood in front of the crowd. "I should have done this first thing," Elven began. "And for that, I apologize. It would have saved us a lot of time, but here we are. Many of you recognize my name. And most of the time, people think that's a bad thing."

"You're damn straight!" someone shouted.

"But it ain't because of my doing," Elven continued. "I am not the same man as my father, and I do not believe a child should live and die by the sins of his father. Judge me by my actions is all I ask."

The crowd didn't seem to protest so much now, but there were still rumblings.

"And what are you doing here?" someone asked. "You ain't sheriff now, so how do we know you ain't just trying to come for our mineral rights?"

"Hell, I'll sell you my rights right now!" someone else yelled.

"Shut up, Josiah! You ain't got shit to sell. None of us do," a voice retorted. "But just because we ain't got the rights don't mean we want a mine put in. They'll blow the top off that mountain and make a mess of our homes."

That was a new one, Elven thought. Was that really what all

these people were afraid of? Most people wanted the jobs that came with a mine, but these people were different. They didn't care about the money and jobs; they cared about their homes and what would happen to them. Of course, if they were afraid of mountaintop mining, he didn't blame them. Cheapest and fastest usually meant the most destructive.

He didn't want to go into the details of how it might not be so bad with other mining methods. He knew enough about the process from his parents, but bringing all that up would only make him look guilty of the very thing they were afraid of. Something that he had absolutely no involvement in.

"I can assure you that I ain't here on behalf of anyone other than myself," Elven said. "And I have no interest in mineral rights or trying to turn this into a mining town. The last thing I want to do is disturb your way of life out here."

"Then why the hell are you in Old Knuckle? It ain't a place for sight-seeing!"

A lot of laughs from that one, and Elven joined in with them. It did seem like the tide was turning, just a little bit, in his favor. He'd take whatever he could get for goodwill coming his way right now.

"Some people in your fine community decided to *reach out* to me," Elven said, smoothing over the details of how he actually got up here. "They said that some girls had gone missing, and one of them was found dead."

"Oh, come on," someone protested. "This is some bullshit. They left town, and the other wandered into some bear's territory. No mystery there."

Elven shook his head. "They wanted to get my opinion on it, so I told them I'd look into it. I said if I found enough that told me they were right and that something was amiss with Shayla's death, I'd stick around to help them figure it out."

"So what are you still doing here?" Roy Leven asked, stepping into the front of the crowd.

Elven locked eyes with the man. He wasn't going to throw down right here with him, not unless he was given no other choice. But he could tell that Roy wasn't here to listen. He was here to oppose.

"I spoke to Maybelle Perkins, and I spoke to Ronnie Vaughn," Elven answered. "We surveyed the scene where Shayla's body was found, and after all of that, I've come to the conclusion that it wasn't just an animal attack but something more sinister. I'm treating this as a murder investigation and a missing person's case. Just like I would have when I wore the badge."

Roy glared at him. "What's your reason?"

"Yeah, what evidence you got?" another chimed in.

Elven wanted to reveal the missing doll that had been hanging in the tree. Tell them about the wings that were put on it that couldn't have been done by a child who'd just happened across the doll in the dirt. It was far too intricate to be a kid's handiwork. But if he said that, he'd be giving the killer the knowledge that he and the others knew. And then they could easily divert from the usual path and would lose the little bit of an advantage they had.

Still, he had to give them something.

"We have some evidence that we found on a second review," Elven said, which may have been a misstep, but it was out there now. "The girl's body had marks on her skin that weren't in line with an animal fight."

That didn't seem to be enough, per the crowd's skeptical glances. So he had to go with the other option. Reason.

"And then there's the question if these three girls were such good friends, were they together?" Elven asked. "And if they were together, then why not three bodies?"

"Because the others left town!" someone replied.

"And they left their friend to die?" Elven asked, shaking his head. "I think from what I've seen of Old Knuckle so far, people here are good, and they're kind. And if any one of you were to die, don't you think your friends would do what was right and tell someone?"

There were some murmurs from the crowd, like they were really giving his words a thought. Even Roy didn't seem like he wanted to push against that logic. Elven may have buttered them up just a little to buy into it, but he meant every word. The people in town were just trying to get by like everyone else. Wanting to keep to themselves didn't make them bad people.

"You're still not from Old Knuckle," Roy said. "And I don't trust a single one of you if you ain't from here."

"I felt the same way," Bear admitted. "Until I found out that this is the man who put Hollis Starcher behind bars."

More rumbles, but this time of excitement. "No shit?" someone asked.

Elven nodded. "He's locked up, waiting for his trial right now."

Even Roy lifted an eyebrow, giving a single nod. "I ain't gonna argue with that," he said. "But you make one misstep, and I'll be the first to run you outta here. You hear me?"

Others joined in, but it seemed like Elven was being accepted. For the time being.

"Loud and clear," Elven said. "Thank you, everybody. I won't let you down."

The crowd started to disperse, and Bear clapped him on the shoulder. "Seems like we've bought a little bit of time for now," he said. "You sure can work a crowd. How long it'll stick, well, that's anyone's guess."

Elven nodded, wanting to gloat a little, but he couldn't help but focus on someone in the crowd who'd caught his attention. He was a larger man, tall and burly, almost like Bear. He was bald, and he kept his head low. He glanced at Elven, but as soon as he locked eyes, the man averted his to the ground and turned around, walking away.

"Now, come on. I want to show you something," Bear said, pulling Elven away.

Elven looked back, but the man was already gone.

CHAPTER TWENTY-THREE

Bear led Madds, Benson, and Elven away from the center of town and to some back roads that Elven hadn't explored yet. Of course, that meant probably ninety percent of Old Knuckle for Elven, but the other two didn't seem bothered by where they were headed.

Once they arrived, Elven figured out why. It was a small cabin, maybe smaller than Benson's trailer, but it was where Bear called home. Elven knew it immediately once he spotted the sign out front, which was a little carved bear holding a sign that said "COLTER." It was far cuter than Elven had expected from a man who looked like Bear, but then again, people were complex creatures. Not everything was right on the surface to see.

There was a fence surrounding the majority of the land around the cabin, but it was made up of small wire that could easily be missed unless you were looking for it. At the front, however, there was no fence. Just a wide opening where a lot of vehicles could be parked, with little half-logs chopped in a line, like a little parking lot of his own.

"Get a lot of company?" Elven asked as they walked toward the door.

Bear nodded. "When you take the mantle of, well, whatever the hell I am to this place, you get a lot of visitors. People like someone to look up to that can help solve their problems when they can't find one."

"How'd you come into that title?" Elven asked. "Whatever it is they call you here, that is."

"Long story," he said. "But mostly because of who my pawpaw is. Then my daddy, of course. I guess it runs in the family. The benefits of the last name, right?"

Elven cocked his head. "You've seen where that gets me. So I'll take your word for it."

Bear opened the door for the other three and let them filter in before him. The cabin was small but surprisingly roomy for four people. It was just one big room, but it was sizable. A heavy cast-iron stove sat against the wall next to a small counter and a handful of cabinets. There wasn't a table, but Elven spotted a TV tray unfolded in front of the couch facing the television. He wasn't sure what kind of signal they got up here, but he spotted a DVD player next to the TV. Elven wondered what the likelihood of satellite was up here, but more than that, what the likelihood of them paying for it was.

And to the left was a curtain that was half pulled out. Elven could see the twin bed and small dresser where the curtain didn't cover. It was homey, cozy even. There was no bathroom, but out the window on the back wall, he saw what seemed to be an outhouse. Elven didn't envy that situation, especially in this cold. Or even worse, when it finally snowed.

Bear closed the door and went to his dresser. He pulled it open and took the Troll doll out of it. Elven had let him keep it as part of the deal. Bear was who people trusted in town more than anyone, so if word got out that the outsider had it in his possession, the people wouldn't be big fans of that. Besides, Elven hadn't known what kind of sleeping situation he'd be in and didn't want to risk losing it, leaving Bear as the best option to hold onto it.

And just as Elven had suspected, it was still in his possession.

"I wanted to show you this," Bear said. "Now, don't jump to conclusions or anything, but I was studying it last night and noticed the stitching."

"What about it?" Elven asked.

"Like I said, it doesn't mean anything," Bear said. "But it's pretty nice. The way the small gown is stitched around, and then look at these wings. I know it looks like some twigs holding it together, but the fabric that's on it, I ain't never seen anything like it."

"So what are you thinking?" Elven asked.

"I'm thinking that whoever did this isn't new to sewing."

"Cora?" Benson asked immediately. "You think she murdered Shayla and hung this up there? No way."

From the way Benson was crossing his arms and shaking his head, it was clear how he felt about it. Elven had only just met the woman, so he had no opinion of her. But even Madds looked a little reluctant to join in on Bear's theory.

"I'm with Benson," she said.

"I ain't saying she did this," Bear said. "What the hell does *don't jump to conclusions* mean to you both?"

"Then what are you saying?" Benson asked.

"That we go ask her," Bear said. "See if she has seen anything like this, and see if she might know anyone who could stitch like this."

"I don't disagree," Elven said. "If you think this is a lead, then let's follow it. I have nothing else to go on. 'Cause if this doesn't work, we'll need to start canvassing the area, looking for other dolls or keepsakes strung up in trees. And if we do that, then we'll need a lot more numbers to do it. And that means—"

"We'll have to tell everyone about the doll," Madds finished for him.

Elven nodded. "So let's go pay a visit to Cora."

______

CHAPTER TWENTY-FOUR

______

Cora's eyes widened when she saw the four people on her doorstep. Elven was pretty sure that Bear and Benson weren't the cause of her surprise. After her little tiff with Elven in the town center, he figured she was ready to give him another earful. He wondered if Madds had any issues with her while living here, or if she got a pass because her last name wasn't Hallie.

Either way, Cora stepped aside and let everyone in. "Just make sure to wipe your feet, please," she said, pointing down to the small floor mat just beyond the doorway.

Everyone did as instructed and then filtered into the open room. The trailer was messy and organized at the same time. It was clean, and everything seemed to have a place, but the space just seemed inconsistent and unplanned. Folded laundry on a recliner, a stack of books on the floor in a corner. And there was a table to the right of the television with baskets surrounding it filled with various fabrics. A sewing machine sat right on top of the table.

"Sorry for the mess," Cora said, scurrying around and starting to pick things up.

"Cora, don't bother yourself none," Bear said, waving a hand at her. "We came over unannounced. Besides, we know you've got your hands full with everything."

"Ain't that the truth," she said, shaking her head.

A door on the right opened up, and the man Elven had seen earlier stepped out. His shoulders were rounded, and he had a sheepish demeanor, not making eye contact with anyone other than Cora. In his hands, he held a bundle of clothes. Most of them were wrapped tight, and Elven couldn't make out much of them, but a piece of floral material dangled loose.

"They're all good," he said. "Thank you, Cora."

"Don't trouble yourself none about it, Quentin," she said. "If you need anything else, you know where to find me."

He smiled and turned, again not making eye contact with Elven or any of the other new people who had just entered. In fact, he seemed to do everything he could to shimmy by, as if he was hoping to avoid any attention. And then he was out the door without another word.

Cora slapped her hands together. "Oh, darn it, it's almost time for food, too, but I can push it another twenty minutes. I'll just put a video on."

"Take your time," Bear said, seeming to know what she meant.

Cora walked to the bedroom on the left, just next to the sewing table. There was some commotion that sounded like she was messing with something heavy. Then a couple of clicks.

"There we go," she said. "We've got some company."

She wheeled out a man in a wheelchair. Cora looked to be in her late fifties, and this man was much older than that. Time clearly had not been kind to him. He was balding on top, wrinkles covering his face, and he gave no response to the sudden change of scenery. His eyes wandered around, but he didn't move a muscle.

"Howard, how are ya doing?" Bear asked.

Howard's eyes gave a quick glance to Bear, but then wandered off so that Elven couldn't be sure if he had actually been aware of the greeting or not.

"Some days are tougher than others," Cora said. "After the last stroke, it's mostly been the tough ones, though." She positioned Howard so he was facing the television and kicked down the lock on the chair. Then she turned the TV on, messed with the DVD player, and put on an old western. "We'll do some TV before food, okay?"

Howard's response was a string of drool creeping out of his mouth, dripping down his shirt. Cora smiled lovingly at the man and wiped at it with her hand, then wiped her hand on her pants. He made a bit of a fuss, pulling his head back and groaning, the first reaction Elven had seen from him so far.

"Thanks for your time, Cora," Bear said.

"It's nothing," she said. "The things we do for our parents, right?" She turned to Elven, who held his hat in front of him. "And you, Elven Hallie. I guess I owe you an apology, don't I?"

Elven was sure he looked as surprised as she had when they first showed up. "You don't owe me anything, ma'am," he said.

"Well, let me do it, anyway," she said. "I should have given you a chance, but living in Old Knuckle my whole life, well, it has a way of boiling things down to one judgment. And a last name shouldn't be what I judge someone on. I hope you can forgive me for that. You're just trying to help, and so far as I can see, this town needs all the help it can get."

Elven nodded. "Water under the bridge."

Cora smiled. "Good, and I should have known, anyway. Madds here hasn't been so bad since she showed up. So why shouldn't you be the same?"

Elven glanced to Madds, who had a big smile on her face. He wasn't sure if it was from appreciation or if she was rubbing it into Elven, that people liked her more than him. He couldn't help but smile. It might have all been in his head, but it also seemed like a very Madds response.

"She has a way of presenting herself a lot better than I do, I suppose," Elven said.

"So, what brings you all down here?" Cora asked. "I'm guessing you don't all need a custom fitting."

Bear chuckled. "Nothing like that. But it is related to sewing. Was hoping you could take a look at something."

"We're also hoping that you can use a little discretion," Elven said. He still didn't want everyone knowing about the doll. Bear confirmed this with a nod.

"I can do that," she said. "Let's see it."

Bear pulled out the Troll doll with the small dress and wings attached. He handed it over to Cora, who took it delicately and studied it. "This was found near where we found Shayla's body," Bear explained.

Cora nodded. "I recognize it."

"You do?" Elven asked.

"The doll, anyway," she said. "Sometimes Shayla would come in here, and she would always be playing with the crazy hair on this thing. Kind of like a nervous response that helped soothe her. At least, that's what it looked like to me."

"What would she come in here for?" Madds asked.

"Same thing everyone else does," Cora said. "Mending clothes if they couldn't do it themselves. Sometimes I would make stuff for Maybelle, so she came to fetch it." She pointed to the wings and clothing. "These are new, though."

"That's what we came to ask about," Bear said. "We figured the same thing. The stitching looks intricate."

Cora nodded, studying the doll. "Sure does," she said. "The dress is basic. Most people in Old Knuckle have some sort of passed-down knowledge about sewing."

Bear scoffed. "I wouldn't know the first thing about it. It's why I come to you with the holes to patch up."

"Well, Bear, we won't hold that against you," Cora said with a smile. "You've got a lot of other skills that are needed. But most everyone else can handle the small things."

"What about the wings?" Elven asked.

"That's where this gets tricky," Cora said. "I deal with fabrics. This here is paper-thin, almost soft like a cloth. But I can tell right away that it ain't."

"How so?" Elven asked.

She pinched at it and gave a small tear. "Anything like this would just fall apart if it were fabric. Not sure what exactly it came from, but this here is skin."

She held it up to the light dangling in the room. It became translucent.

"How did you figure that?" Elven asked.

"My pop did some taxidermy in his day," she said. "Clearly, he's not able to keep up with that now." She stole a glance at him, his rapt attention on the television now. He smiled as he watched, completely enthralled, which confirmed her statement.

"Well, considering he's not up for it, don't suppose he's got a rolodex of taxidermist buddies around here, does he?" Elven asked.

She smiled, shaking her head. "No, but you don't need that from him. Everyone around here knows about Shamus."

Bear sighed. "Yeah, we do," he said. "We just don't know where he calls home most days."

"You know who does, though," Cora said, and it wasn't a question. It seemed like everyone knew who was connected to who in Old Knuckle.

"Yes, I do," Bear said.

CHAPTER TWENTY-FIVE

"Now generally, it wouldn't be a problem to come here," Bear said, getting off his ATV. "We have some differences here and there, but overall, we get along. They generally back Roy on everything, though, so that adds to issues whenever Roy and I butt heads."

"So what's the problem?" Elven asked.

"The problem is that you threw Roy down on the ground, put your foot on his throat, and then you and Madds here went and pointed guns at them while being completely unprovoked."

"I wouldn't go so far as to say we were unprovoked," Elven said. "I was feeling pretty darn provoked, to be honest."

Bear laughed. "Yeah, well, maybe I should have said unprovoked physically."

"Can't argue with that," Elven said. "Is that why you told Benson to stay in town?"

Bear nodded. "He's a good kid, so I let him come around and feel like he's a part of it," he said. "But when it comes to the possibility of getting into a fight, I want to try to leave him out of it. He's still too connected, what with his sister missing and all."

"Couldn't agree more," Madds said.

"So what's the plan, then?" Elven asked. "You think the Morrison brothers are gonna give us some grief just for stopping by?"

Bear looked ahead at the property and shrugged. "Me? No, not at all. But you two? I mean, maybe it's best to just stand behind me."

"Fair enough," Elven said.

He put his hand on the butt of his gun, following closely behind Bear. But Bear stopped when he saw it.

"Now I don't know what you just heard me say, but it wasn't to be ready for a gunfight," Bear said. "I am trying to keep everyone here docile and friendly. Just because they got differing views don't mean you need to pull a gun on them."

Elven shrugged. "Don't intend to. But I wanted to make sure they knew the implication."

Bear stared Elven down. "I can see why you lost the election in town."

Madds let out a cackle, and quickly covered her mouth. "Sorry, that was pretty good," she said, still giggling.

"You gonna keep your shit holstered?" Bear asked.

Elven raised his hands. "Fine, but if they draw—"

"They won't," Bear said. "I don't know if they've ever hit anything on their hunting trips as it is."

"All good until they get lucky," Elven said, but he nodded. "But I hear you."

Bear shook his head, grumbling something about wishing he was doing this on his own. Elven couldn't help but bust Bear's chops, but there was some truth to it. He didn't know anyone up here, but they all knew him. He might have won some people over with that little speech in town, but he was sure he hadn't won over Roy or the Morrison brothers.

Still, he was a guest in their community. So he'd follow Bear's lead.

The overall property where the Morrisons lived was big by the look of the fence that sprawled out in both directions, but the terrain was almost uninhabitable. Lots of rocks and uneven ground. It was a wonder that anything had been built on it like this. And what was built looked very small. A one-bedroom at most, but pulled up right next to it was a motorhome on blocks.

"So why do these guys know where Shamus is?" Madds asked. "Nobody else knows where he's at? Kind of strange, isn't it?"

"He's their cousin," Bear said. "Third cousin, to be exact. And it ain't strange. Shamus moves around a lot between a few different places. If you knew Shamus, that would be the least strange thing about him."

"Not sure I'll ever get used to what Old Knuckle considers normal," Madds said.

Bear walked right up to the door of the small building and pounded his fist on it. "Shawn, Nolan, you boys home?" he shouted.

It was the first time Elven heard the first names of the Morrison brothers. He'd been beginning to wonder if these men even had them, from how everyone around town referred to them by their last name.

"Bear? That you?" someone asked through the door.

"Yeah, and I'm with a couple of friends," Bear said. "But we ain't here for anything other than a conversation, so don't come pointing your rifles at us any."

"Why not? Last time we ran into you, that's how we were treated."

"Last time ain't this time," Bear said. "Now, come on out."

The door opened, and the brothers peered out to find Bear. The first brother looked over his shoulder and saw Elven.

"Oh, come on, Bear," he groaned. "You didn't say nothing about bringing him."

"I told you I had some friends with me," Bear said. "Now, quit your bitching and come answer some goddam questions. We ain't got all day."

Both brothers came out, and just as Bear had said, no guns were drawn. Instead, they crossed their arms over their chests and scowled down at Elven and Madds.

"What you wanna know?" one said.

"Where can we find Shamus?" Bear asked. The brother on the left rolled his eyes. "Shawn, I'm asking nicely."

At least Elven knew which brother was which now. Not that he intended to set it to memory in the long run.

"Why you wanna know?" Nolan asked.

"We need his expertise," Elven said.

"I ain't talking to you," Nolan barked, glaring at Elven. Elven rolled his eyes, already too impatient for this, but he let Bear handle it.

"You heard him," Bear said. "Need to know something about taxidermy from him."

The brothers exchanged glances and shook their heads. Shawn went ahead and answered for them. "Go ahead and look for him all you want. But we don't know where exactly he's at. Even if we did, not sure I'd tell you."

"Maybe we would without your *friends*," Nolan added. "We don't buy what you fed all those people out there this morning." This time, he was staring right at Elven when he said it.

"So now you are talking to me?" Elven asked.

Nolan lifted his nose up and looked to the side.

"Look, you can hate me all you want. But the sooner we find this out, the sooner I'll be out of this town, and you'll never have to see me again."

This seemed to get a little more attention from the brothers. Apparently, they hadn't thought that far ahead.

"He's not lying," Bear said.

"Why you wanna know about taxidermy?" Shawn asked. "You know something you didn't tell the rest of the town, don't you?"

Nolan grinned. "We ain't telling you until you tell us."

Bear groaned and turned to both Elven and Madds. Elven didn't want to let them in, but it may be the only way. Still, he wasn't sure the brothers could be trusted.

Bear, however, didn't wait any longer for an answer. Turning back, he showed the boys the doll.

"We found this with Shayla's body," he said. "We didn't want everyone to know so they didn't get spooked."

Shawn studied it closely, but he didn't reach for it. Elven hoped that Bear would have pulled it back if he had. "What kind of skin is that?" Shawn asked.

Bear finally did pull it away, stuffing it back in his jacket. "We don't know. That's why we want to find Shamus."

"It's decent work, but Shamus didn't do that," Shawn said. "He stays away from most people. No way he's wanting to cause problems with them. He ain't like that."

"We aren't saying he is," Elven said. "But he could know someone who might have made something like this."

The brothers exchanged another glance. They looked unsure, their heads tilting like they were weighing a decision. Finally, they turned to Bear.

"We don't trust you won't pull a gun on him," Shawn said, poking his finger into Bear's chest. If it were Elven, he'd consider that to be *provoked*. "He's our cousin, so we gotta look out for our—"

Bear grabbed Shawn by the collar and threw him to the ground. This surprised everyone. For a man who just gave Elven a lecture on keeping his cool, he sure lost it just now. Apparently, Bear felt *provoked*, too.

"I'm done playing this game with you," he spat in Shawn's face. "Now, tell me where Shamus is."

"Get off my brother!" Nolan screamed, jumping on Bear's back, trying to pull him off.

Bear threw an elbow behind him, popping Nolan in the mouth. He stumbled backward, holding his teeth. Bear then went back to Shawn and punched him across the face. He threw three more before Nolan was back on him.

This time, Elven grabbed Nolan and yanked him off Bear, but he didn't throw a punch. He was just letting Bear do what he felt he needed to do. But if it went further, Elven might be pulling Bear off Shawn next.

"We don't have time for this shit anymore," Bear growled. "There are two girls still missing and a killer on the loose. I just want to ask Shamus some questions. Now, tell me, or I'll start cutting pieces off ya!"

Shawn didn't say anything, and Elven wondered if he'd been knocked unconscious. But Shawn didn't have to—Nolan was already on it, holding his hands up so that he didn't start getting the same treatment as Elven held him back.

"Alright, I'll tell ya! Just stop hitting my brother, alright?" Nolan's voice quivered with fright.

Bear stood up. "See, wasn't that hard," he said, smoothing his hair back.

Elven wasn't sure what he had just watched. Was it necessary? Maybe to a point. A little nudge or two in the direction was one thing, but this? This was edging close to being over the line. A quick glance to Madds told him that she felt the same way.

The way Bear had snapped from cool, calm, and collected to whatever this was had Elven leery about who he was really working with.

CHAPTER TWENTY-SIX

After another ATV ride to the middle of nowhere—while already being in the middle of nowhere—Elven, Madds, and Bear found themselves at the start of a hiking trail. It was where Nolan had told them to go, even though he'd made sure to let them know that Shamus may have already taken off by now. But this was the last place the brothers had heard he was at.

Of course, right here at the beginning of the trail wasn't where Shamus would be. It was at the other end of the trail. The one where it was too overgrown and tight to get any vehicles through it. From here on out, they'd have to go on foot.

And according to the brothers, it was going to take a while.

If they left now, they might make it to where Shamus was before the sun went down. Getting back to town, however, was a different story. It would be nightfall by the time they reached the center of Old Knuckle. Elven just hoped that they could make it back off the trail before that happened. He had some strong doubts, though, with the way the sun was setting so early.

Bear had a canteen that he'd pulled off his ATV, strapping it to his belt. But neither Madds nor Elven had any sort of supplies.

Neither one of them had been planning on an excursion like this today, but neither said a word about it. After watching Bear lose his cool, Elven figured they were both processing it.

Most of the walk had been in silence. Madds and Elven had exchanged a glance here and there, unsure of what to say to each other. Madds was the one who had been working with Bear for a few weeks, and had been living in the same town as him for a few months now. So he figured if anything like this had happened before, she would have filled him in on his temper.

But she hadn't. And from the way she looked, she was just as caught off-guard as he was.

After a few hours of hiking, Bear suggested they stop and take a breather. He popped open the canteen, took a swig, and handed it to Madds. She gulped greedily for a few seconds before handing it to Elven, who took his fair share as well.

Finally, Elven figured enough time had passed for them to discuss it. "So, did you want to fill us in on what just happened back there?" Elven asked Bear. "I thought we were keeping our cool."

Bear shook his head. "I told you not to pull your gun," he said. "I didn't want anyone getting shot."

"Really? Cause I thought you made comments about how I got physical unprovoked?" Elven said.

Bear nodded. "I suppose I did," he said. "But that was before they had all the information. Those boys knew we had a killer on our hands; we showed them the evidence and everything. What you did with Roy was just throw your weight around for no reason."

"But you had a reason?" Elven asked.

"You're damn straight I did," Bear said. "Those Morrison brothers are a couple of idiots who were stalling this investigation, as you call it. I cut through the bullshit and handled it."

"Even when I was provoked, it was just a poke, what I did," Elven said. "Your response was over the line."

"I got us the information we came for, didn't I?"

"Bear, this isn't like you at all," Madds said. "In this entire time I've known you, you've been pretty collected."

"That was before," Bear said.

"Before what?" Madds asked.

"Before I was certain that someone from our own community had a hand in this," Bear said. "Until we found that doll, we just had a bunch of guesses and speculations. But now? We know someone did this to Shayla. The longer we waste time, the less likely it is we find Sadie and Lila."

"Is that why you asked Benson to stay behind?" Elven asked.

Bear nodded. "He doesn't need to see this," he said. "Old Knuckle has a way of handling its own business, and maybe you're starting to see a little bit of that. I'll ask nicely, I'll be patient to a point, but I ain't gonna be jerked around."

"Next time, maybe just fill us in on what might go down," Elven said. "That way, we're prepared."

Bear took a deep breath and let it out slowly. "I think it's safe to assume that from here on out, you might want to be prepared," he said. "That filled in enough for you?"

Elven nodded. "I'd say so."

"Good," he said. "Come on, we're losing daylight."

CHAPTER TWENTY-SEVEN

After another hike that lasted about twice as long as the first leg, they came up to a spot that had a sign posted. The spot looked no different than any of the others along the way—heavily forested, chirping birds, and even a little bit of running water in the background. They must have been near a river, or maybe a brook, but nothing that Elven could see.

The sign read "TRESPASSERS BEWARE."

"That's a little ominous," Madds remarked.

Bear nodded. "I don't disagree with you on that one."

"Is this area owned by Shamus? Or owned by anyone at all, for that matter?" Elven asked.

Bear shrugged, surveying the area. "A lot of old hunting cabins are still standing from God knows when. It's possible Shamus owns one or more of those. Or for all I know, he's squatting in one."

"I don't see a cabin anywhere, do you?" Madds asked.

"Oh, I'm sure there's one somewhere through all this," Bear said. "The only thing we have to worry about right now is what that sign means exactly."

"Think we're likely to be shot?" Elven asked.

Bear slowly worked his way forward past the sign. "Maybe, or maybe it's all scare tactics," he said. "But keep an eye out for anything unusual."

"That sounds comforting," Madds said. "What's unusual in the woods?"

They walked forward, this time at a far slower pace. "Shamus!" Bear yelled out. He then looked over his shoulder to the other two. "Might as well make the announcement now. Maybe he'll come out and have a chat with us."

There was no answer, though. Only a breeze through the trees followed by a few chirps of a bird.

Bear shrugged. "Was worth a shot," he said. "We're coming to have a conversation!" he yelled again. "That's it! Nothing more than that, so we'd like to not get shot!"

He continued shouting to the woods, but got no answer back.

Bear took a few more steps, but Elven spotted something near his foot. Elven wasn't sure if what he saw was correct, but Bear was half a step away from putting his foot down on whatever it was. Just before Bear's foot landed, Elven grabbed him and yanked him back.

Bear stumbled backward, landing on his ass. He climbed to his feet, red growing over his face where his beard didn't cover. "What the hell was that?" he demanded.

Elven bent over, picking up a stick from the ground and pointing with it. "You said keep an eye out for anything unusual," he said. "How about this?"

He shoved the stick down, and it suddenly snapped right in half with a loud *clang*.

Bear jumped back at the sudden noise. The three of them got closer to it, shoving some of the tree branches out of their way. That's when they saw the massive bear trap, the teeth of it clamped shut right where the stick was broken.

"Holy shit," Bear muttered.

"Are those even legal out here?" Madds asked.

"Legal isn't the biggest concern out here, if you hadn't figured that out yet," Bear said.

"Still want us behind you while you lead?" Elven asked.

Bear chuckled and motioned ahead of him. "If you want to take point, I'll be happy to let ya."

Elven held a hand up. "I think you've got a good handle on it. You know Old Knuckle better than us, after all."

Bear grinned. "Good looking out."

"Don't mention it," Elven said.

The three of them kept a look out ahead of them, their eyes glued to the ground and scanning around every so often. Elven wasn't sure what type of traps Shamus was using, but he doubted there would be any large logs or deadfall traps set up like in some crazy survival movie. He still didn't want to make assumptions and end up with a spike through the chest, though.

They spotted a couple of other traps on the ground, so no more close calls this time. The babbling water grew closer as they inched their way forward. Finally, they came to a small clearing, where they spotted an old hunting cabin next to a creek.

It was a beautiful spot, but it was hard to enjoy it after the series of death traps they'd just walked through.

And then they spotted a man who looked like he hadn't showered in a month. He had long, ratty hair and a beard to match. He was up higher where the creek bed opened up. Once they started toward him, that's when he spotted them.

His eyes going wide, he glanced around like a scared animal, unsure where to go next.

"Shamus, we're just here to talk," Bear said, raising his hands.

Elven hoped that's all they were here for. But if Shamus gave Bear any trouble, then Shamus might be in for a rude awakening.

And, of course, Shamus didn't seem to believe him because he lunged for the trees, away from the creek. Elven didn't want Bear to get into it with him, so he drew his pistol and fired it in the air. Bringing it back down, Elven pointed it at Shamus.

"Show me your hands!" Elven yelled.

Shamus froze at the sound of the gunshot. He lifted his hands slowly, looking at the tree line. The three of them walked toward the man, and that's where they saw a rifle resting right next to a tree.

"I told you we were just here to talk," Bear said. The tone of his voice was verging into a territory that Elven wasn't comfortable with.

"That's enough, Bear," Elven said. He directed his next question toward Shamus to avoid any further conflict. "Why didn't you come when we called you?"

Shamus turned his head around, his arms still raised. "You were calling for me?" he asked. "I don't hear too good out of this side."

"We're just here to talk," Elven said. "So if you're up for it, I'd like to take my gun off you. What do you say?"

Shamus nodded. "I'd very much appreciate that."

"You gonna behave?" Elven asked.

"Yes, sir," he said.

Bear bent over and picked up Shamus's rifle. "I'll hang onto this for now, just in case," Bear said as Elven holstered his gun on his hip. Bear turned toward Elven slightly. "Don't you ever tell me what's enough, you hear?" he hissed. "In Old Knuckle, I run things the way I see fit."

"Just trying to save your fists from further bruising," Elven said, beginning to see the cracks in Bear and his way of seeking justice.

"And now it's my turn," Madds said. "Let's ask our questions and get moving."

Both men seemed satisfied with that suggestion. Shamus watched them, still frightened-looking, still with his hands up.

"You can put your hands down now," Elven said.

Shamus did as he was told. "Thank you," he said. He was timid, which may have been because of the gunshot, but Elven wasn't completely sure that was it. He just seemed like he preferred his own company over anyone else's.

"So what you wanna ask me?" Shamus said.

Bear pulled the doll out. "What do you know about this?"

Shamus studied it a moment. The way he looked, Elven was sure that he had never seen it before, which meant he wasn't their guy. But still, they needed to be sure.

"Madds, you wanna go check out that cabin?" Elven asked.

"Sure," she replied. "Keep me posted on what you hear."

"Make sure to keep an eye out for any other traps," Bear warned.

Shamus looked up as Madds started walking toward his home. He stepped toward her, but Elven stepped in his way.

"What's she doing?" Shamus demanded. "That's my cabin."

"Not sure if you've heard, but there are two girls missing in town," Elven said.

"And another one who turned up dead," Bear said. "That was hung above her corpse," he added, gesturing to the doll.

"So you think I had something to do with it?" Shamus asked. "I've been out here for months. I don't know shit about what happens in the community."

"We just want to rule you out," Elven said. "You don't have anything to hide, do you?"

Shamus shook his head. "I just don't like my things being messed with."

"Unless there's a couple of girls stashed away in there, she won't touch anything," Elven reassured him. "Now, what do you know about that doll?"

Shamus turned his attention back to the doll. "Nothing," he said. "Never seen it before."

"What can you tell us about who might have made it?" Bear asked. "Assuming it ain't you."

Shamus laughed this time, as if what Bear had said was absurd. "I'm not this sloppy," he said.

"What do you mean by sloppy?" Elven asked.

Shamus got close to Elven, lifting up the doll and pointing to the wings. "Well, for starters, I wouldn't have stitched it this way," he said. "It's far too exposed. I like to keep the stitches hidden. Under bellies, or natural seams like the crease of a leg. That sort of thing.

Which brings me to the other reason. I like realism. This is some abnormal shit. Dolls? Ridiculous."

Madds came out of the cabin. She'd spent barely any time inside, which was either a good thing or a bad thing. With how casual she was, Elven figured it was good for Shamus, bad for them.

"Too small for more than one person," she said. "No sign of anything other than him."

Shamus grinned. "See?"

"Any ideas who might have done it, then?" Bear asked.

"Specific people? Ain't a clue," he said. "But I can tell you that you're looking for someone who's either lazy or not advanced."

"Why's that?" Elven asked.

"The skin here, the way it was tanned was by salt," Shamus said, gazing at the doll. "It's not a bad job, just basic. I like to use hardwood ash. It helps remove the hair if I'm going for that kind of look. And then there's the skin itself."

"What about it?" Elven asked.

"This ain't from no animal," Shamus said. "It's human."

CHAPTER TWENTY-EIGHT

Just as Elven had suspected, nightfall came quick. They were lucky enough to make it most of the way back through the hiking trail before it became too dark. By the time it was properly dark, the trail was far easier to navigate the closer they got to their ATVs, so it didn't cause too much of a headache.

The drive through the night, however, was a little more difficult. Luckily, the headlights on the vehicles were good enough to help them navigate back to town. And Bear confidently led them back, reassuring Elven and Madds that he practically knew all the twists and turns of the various roads near Old Knuckle by heart. They took him at his word and weren't let down.

In fact, it wasn't the roads, pathways, or nightfall they had to worry about at all. It was the people. Because once they made it back to the more populated regions of Old Knuckle, they were met with a much bigger roadblock than they had expected.

Roy Leven stood, waiting for them. But unlike their previous run-ins with Roy since Elven had set foot in Old Knuckle, he had a lot more people than just the Morrison brothers with him. He had practically the whole darn town.

There were no pitchforks in sight, but Elven could tell by the group's demeanor that they weren't far from picking them up. Lanterns, flashlights, and a few ATVs lit up the town center. Madds and Elven pulled up next to Bear.

"What do you think is going on here?" Elven asked.

Bear shook his head. "Guess we're about to find out." He nodded to Roy. "Roy, something happen while we were out?"

Roy stepped out from the group and approached Bear. "You and I don't always see eye to eye. That's fine. We got differing opinions, as we should. But we both have always kept Old Knuckle at the heart of our concerns."

"Agreed," Bear said. "What are you getting at?"

Roy waited a moment, like he was pausing for dramatic effect. He looked Bear up and down, his face twisting in disgust. Elven was growing impatient with this, so he could imagine that Bear was feeling the same, if not worse. Finally, Roy spoke.

"Differing opinions is one thing, but keeping secrets is another," he said.

"Roy, I don't have the slightest clue—" Bear began.

"Where is the doll?!" Roy shouted, making sure that everyone in the area could hear him. He turned around, now addressing the crowd, even though the words were still meant for Bear. "We try to keep things simple in Old Knuckle, don't we?"

"That's right!" someone shouted, which caused a few others to cheer along.

"We look out for our own and don't let outsiders get in the way of that!" Roy continued on. "But our very own Bear Colter has done just that. He's too busy playing police, entertaining some new faces, while the rest of us are kept in the dark! How is that right?"

"It ain't!" another shout came.

"No, it is not," Roy said, and turned back to Bear. "Now, are you gonna show us the doll or what?"

Elven could see the fire in Roy's eyes. Bear growled, and Elven wondered if they were in for a fight right now. With Roy amping up the rest of the locals, he didn't think this would end well for the three of them. The people here could get the upper hand over Bear, and he'd be fine. He was one of them, after all.

But Elven and Madds? Well, Elven hoped it wouldn't go that way. Still, he wanted to be prepared.

He leaned toward Madds, whispering just behind her ear, "Be ready to gun it if it starts to get too dicey."

Madds's hand was on the throttle, gripped tight. "Didn't want to assert dominance this time?" Madds asked, a little too snarky for Elven's liking in the moment. Seeming to sense his irritation, she shook her head and glanced back at him. "We're on the same page."

He nodded, but Bear held a hand out like he'd heard them. Or maybe he'd just picked up on the overall tension.

"Alright, no need for pushing it further," Bear said. He dug the doll out of his jacket and held it up. "We found this above a spot where we believe Shayla was buried. Or where someone tried to bury her, anyway."

"You kept it from us?" someone yelled. "Why not just tell us? We would have believed you instead of all this shit."

Bear sighed. "I wasn't sure if—"

"You can't decide for everyone, Bear," Roy said. "It ain't fair to us all. We might look to you for guidance, but we didn't elect ya to be the end-all-be-all of Old Knuckle, did we?"

"Hell, no!" everyone shouted, almost in unison.

"We could have been looking for the other girls!" another voice shouted. It was too dark for Elven to make out who was saying what, other than Roy, who was right up front, leading the charge. There were some clear politics going on, even in this small community.

"Now you want to start looking?" Bear asked, his voice booming over the crowd. "We told you that we were dealing with foul play. But nobody wanted to believe us! I thought my word was good enough to convince you."

Roy shook his head. "Nobody wanted to believe you, Bear. It wasn't that they didn't; they were just scared. And then you went and lied to us all. Maybe your word ain't worth as much as everyone thought."

Bear was about to reply, but Elven knew it would only be met with more arguments. Bear wasn't doing himself any favors, and Roy was just running with it. Elven may have some reservations about working with Bear now, but he was still better than the alternative.

"It was my fault," Elven said, trying to match the volume Bear's volume. It was close, but he couldn't quite roar like Bear. Still, he got some of their attention. Maybe just not the right kind of attention.

"Oh, we have no doubt about that," Roy said snidely. "But go ahead, tell us why you thought you knew better than the good people of Old Knuckle."

Elven got off the ATV and walked in front of it. He didn't want to look like he was using Madds as a shield. But by doing so, he was risking his speedy getaway if he needed one.

"I told Bear not to tell anyone about the doll because it was still part of an ongoing investigation," Elven said. "Not everyone needed to know about it because it wasn't important for everyone to know. It gave us the leverage to find leads without giving away something we knew about who was responsible."

"And have you caught the person yet?" Roy asked. "Did withholding that information tell you anything?"

Elven took a deep breath. He certainly wasn't going to admit that they were another dead end. And he didn't want to reveal what little they did know about the taxidermy lead. He opted for the political route: be noncommittal.

"We have a few new leads that we are still working through," Elven said. "For now, we ask that everyone please give us some time while we try to—"

"I think we've all heard enough from the former sheriff," Roy cut him off. "I can see why his title is *former* after all this."

Elven kept silent, not taking the bait.

"Tomorrow, we'll organize a search party at daylight," Roy

continued. "Anyone interested in helping, show up right here at that time."

Elven had to admit it wasn't a bad idea. But there were tons of woods to search, and nobody even knew what they were looking for other than a body or a random toy strung up in a tree. Still, he could think of worse ways to use the power of a community.

Of course, it only took giving up their one piece that the killer didn't know they had. Now all bets were off.

He just hoped that it wouldn't bite them all in the backside.

CHAPTER TWENTY-NINE

Auriel waited until everything was quiet in the cabin. The Keeper sometimes stayed up late, listening to his radio. She'd seen it before, a small radio that sat on the counter. It had a little handle on the side that reminded her of a truck when the window had to be rolled up or down. He had shown it to her and told her that it didn't need batteries or to be plugged into the wall to work. That all he had to do was crank the handle a bunch of times, and then he could listen to it.

She'd asked how long that would last, and he said for a while. Then he would crank it some more and do it all over again. It was really neat, but she also thought it was tiring and a waste of time. Why not just have it plugged into the wall? Then he wouldn't have to crank it at all.

When she'd asked that question, he only smiled and rubbed her head, telling her how special she was, and that not everything had power, like the cabin. He reminded her the old ways worked best. Putting in a little effort and hard work made everything better, and worth far more than convenience.

She didn't understand that, but once again, she nodded and

smiled like she did. It seemed to make him happy, and that's when she liked him best.

She couldn't fully make out what he played on the radio. At least, not at night. The sound carried down into the basement, but it was mostly mumbles and almost chanting sounds. One time, she ventured out and could hear it a lot more clearly. It reminded her of a preacher reading from the Bible. She didn't understand what it was all about, but she knew that it had something to do with God and Satan.

That's pretty much all The Keeper talked about while they were at the cabin. Once they got back to the community, it was different. There was still a lot of Bible discussion, but they never talked about the work he did while he was at the cabin. And they never used their angel names in town, either. That was only for work.

Another rule she didn't fully get, but that was life. Being a kid was nothing but rules to follow, with little explanation as to why.

Once the radio stopped its mumbled preaching down in the basement, she knew that The Keeper had fallen asleep. That was one good thing about using the handle to power the radio instead of plugging it in. If it was powered by the wall, then it would ramble all night, and she'd never know when it was safe to explore.

Again, Auriel knew it was breaking the rules, but she was too excited to care. She had met Dina and made a promise that she would come see her again. Dina was really sweet, too. She was much older than Auriel, but that was okay with her. She didn't have a whole lot of friends, especially when they were out here doing the work. So it was something special to get to see her again.

Just as she had the other night, Auriel snuck into the hallway, this time not needing to pee. She'd made sure to take care of that just before bed. She'd almost burst from holding it all night last time. But like last time, The Keeper had left her door unlocked.

She crept her way to the door where Dina was locked inside, and she shoved the bar up again, pinning it against the wall so that it didn't move back down. There were no sounds coming from the room, though. No sobs or cries. She hoped that Dina was still inside, but she was sure she was. If not, it meant that The Keeper had already finished his work with her, which would make Auriel sad that she didn't get to say goodbye. But The Keeper had told Auriel that she would be there for the work this time.

And she knew that he kept his word when it came to the work he did.

She poked her head inside, and just as she had thought, Dina was still inside. But she laid on her side, her breathing heavy while she slept. It was dark, but Auriel could see her eyes moving back and forth behind her eyelids like she was having a dream. Dina didn't seem settled, so Auriel figured it might be a bad one.

Auriel stroked Dina's brown hair gently, trying to calm her down while in the dream. She rubbed her head softly, and that was enough to wake Dina. The woman opened her eyes and sprang upward, almost ready to scream. But Auriel put her hand over her mouth to muffle any noise that might escape. She put her finger to her own lips and softly shushed her, adding a smile.

When Dina fully met Auriel's gaze, that's when Auriel saw the other side of Dina's face. She had a large bruise covering her cheek and a gash just over her eye along the brow. It had been stitched up crudely, the ends of the string poking out in different directions from the small knot. Auriel frowned at the sight, knowing it must have hurt when Dina got in trouble with The Keeper.

"I'm sorry that happened," Auriel whispered.

Dina shook her head. "It wasn't your fault," she said, adding a pained smile. "You came back."

"I promised I would."

Dina wiped a tear away from her eye. "And you kept your promise. Did you get in trouble?"

Auriel shook her head. "I made it back to my room without him knowing I was out."

"I'm glad. I wouldn't want you to get hurt, too," Dina said. She winced when she tried to smile.

"Are you okay?" Auriel asked.

Dina shook her head. "I need to leave," she said. "My family, they're probably missing me right now. I want to get back to them."

Auriel frowned. "We can't—"

"Auriel, I need your help." Dina grabbed her hand. "Is my friend still here?"

Auriel nodded.

"Will you take me to her?"

Auriel wasn't sure about that one, but it was no different than going into Dina's room, right? Maybe she could break the small rules without breaking the big ones still. Having another friend would be fun, too, so why shouldn't she?

"Okay, but we need to be real quiet when we leave," Auriel said.

Dina nodded and climbed to her feet, pulling herself out of the blanket. Her legs were long and pretty, but bruised from the hard floor. Her feet were bare and dirty. The Keeper would take her out in the daytime sometimes to get some fresh air, but he never gave the angels shoes when he did so. He said it was to keep her and the other angels grounded, but when he gave Auriel shoes, she'd asked him about it. He told Auriel that he knew she wouldn't run away from him. So she knew that there were other reasons he hadn't told her before.

They snuck out into the hallway, Dina behind Auriel. And like she'd promised, she stayed quiet. It wasn't too risky because the door was right across the hallway. And this time, Auriel didn't have to use her trick to open it. Dina was able to lift the bar for her, making sure that it didn't make any noise.

They opened the door, and for the first time, Auriel saw the other angel The Keeper had brought here. She was about Dina's age and had short brown hair. She slept, but as soon as they entered, she woke up and held her hand out, like she was shielding herself from something, or someone.

"Oh my God," Dina whispered, quickly running to her friend. "Come on, we need to get out of here."

"Where are we?" Dina's friend asked. "Where have you been?"

"There's no time," Dina said. "Let's go."

Dina helped her friend up to her feet, and they went to the door.

"Wait, you can't leave," Auriel protested.

"We have to go," Dina said. "You can come with us. We'll find your mom and dad."

Auriel shook her head. "No, you won't," she said. "My mama is in heaven. And my dad is... well, we just can't go!"

Auriel knew she was being too loud, and the way that Dina looked at her, she knew it, too.

Dina swallowed hard. "It's okay, Auriel. We'll be really quiet, okay? We just want to go outside and look at the stars. Can we do that?"

Auriel wasn't sure. She knew they couldn't leave, but Dina was her friend now. She wanted to believe her so badly. "It's dangerous. He might wake up."

Dina nodded, understanding. "We're going to be super careful, I promise."

And then Dina started heading into the hallway without waiting for Auriel to give her blessing. Auriel slowly followed them, knowing it wasn't a good thing, but she just couldn't stay there alone.

The two women went up the stairs slowly, making sure each step supported their full weight before taking the next one. Auriel knew it would, but they were smart to test them. The steps could sometimes be squeaky, and any sort of noise like that would surely wake The Keeper.

After what felt like forever, they finally reached the top of the stairs. They crept forward, Auriel staying close behind them, her curiosity getting the better of her. As soon as she looked into the living room, she knew she was in trouble.

The Keeper stood there, holding his long gun, the one that scattered shot everywhere and looked like it had two dark holes on the end. He didn't point it directly at the three angels, but held it firm. Auriel knew he'd never point a gun at her, but the other two? No question about it.

"Auriel!" he screamed. "Get to your room!"

Auriel took off running downstairs, knowing she was in big trouble. She didn't know what her punishment was going to be, but she knew it would be bad.

But not anywhere near as bad as Dina's or her friend's.

And just as she thought that, she heard Dina's scream echo down into the basement. It was far more shrill and scary than anything Auriel could imagine. Her friend screamed next. And then she heard the sounds of fist against flesh. And shortly afterward, a couple of loud thuds.

Auriel ran to her room, burying her head under her pillow, praying to drown out the noises. And praying that her punishment was swift and painless.

CHAPTER THIRTY

The night before, Elven made it back to Ginny Tiller's cabin and fixed himself a plate. Madds did the same, and from the look on her face, it was clear she wanted to talk about something. Elven could tell it wasn't about the case they were working, either. He had spent enough time with her to know that look when he saw it.

Or at least, he thought he had. She'd proven to him that maybe he didn't know her at all. Still, he went with his gut and took his meal to his room to eat in silence. He was in no mood to have a conversation about the past and hear some more excuses about why she'd done what she'd done. She may need closure, but he wasn't going to be the one to give it to her.

He'd been left hanging himself for far too long, and at this point, he was over it all. That's what he told himself, anyway.

But either way, Madds's feelings weren't his priority anymore. She'd made that decision for him.

Besides, he had his mind on plenty of other things, and the last thing he needed was a distraction from all that was happening. Yesterday morning, he thought he was finally winning over the town, even just a little. On top of that, they had a handful of new leads to look into.

But by the end of the day, the leads were all dead ends other than one small bit of information about taxidermy that sounded like it could fit any hobbyist. And even worse, the town had flipped even further in opposition to him. He found it interesting that small towns loved their secrets, yet if he tried to keep one from them, he became the villain in their story.

He could understand where they were coming from, but he had a job to do, and that's the same way he would have done it in Dupray when he was still the sheriff. But it didn't matter to them. These girls were their neighbors, friends, and family. They were far too invested emotionally to think logically.

So to say that he was dragging his feet to get ready that morning might have been a bit of an understatement.

He showered and meditated first thing, trying to reset the day, even though it was literally just starting. That's how bad yesterday had felt, like a hangover trying to overtake everything he had to do for the new day at hand. But he felt much better after getting ready. All he needed to do now was have something to eat, and he'd be ready to start fresh.

What surprised him most when he went to the living room, however, was that Madds was already seated with a plate of food. She'd even taken the liberty to dish out some for Elven. The plate was steaming, sitting right in front of an empty seat along with a cup of coffee. She was fully dressed and even looked perky, or at least wide awake. Her hair was in a bun, like she was prepared to dive right in and not let anything get in the way.

Ginny came out of the kitchen with a smile, patting Elven on the shoulder as she passed. "Looks like you're the one who got the beauty sleep today," she said. Then she headed straight upstairs, like she did the day before.

"Hopefully, it shows," Elven said dryly as she walked away. He picked up the cup of coffee and took a sip. It was still hot, but just cool enough that he didn't burn his tongue.

"Don't think you need any help there," Ginny said, her voice drifting down the stairs. "Any more, and I'm sure you'll let it go to your head."

Elven laughed, then pulled out the chair to sit. Seeing the food made him even hungrier than he was.

"Too late," Madds said with a smile. But Elven wasn't in the mood to banter. At least, not with her.

Elven picked up a piece of bacon and chomped at it, then proceeded to cut up the biscuits, gravy, and eggs on his plate. He stabbed a few pieces and shoved them into his mouth, leaning back and sighing. It was delicious. Simple food made right. That was one thing about small towns and families in Appalachia that he'd always loved.

"I was hoping we could talk," Madds said, not even letting him swallow.

Pulled from his brief moment of enjoyment, he locked eyes with her. He swallowed his food and shook his head. "About the case?"

She shook her head. "I want to apologize," she said. "I want to explain what happened and why it happened."

"Madds, I know what happened," he said. "I was there, remember?"

"But you don't—"

"I don't need more excuses about it," he said. "What's done is done. We already talked about it when you showed up at my room in Dupray."

"Being held with a gun in my face isn't what I'd call talking about it."

"No, it's what you call convincing me to work on a case."

Madds grumbled. "Look, I wasn't trying to start a fight with you this morning. I just thought if we buried the hatchet on this thing, we could work together better and figure it out."

"I think we're working together just fine," he said. "Do you not trust me to have your back?"

"I think the better question is, do you not trust me to have yours?"

"I've got your back, and you've got my back. That's as far as this needs to go."

Madds slammed her hand on the table, clearly frustrated. "Jesus tits, Elven. There's so much more to you and me than just working together that we need to discuss. You're being far too stubborn if you can't admit that."

She was seething now, her chest heaving up and down like she'd just run a marathon. He knew he was being stubborn, but he still wasn't ready to give in. Instead, he just watched her, unsure of what to say next.

But he didn't have to, because the buzz of an ATV engine came to distract them. Someone pulled right up to the front door and burst through. It was Benson, and he had a look on his face that said more than his words could. Still, the kid gave it a try.

"You gotta come," he said. "It's bad."

CHAPTER THIRTY-ONE

He'd never seen the girls in person, but when he first arrived in town, Benson had shown Elven a picture of Lila, Sadie, and Shayla all together. It was from Lila's social media page. People rarely framed pictures these days, but plastered tons of them all over digitally. They had looked so happy together, posing near a waterfall on some hike they'd all gone on.

Shayla was dead now, and even then, Elven had never seen the body. She was buried before he got there. It wasn't how he would have handled it, but he understood it. So he only ever saw pictures for that, too.

But the other two were just missing. Up in the air, so to speak. There was always a possibility that they were alive. A possibility that they weren't even part of what had happened to Shayla. But as much as Elven was hopeful, it would be one heck of a coincidence for them not to be a part of it. And because of that, there was a large part of him that knew they were unlikely to find the other two girls alive. With how much time had passed since the girls had been gone, they were just playing the odds at this point.

While he wanted to find the person responsible, they were also looking for the girls. The part that never said it out loud figured they would be looking for another grave that wasn't deep enough and just hadn't been located yet.

But as soon as Benson led them to the spot in the woods, he found out just how wrong he was.

"Oh my God," Madds said from behind Elven. He'd demanded to drive this time. Having been a full day in Old Knuckle, he figured he could get around just as easily as she could. Wrapping his arms around her was wearing on him, though he wasn't sure that her wrapping her arms around him made it any better.

But now wasn't the time to focus on that. As soon as he pulled up to the scene, his mind focused on nothing other than the carnage in front of him. And Benson had been right.

It was bad.

She didn't look like the picture he'd seen. There was no smiling face. There was no hair braided in a ponytail. There were no friends surrounding her, enjoying her company.

There was none of that, because she was dead.

But there also wasn't a grave where she was buried. No trinket hanging in a tree above her with some makeshift wings out of skin and thread.

That's because it was Sadie Vaughn's body that hung in the tree. And she was the one with the wings crudely sewn onto her back.

It was awful. Not only because of what had been done to her, but also because Roy Leven had done just what he said he was gonna do. He'd formed the search party to look for something that might tell them what had happened to the girls.

And they'd sure found it.

It felt like half the town was out there, staring up at Sadie Vaughn dangling in the tree. The rope that held her was wrapped around her neck, digging into her skin as her full weight pulled taut against it. Her arms were slack by her side. Her head was slumped, but her face was covered in makeup.

She looked as if she'd been beaten, maybe even tortured. Cuts littered her arms and legs, from what he could tell. But the dress she wore covered most of her other flesh, so Elven couldn't be certain what had happened to her.

"We need to get everyone out of here," Elven said.

Madds picked up on the necessity immediately, shoving whatever problems they had between the two of them out of her mind for now, clicking straight into cop mode. Madds still had the training, and she was a good officer.

But this was far beyond what the two of them were used to dealing with. They needed to call in an expert. The FBI had teams who could handle this far better than Elven could. And he might even suggest that or call it in himself. He knew that nobody would jump on that idea if he brought it up.

But for now, he needed to keep the scene clear. There were people who were crying, while some were walking around far too close to the body. Most just stared up at the trees.

"Alright, I need everyone to back up," Madds called out, her voice firm and commanding.

Not many people listened, though. They were transfixed on the girl.

Elven grabbed Benson and pulled him in. "I need you to help get everyone back out of here," he said. "This is a crime scene, and we don't need anyone getting any ideas while we try to figure out what happened. Can you do that for me?"

Benson swallowed hard, but he nodded. "I think so," he said.

Elven watched as he joined Madds, trying to hold his hands up and motion for people to move backward. Some of them were starting to listen.

Elven spotted Bear standing near the tree where Sadie hung. He had a knife in his hand, like he was going to cut her down. Elven wanted to get a look at everything before they did that, though. It might not make a difference, but it was better to take any precautions possible. This was a far different scene than the one he'd been told of when they found Shayla.

"Bear, hold on," Elven said, walking toward him.

Bear stopped what he was doing, then looked to Elven. His eyes were bloodshot and moist. It was clear he'd been crying.

"I don't know what to do here," Bear said. "I'm so far in over my head on this thing that I can't come up for air." He held out the long pocket knife, his hand shaking.

Elven nodded, taking the knife from Bear and closing it up. He handed it back to him. "Just take a breath for right now," he said. "Take a minute to collect yourself. There's too many people around right now to see you. Nothing's wrong with a man crying, but these people need to have confidence that we know what we're doing. Even if we don't have a clue right now."

Bear did as he was told, understanding what Elven was telling him. "Sorry," Bear said.

"You've got nothing to be sorry for," Elven said. He was beginning to understand Bear even more. He may have a temper at times and be looked to as a leader at other times, but he was still a part of this tight-knit community. And he truly cared about the people in it.

"You really fucked things up this time," a voice said from behind Elven. He turned around, and unsurprisingly, it was Roy Leven. "Look what your secrets did to this place."

Elven was far too busy to deal with whatever Roy thought he was doing. Making a scene? Telling Elven off? Wasting everyone's time was all Elven could think of.

"This is the very thing I was trying to avoid by keeping that secret," Elven said, growling through his teeth. "That little stunt you pulled in front of the whole town showed everyone our leverage. The killer included. You think this is a coincidence that we found Sadie like this? No, this is the killer being cocky. They've got nothing to hide now, and they knew you were gonna be searching these woods."

Roy's eyes were on fire, like he was ready to give Elven as good as he was getting. "Whoever did this killed two of our girls already and—"

"Exactly!" Elven yelled. At this point, he knew he was drawing attention to himself. It was the exact opposite of what he needed, but he didn't care. The more Roy Levens stood in his way, the longer it was going to take to get anywhere with this case. So he needed to get this done and over with here and now.

"But you know the thing that is obvious to me, standing right here under her body?" Elven continued. "She wasn't killed weeks ago like Shayla. If she was, she'd be decaying and stinking to high heaven." He hated talking about the poor girl this way, but with how close everyone was, he wanted to have the biggest effect with his words. "She was more than likely killed last night. This is a statement. And you know who they're making it to? 'Cause it ain't me for showing up, and it ain't Madds, or Bear, or Benson. They're making it to you." He poked right down on Roy's chest. He knew it was risky, and he might just push the man over the edge, but he did it, anyway. "They're telling you that you don't have any control here. That they can do whatever they want, whenever they want. And it doesn't matter how many people know it, how many people you loop in on it, because we ain't anywhere closer to finding them now that their secret is out."

Roy looked like he was ready to throw a punch. If that's where this was going, Elven was ready to throw down right here and now if he needed to. But instead, Roy just shook his head. "You don't belong here," he said.

"Believe me, I know it," Elven said.

"I just hope you know what you're doing next," Roy said. "'Cause this town can't take much more of this." He turned around and hiked up the hill, disappearing to the path where Elven had seen a number of ATVs parked.

Elven looked around, finding Madds and Benson had worked together to get the majority of the people back away from the scene. Bear had collected himself enough that he wasn't shaking any longer. And the tree where Sadie was tied up didn't have anything of note on it. But at least this way, they could examine her gently, away from too many prying eyes.

"Alright, let's get her down from there," Elven said. "We can do it together so she doesn't hit hard."

Bear nodded, pulling his knife back out. "Thank you."

"Don't thank me yet," Elven said. "There's still another girl out there."

He watched Benson in the distance, still helping Madds. He wasn't asking questions, and he was doing as he was told. Elven was grateful that it wasn't Lila they'd found. He could only imagine how upset Benson would be right now if it had been.

But they would still have to tell the Vaughns about their daughter.

CHAPTER THIRTY-TWO

Madds and Benson had gotten one side of the crime scene sectioned off. The people had either lost interest in looking at the dead girl hanging from the tree, or they understood that it wasn't something they should be gawking at. Madds wished they had some caution tape, but this wasn't a regular kind of case. She wasn't a deputy anymore, Elven wasn't the sheriff anymore, and nobody else here was technically law enforcement.

The fact that they were doing this themselves broke a lot of laws as it was. But she knew that there was no other way to do it. From how everyone talked, they would shut their mouths and not say a word if any official law enforcement got involved. They were a stubborn community, and Madds didn't fully understand it. She would do whatever it took to find her loved ones if they were missing and at risk.

But the people of Old Knuckle? They might say they would, but in the end, it was a lot of lip service and empty promises. Ultimately, they were just afraid of things changing around here.

She looked to Benson, who was holding his arms out a few feet away from her, asking a couple of people to move back just a few feet.

Once they did, they'd be just out of sight of Sadie's body. He was a good kid, but she could see the fear written all over his face. Lila was at the top of his mind.

"How you holding up?" she asked, walking up behind him.

He shrugged. "I knew Sadie pretty well," he said. "From hanging out with Davin when I was younger, and she was at the house a lot to see Lila. So not great, I guess."

She hadn't even thought about his connection to Sadie. Everyone in Old Knuckle knew everyone else. He was in the thick of it even more than most people, it seemed.

"I don't know how Davin's going to take this," he said after standing in silence for a moment.

"What's up with him?"

Benson shrugged. "We used to be friends, but grew apart. That's it."

She nodded. "Is he close with his sister?"

He shrugged again. It was starting to be his usual response, but then again, he was eighteen years old. He didn't have an opinion on much.

"Not like me and Lila," he said. "We grew closer when our parents died. Davin and Sadie, though, they all sort of went separate ways in that family. They ain't even have anything to break them apart like we did. Some families just aren't good, I guess. The people are, but the problems tear them apart."

So much for Madds's theory about eighteen-year-olds. Benson was turning out to be more insightful than she gave him credit for originally.

"But Davin?" Benson continued. "He's got a temper on him. Just never thought I'd be on the receiving end of it." He pointed to his eye. "Things got hard for him after my mom passed. He didn't have someone like Lila to lean on."

"I'm sorry," Madds said. "If you want to go home, everyone here would understand."

Benson shook his head. "As long as Bear lets me be here, I'm here.

Last night, he'd asked me to stay behind, but I didn't want to. He said it would be dangerous for me." He sighed. "I'm probably just messing everything up, anyway. I don't know what the hell to do to fix any of this."

Madds grabbed his hand. "You're doing everything you can to help," she said. "This isn't something that you should know what to do. It's not something anyone should know, honestly. This isn't just some random murder. It's clear there's a message or a pattern. I think it's clear to everyone that this was no accident now."

Elven walked up the small hill where they stood and approached gently. He cleared his throat, pulling their attention.

"Hey, Madds, can I have a quick word?" he asked. She took a look at Benson, who nodded and started to turn around.

"Don't wander too far," she said to Benson before she stepped away with Elven.

"How's he doing?" Elven asked.

"Better than expected, honestly. But still not great," she said.

He nodded. "We have to notify the Vaughns before word gets back to them, if it hasn't already. Bear says he'll go, but I think one of us needs to be with him to see if anything turns up."

"You don't trust Bear?" Madds asked.

He shook his head. "No, I think he's on the up and up here. But the Vaughn family was a little off. And then—"

"Davin," she said.

He nodded. "Davin. If Bear matches his temper, then I don't know what'll happen. I can stay at the scene if you want, or—"

"No, I'll stay here," she said, motioning her head to Benson. "I want to be here with him. He's still just a kid, and I think me being around helps. Call it my sisterly vibe, I guess."

Elven nodded. "Agreed," he said. "We'll be as quick as we can."

And then Elven left her there. At least he trusted her to work the scene without him, not that there was a lot to do. It was mostly just keeping people away from the body.

As soon as she went to Benson, though, he met her eyes with tears in them. He'd gotten a moment alone to think, and he was spiraling. "What about Lila?" he asked. "Do you think we're going to find her hanging up like this next?" His eyes welled with more tears. "Is she dead already?"

"Hey, don't do that, okay?" she said. "There's no point in speculating on any of that right now. The best thing you can do is hold out hope to find her. She doesn't need you giving up on her now, alright?"

He sniffled and wiped at his nose, nodding. "I know, I know," he said, but he sounded completely deflated.

"Sadie was found just now, looking like this," Madds said. "She hasn't been here for long. It was just overnight, and she sure as hell wasn't killed, stored somewhere, and then brought out for this. She was alive until last night."

"So what does that mean?" Benson asked.

"It means that Lila isn't here," Madds said. "Someone kept Sadie alive until last night for whatever reason. So they're keeping Lila alive, too. There's still time to find her."

Benson looked a little bit encouraged, but his face fell again. "We're just running out of it."

CHAPTER THIRTY-THREE

Elven and Bear pulled up to the Vaughns' trailer. It was left in the same state since they were there a couple of nights earlier. They weren't big on picking up their mess, it seemed. The tobacco remnants were still on the makeshift patio out front. The chairs were still disorganized from when they sat in them. The only new thing was a plate on one of the Adirondack chairs, nearly licked clean, and a plastic cup that had been tipped over, staining the stones underneath them with a brown liquid.

The Vaughns hadn't been doing well since Sadie went missing. Or maybe that's how it always was. From the way Benson had spoken about them, they had problems long before this case started.

But they were people who didn't deserve to have the news told to them that they had to tell. Nobody did, as far as Elven was concerned.

And the way Sadie was killed? He didn't want to tell them the state she was found in. It was terrible, and it wasn't anything that a father, mother, or brother should ever have to picture. It would only cause nightmares for the rest of their lives. At least they hadn't been there to see it themselves.

Bear was thinking the same exact thing, because he held out a hand to Elven before they walked up the stairs toward the front door. "Let's keep how we found her between us," he said. "At least right away. It's a lot to process all at once, I think."

Elven nodded, but he knew it was only a matter of time. They would find out sooner than later, and maybe not telling them was selfish of them. "Word's gonna get out," Elven said. "The whole town saw it. Maybe it's better from us than the whispers through Old Knuckle."

"I know," Bear said. "But let's at least wait until we know if the hanging is what killed her or if it was something else. We'll take a look once we take her body into town."

Elven nodded. "I'm with you on that."

"Good," he said. "Then let's rip this band-aid off." He took the steps up and knocked on the door, waiting for someone to answer.

Ronnie pulled the door open, a grease spot on his white tank top and a beer in his hand, not caring that it wasn't even lunchtime yet. Elven had an idea the man might be reaching for something a little stronger in a few minutes, once he'd been given the news.

"Ronnie, can we talk with you?" Elven asked.

Ronnie nodded. "Let me get my coat. The way we get to yapping, I'm sure I'll freeze my nuts off out there."

Bear clearly didn't feel like joking, but he did speak. "And you'll want to get Darlene, too."

Ronnie stopped in his tracks. Elven thought he might turn around, but instead, he only nodded. "It's Sadie, ain't it?"

Bear didn't answer, and neither did Elven. Bear was right. He wanted both the parents in on this one.

"Might as well just come on in, then." Ronnie waved them inside.

Benson's place was a kid who didn't know how to keep a clean house. But the Vaughns' trailer was a home that was slowly falling apart. It was clear that people lived here, but the walls had been closing in on them for years.

The only spots to sit were the recliner and the left side of the couch. They were well worn in, sunken down from continuous use. Everywhere else was filled with some sort of junk. It wasn't dirty plates or anything rotting. On the couch were a couple of broken radios, like someone had taken on the project of trying to fix them up, and everywhere else were various other electronic items like it. In the corner of the living room was a washing machine drum with welded-on legs, like it was soon to become a fire pit.

"I'll go get her," Ronnie said, and waved around the room. "Feel free to make yourself at... whatever." He shook his head and walked down the hallway.

Elven and Bear stood in silence, exchanging one glance while they waited. Neither one of them chose to sit down. They weren't comfortable enough to do that, but also, if they did, there'd be nowhere for Ronnie or Darlene to sit. Besides, they didn't want to stay long.

They heard footsteps come down the hallway, but they were far heavier than Ronnie's when he'd disappeared down it the first time. It's because it was Davin who came into the living room. He was dressed just as sloppily as Ronnie was, but without the beer in his hand.

"What the fuck are you two doing here?" he snapped, blowing into the kitchen, past the mess of the living room. He pulled out a beer and popped the tab, taking a long guzzle. So much for no beer in his hand, Elven thought.

"They're here about your sister," Ronnie said, emerging from the hallway with who Elven assumed was Darlene.

"Welcome," she said with a half-smile. She was pretty, but her facial features looked slack. Her eyes were half-open, and her words were ever so slightly slurred. If Elven was anyone else, he might not have picked up on it. But in his line of work, he'd seen a lot of people who were addicts, so he knew the signs. Darlene was clearly on something.

Her arms weren't littered with track marks, and with what Benson had told him about the family, he figured she was on pills.

That was the easiest and most popular thing to get up in the hills. But she was still coherent enough to understand things happening around her, so Elven wasn't going to voice a concern. Just because she had a problem of her own didn't mean she wasn't worthy of hearing that her own daughter had been found dead. Better from him than the town, anyway.

"Well, it's good that you're all here," Bear said.

"Just tell us what happened," Ronnie said. "If you'd found Sadie, then she'd be here, right?"

"What about Sadie?" Darlene asked, plopping down in the empty spot on the couch, the pile of radios jostling as she did. "Didn't she leave town? Is she back?"

"No, ma'am," Elven said, sharing a glance with Bear again. He cocked his head. If Bear gave him the nod, then he'd say it, but he wanted to respect the dynamic. This was his town, after all.

Bear gave a single shake of his head, telling Elven he would handle it. "We found Sadie this morning," Bear said. "I mean, we, uh, we found *her body* this morning."

Darlene shook her head. "I don't—what?" she asked. It was like she was struggling to come out of the fog, but Elven could see the wheels catching up. "Her body?" Her chin quivered at the mention.

"Yes, ma'am," Elven said, taking over for Bear, who was showing signs of breaking just as he had at the crime scene. "She was murdered."

That's all it took for Darlene to lose it. She might have been high, groggy, and slow to register, but she was coherent enough. And she'd just lost a daughter.

She let out a long wail that came out from the deepest part of her soul, etching a noise through her throat like a growl. "My Sadie!" she screamed. "What happened? Not my baby!"

Ronnie grabbed her and held her in his arms as she curled up into herself. She continued to cry, but she could produce no more words. Ronnie looked up at them, his own eyes wet and his face red as he clenched his teeth. He was sad, but more than anything, he looked angry.

"Who did this?" he asked.

Bear shook his head. "We're still working that out."

"I can't believe this," Ronnie said, but he looked down like he wasn't directing it at anyone. Other than himself, that is. "I thought she'd run off, that's it. I should have been out there looking for her. I should have done more."

Elven glanced at Davin, who had gone quiet. He stood, holding the open can of beer, staring at his parents. He wasn't sure if it was his parents' reaction that had caused his frozen state, or if he had wandered into his own mind, making statements and accusations quietly to himself.

"It's not your fault," Bear said. "And it won't do any good to blame yourself."

"I know I'm not responsible for this," Ronnie said. "But someone else sure as hell is, and when I find them—"

"You'll what?" Davin finally asked, his anger raging beyond what Ronnie's was. "Sit around, drinking yourself to death while Mom keeps self-medicating?" He shook his head, then threw the beer hard at the counter. Beer splashed everywhere, reaching all the way to the other wall. "And you?" Davin seethed at Elven. "What the hell good are you for if you ain't gonna have the slightest clue who killed my sister?"

Elven wasn't going to argue with the kid when he was in a lot of pain and nowhere to put it. But Bear decided to try to calm him. "Davin, we are going—"

"Oh, shut the fuck up. You're no better than this asshole," Davin said, gesturing at Elven. "The great Bear Colter is here to make the community great, but in reality, you have no fucking clue what you're doing. That's why you brought in this outsider—because he's better at it than you." Davin nodded at the two of them. "And that's not saying a hell of a lot."

"Davin—" Elven began.

"Why don't you get out of our fucking town and let everyone else figure this mess out," Davin said, growling at Elven. "We don't need either of you for this shit."

Before anyone could say anything else, Davin blasted past them out the door. They heard the ATV fire up and head off into the forest. Ronnie didn't say a word, just continued sitting with his wife, rubbing her back.

She was starting to calm down, but Elven knew that it was just her body exhausting itself. This loss would stick with her forever.

CHAPTER THIRTY-FOUR

ANGRY WAS AN UNDERSTATEMENT. BUT ULTIMATELY, HE KNEW that he hadn't explained it well enough to her. She was still so young, and in the end, it was something she needed to learn for herself. Punishment wasn't the only way to reinforce things. Perhaps this was on him for not being transparent. He was going to use this as a teaching moment.

When he heard the rustlings the previous night, he knew that the girls—no, the angels—had gotten out of their rooms. There was only one way for them to do that, as far as he knew, and that was to open the door from the outside.

He clearly hadn't done it. So that left one other person.

Auriel.

She had a lot of things that had gone wrong in her life already at such a young age. It was difficult to guide a young child, *a young angel*, without a motherly figure to guide her. So this was his fault in so many ways.

But it was also the hand he had been dealt.

He knew God would provide for him. For them. So he only needed to trust that this was all happening for a reason. He was doing the work that had been asked of him. That had been placed at his feet when he himself was young.

And then he was going to do the same for Auriel someday.

He paced the room as Auriel sat in the corner of the room, facing the wall. He'd lost his temper already last night, yelling at her, giving her the whooping his anger unleashed, and now she was having to think about what she had done.

He made her watch what he'd done to one of the angels last night, too. He remembered the first time that he'd witnessed it. It stuck with you the first time. And as much as it bordered on horrible, there was something about it that was also so pure.

He stared at the back of Auriel's head, thinking about how it shouldn't be a punishing moment. It should be something to be celebrated. And that was where he knew he went wrong.

But there was still time to rectify that.

"Are you hungry?" he asked Auriel.

She didn't speak, but took a deep breath, her shoulders raising as she held it. Finally, she shook her head, still facing the wall.

He smiled, knowing her response was one of fear. One of not wanting to disappoint him. But he also didn't want her to fear him.

"It's okay to be hungry," he said. "So what do you say?"

She hesitated again, but slowly nodded her head up and down.

"Good. You can come out of the corner, Auriel."

Auriel was hesitant, but she did as she was told. She was a good girl, after all. She was just young, curious, and confused at times. But she was still the most important person to him, and that was saying a lot. Her life was even more important than his own.

"I'm sorry, Da—"

She stopped, covering her mouth with her hands. Her eyes welled up, like she was in trouble again.

"Hey, hey," he said, kneeling down. He tried to keep his voice as calm and comforting as possible. "It's okay. Sometimes we make mistakes. We aren't God. But we try to be as godly as possible. Trying is all we can do. You're not in trouble, okay?"

She nodded rapidly. He reached out to her and gently pulled at her arms so that her hands came off her face.

"There. Now let me see that pretty smile God blessed you with."

She sniffled, still clearly dealing with other emotions. But she did as she was told again. A smile crept up on her face, but it still wasn't as wide as he knew it could be.

"Is that it?" he asked. "Do you have anymore?"

"No," she said, shaking her head. It grew ever so slightly when she spoke, though, like she understood she was entering playful grounds, but wasn't ready to reveal it yet.

"I think there's more where that came from," he said. He grabbed her and started to tickle her all over.

"No, don't tickle me!" she squealed. She squirmed in his arms and giggled her heart out. "Stop, stop, stop." Her voice wasn't distressed at all, but loving the attention. Loving to play the game.

Finally, he stopped tickling her once she had just about been squirmed out. She was panting, catching her breath from all the excitement. He truly did love her.

"You're my number-one angel," he said. "You know that, right?" He spun her around so he could look her in the eyes.

She met them and nodded with a smile.

"And nothing will ever happen to you. I promise you that. But only as long as you stay here. You know that, too, right?"

She nodded again. "Because angels are never supposed to leave, right?"

He smiled wide. "That's right," he said. "Old Knuckle is the place for angels, and we need all that we can get."

"And that's why the other angels are here?" she asked. "Because they tried to leave?"

He frowned and took a breath, sighing. "That's right," he said. "Sometimes they do try to leave, and that's what my job is for. To make sure that they never do. Last night was one of those moments."

Auriel weighed something on her mind. He could tell by the way her eyes wandered over the ground, like she was thinking and not quite sure how to put the words together. She did the same thing back home, where he called her by her given name, not her angel name. He could finally see the words coming to her.

"So you kill them?" she finally asked. "They have to die if they try to leave?"

He grabbed her and held her in a tight hug. "No, honey," he said. "Well, I guess in some ways, yes. Like the way that we won't see them walking around again."

"Like Pappy?" she asked.

He smiled, letting it slide to refer to him as her pappy. Technically, he was at this point, but generally, he liked to keep this life separate from the one everyone else saw. She was still a little young to understand that, though.

"Yes," he said. "Like Pappy. He isn't here physically, but he's still here in spirit, right?"

"Right," she said with a nod.

"And so are the other angels. After I'm done with them, they will never leave this place. Their presence, aura, spirit, is always locked to Old Knuckle," he said. "You understand that?"

She nodded. "I understand," she said.

He hugged her again, choosing to believe her. There was still one more angel to work on, for this trip, at least. But he still had to wait for the right moment. Wings took time, and he needed to rest up. And then, when it was finally time, he knew that he could help Auriel see the truth, and her future to come.

CHAPTER THIRTY-FIVE

THE SCENE HAD BEEN COMPLETELY CLEARED BY THE TIME Elven and Bear made it back to Sadie's body. Elven wasn't sure how they'd managed it, but he got the feeling that the entire town had enough respect to let them figure things out. There was only so long they could stare at the dead body of one of their own before it became too much. The shock had worn off, and the reality hit hard. This was far too close to home for any of them. Elven imagined they were going home, spreading the information like wildfire, and battening down the hatches in their own homes.

Elven hoped they would get a lot more information than they currently had, but after surveying the scene, he was sorely disappointed. Being in the dark about this was not great for the community. It would lead to a lot of accusations soon, and he knew it. They needed to find something, anything, to give them a little bit of peace before everyone turned on each other for reasons out of thin air.

Though, he knew that once they had the smallest detail, if it caught on in Old Knuckle, it might be even worse than no detail at all. They could all focus their efforts on the wrong person just because of one single thread that carried no weight. And then all bets were off on how everyone would react.

They'd walked the area like they had when they found the doll hanging in the tree, but this time, Elven was pretty sure they weren't looking for any trinkets. The girl had been strung up, so there was no marker needed to find a body. Not unless there was a second one buried somewhere, but to him, that wouldn't make any sense. This was a statement, and it wasn't just so the killer could hide a different body.

Benson had stuck around, even though he was too vested in this case. There were only so many times they could tell the kid no before he would stand up for himself and run off to do who knows what and get himself in far more trouble than it was worth. Besides, he was someone that Elven could trust, and he'd done a decent job with the instructions he was given earlier.

Once everyone scanned the surrounding woods, they met back at Sadie's body, which they'd covered with a blanket after finding no evidence around her, either. Even with such a shocking display, the killer had done their due diligence this time and didn't leave any crumbs, so far as he could tell.

But then again, maybe he was missing something. And that's what he wanted to pitch to the others.

He swallowed hard, knowing this was going to ruffle some feathers. "I think this has gone too far," Elven said.

"No shit," Bear said.

"I'm glad you agree," Elven said. "That's why we need to bring in some more help."

Benson looked confused. "I think a lot of people in town are willing to help out," he said. "But who do you think we can bring in? Roy? I don't think he has anything to do with this, but, well, he's kind of an ass."

Madds smirked at the comment. Bear, however, didn't seem thrilled at the topic of conversation. "He doesn't mean someone from the town," Bear said, picking up on it immediately. "And my answer is no."

"It was one thing when we weren't sure there was someone responsible for Shayla," Elven said. "And then when we thought there was, we didn't know exactly what we were dealing with. But we have a much clearer picture after this whole display." He motioned to the tree where Sadie had been hanging that morning. "I'm in over my head on this one. We all are."

"What are you saying?" Madds asked.

"I want to call the FBI," Elven said.

Madds immediately tensed up. "Elven, I—"

"You can leave, Madds," he said. "I don't care. At this point, there's one more girl out there." Elven watched Benson grit his teeth at the mention of his sister. But that was good, because he knew the stakes. "Who knows how many more times this will happen, too. This isn't just a random murder, or an enraged ex-boyfriend, or even an accident someone is trying to cover up. This feels like a serial killer."

"Doesn't there need to be three killings to classify that?" Bear asked.

"Do you want to wait for another one?" Elven asked pointedly. "At the very least, this was a message left by someone who wanted everyone to see it. Intention was put into this display. And they ain't scared of us getting close."

Benson looked unsure, but Bear looked downright angry. Elven turned to Madds, motioning with his hands between them.

"Finding who is responsible for this is far more important than our issue. I'd rather stop a killer than fulfill my own vendetta, whether it's justified or not."

Madds nodded, staring down at the girl's body. "I'm in," she said. "And I'm staying to see this through. You're right. Saving the rest of these people and catching the motherfucker who did this is more important. Even if it means going to prison for my mistakes."

Elven stared her down, seeing how genuine she was. A small smile crept over his face, and his stomach sank. She was serious, and he respected it. She wasn't just trying to save herself, and it reminded him of the woman he had once shared a bed with. Who he'd shared his heart with.

"No," Bear said again, shooting it down.

"Bear, this is far too—"

"I know it, but we can't," Bear said. "It isn't because I don't agree with you. Hell, I know how in over my head I am on this one. That's why we brought you two in on this. That alone was a struggle, and people still don't want to give you the chance. What do you think they'll do when we bring the FBI up through these hills?"

"I know they won't like it, but they'll see why," Elven said. "They won't be here to do anything other than to catch this person. The FBI isn't surveying for minerals. I think the people are smart enough to know that."

"It doesn't matter," Bear said. "They'll cover this whole thing up to keep it quiet from the outside world. Word gets out there's a serial killer here, then the news crews come, their way of life is on display, and then the attention is here. Once that happens, there's no putting that genie back in the bottle. And when I say *cover it up*, I mean it. We'll have absolutely nothing to work with, and we'll be worse off than when we started.

"I hate to say it, but right now, this little group we got standing right here is all we got," Bear continued. "So if we're this far in over our heads, then we better start swimming upward and get above it. Otherwise, there's no hope for finding Lila."

Elven didn't like that answer one bit, but Bear had made his point. Elven nodded, understanding where they stood, but it didn't mean that he was going to go along with it for long.

He would just have to figure out how to inform the FBI and get them up there before the town could do anything drastic. The problem was, there was no cell service, and far too many questions would arise if he left town. It was much easier said than done.

CHAPTER THIRTY-SIX

Elven hadn't been here when Shayla's body was found, so he didn't know what protocol the town had followed, if any. But he was surprised to hear that they intended on bringing Sadie back into town to get pictures and do an exam of the body. The way Bear seemed unsure of the whole matter told Elven that this wasn't the usual occurrence. More than anything, he figured it was Madds's doing last time that had set the tone for what was to happen this time.

As much as he felt they needed to bring in people with far more expertise than his own, he was glad that Madds had found a home here for the time being. If it hadn't been for her, this case would never have made it as far as it had now. And nobody would know that there was a killer loose in their community.

He was sure that Sadie's body would have been buried, perhaps better than Shayla's, and their secret would have stayed buried for years to come. There would have been no reason for a message to be sent to him or anyone else.

They attached a trailer to Bear's ATV and brought it into town. That was also better than draping her across the back of it, like some sort of old western where they carried a dead body on horseback.

They may not have had all the tools at their disposal, but they were going to do things as best they could while trying to avoid any short-cuts so they didn't screw it up.

They brought Sadie's body to a shed just outside of the center of the community. It was surprisingly cold, still connected to power, and had a large walk-in freezer inside. Elven wasn't sure if she would be stored there for a while or if this was just a holding place for the time being.

There was a large metal table right in the center of the room. A sink was in the corner, and a couple of tables lined the side. Elven thought it looked similar to a medical lab of sorts, but with the hooks dangling from the ceiling, all clustered together in the back, he figured it was more of a butcher shop than anything else.

He didn't ask questions about what the room was, but when a woman with red hair and freckles all over her face he hadn't seen yet came into the room, he lifted his eyebrows toward Madds.

Bear must have seen it as an invitation for an explanation. "This is Jessa. She's our local catch-all of sorts."

Jessa smiled and held her hand out. "Mostly working with yarbs and the like," she said. "They called me in on the last one, so I guess they think I can help on this one." She was soft-spoken and far gentler and kinder than the medicine woman in Monacan he'd dealt with before. "Not sure what there is, but I'll take a look if you want."

Elven nodded. "You have experience looking over a body?"

"Mostly ones that are alive," she said. "I do all the checkups around here."

It was gonna have to be good enough for Elven, even though he worried about muddying a crime scene or evidence. But they were far past that at this point. They were going to do what they felt was right, with or without Elven.

"Benson, can I get you to run down to my greenhouse and gather me some rosemary?" Jessa asked.

Benson nodded, but scrunched his face. "Rosemary's the one with the little spriggy things, right?"

"That's the one," she said.

Elven hoped that their definitions of "spriggy things" were the same, but they knew each other better than he did, so he didn't protest as Benson headed out the door.

"Rosemary something special for this?" Elven asked once Benson shut the door.

"It symbolizes the soul's immortality. The scent is also useful for decay," Jessa said. "But mostly, I just wanted Benson to leave the room so we could strip this poor woman down and give her some decency. He doesn't need to muddy his mind with the images."

Jessa was thoughtful, he'd give her that. Both Madds and Jessa started to strip the dress off the young woman. Bear and Elven turned so they could also give her some semblance of privacy, even though they'd be turning right back around to look at the body for any marks. There was just something about taking the young woman's clothes off that didn't feel right for their eyes.

"All clear, boys," Madds said after a bit of rustling.

Elven and Bear turned back to see Sadie, now completely uncovered, lying on her side. Her body was bruised, and not just from a tumble. It was clear she had been beaten. Tortured, even. And then there was the skin that was missing from her back. It was one large piece, just carved off of her.

The makeshift wings were no longer connected to her, but on the table nearby. They were the same material as the small ones attached to Shayla's. And that meant they were made of skin, but they were a different shade than Sadie's own skin. Just slightly tanner. Madds took pictures of everything as she saw fit.

"Does the process make the skin darker?" Elven asked.

Bear shrugged. "You and I know about the same amount on taxidermy," he said. "Jessa?"

She shook her head. "Not my expertise. But the area that she's missing the skin from is the same size."

"I don't think she was killed until just yesterday at most," Elven said. "There's no decay. I'm no expert on the dead, but I've seen bodies one week old, and they didn't look this fresh."

Bear nodded in agreement. "I bet it takes a while to make skin look like that," he said, pointing to the wings. "The tanning, or whatever you call it."

"We could go get Shamus," Madds suggested.

"Christ, I don't know if we can even hunt him down again," Bear said.

"We should have brought him in," Elven said.

"Well, we didn't," Bear replied. "And now I'm sure he's up and moved from where we found him. If I were the recluse type, I know I would. Even then, that hike took a whole day that we don't got right now."

"Anyone else an expert on taxidermy around here?" Madds asked.

"Cora pointed us in the right direction before," Elven said.

Bear nodded, chewing the inside of his cheek. "She did say her family had done it in the past. She's no expert, though."

"But she could probably tell us how long the process takes," Elven said, knowing they didn't have much else to work with. But he needed to know.

"Is it even that important to find out?" Bear asked.

Elven nodded. "It is," he said. "Because if this wasn't her own skin, then it means he took this chunk for a reason. And if it's what I'm thinking, then we know the minutes left on the clock that's currently ticking."

CHAPTER THIRTY-SEVEN

"I don't know how much help I'll be," Cora said, standing outside the shed where Sadie lay. "I told you my family used to do this kind of thing on the side. It wasn't the type of thing that got passed down far. The idea of working with dead animals wasn't really my idea of fun. I like to stick to sewing fabric."

Benson stood with them outside as they spoke to Cora. Elven and Bear had headed off Benson before he came inside the shed after fetching the rosemary requested by Jessa. That's when they'd asked him to go get Cora for them. He was more than happy to do so. Elven was sure that he wanted to help in any way he could, but being sent out of the shed was also what the kid wanted most. He might put on a brave face, but Elven was sure Benson was hesitant to see Sadie's body in worse shape than he already had. It probably reminded him of his sister more than he would admit.

Elven smiled at Cora. "I understand. But you were able to identify those wings as skin before any of us were, so you've got more knowledge than the rest of us."

"And you need me to look at the poor girl? Sadie Vaughn... I can't believe it," she said. "I heard about how you found her. Everyone in town is saying it. Up in a tree? My Lord." She shook her head, her eyes soft. "I knew both girls in some way. It just won't be the same not seeing them around anymore."

Bear nodded. "Think you'll be able to handle it? I hate to ask, but we don't have much else in the way of resources for this one. But the image might stick with you."

"If it'll help, then I'll do whatever it takes," Cora said. "I don't want any more girls to end up this way. And if it costs me some unrestful nights to do it, then so be it."

Elven and Bear nodded to each other, agreeing that she was about as ready as she would ever be. Elven placed his hand on the door, but Benson stopped him before he could open it.

"Uh, if it's alright with you, I, uh, I..." He trailed off, looking uneasy.

Elven nodded in understanding. "Why don't you stay out here, Benson? Let us know if anyone comes around snooping. Don't want any prying eyes."

Benson nodded. "Yeah, I can do that. Thanks."

Elven smiled, both of them knowing what the other needed. He and Bear opened the door and escorted Cora inside. Immediately, her hand went to her mouth.

"Oh my," she whispered, her eyes going from the girl, then to Madds, then back to the girl. Jessa had left after she said there wasn't much she could decipher from the body.

Cora closed her eyes and whispered to herself a little prayer. She opened them again and nodded. "Okay, what did you need my help with then?"

"There are more wings, like the ones we found with the doll," Elven said. "But these are much bigger." Elven walked to the side of the table, showing Cora.

She nodded. "I'd say so," she said. "And these were on the girl?"

"Attached to the dress," Bear said.

Cora nodded. "I see," she said. She studied the wings, then took a long look at Sadie's back where the skin was missing. "Interesting."

"What's that?" Elven asked.

She went to the wings, pointing. "There's what looks to be a sort of imperfection on the wings here," she said. She pointed to a spot that looked faded, like a line across the back. It wasn't super pronounced.

"What is that?" Elven asked.

"Well, I'm not an expert, like I said. But it looks like it was something on the skin before. It goes right to the edge of the wings," she said. "Did Sadie have some sort of scar on her back? One that would have extended further than this goes?"

Madds helped angle Sadie's body so they could get a good look at her back without flipping her over on her face. Elven, Bear, and Cora studied the areas around her back, but so far as Elven could see, no scarring matched the pattern on the wings.

"Doesn't look like it to me," Bear said.

"Me neither," Cora agreed.

"So this isn't her skin," Elven said.

"That's my theory," Cora said.

"How long does it take to do this? Can it be done in a couple of hours?" Elven asked.

She shook her head. "Not as far as I know. I'm sure there are quick ways of doing it, but even then, it would probably take a couple of days at minimum. And then there's making this sort of contraption with it, too." She pointed to the wings. "But it could even go a couple of weeks, depending on the method."

"So it wasn't Sadie's skin," Madds said.

"And by the size, I can't imagine it was from anyone they were trying to keep alive right now," Elven said. "But worse things have happened."

"What are you thinking?" Madds asked.

"I think this skin is from someone no longer drawing breath," Elven said. "My money is on Shayla Perkins."

"Oh my," Cora said again, cringing. This was probably too much for her to handle at this point. Elven didn't feel they needed anything more from her.

"Thank you, Cora," he said.

"I'm sure you've got to get back to your father," Bear said. "Thanks for coming by. Are you gonna need an escort home?"

She shook her head. "No, I'll be able to make it. Thank you, though."

Bear nodded, holding the door for her.

"If you need anything else, please don't hesitate to ask," she said before starting to head out the door. She paused as she stared in the corner where the dress was wadded up along with some of the herbs Benson had brought. It was a lot to take in, Elven knew. Then she was out the door and on her way home.

Madds had waited until she left, which was a good thing because her wording was not the most gentle. "I took pictures of Shayla, but she was, well, too chewed up to know for sure if the skin came from over."

"I'll talk to Maybelle and see if she had any scarring on her back," Bear said.

"That'll be good," Elven said. He went to the door and opened it a crack so that Benson couldn't peek inside. "Benson."

"Yeah, Elven?" he asked, his demeanor perking up at being needed.

"Your sister," Elven started, trying to be as tactful as possible. "Did she have any scarring on her back? Maybe like a long streak?"

Benson shook his head. "Nothing like that," he said, then snapped his fingers. "Shayla did, though."

Elven cocked his head, curious as to how he knew that so well.

Benson tucked himself into his shoulders, suddenly sheepish. "When I was younger, we all went down the river and swam together."

"And you remember this still?"

Benson sighed. "At twelve years old, seeing that amount of skin on a teen girl sticks with you," he said. "It was like... what's the word for like when you..."

"Awakening," Elven said.

Benson nodded. "Maybe don't spread that around?"

"Your secret's safe with me," Elven said with a wink, and Benson looked relieved. Elven closed the door and went back in.

"Guess we have our answer," Elven said, confirming his theory. "Now we know."

"What do we know exactly, other than the skin was from Shayla?" Bear asked.

"That big piece of skin that's missing from Sadie," Elven said, pointing. "The killer is going to do this again to someone else. We know Lila is missing, so we can safely assume it's her. Which means—"

"She's still alive," Bear said.

"And we have maybe a couple of weeks at most," Madds said.

"And at worst, a couple of days," Elven added grimly.

CHAPTER THIRTY-EIGHT

It had been a long day already, and it was still going. By the time they had finished up with everything, the sun was setting again. They'd spent a lot more time at the crime scene than Elven had originally thought. His stomach grumbled, and he realized that once again, he'd skipped lunch.

Stress and staying busy had a way of keeping your mind off of things like that.

But he was going to have to call it a day soon. They couldn't do much once it was dark, and they still had no new leads. At this point, he was thinking they would just have to search every dwelling in the place. Of course, he was sure that a lot of people wouldn't consent to a search, and it would take a long time. But what else did they have?

As the four of them walked together toward the center of the community, Benson voiced his own opinion on wanting to get a bite to eat. There were no restaurants in Old Knuckle, which would have been a perfect place for the foursome to gather and discuss their theories on what was happening with the case. Ginny Tiller's might be the only spot for that, but just as Elven was about to suggest it, Bear said they could all swing by his place and he'd grill them some steaks he had in the freezer from a previous supply run.

Madds giggled and shot Elven a look, fully aware that he didn't eat beef. She didn't out him, though Elven would have preferred she had. Now Elven would have to figure out a way to politely decline Bear's offer. He didn't mind sitting there while they ate to discuss the case, but it just meant he would have to wait that much longer until he could grab dinner once he returned to Ginny's cabin.

But they didn't even make it that far, because the community center seemed extra lively this evening. Elven should have known it would be after the discovery early that morning. They were going to have some sort of meeting or announcement to quiet wondering minds, or more likely, running mouths.

Of course, there was Roy Leven, right in the middle of all the commotion. It seemed like anything that was going to blow up in Elven's face in Old Knuckle somehow involved Roy. And there were far more people in the center than the other day when Elven had, more or less, convinced them to let him stay and investigate.

Somehow, he didn't think that this gathering was going to go the same way. At the very least, he knew he wouldn't have to convince anyone that there was a killer in their midst. That was pretty obvious to them all at this point. He just wondered what they would argue about now, how they could spin it so that Elven was somehow responsible.

The four stopped, surveying the crowd to see if they could sense which direction this was going. But they couldn't.

"Well, better just get this over with, I guess," Elven said reluctantly, leading the way.

As soon as they reached the boisterous crowd, all attention was on Elven. "There he is!" someone shouted. "What are we supposed to do now?"

Bear raised his hands, taking the lead. Elven was happy enough for him to do so. Maybe it would soften them, coming from one of their own.

"As most of you know, we found Sadie Vaughn this morning," he said.

"We saw her! She was hung from a tree and had wings attached to her!"

Bear nodded. "That's right," he said. "But we can't jump to conclusions. Someone who calls Old Knuckle home is doing this."

"This didn't happen until she showed up!" a woman said, stepping out from the crowd. She pointed directly at Madds. That surprised Elven, and by the look on Madds's face, it sure surprised her, too.

"Hold on," Bear said. "I just said we can't jump to conclusions, so let's not do that. Pointing fingers isn't gonna get us anywhere."

"Then how do you explain it?" the woman demanded.

"Bonnie's right! Old Knuckle was fine before she showed up," a man said, joining in and standing next to Bonnie.

Bear's mouth pressed into a straight line as he stared the pair down. A few more shouts, and the crowd was slowly shifting against Madds. And Elven had thought she was carving out a spot for herself with the people.

It just showed him what a bunch of scared people were capable of when they didn't have any answers.

"Everybody, Bear is right. We can't go around blaming people just because someone is an outsider."

It was Roy Leven. Another surprise for Elven. He couldn't even keep up with the twists happening right now.

"I can assure you that Madds here is only trying to help us," Roy continued. "She's been at it since we first found Shayla. Why would she be bringing in Elven on the case? Why would she be pushing so hard to find a killer when no one even thought a person did this in the first place?"

Roy was speaking the most sense of the crowd, and the woman—Bonnie—and the other man didn't have a response to that. But they did have more questions.

"Then who is it?" Bonnie asked.

"That's what we're trying to figure out," Elven said, finally breaking his silence. "We have some evidence that we're sifting through and think we will have some leads we can follow up on first thing in the morning. But for right now, the best thing is for everyone to go home and not stay out. Like you said, someone is responsible for all of this."

"As far as I'm concerned, Elven here is the only one we can trust," Bonnie said. "Everyone else was in town when this happened."

"That makes sense," the man next to her said. "Everyone else needs to stay home. Anyone out ought to be considered a suspect. What do you think, Elven?"

Elven couldn't believe what was happening. First, they don't want anything to do with him. They'd considered running him out of town, or even worse. But now? Now he was all they had. An outsider was all they were willing to trust.

So much for the unwritten rule. Old Knuckle seemed to be falling apart, and they were looking at him to save it. But he was just as much in the dark as the rest of them.

Not that he was going to tell them that.

CHAPTER THIRTY-NINE

ELVEN TRUDGED INTO GINNY TILLER'S CABIN, EXHAUSTED. IT seemed that in Old Knuckle, that was just going to be the way—constantly working with almost no breaks in between. He just hoped that it wouldn't be for long. And that all his efforts would amount to something.

Because right now, he felt like he was spinning his wheels and getting nowhere.

Elven and Madds had continued to speak with the crowd for a while, but mostly, the discussion was full of ideas about where to look and how to do it. None of it mattered, though. The people had very little evidence to point them in any meaningful direction.

But the fact that they were willing to speak with Elven about it went a long way. They were finally willing to let him—an outsider, a former sheriff, and a Hallie—help their community. Not only that, but they were eager to throw ideas at the wall for him to run with. He wasn't going to turn that down after all the grief he'd been given upon arrival.

Still, it was a long night, and once the crowd had finally dispersed, Elven and Madds had no energy to head to Bear's to eat those steaks. Or at least, for Elven to watch them eat the steaks and wish he had his own meal. Bear and Benson wanted to head in for the night, anyway. So they all took rain checks on the meal for another night and went their separate ways.

Luckily for Elven and Madds, they knew there would be a meal waiting for them when they got back. It might have been sitting out for a while, but it was good enough for them. Ginny's cooking hadn't disappointed yet, and its being cold wasn't going to be a deterrent for them.

Elven and Madds entered the kitchen together in silence, ready to grab a plate of whatever was in the Dutch oven waiting for them. Elven turned in the tight galley and nearly bumped into Madds.

"Sorry," he said, shaking his head as he let out a long yawn.

"It's okay," she said, stepping around him to let him through. She slapped a spoonful onto her plate. "I can take your plate and get you some if you'd like."

He handed his plate to her. "That'd be nice, thank you."

She nodded, repeating the process and handing it back to him. It smelled good, but he had no idea what it was other than something with shredded chicken. It seemed almost like a pot pie without the crust.

"Seems everyone is on your side now," she said. "Not an easy thing to manage."

He smiled. "Guess not," he said. "But I don't think they're going to like me after what I'm thinking about doing."

"You still want to go to the FBI," she said. It wasn't a question. She knew exactly what he was thinking.

He nodded. "It's the best thing for the girls. I'm used to dealing with trespassers, petty theft, drug dealers, and run-of-the-mill murderers with specific motives that aren't like these." He shook his head, like he still couldn't believe where this case had gone to. "Serial killers aren't my wheelhouse. Maybe if we had more leads, or evidence, or just something to go on, I wouldn't feel this way. But we don't." He locked eyes with Madds. "Please don't say anything to Bear or Benson."

"I don't plan on it," she said. "I agree with you, Elven. And I meant what I said, too. I'll do whatever it takes at this point, so you can still count on me sticking around."

"I'm sure they could use your help," he said.

"What I will say, though, is that Bear is right, too," she said. "Those people will do anything to keep things a secret in Old Knuckle. To keep the outside world out of their business. I think everyone wants Lila found, and the person who's doing this caught, but they really do value their privacy."

"I know it," Elven said. "That's why I need to contact the FBI without them knowing. I just haven't figured that part out yet. I'm sure there would be questions if I just disappeared from town."

Madds nodded. "There's a supply run coming this way. Should be tomorrow," she said. "Maybe there will be too much of a distraction with her here, and you can sneak off? Kind of a long shot, but it's all I've got right now."

"Supply run?" he asked. "Is the woman's name Paige?"

Madds shrugged. "I don't know. Never met her. She's kind of petite and looks like she's always in a rush, I guess. Almost frazzled, I'd say. I keep my distance, though."

She lifted her eyebrows, not elaborating on the reasons, but Elven already knew them. Because if someone in town had even whispered about Madds being around, he'd have been all over it.

"I guess you could say I assimilate pretty nicely here," she added.

Elven smiled. "If it is Paige, I might be able to get a message to her. I guess we'll find out tomorrow."

"Think that'll be enough for the FBI to come?"

"I don't know for sure," he said. "And quite frankly, I'm too tired to worry about it right now. I just want to eat this and lay my head on a pillow."

She nodded. "I'm with you on that one."

He started to make his way to his room, intending to finish the plate in his room again. Madds followed behind, looking like she was going to do the same in her room. He stopped at the door, turning to face her.

"Madds," he said. "Thank you. For sticking around, I mean."

She nodded, offering a half-smile, but didn't say anything. Then she disappeared to her room.

CHAPTER FORTY

ELVEN LET OUT A LONG YAWN AND GOT UP IN THE MIDDLE OF
the night, heading out of his room and down the hallway. He'd opted
for boxer briefs tonight. He wasn't used to having clothing on him
when he slept, but since this was a shared house, he hadn't wanted to
risk wandering out in the hallway in the buff, forgetting that he
wasn't the only one there.

The house was warm, which was a good thing. Nothing was more
jarring than stepping out into the cold while still half-asleep. The
house was also very quiet. The only sound that could be heard was
the crackling of wood inside the stove that heated up the whole place.

He stood in the bathroom, relieving his bladder, and looked up at
the ceiling. He couldn't wait to climb back into bed and finish his
night of rest. He just hoped that he still had a lot more hours to go
instead of one. He hadn't bothered to check the clock when he
got up.

He reached for the flush handle on the toilet, but as he was about
to push it down, a noise in the house caught his attention. At first, he
thought a log might have fallen inside the wood-burning stove, but

then, there was a click of metal. Not a gun, but a latch. After a brief moment, he heard the floor creak.

It sounded like someone had opened the front door and walked inside Ginny's cabin. He highly doubted that it was Ginny herself. If that were the case, there would have been creaks along the stairs first. Maybe he was just too tired to notice them, though.

He quickly flipped off the light inside the bathroom just in case anyone had broken in. The way Ginny seemed to rarely lock up, he doubted there was any "breaking" involved. He pressed himself against the wall and slowly twisted the doorknob until it disengaged from the doorframe. It swung inward gently and slowly. He put his foot out to stop it from going too far and drawing any unwanted attention.

He peeked through the open door down the hall, but his eyes were still getting used to the darkness again. He couldn't make much out, but so far as he could see, nobody was in the hallway. Maybe it was just his mind playing games on him, and he was being overly cautious.

Since the hallway looked clear, he quietly left the bathroom and headed for his room. He was going to check the house out, but first, he needed his gun. He pushed his door in and took two steps toward the nightstand where his gun was tucked into the drawer.

Before he could reach it, however, a creak came from behind him. This time, there was no mistaking that noise. Someone was here.

He had no time to make a move—whoever was behind him was already making theirs. They hit him on the back of the head with something heavy, and Elven was unconscious before he hit the floor.

"ELVEN! ELVEN!" Madds's voice screamed. It was distant, coming in and out, like he was being pulled out of the water. Then it got closer and closer until he opened his eyes and saw that it was Madds screaming, but she wasn't distant at all. She was beside him, kneeling over him. But they were no longer in the cabin. They were outside, the headlights of a few vehicles shining directly at them.

He blinked a few times, still unsure what was happening.

"What's happening?" Elven asked, still trying to make sense of it all.

"What's happening is you've been sticking your nose in places it don't belong," a man said.

Elven looked up to find three men standing over them in ski masks. Elven was still on the ground, but he understood now.

"Ginny?" Elven asked, not seeing her anywhere.

"Don't worry about her," one of the men said. "She ain't who we're after. She's tied up night and tight."

"Go fuck yourself," Madds spat at them. She was bleeding from her nose, and Elven wondered how much of a beating she'd taken to get to where they were now. He might have been the lucky one by being knocked out cold.

One of the masked men laughed. "We told you to stay out of Old Knuckle," the man said again. "And now we'll make sure you really get it."

Elven started to climb to a kneeling position, but he was too slow. Before he could get up, the man struck Madds across the face with his fist. She landed on the dirt with a thud. She let out a groan, grabbing at her head.

"Hey!" Elven yelled. He finally was up, kneeling and reaching for her.

"Don't worry, we aren't leaving you out of this," one of the men said. When Elven looked up, he saw a boot heading his way, just before it connected with his jaw. He fell on his side, next to Madds.

She reached out to him, dealing with her own injury at the same time. He grabbed her hand, and that's when the rest of the beating came.

They kicked and punched at each of them. Sometimes, they took turns. Other times, they did it at the same time. Elven tried fighting when he could, even catching a foot once or twice. But as soon as he did, another blow came from a different direction.

Madds tried, too. But just like him, her efforts were useless. They had them in a bad spot, knocking them to the ground and not letting them back up.

Elven had been dealt beatings before, but this was something different. The three men who did it were having fun. It was like a game to them, not just a fight.

But they also were tiring themselves out. Elven's head throbbed, his body ached, and his limbs felt like they'd been detached from himself. But he was holding back what little he had left, waiting to see if he could make any moves.

And then one presented itself.

One of the men got close to them, leaning down. "Stay out of Old Knuckle," he said. His breathing was labored, like he hadn't had this much exercise in a while. "Maybe you'll listen now."

He lifted his leg, ready to stomp on Elven. The other two were also panting, but they weren't ready to quit, either; they were just slow enough that Elven knew he could try again.

Elven grabbed the foot of the man who'd lifted his leg. He pushed it as hard as he could, making him fall on his backside.

His two friends were already on Elven, but Madds knew the score. She must have been saving what little she had, too, waiting for the right moment. And the right moment was now.

She grabbed the legs of both men as soon as they grabbed Elven. Putting all her weight into it, she made them trip, pulling them down on the ground with the rest of them.

Elven didn't waste any time, still holding the attacker's leg up and throwing direct punches right to his groin. It was dirty, but so was clocking someone in the back of his head and dragging him out in his underwear. He continued to punch as many times as he could.

"My fucking nuts!" the attacker yelled.

That's when Elven saw the gun on the man's hip. He'd never drawn it, which meant their intentions weren't to kill them. Just to scare them off. But now the man's hand went for the gun on his hip. He slid it out of the holster, but Elven grabbed his wrist and twisted until the attacker dropped the gun. He squealed out something Elven never even knew was possible from another person.

Elven was too disoriented to know where the gun had landed in the dirt, but it didn't matter. One of the attackers crawled away as Madds held the other one in a chokehold. He struggled, and Elven could see he was slowly getting out of her grip because she was so exhausted and beaten down.

The one who had just taken the beating to the crotch did the same, but Elven was too weak to grab him. He was surprised his attacker could even move at this point, but the will to stay alive—or protect the family jewels from complete destruction—was a great motivator.

Elven felt around in the dirt, trying to find the gun. It was too dark, and his vision was too blurred. He didn't want to let them get away, but at this point, it seemed likely. The one who Madds had in a hold had slipped free, and now he, too, was on the run.

"Help him on top!" someone yelled, pointing to the one who could no longer stand because of Elven.

The two friends lifted the injured one and threw him over one of the ATVs. The leader fired it up and took off, the other two joining on their own ATVs and revving the engines. They were leaving before Elven could even get to his feet.

Madds, however, had a little more in her to give. Somehow in the thick of it all, she had found the gun Elven had been searching for. She stood up and fired three shots. Her aim was so far off that two of the bullets disappeared into the forest, not a single hit against a tree. The third bullet, however, managed to hit the back of one of the ATVs. The metal clanged as it was pierced. But it did nothing to slow them down.

Before she could steady herself any further, they were gone into the darkness. And that's when Madds fell to the ground.

Elven spat out a mouthful of blood and crawled to her. "Madds," he choked out. "Madds, stay awake."

He wrapped his arms around her, struggling with her weight, and stood up on both feet. He steadied himself, not knowing how much left he had. But all he needed was enough to get inside and get Ginny Tiller untied.

Once that was done, which was all a blur, he collapsed on the floor next to where he had laid Madds.

CHAPTER FORTY-ONE

Both Elven and Madds had a rough night, struggling to stay awake for most of it. Ginny Tiller had radioed Bear, who had radioed Jessa. Both of them showed up at the same time, about four in the morning. Elven figured their attackers had run off around an hour earlier.

Jessa did an exam on them both, finding numerous issues. She applied a ton of different concoctions from herbs, paste, and other things that Elven didn't think to ask about. All he knew was that he was in immense pain, and this woman was trying to alleviate all of that.

She did the same for Madds, whom he demanded she take care of first. She put up a fight about it, saying that Jessa needed to stitch up the large gash Elven had on his back before she could do anything else. He had no idea how bad it was since he couldn't see it and his entire body radiated pain, but by Jessa's face, he figured it was down-right awful. He let her stitch him up, but once she was finished, he made sure Madds was taken care of.

Ginny was a great help, too. She boiled rags for them and made for a great nurse to Jessa. On top of that, she brewed some of the nastiest-smelling tea Elven had ever sniffed, but once it went down, everything felt alright. Another thing he didn't ask about, since he had a feeling there was something a little on the less-than-legal side in it. With how much better it made him feel, though, he wasn't going to protest a single word.

Bear helped where he could, but he was more concerned with who was responsible. Elven told him everything he knew, which amounted to a whole lot of nothing. Three men, on three ATVs, and one who now had crushed testicles.

That one made Bear snort a laugh. Elven couldn't help but do the same, but immediately regretted it when his ribs throbbed in pain against his diaphragm.

"I did hit one of the ATVs with a bullet," Madds said. "Don't hold it against me for my aim being shit."

"Madds, the fact that you were able to stand and fire the gun after all this... well, you're a hell of a lot tougher than you look," Bear said.

"I'll make sure to put that on my resume," Madds said. "'Can take a beating like a champ.'" She winced as she pretended to type.

Jessa shook her head and put an ice pack against Madds's face. "Is there anything else?" Jessa asked. "Because these two are gonna need some real rest. So far as I can tell, there's a minor concussion, but nothing that we need to be too concerned with. We'll keep an eye on them for now."

"How about internal bleeding?" Elven asked, grabbing his side as he twisted.

"Can't really tell that one yet," she said. "You could go in town to be sure. But I figure we could also give it a day and see if there are any signs. If they're there, you'll know it."

"Fantastic," Elven said, his tongue prodding against a tooth. It felt far too loose and was grazing the inside of his cheek at an odd angle. He put his fingers in his mouth and gave it a push, tearing at the last couple roots that tried desperately to hang on. He spat it out, catching the worried look on Ginny's face.

"Sorry about that," he said. "Didn't mean to make a mess of your floor."

"Son, a mop can wipe that away easily, but it can't do the same for that face of yours," she said. "I'm just sorry that it happened."

"You and me both," Elven said.

"Christ, I'm surprised he's not complaining about how he looks now because of it," Madds said.

"A lot's changed since you left," Elven said.

"Apparently," Madds agreed.

Bear took a look at the two as they both continued their banter. "For as beat to shit as you both are, it seems like you're doing alright if you can squabble like this. Take the day to rest. I'll handle anything in town if it turns up," he said. "And I recommend locking the door. I'll send Benson by to keep watch while I'm not here, too."

Elven didn't think Benson would do much to scare anyone off. On the other hand, the kid was pretty demanding when he held that gun to Elven when they first met. So maybe he was underestimating the kid. Either way, Elven wasn't going to argue with Bear. Knowing someone else was there might be nice, and he could actually focus on resting.

"Thank you, Bear," Elven said.

"Don't thank me yet," he said. "Now we've got a lot more work to do because of this."

CHAPTER FORTY-TWO

Ronnie Vaughn woke up on the recliner, like he did most days. The sun shining through the window was usually the culprit for the rude awakening, and today was no different. There was a hole in the curtain at just the right angle. He'd always meant to fix it, but he was all thumbs with a needle. He'd thought to take it to Cora, but he had almost no money to pay her. Though, knowing Cora, she probably would have done it for free.

But if he had done that, then he'd get stuck in a conversation with the woman, having to make up lies as to why Darlene couldn't do it for him. It got tiring, and he was sure that everyone in town knew the real reason that Darlene was no help around the house. He just didn't want to face it, and it was far easier for everyone to pretend so he could save face.

In some ways, it was funny how a secret could also be the most obvious thing to the whole community. And maybe that's why it was a community. Because everyone played along so that he could keep that secret.

He managed to pull himself out of the chair and onto his feet. He existed on a perpetual hangover, but it was never a bad one. He could drink a twelve-pack at night and be mostly fine the next day. He stuck to light beer for that very reason. Anything heavier would fill him up fast, and it would also make for a whammer in the morning. Besides, why spend more money on something like that when the low-end stuff gave the same result he was going for?

He stumbled down the hall toward the bathroom. Nature was calling, and so was a shower. He'd sweat all the booze out overnight, soaking it into the chair and through his undershirt. Every time he moved his arm, he caught a whiff of himself, and it nauseated him. His mouth tasted like stale beer, and he couldn't wait to replace that taste with a fresh one.

He passed Davin's room, where he saw him lying on the bed. He hadn't even heard him come home the night before. He usually stayed out at all hours, doing God knows what. But he stayed out of trouble. Ronnie knew it because trouble never followed him home, so Ronnie never felt the need to complain about it. Between dealing with Darlene and now Sadie's disappearance-turned-murder, Davin staying out of his hair was the best thing he could do.

On the left was Ronnie and Darlene's room, though he couldn't remember the last time they'd actually shared it. He didn't like being around his wife when she was on the pills, and that meant he almost never liked being around his wife. She wasn't the same woman he'd married, and because of it, he never felt like the man she'd married. It was a vicious cycle, and he knew it was only driving them further and further apart.

He rested his head on the door frame, thinking he ought to say something. Losing their daughter was going to be even harder on their marriage, and if he didn't do anything to help it now, he knew he would only lose Darlene completely. He sighed, kicking himself for being such a coward.

"What good is a man if he can't even talk to his wife?" he whispered to himself. He hit his head on the wall gently, urging his stupid brain to kick into gear and go in there. She might be asleep and not like the interruption, but he was going to be there for his family. Beer could wait. Hell, beer should probably fuck right off.

He knew he was on the cusp of everything, or nothing at all.

He pushed the door open all the way, seeing the state of the room. They hadn't done laundry in months, and they hadn't put clothes away in years. But that wasn't important now. He saw his wife on the bed, lying on her stomach. She tossed around when she slept, but nine times out of ten, she always ended up sleeping on her belly. He could never do that, finding it far too uncomfortable.

"Darlene," he whispered. "I don't know if you're awake or not, but I want to talk to you."

He stood, waiting to see if she lifted her head at the sound of his voice. She didn't stir.

He walked into the room, jostling the bed with both his hands. He didn't want to startle her, but he needed to wake her. Her body shook, but she still didn't move.

He cleared his throat. "Darlene, honey, are you awake?" His voice was much louder this time, but it didn't matter. The pills always had this effect, zonking her out for hours in the day.

He sat on the bed, slumping his shoulders as he did. He reached out and hesitated. The thought of having this conversation still troubled him, but finally, he went for it. He placed his hand on her back, ready to gently stroke or even shake her, if that's what it took.

And as soon as his hand touched the bare skin on the small of her back where her nightshirt had pulled up, he knew something was wrong. She was cold to the touch.

"Darlene?" he said, his voice no longer gentle but worried. He shook her hard, not caring if he startled her. In fact, he hoped she was. If he saw her jolt right up, only to be yelled at, he would be the most relieved man in the world.

But that didn't happen.

He ran to the side of the bed where her head lay, her body in a complete diagonal on the full-sized mattress. And then he saw her face, turned to the side. There was a puddle of vomit right next to her mouth. Her face was blue, and she didn't draw breath.

"Darlene!" he yelled out. He grabbed her and flipped her over, and her head flopped to the side. He shoved his fingers under her jaw into her neck. There was the faintest thud against his finger, or that's what he told himself, anyway. But he had to think it. She wasn't gone. She couldn't be.

Not yet. But if he didn't do something right now, she would be.

"Come on, baby, come on," he said, lifting her up with all his might. He had no idea what to do, but someone else would. Maybe Jessa or Cora. Hell, it didn't matter. Anyone would do, they just had to save her.

He carried her in his arms straight through the house and down the stairs. He put her across his lap on the first ATV next to the door. The key was inside, and he turned it on, the engine revving up.

"Stay with me, baby," Ronnie begged his wife. "Please, baby. Don't do this to me." And then he was off on the trail, heading straight for the town center.

CHAPTER FORTY-THREE

Bear was on a new mission now, but just like the previous one, he had no idea where to even begin looking. The people who'd attacked Elven and Madds could be anyone. To be honest, he was surprised it hadn't happened sooner. Most people weren't keen on outsiders meddling in the affairs of Old Knuckle. But what surprised him most was that it was after everyone seemed so accepting of the newcomers.

Sadie's body strung up was one hell of a message sent from someone who could only be pure evil at this point. The rest of the town had to think so, too. So for someone to attack Elven and Madds after that, well, it felt like it was more personal than anything else. Either that, or they thought he was getting a lot closer to figuring it out than they realized.

That could be a good thing, except for the fact that none of them knew what exactly they'd done or found to make anyone think that.

After being called to Ginny Tiller's cabin, Bear hadn't gotten any sleep afterward. His mind kept him awake, the wheels turning, trying to figure out so many different things. Most of all, he was wondering what the hell had happened to his community. It wasn't long ago that most people got along. Sure, there were always differences, but they were minor. Now people were getting beat up as a warning, and girls were being strung up in trees for some sort of sick show.

Bear Colter was afraid that Old Knuckle may never be the same after this, or if it could even survive it.

He walked through the town center, not expecting to see or hear much. But he figured there would still be questions after last night. He didn't think he could answer any of them, but the last thing he needed was for anyone trying to bother Elven down at Ginny's place after what had happened. He wouldn't be surprised if Elven and Madds needed to sleep for an entire week while their bodies tried to heal up. Of course, they didn't have that kind of time, but he would do his best to give them what little respite he could offer.

Just ahead, he spotted Paige. He had forgotten all about delivery day, with everything going on. And from the looks of it, so had most other people. Generally, when there was a delivery from town, people were all about, trying to help unload and get a peek at what might be available for them to use. Today, however, had a very low turnout.

"What's up with today?" Paige asked Bear when she spotted him as she unloaded the trailer on the back of her ATV. She had been making deliveries up here ever since her husband had died, taking over for him. She was one of the few people Old Knuckle trusted who didn't live in town. She was a Godsend whenever she came through, restocking the things people needed, making it so they didn't have to go into town themselves. Most people refused to make that trip for one reason or another.

Bear shook his head. As much as he trusted Paige, he wasn't going to tell her what was happening in town. She didn't need to trouble herself with it, and he didn't need one more possible leak to tell the authorities so they could come through and dust up the entire town.

"Just been some issues lately," he said.

Paige nodded, leaving it there. "Hey, Quentin, can you put those bags of flour over there?" she asked, turning to Quentin, who had come out from behind the side of the building where Paige had parked.

He gave a nod, but then spotted Bear. He quickly dropped his gaze down to the ground. Grabbing a bag of flour, he disappeared again. Bear had always known Quentin to be a bit standoffish, but this felt a little different. He was going to ask him a question, but his attention was quickly pulled away from the sound of an ATV ripping through town.

The engine of the ATV roared louder than usual, like whoever was driving it gave no care for the engine and was pushing it to its maximum limits. Bear wouldn't be surprised if they ended up doing some real damage to the machine. He ran toward the noise, holding a hand out for Paige to stay where she was. But he also wasn't sure what to expect, so he tucked himself next to a trailer a few twists of the path down the way, placing his hand on his gun. He needed to be ready for any sort of surprise after what had been happening lately.

But it wasn't a threat at all. Instead, Bear watched as Ronnie Vaughn rolled off the trail from his house and made a sharp turn toward the center where Bear stood. He didn't slow down one bit, the two wheels on the vehicle's right side lifting off the ground about an inch. He was lucky that he didn't tip the whole damn thing on its side and get caught underneath it.

But once Ronnie saw Bear, he stopped the ATV, and that's when Bear saw the body draped across his lap. It was his wife, Darlene. And she didn't look good at all.

"Help!" Ronnie screamed. "I need help! Bear! Bear! Come on, help me get her down. Is Jessa around?"

Ronnie was frantic. Bear ran up to him, ready to offer whatever help he could. Ronnie lifted Darlene up, and Bear took her in his arms.

And that's when he realized that he couldn't offer any help.

"Ronnie," Bear said. "What happened?"

"The pills. She took too many, I think," he said. "She threw up, and now... now... now I need your help!" He was stumbling on his words, but he made enough sense.

Bear laid Darlene down on the dirt a few feet away from the ATV while Ronnie jumped off the vehicle. He looked down at her and saw what Ronnie was talking about. She had vomit on her face and down her front. But Ronnie didn't seem to understand that there was nothing anybody could do at this point.

Bear checked for a pulse, and he didn't feel a single thump of the vein against his finger. Darlene's eyes were open and glassy, staring up without ever moving. Her mouth hung open. And her skin, it was pale blue, completely cold to the touch. That may have been from the ride over and exposure to the winter air, but with all the other details, Bear figured she was already dead. Or she'd died on the ride over, and Ronnie hadn't noticed.

Bear stood up as Ronnie rushed to her side. "Ronnie, I'm sorry."

Ronnie shook his head. "What are you doing? Do something! Help her! Somebody help us!" he screamed.

A few people came out of their homes as others rushed to see the commotion, but once they saw what was happening, they stopped. There was nothing they could do but stare and offer pitying looks.

"Ronnie," Bear said, putting his hand on the man's shoulder. "I'm sorry. But she's gone."

Ronnie sobbed, his shoulders bouncing up and down against Bear's hand. "No," he wailed. "No, no, it can't be. I can't lose you, Darlene."

There was no response from Darlene, of course. Bear didn't know what else to say in this moment, and really, there was nothing for him to say. He couldn't bring back Darlene, and he couldn't make Ronnie feel better about losing his wife. Ronnie had just lost a daughter, and now he'd lost a wife. Even with all their problems, nobody deserved to go through that.

Bear didn't want to say he was sorry again. It seemed like that was all he had been doing. Instead, he thought about what he might be able to help with.

"Can I give you a ride?" Bear asked. "We'll take Darlene to Jessa's, of course. But maybe I can pick up Davin, and you guys could talk?"

"Oh my God," Ronnie gasped, wiping at his face. He turned his face toward Bear, his eyes bloodshot and snot dripping off his nose. "I didn't even say anything to Davin before I left. I just—I just came here."

Bear nodded, then turned his attention to the ATV that Ronnie had ridden in on. Something caught his eye. It might not have been anything unusual at first, but after the story Elven and Madds had told him, it seemed pretty damn pertinent now. There was a single bullet hole on the backside of the ATV. But Ronnie didn't look like he'd been beaten, or done any beating himself. His fists weren't bruised or bloody at all.

And then Ronnie clarified the entire thing for him. "Fuck," he cursed. "I didn't even think and took Davin's ride, too. I just wanted to get here."

"That's Davin's ATV?" Bear asked.

Ronnie nodded. "It was the closest to the door," he said. "What am I gonna tell him now? About his mother, and right after his sister."

Bear wasn't sure what to say to that, because his mind was on the fact that Davin's ATV was the one with the bullet hole in it. That meant that Davin was part of the trio who attacked Elven and Madds last night.

"I don't know, Ronnie," he finally said. "But let's get you up and get Darlene out of here before too many people come gawking."

But Ronnie remained next to Darlene. "We keep trying to be isolated out here, as if somehow that'll keep us safe from everything out there. But we're just kidding ourselves. Nothing is safe. Not no more."

Ronnie gave his wife one last hug before getting up.

CHAPTER FORTY-FOUR

Elven wasn't sure if he had actually gotten any sleep, or if he was stuck in the between stage. The one that felt like a fever dream laced with reality. He could hear things in the cabin, and at the same time, he was in a dark place, drifting around. The whole thing felt like one massive trip, and part of him wondered if it was from the beating he'd taken, or if that tea he'd drank was made from mushrooms.

Either way, he felt horrible as he lay in the bed, tossing and turning, his body screaming at him every time he moved. Jessa had covered his body, nearly head to toe, with some sort of salve that was supposed to be good for all his cuts, bruises, and general aches. With how he felt now, he hated to think how badly he would have felt without it.

But more than anything, he figured it was his mind wandering that was keeping him from drifting off into a solid slumber. There were a lot of questions about who'd made the attack, and for what reason. They clearly weren't trying to kill him. If they were, they could have just shot him and Madds and been done with it. Maybe they still would have, but wanted to make them really feel it first.

Elven wasn't so sure, though. He thought they were just giving them a warning. Like the man said, they had tried to tell them to get out of town and Elven just hadn't listened. So maybe it was just trying to get him to listen.

If that was the case, then what for?

Before he could answer that question, a knock came on his door, soft but firm. Elven sat up, his head rushing as he did. "Yeah, come on in," Elven choked out.

He expected Ginny to come in, possibly with some food. Or at the very least, Madds, checking in on him. But it was neither.

Bear Colter stood in the doorway, blocking nearly all of the light from the hallway with his large body. "Hate to bother you," he said.

"But you're gonna, anyway," Elven said with a smirk that cost him a stabbing pain in his cheek.

"Figured I'd let you have the option before I followed a lead on my own," he said.

Now Elven was intrigued. "A lead?" he asked. "On Sadie Vaughn?"

Bear shook his head. "Don't know that yet," he said. "But a lead on who did this to the two of you." His finger drifted, pointing to Elven and then to Madds's room. "Could be connected to the murders, but that depends on why you think they attacked you."

Elven nodded. "Was just trying to figure that one out myself," he said. "You think this is a solid lead? Or just something you're trying to sniff around?"

"If you consider finding the ATV that was here last night and knowing the owner of it a lead, then I'd say it's solid," Bear said, and Elven couldn't disagree with that one. "Found it during this morning's delivery. It's been a morning, to say the least."

Elven sighed, forgetting all about the delivery and his hope to pass a message to Paige. But if this lead was as sound as Bear said it was, maybe he could follow it up before doing anything drastic like he had planned.

"After last night, I'd say they're willing to take this pretty far," Elven said. "So you're gonna need my help."

He slowly climbed out of bed, grabbing at his side as he stood upright.

"You sure about that?" Bear asked, frowning. "You seem a little worse for the wear than I realized."

Elven waved him off. "You knew how bad it was. If you really thought that, you wouldn't have come."

Bear nodded, and Elven knew he'd caught him. The man wanted the help, and Elven was happy to give it to him.

"What about her?" Bear asked.

Elven put his pants on, holding back a wince as his body told him this wasn't the best idea. He was going to see this one through, though. He walked into the hallway, moving past Bear to Madds's door. He debated knocking, but when he didn't hear any noise from inside, he went for the doorknob. Cracking the door open a sliver, he peered in to find Madds sound asleep in bed. She apparently hadn't had any of Elven's trouble falling asleep.

Elven slowly closed the door, leaving her inside. He shook his head as he went back to his room to finish getting dressed.

"Let her sleep," Elven said. "She's been through enough for now."

CHAPTER FORTY-FIVE

Elven took the ATV, leaving Madds without her own ride. But that was fine because he figured she wouldn't need it. And if she truly did need one, Benson was still there. He'd fallen asleep on the couch, his gun beside him on the floor, while Ginny rummaged around him, making breakfast for everyone. She told Elven that as soon as she finished cooking, Benson would be wide awake, probably eating half of the meal she'd prepared. The woman didn't seem bothered by what had happened the night before, either. Elven could tell she was a lot stronger than most.

They rode all the way out to the Vaughn residence, which was now just a quiet shell. Ronnie was still in the center of town at Jessa's house, preparing Darlene for whatever needed to be done. Mostly cold storage until it was time for the funeral. Now both Vaughn women were in the same place, which, Elven supposed, was exactly what Darlene had wanted after hearing about her daughter's death.

But instead of riding right up to the place, he and Bear hung back, just out of view from the trailer. However, they could still see it through the trees.

"Think we're far enough back?" Elven asked, wanting to double-check.

Bear nodded, handing him a set of binoculars. "Yeah, this is fine. Someone would have to really be looking to find us, and in Old Knuckle, I don't see much reason to do that."

Elven looked through the binoculars and watched the trailer for a moment, confirming that Bear was right. Nobody was trying to see if they were being watched.

"So what's the plan, then?" Elven asked, rotating his shoulder a few times to keep it lubed up. It had swollen some after last night's events.

"You're asking me?" Bear asked. "Isn't this your thing?"

"You brought me here," Elven said. "I thought we'd go talk to Davin and find out."

"All you'll get is an earful of bullshit with that one," Bear said. "You ask him about the bullet hole, he'll say someone must have taken his ATV."

"And brought it back?"

Bear chuckled. "Hey, don't grill me. I'm just telling you what he would say. Like I said, earful of bullshit."

"Fair enough," Elven said. "So what, then? Just sit here and wait for him to come out?"

Bear nodded. "Pretty much," he said. "Reckon we should follow him to wherever he's heading when he goes off into the woods. Who knows, maybe it'll lead us to Lila."

"You really think Davin had something to do with his own sister's death?" Elven asked.

Bear shook his head. "I don't know what to think anymore," he said. "But I do know that he was trying to run you out of town for a reason. And it wasn't just because he doesn't like you. I mean, that might be part of it, but there's something else there."

"Does he know about his mother yet?"

Bear shook his head. "The way Ronnie was talking, he ran out without telling Davin a word about it. And nobody seems to be running down here to fill him in."

As if Bear manifested it with his words, another ATV came down the trail, blowing past the turn-off that Elven and Bear had taken and not noticing them there. The vehicle pulled up to the side of the trailer, and a man got off. Bear took the binoculars from Elven and watched him.

"Know who that is?" Elven asked.

"Looks like Jake Bronson," he said. "One of Davin's friends who usually causes nothing but trouble when he's involved."

Jake pounded on the door, waiting a few minutes until Davin came to it. Instead of letting Jake in, Davin stood on the porch, discussing something with him. Davin didn't seem super emotional, so Elven wasn't sure if he had been told about his mother or not. But he sure seemed pretty angry in general.

"Davin's pissed about something," Bear said, noticing the same thing as Elven.

"No different than I've ever seen since coming here," Elven said.

"Yeah, well, growing up in that family has a way of causing that outcome, I guess," Bear said. "Still don't make whatever he's doing right, though."

Davin pushed Jake, but nothing escalated after that. Davin looked over the railing at the ATVs and waved his hand again in anger. Finally, Davin motioned for Jake to follow him and jumped over the railing, landing on the ground.

"Looks like we'll be on the move," Elven said.

Bear nodded in agreement as Davin and Jake hopped on a couple of ATVs, though not Davin's own, since Ronnie still had that one in town. But Davin didn't let that stop him, and the two of them took off into the woods.

Bear and Elven fired up their vehicles and followed them. At this point, Elven knew how it worked and hung way back, taking it at a slow pace so the revving of their engines wasn't too much of a give-away the young men were being followed. He didn't worry that they'd lose them, either, because the big cloud of dust in the air trailing behind the ATVs showed their location. So they took the route nice and steady, all the way through the twists and turns.

The path eventually led to some overgrown spots that didn't look well-traveled. Bear led the way down the tight pathway between the trees. They were pretty deep in, away from any signs of civilization. He signaled to Elven to stop, which he did.

"Not sure where this is," Bear said. "But it's clearly not anywhere people come too often."

"I can see the dirt in the air stops just ahead," Elven said. "Think we should push on this way, or go on foot?"

"You're onto what I was gonna say," Bear said. "Let's leave these right here. Unless there's another way out on the other side, they won't be able to get past if we line 'em up."

Elven agreed, pulling his ATV as close to Bear's as he could, creating a plug on the trail so nothing could get by. And then they were off on foot.

Elven kept his mouth shut, but the hike wasn't easy on him. His body was screaming to crawl back into bed, but they were in too far at this point. His resilience paid off, because after what felt like hours of hiking, which might have only been thirty minutes, they found a large shed that looked as if it had been dropped from the sky. It was metal and rusted, so it must have been there for quite some time. There were three 4-wheelers outside, along the right side of the building.

"Three attackers, three ATVs," Bear whispered. "What are the odds?" He had a big smile on his face, like he'd just cracked the case wide open. Elven let him have that one.

Music played from a small speaker, but it carried well enough through the large sliding door that was almost all the way open, with only a couple of feet left to pull into the ceiling. A conversation could be heard mixed in, but nothing concrete stood out. Not until they got just outside the door, that is.

Both Bear and Elven pulled their guns out just before reaching the door. They pressed their backs against the wall, exchanging glances to make sure they were on the same page. They were, as far as Elven was concerned.

"Goddammit, Jake!" someone cried out. "Don't fuck with me, my nuts are fucking crushed right now. You said you were gonna bring more ice. Where the fuck is it?"

"Did he just say that?" Bear whispered, lifting an eyebrow.

Elven tipped his head. "I'm sure he's feeling a whole lot worse off than I am right now," he whispered back.

"I've been here all night holding my junk, hoping it's not fucking blown for good," the voice said again.

"Calm the fuck down," Davin said. "If you didn't want to be nursing yourself all night, then you shouldn't have let him get the jump on you."

"Where's the fucking ice?" his friend demanded.

"I left it outside," another voice said. Elven figured it was Jake since he hadn't been hobbling around, holding his crotch when he paid a visit to Davin.

Bear put a hand out to Elven, signaling that he was going to handle this one. And handle it, he did. Because as soon as Jake Bronson came out through the door, ducking just a little so his big head didn't hit it, he was met with Bear's gun sticking right into his face.

"Show me your hands," Bear said.

"Oh, shit," Jake said, suddenly frozen in fear. Jake didn't lift his hands; he just swallowed and stared at the barrel in his face.

"Hands!" Bear shouted.

"Fuck, get rid of it!" Davin shouted.

But Elven wasn't going to let them get away with whatever it was they were planning. He spun around Bear and Jake, pointing his revolver directly through the massive opening. He didn't spot a target first thing, but his eye eventually caught them both. Davin was to the right, behind a table that held some beakers and other cooking items. And the other one, the one with the heavily bruised testicles, sat on a rickety-looking bed frame that housed a filthy mattress.

"Hands up, now!" Elven demanded.

He watched them both hesitate. He knew this wasn't going to be good, and just as he thought, it wasn't. The one in the corner dropped his hand down to the mattress, right where a handgun sat. Elven pointed his revolver and fired before the guy could even lift it up. The bullet ripped right through his shoulder. He fell backward and bounced off the mattress, landing on the floor. The gun stayed where it was.

"I said put your hands up!"

"Motherfucker!" the man on the floor screamed. He writhed in pain on the concrete floor.

Davin, however, slowly lifted his hands. "Okay, okay," he said. "Just don't shoot me."

Bear held Jake in front of him, walking him into the building. Jake clearly didn't want to be shot, either, as he now had his hands up.

"What the hell is going on in here?" Bear asked, his voice more disappointed than angry. It was clear that he already knew what this setup was. Elven knew it, too.

They were cooking meth.

"I think we found the reason they didn't want us sniffing around," Elven said. "Ain't that right?"

"Goddammit, I need some medical attention or some shit!" the one on the floor said.

"Quiet down," Bear barked. He found a chair and put it next to Jake. "Sit and don't get cute."

Jake did as he was told without a word, and Bear walked to the one on the floor. "Saul Willet. Boy, they must be pretty damn desperate to be working with you." He bent over him and grabbed the gun off the bed. Holstering his own gun, he hoisted Saul back on the bed. "Now stay there and shut up."

"I need—"

"You'll get all the medical help you need once we finish up here. But you're gonna have to drive your ass back to Jessa's for that. If that don't cut it, we'll take you to the hospital in Dupray, put a bag of this shit in your pocket, and call the sheriff to pick you up," Bear said. "Until then, shut the hell up."

Saul nodded, wincing and letting his one good hand go between his shoulder and his groin, probably unsure of which hurt more. Elven didn't envy him right now, but he got what was coming to him.

"Is this all your doing?" Bear asked, getting close to Davin.

Davin shrunk, tucking himself back against the wall as Bear grew near.

"Answer me!" Bear grabbed the table and lifted it up, throwing it on the ground. All the glassware shattered against the concrete floor. A tray of crystal went with it, scattering everywhere.

Bear closed in on Davin, towering over him, pushing his body right up against him. He was a very intimidating man.

"I didn't want you finding out about this," Davin said, his voice quivering.

"No shit," Bear said. "But that ain't what I asked. Is this all you?"

Davin shook his head. "H—Hollis," he said. "I ain't supposed to say, but he said if I just made small batches on the side, then nobody would know or get hurt."

Bear slammed his hand against the wall right next to Davin's face.

"Bear," Elven said, not wanting him to take it too far. As much as he hated the drugs, and hated Hollis for bringing them here, Davin looked like a terrified kid.

Bear glared at Elven, but nodded. He took a deep breath and let it out slowly. "Answer this question," Bear said. "Did you have anything to do with Shayla or your sister?"

Davin looked up, shocked. He was crying now. "No, I swear it," he said. "Sadie and I weren't close, but she was my sister. Probably the closest family I had. She grew up the same way as me."

"We just wanted to run you off last night," Jake added, trying to support his friend. "We didn't kill nobody."

Bear sighed. Elven couldn't tell if he was grateful or frustrated. Probably both. But they were back to being at a dead end.

"You heard anything from town yet?" Bear asked Davin, his tone softening.

"Town? No, why?" Davin asked.

Bear turned to Jake, glaring at him. "You didn't tell him?"

Jake only shrugged, keeping his mouth shut.

"Tell me what?" Davin asked, clearly having no idea about his mother.

Elven holstered his gun, knowing it was going to be a rough rest of the day trying to clean all this up and take these young men back to town. He didn't even know what they were going to do with them, but figured there was some sort of way to hold them.

"Son, I've got some bad news," Bear began. "It's your mother."

CHAPTER FORTY-SIX

It had been a very long day. One that Bear was wanting to be done with. On some level, it seemed like it had been successful. He'd solved the mystery of who attacked Madds and Elven, and he had taken down a meth lab and the three men responsible for it.

But on the other hand, it was also a disaster. A grieving family had lost their mother, the community had been betrayed by three of their own with drugs and greed, and, of course, they still had zero leads on who was responsible for the murders.

Elven and Bear had brought the three men—if they could even be called that—into town. Saul was dropped off at Jessa's, where she could dig the bullet out of him and stitch him up. Elven was a great shot, and he'd managed to not hit anything that would cause too much long-term damage. It was up to Saul if he wanted to go to Dupray and be seen at the hospital. Bear meant what he said about alerting the sheriff, too. He had an idea that Saul was gonna find his shoulder wasn't so bad after all.

At the same time, Bear asked Jessa to take a look at Saul's nether regions. The way the kid complained the entire ride on the ATV, Bear had a feeling those were worse off than his shoulder.

But again, probably nothing that Saul wasn't willing to power through.

The other two, Bear hadn't decided yet how he wanted to handle. In the past, when the meth labs had gotten real bad, they either ran them out of town, or the cooks caught a bullet by not obeying their orders. This time felt different.

Davin was in a bad spot. And Jake was just an idiot. Bear had a soft spot for everyone in the community, especially when they were connected to more kin right there in Old Knuckle. Of course, Davin's kin was growing extra thin these days. Maybe it was being too soft, but Bear was willing to look the other way on this one as long as it didn't happen again.

But he wouldn't make that decision on his own. He'd probably bring Roy Leven and a few others in on that call. If they all came to a consensus, the community would abide by the decision they made.

Bear would put that discussion on the back burner for now, though, because Cora radioed him just after he told Elven to go back to Ginny's and try to get some rest. The man had been through a lot the previous night, and there was still far too much left for them to do on the case of the murdered girls.

One thing Bear had to admit, though, was that Elven was a great shot. If that's how he shot, battered and bruised as he was, then he'd love to see him shoot when he was in good health. He made a mental note to make sure he was never on the opposite end of that gun, though.

Bear told Cora to sit tight and that he'd meet her at her house. He knew she had a lot going on with being her daddy's caretaker. He didn't mind making the trek to her, and besides, she seemed pretty concerned about something. When he pressed her about it, though, she refused to say over the radio.

Secrets in Old Knuckle were plenty, but Cora generally wasn't one for them. So it must be pretty damn important.

And when Bear finally made it to Cora's, he could see on her face that she was troubled more than usual. He wondered if it had anything to do with having her look at Sadie's body back at Jessa's. He felt a twinge of guilt wash over him and regretted asking her to come down. But it was done, and there was nothing he could do to take that back.

"Thanks for coming," Cora said, running a hand through her hair. She twirled a finger through it and paced twice after letting Bear inside. She was nervous about something, and maybe it wasn't just the image of Sadie burned into her mind.

"Of course, Cora, you know I'm here to help," Bear said. "Now, what exactly are you needing help with?"

He watched as she debated something in her mind, her eyes shifting like she wasn't sure anymore about what she wanted to talk about.

"I'm sorry, Bear," she said. "I don't even know if I should be saying anything, or if I'm just going crazy or something. But something just don't feel right, and I thought if I called you, I would have clarity. But even then, it just feels like this weight on me, and I can't get it off, you know what I mean?" Her voice was running a mile a minute.

"Cora, calm down, alright? Take some breaths, maybe have a seat," Bear said. "Can you do that for me?"

He placed his hands on her shoulders, trying to keep her in one place. She nodded rapidly, which told Bear that she was nowhere near calm yet. But he managed to get her to sit down on a chair at her small dining room table. There was a large empty spot next to it, which he figured was for when she wheeled her father up to the table to eat with her.

"Where's Howard at?" Bear asked. "Is everything alright with him?" He wasn't sure if it had anything to do with her father, and if not, then at least Bear thought it might take her mind off whatever was troubling her.

He was right, because it seemed to do the trick. At least for a brief moment.

She shook her head. "He's fine," she said, her voice now more even. "In the bedroom, having a rest. He naps a lot more than you'd think. As much of a handful as he is sometimes, he's also a lot easier than most people think."

Bear slid into one of the remaining chairs at the table next to Cora. She was a little too old for Bear to consider anything as more than friends, but he had to admit, for a woman her age who wore no makeup, she wasn't half-bad to look at. Natural beauty was a prize to behold, though he thought that it reflected more who the person was on the inside than the outside. Her taking care of her father the way she did was proof of that.

"That's good," Bear said, watching her nervousness return as she fiddled with her hands. He reached out and grabbed them. "Now, what's all this about? Take it slow and steady if you need. I'm here to listen."

She nodded, this time a bit slower. "I didn't want to cause any trouble, but I felt like I should say something. It's about what I saw yesterday."

Bear nodded. "Sadie Vaughn," he said. "It was pretty horrific, I know."

She agreed. "Yes, but it was something else I saw."

"What did you see?" Bear asked.

"I'm sorry, did you want some tea or something," Cora said, starting to get up. "I didn't even offer, and I—"

Bear squeezed her hand a little tighter, keeping her at the table. "Cora," he said, locking eyes with her. "What did you see?"

She sat back down. "The dress," she said. "I saw it stuffed in the corner of the room. At first, I wasn't sure, but the more I thought about it, the more I knew that I'd seen it before. And it wasn't Sadie's."

Now she had Bear's attention. "What do you mean it wasn't hers?"

"I mean, it fit her, maybe," she said. "But she didn't buy that dress."

"And how do you know this?" Bear asked, now finding himself lost.

"Because I made it," she said.

Bear pushed back from the table, unsure what he was supposed to do with this information. "You mean, you made it for her? Like she came in before she went missing and asked you to make it?"

She shook her head. "Nothing like that," she said. "Sadie never asked me to make that dress for her. But someone else did."

"Who?"

"Quentin Delvers," she said.

"You're sure about that?" Bear asked, ready to go hunt down Quentin right now.

She nodded. "Everyone in town knows Quentin's a little checked out," she said. "But he's harmless."

"So, he just came in and asked for a dress?" Bear asked. "You didn't think that was weird? Quentin's been living alone for as long as I've known him."

"Before that, he had a mama, too," she said. "But no, I didn't think that was weird because it wasn't the first dress I made for him, either. I didn't know what he was using them for. He said it reminded him of his mama, and I didn't have the heart to say anything about it. Most people would hate on him for that kind of thing. They usually found any reason to do so already, and Quentin was always the gentle giant type."

"And now?" Bear asked.

She shrugged. "Now I don't have a clue," she said. "After all that's been happening, I'm wonderin' that maybe I don't know everyone like I thought I did. What the hell has Old Knuckle become, Bear?"

Bear stood up. He had no answer, because he was wondering the same thing.

CHAPTER FORTY-SEVEN

Bear knew he had to get to Elven with this new information from Cora. It was the first time during this case that they'd had a substantial lead like this, and knowing Cora, she was telling the truth. She made dresses and other pieces for people, so she'd be the one to recognize the dress. She would have known what fabric it was, and who she made it for.

Quentin was very peculiar, that was for sure. Just because he was odd, it didn't mean he was a killer. But buying a dress and having a girl end up dead in that very dress? Well, that was a different story.

Bear hopped on his ATV, but before he could fire it up, Roy Leven stood in front of him, blocking his way. Bear didn't have time for this right now, but he knew if he didn't handle it, the problem would only grow bigger.

"Need something, Roy?" Bear asked.

Roy shrugged, adjusting the ball cap on his head. "Depends on what you know," he said. "I heard Cora call you on the radio, and by the sounds of her voice, she sure seemed troubled."

Bear studied Roy, debating on what to say next. He could lie to the man, let him know it was just about what was happening to the community. That wouldn't be too far off-base, but it also wasn't his style. Roy was a pain in his ass, but he was a good man who meant well.

And after all the secrets Bear had been keeping to try to solve this case—the ones that ended up getting out, anyway, and causing a lot of grief to the community—he figured it might be best to bring Roy in on this one.

"Cora gave me some information that she thinks is important to the case," Bear said.

Roy lifted an eyebrow. "And what might that be?"

Bear hesitated.

"Bear, I want to catch whoever the sick prick is that is doing things to those girls as much as you do. I can help on this one."

Bear nodded. "Alright," he said. "She said the dress that Sadie was wearing when she was found was one she made."

Roy shrugged. "Cora makes a lot of dresses."

"She made it for Quentin," Bear said.

Roy's face dropped. "That motherfucker," he said. "You give me a couple of minutes, and I'll round up everyone in town to go down there and—"

"Roy, that's exactly why I didn't want to tell you anything," Bear cut him off. "We don't know that he's involved at all. Just that Quentin had the dress made."

"And that doesn't strike you as weird?" Roy asked. "What the hell does a grown-ass man who doesn't have a wife and daughter need with a dress?"

"We're gonna find that out," Bear said. "But we're gonna do it right."

"And how exactly is that?"

"I need to go get Elven and Madds in on this one."

"You don't need those outsiders to figure this out," Roy countered. "We can go grab the prick and bring him down here and ask him the questions ourselves."

"And what if Lila isn't there?" Bear asked. "What if we spook him, and he won't tell us shit? Then what are you gonna tell Benson about his sister? That you're sorry that she's out there, maybe starving to death or worse, because you wanted to handle this yourself?"

Roy didn't say anything.

"Roy, I promise you that you can be a part of this. No more secrets, no more keeping you in the dark, alright?" Bear said. "But we do this the way I say. That means we get Elven, we get Madds, and the four of us ask our questions."

Roy considered this a moment, but finally, he gave a nod. "I can agree with that," he said. "But I gotta run home to fill up my tank. It's gonna take me twenty minutes to get down there, then another to get back."

"That's fine," Bear said. "I need to get Elven and Madds from Ginny Tiller's. Let's meet at the bend just outside of my cabin. Once we're all there, we can ride together. But I swear to God, Roy, you better fucking wait for me. I don't want you going down there to Quentin's until we come with you, you got that?"

"I hear you," Roy said.

"Then give me your word," Bear said.

Roy rolled his eyes. "I just fuckin' said it, didn't I? But if you need more, then fine. I will not go to Quentin's without you. I'll be sitting at the bend just like you said, and then when you get there, we'll all go together. Satisfied?"

Bear nodded. Roy was a man of his word, even if he was a pain in the ass. So that was gonna have to be good enough for him. And if they were going to get this done in a timely manner, he couldn't babysit Roy the whole time. They'd already wasted too much time as it was.

"Alright," Bear said. "Go fill up and meet us there."

Bear took off, leaving Roy to take care of his business.

Of course, Bear wasn't aware of all the business Roy had to take care of. And he didn't see, nor did he hear, Roy reach for his radio once he was on the pathway.

CHAPTER FORTY-EIGHT

When Bear showed up at Ginny Tiller's cabin, Elven thought he looked far more excited than he'd ever seen the man. Not only that, but he was very antsy, if not outright impatient. He'd busted in, not bothering to apologize for disturbing Elven and Madds like he had that morning.

Elven hadn't realized how much rest he'd gotten after helping Bear track down Davin and bust up their meth lab, but his body had clearly needed it. Waking up in the late afternoon was a surprise to him, but at the same time, he felt far better than when he'd woken that morning. Madds looked even better than Elven, but she hadn't had the same interruption and trek that he'd gone on with Bear earlier. Elven even thought he could get back to the investigation without being in pain the whole time.

And that was a good thing, because Bear had some high expectations of them for that evening.

First, Elven and Madds grabbed a quick bite, and by "quick," they literally ate everything they could while Bear filled them in on what had happened. Elven stretched that time by filling in Madds on what had happened with Ronnie and Darlene, and then Davin.

At first, he thought she was going to be angry that they hadn't woken her up to chase him down with them, but if she was, she didn't voice it. In fact, he suspected she was grateful because she'd gotten to catch up on the sleep and allow her body to recoup. She did, however, make sure to let him know not to do that again if something came up. She must have been feeling a lot better, as Elven had suspected.

But then Bear briefed them on what Cora told them about Quentin, and how Roy was going to be waiting for them.

Elven agreed with Bear that they better move quick, lest they give Roy any other opportunity to mess it up for them. Bear might have had the man's word, but Elven didn't know him other than the few heated encounters he'd had with him. And he was less than impressed.

Benson wanted to come, too, which was expected, though Elven wasn't too keen on the idea. Still, he could go to town with them. Elven just intended to talk him into staying there while the rest of them paid a visit to Quentin.

They rode back to where Bear said Roy was supposed to meet them. Apparently, there was a bend in a path near Bear's cabin that they all knew about, and it led in the direction of where Quentin Delvers lived. Elven let Madds drive this time when she protested after he tried to get on first. She made mention of the trip he and Bear had taken without her, which made Elven smirk. He knew it would come back to bite him somehow.

But Elven let her drive, not minding sitting in the back. He'd had his fair share of driving around, so letting her take on the driving for the evening was a nice break. And much to his surprise, when they drove past Bear's cabin and toward what he assumed was the meeting spot, Roy Leven was right there where Bear said he'd promised he would be.

"Took y'all long enough," Roy said.

"Had to admit," Bear said, "a small part of me worried you were already gonna be pounding down Quentin's door without us."

"I gave you my word," Roy said. "That should be all that needs to be said about it."

Bear nodded. "So it is."

Roy turned to Elven and Madds on their ATV. "I also agreed to do it the way Bear says we do it," Roy said. "And apparently that means letting you two take the lead."

"I don't know what to even say right now," Madds said.

"Yeah, well, don't make a thing of it," Roy said. "I ain't doing this for you. I'm doing it because I respect Bear and I love Old Knuckle."

"We don't know what this is," Elven said. "We are there to ask questions, see if we can take a look around, and find out what he knows about this dress. For all we know, Quentin gave it to Sadie before she went missing, or misplaced it somewhere. I want to give him the benefit of the doubt here, so we don't need anyone shooting from this hip on this. Figuratively and literally."

"Heard," Roy said, throwing a single nod Elven's way.

Elven turned to Benson. The kid was practically salivating at the thought of finding Quentin. Elven doubted Benson had gotten the message as much as Roy, and he might be the one who needed to listen the most. But like he thought earlier, he didn't want Benson coming on this one.

"Benson, I need you to stay here in town," Elven said.

Benson shook his head. "No way," he said. "If Lila is there, I need to be there."

Elven placed his hand on the kid's shoulder as he pulled up next to him. He knew it would be a hard sell, but he figured the others would jump in if Benson continued to protest.

"We need someone in town to keep an eye on things," Elven said. It wasn't a lie, but he made the task sound a little more important than it actually was. The town would do whatever it was gonna do. But it also wouldn't hurt to have eyes on it just in case it went a little too far off the rails. "People are gonna have questions," Elven added, "and if we're all gone, they won't have anyone to answer them. They might start going a little stir-crazy, and knowing we're out, they might get some ideas of their own."

Benson looked like he was going to argue, but his gaze drifted behind Elven to Bear, who must have looked a certain way because Benson deflated.

"What do you want me to tell them?" Benson asked. "That you're out looking for Quentin Delver?"

Elven shook his head. "Just say we're following up on some leads and will be back soon. Can you do that?"

Benson nodded. "Just keep your radio on," he said, looking to Bear. "I ain't like the rest of you where I can talk to a big group of people. If it gets hairy, I don't want to be in the thick of it."

Bear agreed, but none of them knew just how hairy it was about to get.

CHAPTER FORTY-NINE

QUENTIN DELVERS'S HOME WAS ALMOST INVISIBLE FROM THE outside world. If Elven were on his own, he would have flown right by it, never spotting the building from the path. He wouldn't have even seen the turn-off from the way it dipped down a small hill. It seemed that only those who lived here knew about it.

The hill gave Quentin's house coverage, making it look half-buried in the ground. But then the vegetation was just high enough to cover the top of the building from where it sat. Once they pulled onto the small pathway that led straight to Quentin's place, however, Elven saw that the place was actually a lot larger than he'd assumed. It surprised Elven, considering most everyone else had small trailers in Old Knuckle. The largest dwelling he'd seen was Ginny's.

This house, however, was just as big, though without a second story. It was wide and long, and from the outside, Elven could see multiple windows that opened into different rooms.

The crew of four rode up, deciding not to approach on foot. The more they snuck around, the more it might scare the man off. Elven had almost no interaction with him so far, but Bear said he was usually straight with him, so anything other than Bear would set

Quentin off. Elven wondered what Bear meant by "set off," but he didn't ask for clarification.

They drove around and parked their ATVs along the side of the house rather than right up front. There wasn't a large opening for them to park near the door since the bushes had grown too close to it.

"So you think he's going to just talk to us?" Roy asked.

Elven didn't have an answer to that, but he hoped that was how it would go. While he planned on being there to ask questions and dig around, Bear was the one who said that would be the outcome if that's what Elven wanted. Elven had the idea that Roy wanted to ask questions last. What Roy wanted to do first, however, was probably nothing good. Due process didn't seem to be at the top of his list.

"That's what I said would happen," Bear said.

"I never seen anyone have an actual conversation with the man that amounted to much," Roy remarked.

"The same could be said about you," Bear said with a half-smirk, and Elven figured Bear had fun with that zinger. "Quentin might seem a bit simpler in the mind, but if you really want to know him, he opens up. Just gotta find common ground."

Roy rolled his eyes. "You said it. Simpler minds must be the common ground."

"Or maybe I just like to talk about the trees, the wind, the weather," Bear said. "Most people overlook stuff like that, but Quentin has an appreciation for it. If we could only slow down and be so lucky."

Roy didn't argue that point, and Elven even found himself nodding along. But the way Bear talked about the man, it was almost like they were friends. He just hoped that if Quentin did have something to do with the murders, Bear could keep his head on straight to deal with the problem instead of letting his friendship get in the way.

"What the hell?" Bear said, stopping in his tracks as he rounded the corner and spotted the door.

The rest of them caught up and saw it, too. The front door was wide open, but more than that, there were strange marks on the ground. The front of the door was muddy from the shade and the divot in the ground. The water looked like it pooled there whenever it rained, and without the direct sunshine, it held onto that water for as long as it could.

There were lines dug into the mud. Not only that, but there were boot prints and what looked like a tire just on the edge of the mud. Elven saw another path leading in a different direction from the door.

"Is this the only way in here?" Elven asked, pointing to where they'd just driven from.

"It's the quickest way in," Bear said. "But if you want to spend an extra hour, you could get here through that way." He pointed to the other path. "Don't see why anyone would use it."

"Maybe if they were running and knew that someone would be coming the other way," Madds said.

Elven was thinking the same thing.

"Why would he think anyone was coming for him?" Roy asked.

"That is the question," Elven said.

Bear approached the door, knocking on it before entering. "Quentin?" he called out. "You in here? It's Bear Colter. I got some friends here, and we just wanted to ask you something. Can you come on out?"

There was no answer.

"Guess he ain't home," Elven said, trying to avoid the muddy spot in front of the door as he walked inside. Madds and Roy followed behind him.

"Think we should take a look around?" Madds asked. "The door's wide open, so it's not breaking in."

"When you quit being a deputy, you really went all-in, didn't you?" Roy asked with a chuckle.

Elven wasn't going to touch that one, but he decided that it didn't matter at this point.

The living room opened up once they made it past the small foyer. It was surprisingly well-kept. There were knickknacks all about, between the furniture wrapped in plastic sheeting and the various end tables topped with small protective cloths.

"For someone who lives alone and doesn't entertain a whole lot, he sure does keep it tidy," Madds said. "His taste, however, is like my grandma's."

The couches were floral and very dated. The wooden furniture definitely didn't tell Elven that he was a bachelor, no matter what age Quentin was. There was even a grandfather clock against the wall on the other side of the living room. It was possibly the cleanest place he'd set foot in since coming to Old Knuckle.

Except for one thing, that is.

There were various muddy footprints at the entryway, which led to the right. Elven followed them until he came to the small dining set where a tipped-over chair lay on the floor.

"It ain't much, but it looks like there was more than just Quentin here," Elven said.

Before anyone could agree, argue, or add their own two cents, Bear's radio lit up with static.

"Bear, you there? Bear!" It was Benson on the other end. It cut in and out a little, but they could hear him clear enough.

Bear picked up the radio and walked to the doorway where it might have gotten a better signal. "Yeah, Benson. What is it?"

"You gotta get back here," Benson said. "It's going down right now, and I don't know if I can stop this. The shit's gonna hit the fan."

Bear looked confused. "What's going on?"

"It's Quentin," Benson said. "They brought him in, and the whole fucking town knows about it! I gotta go, but hurry!"

And then Benson was out. It didn't take but one second for everyone to head out the door, ignoring everything else in the house and getting to their ATVs. Whatever was about to happen in town, all four of them would need to be there if they wanted to stop it.

CHAPTER FIFTY

BENSON'S EYES WERE AS WIDE AS SAUCERS AS HE BATTLED against the crowd. He'd never seen Old Knuckle like this before. The anger, the confusion, and most of all, the fright. He had watched as the Morrison brothers came driving into town, laughing and boasting as they did. But this time, they weren't with Roy. It wasn't a rarity to see them without him, but generally, when they acted as cocky as they were when they'd driven in, Roy was always in the lead. He was like their protector, of sorts, giving them permission to be their absolute worst.

It wasn't that the Morrison brothers were all that bad, but they could be a couple of dicks when at their worst. Other times, Benson had seen them act just fine. Normal guys who were trying to make it in Old Knuckle like the rest of them. But there was something about being around Roy that turned them into the biggest douches.

But now, they weren't with Roy. Instead, Benson had seen them come into town with someone else in tow. And it didn't look like he was coming out of his own free will.

In fact, he looked downright scared shitless.

Quentin Delvers had his hands bound together, like he was being

248

arrested. Benson knew that Quentin was a suspect, but he also knew that Elven and the rest of them weren't planning on bringing him in unless they found evidence for it. And he also knew that the Morrison brothers had no part in their plan.

This was something else.

"What the hell are you doing?" Benson demanded.

The brothers both just laughed, not paying him any attention. They had come in blowing whistles, of all things, gathering the attention of anyone and everyone around. And unsurprisingly, it had worked. It may not have brought everyone around, but it brought enough.

The Morrison brothers then made a big show, announcing that Quentin had paid to have the dress made. The one that Sadie was wearing when she was found.

That was all they needed to hear to turn on Quentin.

And once they turned, the Morrison brothers lost control of everything. That's when Benson called Bear.

Right after that, Benson clawed his way toward Quentin. He shouted at them all, trying to get them to calm down. But it was no use. He wasn't even sure that any of them could hear him. They hadn't gotten physical yet, but they sure as hell were verbal. Shouts of profanity, angry rants, and heated questions filled the air, and nobody could understand a single thing.

Benson positioned himself between Quentin and the rest as both brothers slid out of the way, the looks on their faces telling Benson that they were spineless trash. They were just as scared as everyone else, and they knew they'd stepped in it now.

"Everyone needs to wait for Bear!" he yelled, holding his hands up.

"Get the hell outta the way, Benson!" someone shouted.

Benson was now the scared one, and more than that, he had his own questions. He looked behind him as Quentin tried to back away, but the crowd surrounded him from all sides now. He cowered, like he was afraid they were going to start throwing punches.

Benson got next to Quentin, grabbing him. "Where is Lila?" he shouted, no longer trying to battle the crowd. If he could get what he needed out of the man, then it would all be okay. "Where is my sister?"

Quentin shook his head, locking eyes with Benson. He looked like a terrified child, and Benson felt wrong all of a sudden.

"No Lila!" Quentin shouted. "I don't know what you're talking about!"

Everyone knew that Quentin wasn't all up there in the head, but he wasn't necessarily slow by any means. He was just peculiar. Hell, some might even have called him emotionally immature. Benson had seen a video about that once, and he figured it had something to do with Quentin's mama and the way she'd treated him. But he was no therapist.

"What about Sadie and the dress?" Benson asked.

Again, Quentin shook his head. Tears were running down his face, and he cried out. "I don't want no trouble!" he said. "I didn't do nothing! Dresses don't matter. I can have all the dresses I want. I don't hurt no one!"

Benson had no idea what he was even talking about, but the way the crowd was now pulling at Benson, he knew that he couldn't manage this alone. He hoped to God that Bear and the others were on their way.

Just as he thought that, he heard the three ATV engines come through to the center of town where the crowd was. He looked up, trying to see over the heads of everyone, and saw that it was them.

"Thank God," Benson muttered. He grabbed Quentin, trying to pull him through the crowd, but they were too strong. "Bear! Elven! Help me out here!"

"Everyone get back!" Elven shouted, but nothing was going to get to this crowd. That's when Benson watched Elven pull his gun out, ready to point it to the crowd.

But before he could, a gunshot rang out through the crowd. Benson felt a warm splatter against his face. His ears went numb, only hearing a high-pitched ringing. He spun around like he was in shock. Everything moved in slow motion.

Slowly, a little bit of sound came back, but it was far too muffled to make out. He only heard some screams as people scattered.

Quentin was falling to the ground, the side of his head blown out. Behind him, Ronnie Vaughn stood, a revolver pointed right where Quentin had been standing. The barrel was practically smoking right in front of him.

Benson swallowed, half-expecting another bullet to fire out of the gun, finding its way straight to himself. The muffled voices of Roy, Bear, and Madds were yelling something, but he couldn't tell. He assumed they were telling people to move or get down, or even for Ronnie to drop the gun.

Instead of firing it, Ronnie dropped it. He raised his hands, and Elven came up behind him, his gun drawn. He watched Ronnie get on his knees and put his hands behind his head.

But none of it mattered.

Quentin was dead.

And if Quentin was responsible, he only hoped that the rest of them had found Lila. Because if not, what were they going to do now?

CHAPTER FIFTY-ONE

Bear grabbed Roy Leven by the collar as soon as he set foot in his cabin. He got right in his face and shoved him against the wall.

"I know you radioed those two fucktwat brothers you have follow you around everywhere," Bear growled. "This is why I said to let us handle it. You gave me your goddamned word, Roy!"

"And I kept it, didn't I?" he spat, as defiant as ever. "I waited there and went with you. You never said nothing about sending anyone else to grab that freak."

Bear grinned, almost like it was funny. But Elven knew that look. It was the look of a man who had just about snapped. The next thing Bear was bound to do was something incredibly reckless. And, quite possibly, something he couldn't take back.

Bear's hand went to his gun on his belt. He wrapped his hand around it and pulled it up, just about ready to shove it in Roy's face. Bear was so angry, he had his finger already on the trigger.

Elven wasn't going to let him ruin his reputation—and his life— with one mistake. Elven grabbed Bear's hand as soon as it came up and twisted it to the side. He pinned Bear back, yanking the gun from his hand. Of course, Bear was far bigger than Elven. He might have gotten the jump on him, but it didn't last.

Bear pushed back with all his weight and shoved at Elven. He broke free almost immediately, which was fine with Elven because he no longer had his gun. But he also came back swinging.

Elven took a fist to the chin before he could get a word out.

"Don't you fucking touch me in my own house," Bear growled. He spun around to Roy, who was already on the move, placing himself closer to the door. He raised his finger to the man. "You fucking set foot out of here right now, and I swear to God I will tear you apart with my hands the next time I see you. Now fucking sit!"

He kicked a dining chair between Roy and the door. It skidded against the floor and hit the wall.

Roy watched him for a second, debating on his next move. Elven could see the fear in Roy's eyes, and he assumed the man had never seen Bear this far gone. Roy sat his backside right down on that chair, opting to take Bear at his word. Probably the smartest choice he could have made.

"Bear, you need to calm down," Elven said. The man dealt one hell of a punch, but Elven had already been down that road while in Old Knuckle. One more wasn't gonna set him back.

"My gun," Bear said, holding his hand out.

Elven shook his head. "Not until I get your word that you'll calm down and we can talk this all out."

"I ain't gonna shoot him," Bear said. "But you don't give me that gun right now, you're next on my list to tear apart. You hear me?"

Elven watched him, cocking his head. After a moment, he slapped the gun into Bear's large hand. Elven put his own hand on the butt of the revolver at his side, hoping to high heaven he didn't have to draw it. But Bear kept his word, and he tucked his gun into the holster on his belt. He let out a huge yell of rage, kicking another chair, sending it into the opposite wall where one of the legs broke off.

Bear turned to Roy, but he didn't charge at him or try to hit him. But he sure didn't let up from the yelling.

"What the hell are we supposed to do now?" Bear demanded. "There's still one girl missing."

Roy shook his head. He clearly hadn't thought that one through. "We go find her," Roy said. "But now there won't be any more missing girls."

"We don't know that for sure," Elven said. "We haven't even gotten a good look at Quentin's place."

"Then I suggest you do that," Roy said. "Hell, maybe you'll even find the girl."

Elven didn't like Roy's attitude. He considered leaving and letting Bear do whatever he wanted with him. But it would do no good at this point.

"What about Ronnie?" Elven asked, his voice calm, speaking to Bear.

Ronnie was outside, his hands bound, sitting against the wall while Benson watched him. Nobody thought he was a threat anymore, but he had just murdered a man in plain sight, so they couldn't not have someone on him.

Bear shook his head. "This kind of thing has never happened," he said. "Killing someone, but for reasons that we all understand. Not like we have a jail cell to hold people here."

"You can't just let him go," Madds said.

"Why not? Far as I'm concerned, he did this town a favor and was justified in doing it," Roy said.

Nobody wanted to hear from him, though, and Bear shook his head. "I never said we were going to," he said. "For now, we'll leave him here. He's been cooperative. Don't think he much cares about what happens to him now."

Elven agreed. Ronnie did what he came to do. Losing a wife and daughter gave him little to no ambition to do much else. And Davin was on the way out, too, it seemed.

"This town has torn that family apart," Bear said. He turned to

Roy. "Get out of my sight. Whatever happens from here on out, you are not invited to be a part of it."

Roy was going to speak, but by the look on Bear's face, he decided otherwise. Elven figured everyone knew he was getting off far easier than he should have. But he left the three of them there.

"We should go look again at Quentin's place," Elven said.

"Maybe something there will tell us that he really was guilty, and then maybe we find Lila," Madds added.

It was getting late, but they all knew it was the only thing left to do.

CHAPTER FIFTY-TWO

After what she had done with the two other girls, Auriel had no expectations that her door would be left unlocked. She didn't even want to test it. She'd gotten in too much trouble, and the last thing she wanted to do was get into any more of it. She knew that The Keeper could have done far more than what he'd done to her. She had gotten off very easy. But then again, she loved him, and she knew he loved her.

Whatever punishment she got was deserved, and however she was spared was a gift. One she wasn't going to take for granted.

But part of her was still sad. She liked Dina. More than any other angel she'd met before. And she thought that maybe they were true friends. She didn't have much of those in town. At least, not ones who understood her situation.

Dina, though, was in a very similar one with her now.

But Auriel knew that Dina's time in the cabin was coming to an end. She just hoped that she could say goodbye before then.

She thought that it would have happened to her the other night, but instead, he'd picked Dina's friend. Auriel hadn't even learned her name. But that was okay. It meant she had at least a little more time with Dina.

She could hear the footsteps coming down the stairs and head toward her room. The bar was lifted, which told her that she'd been right about it being locked. But she was curious as to why it was being opened now. Had he changed his mind and decided she needed further punishment?

The door opened up, and she knew she was going to find out soon enough.

The Keeper stood there, a solemn look on his face. He carried a lantern and looked like he had been sweating.

"Come on, Auriel," he said. "It's time to learn."

She sat up from her bed, hesitant to join him. *Learn?* What did that even mean?

He held his hand out, expecting her to take it. She knew better than to argue or try to defy him. Besides, whatever he had in store wasn't going to be bad for her. She trusted him, or at least she told herself she did. That's what he told her to do, after all.

She climbed out of bed and took his hand. He gripped it softly, rubbing his thumb over her skin for a brief moment before giving her a nod. "Let's go," he said.

They walked down the hallway toward the stairs. All the other rooms were open, and when she looked into the room where Dina had been, it was completely empty. Confused, she looked up to The Keeper. He didn't look down, though, only ahead. She decided not to ask where the other girl had gone.

They walked up the stairs and through the small room toward the door that led outside. There were no signs of struggle, so whatever had happened to Dina, all had been according to his plan.

The cold bit against her skin as soon as they went outside, but she was too focused on the scene to be bothered by something like the temperature. Because she knew tonight was the final night for Dina to be here with them.

At least in bodily form. She would always be here in spirit, tied to

Old Knuckle forever. That was the point of this, after all. All The Keeper's work was to keep the angels here. They would never leave Old Knuckle again.

Dina was outside, her hands tied together. Her bindings were tied to a tree just on the outside of the clearing where the cabin sat. She had tears running down her face and was pulling against the rope like she was trying to escape. Auriel knew that was useless, though. The Keeper was good at tying knots.

She couldn't help but feel sorry for Dina. She was clearly afraid. Probably because she thought she was going to die. Auriel thought the same thing, but after The Keeper's explanations, she knew that wasn't the true case. It was just a transition. That was all. Nothing to be afraid of.

Even so, Auriel couldn't help but feel a little pang inside her. One that told her to be afraid, too. The outside world had told her that dying wasn't a good thing, but something to be frightened about. It was hard to think otherwise. But maybe it was just the unknown. After all, she had never spoken to anyone who had died. And no matter how much she tried, she never heard the voice of God like The Keeper said he heard.

Maybe that would come sometime when she was older. Or maybe she wasn't meant to hear it ever.

"Why are you doing this?" Dina asked.

The Keeper brought Auriel closer to the other angel, letting go of her hand and leaving her a few steps behind him. He smiled. "Because angels should never leave this place," he said. "And that's what you were going to do, wasn't it?"

She shook her head. "I don't know what—"

"Don't lie," he said. "You were going to leave Old Knuckle. I know it. And Old Knuckle needs all the angels it can have. This is the only way to ensure that you never leave."

He pulled out a large hunting knife off his belt.

Dina contorted her face, and at first, Auriel thought it was confusion. But instead, it was because she was putting all her strength into something. And that something was breaking free.

The rope that had been wrapped around the tree broke free, the center of it completely frayed apart as if Dina had been rubbing it together for a while before he'd come back. And The Keeper didn't expect it.

He had the knife in his hands, but he had been caught off-guard, never getting the chance to raise it. Dina rushed into him, lifting her foot and kicking him in the chest. He fell backward, landing on his back. He let out a yell, and then his head hit the ground behind him.

Auriel froze, unsure what to do. She'd never seen him like this before. He had his eyes closed, but he groaned, so she knew he was still alive. She thought about rushing to his side to ask if he was okay, but all she could do was look back at Dina.

"Come with me," Dina said.

Auriel opened her mouth, wanting to protest. But the fear inside her bubbled up, telling her that maybe this wasn't right. That maybe going with her friend was what she was supposed to do.

"Auriel," Dina said. "Please come with me. We can go together. But we have to go now."

Auriel looked to The Keeper on the ground. He was starting to roll his head. But she saw the knife just next to his hand. He'd dropped it during the fall.

She quickly grabbed it and ran to Dina. She helped her cut the rope apart so that her hands were free.

"Auriel!" The Keeper yelled. He was beginning to sit up, now angrier than she'd ever seen him. She might have made a mistake, but it was too late for that. "Auriel, stay here!"

Dina wrapped her arms around Auriel, lifting her up against her chest. And then the two of them were running through the woods.

CHAPTER FIFTY-THREE

Elven, Madds, Benson, and Bear rummaged through Quentin's cabin as much as they could. Elven thought about asking Benson to stay behind, but with the idea that the killer was now dead and Lila still missing, there was no way he would. He didn't blame the kid, either. If someone had told him to let them handle it, he would have told them off and been leading the charge to find her.

He wasn't going to make Benson have that kind of standoff with any of them. It seemed Bear was of the same mind, because he explained that they weren't going to tear apart the building, looking for Lila. They needed to find a small piece of evidence that might point to where she was.

But they did scour the entire house, looking for her first. They never found her there, but Elven didn't think they would. Between the Morrison brothers scooping up Quentin and them being there earlier, even if briefly, someone would have stumbled upon her if she had been here.

On their full walkthrough, the house was just that: a regular building. No secret compartments where Quentin could stash three girls all at the same time. And there were absolutely no signs that anyone other than Quentin had been there. Not including the small signs of a struggle, which now made sense given how Roy had informed the Morrison brothers to come get him.

Now they were searching for evidence. And there wasn't a whole lot to be found.

That is, until Madds called out from the bedroom. The four of them headed toward her voice and into the room. It was filled with older furniture, just like the rest of the house. The carpet was a deep shade of green, and it smelled of mothballs and potpourri.

"He used to live with his mother," Bear explained. "She passed a few years back, but it was clear Quentin wasn't into redecorating."

"I'm not too concerned with how the house is decorated," Madds said, walking out of the closet, holding a small shoebox. "But that might explain all the dresses in the closet."

"Surprised he has that," Bear said. "Other than the furniture, when she died, he got rid of all her things. Brought them down to sell and give away whatever she had. I used to think they had a good relationship, but after she died, it seemed like he was a lot happier. Showed up around town more. Even if people thought he was odd, he wanted to be around them more."

"Maybe she was controlling," Madds speculated.

"It doesn't matter the reasons," Elven said. "I think we're a little past that now. What did you call us in for?"

She hoisted up the shoebox. "Do these look familiar to you?" she asked, setting the box down on the quilted bed.

The three men drew closer as Madds backed up. Inside were two trinkets. Elven wasn't sure what else to call them, really. One was a small mirror, almost like a compact, but made of rusted metal. The other one was a strip of fabric, like a blanket. It looked very torn up and ratty. It wasn't much of anything that Elven would have identified himself, except for one thing.

Both of them had small wings attached to them. They were both beat-up and a little ragged, but they were in the same fashion as the wings they'd seen on the doll that had belonged to Shayla. And the much bigger wings they'd found on Sadie.

And the material used might have been older and brittle, but he had an idea that it was also human skin.

"Does this mean that Lila..." Benson couldn't even finish that sentence, but they were all thinking the same thing. These were probably grave markers.

"We don't know that," Elven said. "And there's two of them. Sadie didn't need one, and we found Shayla's already, so this could be anything."

"That's right," Madds said from the closet again. She came out, waving a spiral notebook. She slapped it down on the bed next to the box. It was open to a page full of doodles. Small drawings of the forest, and in the trees were wings dangling from the branches. He had drawn the setting where these had been placed.

"This could mean anything," Bear said. "Any spot in the forest looks like this, and without the markers, how will we know it?"

Elven spotted what Madds was going to say next. He beat her to it, placing his fingers along the small numbers in the margins. "There's numbers here. The handwriting is bad, but by the way it's written, these look like coordinates."

"Anyone have a GPS?" Bear asked.

Madds grinned, slapping down another item right on top of the notebook. "Looks like Quentin had it all prepared," she said.

Elven wasn't much for the showy approach like Madds, but he was glad they had somewhere to look. "Let's go grab some shovels and get to work," he said.

CHAPTER FIFTY-FOUR

Auriel held onto Dina as tight as she could. She felt like she was flying through the trees with how lightning-fast Dina was running. She wasn't even sure how Dina was able to run like that. She had no shoes on her feet, and when Auriel looked down, she could see they were covered in brown mud and deep red, like the color of blood.

She wondered if The Keeper was after them, but she knew that he would be. Once an angel tried to leave, it was his job to stop them. It was his job to keep them tied to Old Knuckle forever. He'd told her that countless times, which made her wonder what would happen to her.

She wasn't trying to leave Old Knuckle. She just wanted to see her friend again. Or keep seeing her. They didn't have to leave at all. They could just play together back in town. Wouldn't that be alright?

Or was it too late for all of that? Would Dina ever understand what had happened to her and her friends? Would she be able to forgive him for doing all that?

Or would she just try to leave again?

Maybe this was a bad idea after all. But it was too late for that now. She was with Dina, flying through the woods.

"Dina!" The Keeper's voice could be heard in the distance. "Dina!" It was growing farther and farther away.

Maybe this was working. Maybe they would get back to town.

She couldn't help but feel bad about it, though.

Dina slowed down, panting as she struggled to carry Auriel. Finally, she came to a spot.

"I need to stop for a second," she said. She set Auriel down next to a small boulder and sat down on it. She grabbed at her feet. Auriel could see they were torn up pretty bad.

"Are you okay?" Auriel asked.

"I'll be fine," she said. "We just need to get to town. I don't even know if we're going in the right direction or not." She looked up at her. "Do you still have that knife?"

Auriel nodded, handing it to Dina. "Here," she said. It was large, and she'd managed to hold it tight during the run without cutting anyone. She almost didn't want to hand it over, but Dina looked very concerned.

Dina dug into her foot with it, almost slicing it open. She grit her teeth and dug further, nearly screaming as she did. Finally, she pulled out a large twig that had embedded itself into the sole of her foot. It gushed blood, and Auriel thought it looked bad.

"Maybe we should go back," Auriel said.

Dina shot a look at the girl. "What? We can't go back there," she said. "He's fucking crazy. He killed my friends, and he's going to kill me next. Maybe even you."

Auriel shook her head. "No, he didn't," she said. "I know it seems like it. But really, he saved your friends. They're angels. We all are. And we don't die like people. Our spirits are just bound to Old Knuckle, and Old Knuckle needs us to stay. That's why he's doing it. Angels aren't supposed to leave."

Dina swallowed hard and looked at Auriel. For the first time,

Auriel wasn't sure what to think, because Dina wasn't looking at her like she was a friend. Instead, she was looking at her the way she'd looked at The Keeper.

CHAPTER FIFTY-FIVE

The foursome found the first spot in the forest by plugging in the coordinates and using the GPS to guide them. Most of the way had been reachable by ATV, but they still had to get out and hike the rest of the way.

It was like Bear had said, just any other spot in the forest. It didn't stand out. It didn't even have a single marker, or multiple bottles like where Shayla had been found. This area was untouched, or at least, hadn't been touched in a long while.

If Quentin had done any digging here, it hadn't been in a very long time.

But that didn't matter now. They had the spot, and it was just under a tree. So they got to digging. Most of it had been in silence. They battled against the cold, but that didn't last long. All the effort they put into the ground with their shovels had heated them up so much that Elven stripped off his outer shirt. Everyone else did the same rather than sweating through their clothes.

After a while, they finally came to the end of the digging.

But they didn't find a corpse. No, it was a skeleton. Whoever had been buried here had been long dead. There was no way this person was Lila.

"I don't even know who this could be," Bear said. He wiped the sweat from his brow, shaking his head. "They've been here too long now."

"This ain't Lila, right?" Benson asked. He was right, but he was still confirming.

"It's not her," Elven confirmed, watching Benson's reaction. He looked relieved and also disappointed at the same time. The poor kid just wanted answers, and instead, they were only digging up more questions.

They continued to excavate the grave, making sure not to disturb the bones too much. Elven felt like an archeologist, but instead of uncovering a lost tomb, they were uncovering someone nobody knew was even missing.

Finally, he found a small metal clasp. It was rusted but shut. Elven pried it open, and inside, found a few dollars and a small card. It was a license. Most of the information had been rubbed off, but there was a clear name on it.

"Rebecca Ellison," Elven said.

"Holy shit," Bear said. "Ellison?"

Elven nodded and tossed it to Bear. "Know her?"

Bear shook his head just after catching it. He studied it a moment, running his fingers across it like it might make more sense to him. "I mean, I know of her," he said.

"Who is she?" Benson asked, clearly in the dark as much as Elven and Madds were.

"I was just a kid, but she was the talk of the town for a bit there," Bear said. "She went missing, and everyone just said she ran off. Escaped Old Knuckle, or something like that. I was too young to care. This was like at least forty years ago."

"This has been happening for a while," Elven said. "And there's still one more spot we need to dig up."

CHAPTER FIFTY-SIX

"That's not how any of this works," Dina said. She still fixed her gaze on Auriel like she was crazy while holding her foot tight to stop the bleeding.

Auriel didn't like the look she was giving her. That wasn't how friends treated each other.

"That's what he told me," Auriel said. The cold was now cutting into her. Her decision to run was proving to be a bad one. "What else is it, then? He isn't just killing people. He can't be."

Dina's eyes softened. "That's exactly what he is doing."

"No!" she screamed. "He's The Keeper. He's my daddy! He is doing what God told him to do. You don't know what you're talking about, Dina."

"My name isn't Dina!" she said, her voice raising at the name. "Stop calling me that. My name is Rebecca, and I live in Old Knuckle. I'm just a girl who wanted to get out. I'm not some stupid angel. And your daddy is batshit-crazy, do you hear me? He's been lying to you this whole time. I'm sorry, but that's the truth."

"You aren't supposed to say your name!" Auriel screamed.

"You're supposed to use your angel name. You're Dina. You're Dina. You're Dina! And Dina is a liar!"

"Calm down," Dina said, holding her hand up. "He's going to hear you and know where we're at."

Auriel stood up. She was done playing this game now. She had made a huge mistake, and she was willing to take whatever punishment she got for it. But she needed to end it and fix it however she could now. She stood straight up and screamed at the top of her lungs.

"Keeper! We're here! We're right here!" Auriel's voice shouted from her throat so hard, it grew sore right after.

"I said shut up!" Dina yelled.

Dina slapped Auriel across the face. She felt a slight cut from Dina's ring slicing her cheek, but Auriel continued to scream like a banshee. She may not be saying words, but the noise would tell him where they were. And that's all she wanted. She powered through the sting of the slap, not backing down.

"Stop it! Shut up!" Dina shouted. But at this point, there was no hiding anything anymore. Dina's own yells were just as loud as Auriel's screams.

But what Auriel hadn't expected was for Dina to try to shut her up. Dina lunged at her, knocking her down on her back. She covered her mouth with one hand while shushing her. Her other hand wrapped tightly around Auriel's throat, cutting off her breath.

Auriel no longer screamed. Instead, all she wanted to do was breathe. But Dina wasn't letting her. "I'm sorry," Dina said. "I need to leave, and you won't let me."

Auriel struggled, but Dina's body was too strong, too heavy, as it lay on top of her. She wriggled around, but she wasn't going anywhere. She couldn't suck in a breath. Her eyes locked onto Dina's as the older girl's tears dripped down onto Auriel's face.

Auriel had one option, and it was in her hand. She took the knife and plunged it upward, right into Dina's side. Dina's eyes widened at the blade entering her guts. She opened her mouth like she was going to say something, but instead, she just looked down at Auriel. A look of pain, and betrayal.

Dina rolled over onto her back, and Auriel sucked greedily at the air. She filled her lungs with it and coughed as it fired back out. Dina scrambled to get to her feet, but Auriel couldn't let her.

She had to fix her mistake.

Auriel plunged the knife again into Dina, this time straight into her chest. Dina let out a little whimper, looking down at the knife in her. Auriel wasn't sure if she'd hit her heart or not, but it looked close enough.

"I'm sorry," Auriel cried. "I'm so sorry."

Dina fell back down to her back, her chest never rising. Her eyes stared up blankly at Auriel.

"I'm sorry."

Auriel wept, placing her head down on Dina, who never moved again.

CHAPTER FIFTY-SEVEN

"This isn't Lila, either," Benson said. His voice, once again, sounded relieved and also disappointed. Elven knew he didn't want his sister to be dead. He just wanted this to be over with.

The exhaustion on the boy's face told Elven everything. And Elven didn't blame him one bit. He was exhausted himself, and he didn't even have a loved one being affected by this.

"No, it isn't," Bear confirmed. He dug around, looking for anything like they had found with Rebecca's body. But there was nothing to be found. It was just a set of bones.

"Did Rebecca have anyone go missing with her?" Elven asked.

Bear shrugged. "I was a kid, so maybe."

"Anyone in town who might be able to figure it out?" Madds asked.

"There's a few old-timers around," Bear said. "I'm sure we can figure something out. Maybelle Perkins probably knows something. Hell, Howard, too, if he were coherent enough. But don't think I'll get much outta him."

"What do we do now?" Benson asked. "What about my sister?"

Madds shook her head. "There were no other places written in the notebook."

"Could mean she's not in the ground," Elven said, then looked to Benson with soft eyes. "Sorry, I'm just exhausted. I meant she might still be alive."

Benson nodded. "Then we need to find her, right? Where do we look next?"

"Benson," he said apologetically, "I can't even think straight right now. None of us can, I'm sure."

"You're not wrong," Bear agreed, letting out a long sigh.

"You don't look so great yourself," Elven said, placing a hand on Benson's shoulder.

Benson shook his head, his chin quivering. "I can't keep doing this," he said. "Where is she? I just want to find Lila and bring her home. I'll leave Old Knuckle if that's what she wants. I just want to do it with her, whatever it is." He looked up at Elven, his eyes blood-shot, tears running down them. "That's not too much to ask, is it?"

Elven wrapped his arms around the kid, pulling him into a hug. "No," he said. "It ain't too much to ask at all."

Benson buried his wet face into Elven's shoulder, soaking it with his tears. "I'm just so tired."

"I know it," Elven said. He locked eyes with Madds, then Bear. They both nodded, knowing what he was asking.

"I think we need to get some rest," Bear said.

Benson shook his head, pulling away from Elven. "No, we need to look," he said, but his voice sounded like he was going to fall asleep right then and there.

"Benson, you can barely keep your eyes open," Madds said. "I think Bear's right."

"Me too," Elven said.

"We'll look first thing in the morning once we're refreshed. We can barely see anything out here in the dark as it is," Bear said.

"The adrenaline has worn off of all of us," Elven said. "And that's when people make mistakes. I don't want to make any more mistakes when we know what's on the line. You get me?"

Benson nodded. "Neither do I," he said. "I just feel guilty if I fall asleep one more day with her still out there."

Elven put his hand on his shoulder again, giving it a squeeze. "If it's permission you need, then you have it. Get some rest. I'll lock you in your trailer if it's what it takes."

Benson wiped his face and gave a smile. "Thank you."

"Come on," Madds said. "We'll make sure you get home okay."

The four of them walked back to their ATVs. Elven was hopeful they had more to the story, but at this point, it still seemed like another dead end with more questions he wasn't sure they had answers for.

CHAPTER FIFTY-EIGHT

BENSON FLOPPED DOWN ON THE BED AFTER STUMBLING through the mess of a trailer he called home. He didn't bother to strip down at all. Madds, however, took it upon herself to untie his boots. She got him to lift his feet and yanked them off. His eyes were half-closed when she started, and by the time she finished, they were fully closed.

"I'd say this was the right decision," Elven whispered, standing behind Madds in the small hallway.

She nodded. "The poor kid's been through a lot," she said. "I'm just happy we were able to make it here without him passing out on the drive, causing an accident."

Elven nodded. "Think he's okay to be left this way?" Elven asked, motioning to Benson, sleeping on top of the blankets in his clothing. He'd probably sweat through most of the clothing he was currently wearing.

"If you want to strip him naked, be my guest," Madds said. "That's where I draw the line. Besides, I think he can deal with it in the morning and take a shower then."

"Fair enough," Elven agreed. "You ready to go?"

She closed the door to his bedroom and shook her head. "I think I'm gonna stay here," she said. "He's not in a good place. You saw it on his face. He might just need some sleep, but I don't want him waking up alone after all that. I'd hate to think of what he might do, especially after Darlene and Ronnie."

Elven couldn't have agreed more. It seemed like Old Knuckle was going through a lot more than it ever had before, and nobody was equipped to handle it. Not only on a law enforcement level, but on a mental health level, too.

"I think he'll appreciate it," Elven said. "But I need to talk to you about something. Maybe outside, in case he wakes up and hears. I don't want it getting out."

Madds nodded, and Elven led her to the front, holding the door open for her. He closed the door gently, now satisfied that Benson wouldn't hear. He didn't expect him to wake up at this point, but still, it was better to be safe than sorry.

"What's up?" she asked once they were in the clear.

He chewed his lip a moment before saying it out loud. "I think it's time," Elven finally said. "We lost the day after we were attacked, so our plan went south. But then we got a lead and chased it down. I felt justified in doing all that, knowing that we'd lose it if we tried to bring anyone else new into this. But now?"

"Now that Quentin is dead, and pretty much seems like our guy, we've got nothing," Madds said, nodding her head in agreement.

"Nothing," Elven reiterated. "All we can do now is search those woods for Lila. The whole town can do that. But we might have missed something, or even trampled over some evidence that someone better equipped could have used."

"You want to bring in the FBI on this," Madds said.

"I do. The town can try to cover up whatever they want now," Elven said. "They can do that. Hide the bodies, the murders. But I don't believe for one second they'd cover up the fact that someone is still missing. Benson sure wouldn't let that happen, and now that Quentin is dead, I don't think Bear would, either."

Madds sighed. "You might be right. But what about you? Won't this bite you in the ass? Basically pretending to be law enforcement when you aren't that?"

Elven shrugged. "I've been in trouble before. Nothing I can't handle. But it's the same as you, right? You said you're willing to go to jail to get this thing solved."

Madds nodded. "Right," she said.

But Elven had to admit she didn't seem so sure anymore.

CHAPTER FIFTY-NINE

Madds had seen Elven off half an hour earlier, and what he had said made sense to her. But she couldn't sleep because of it, either. Bringing in the FBI would tear this place apart. She was sure nobody would forgive her for it, but she knew that didn't matter. Finding Lila was the most important thing. And after her promise to Elven, Old Knuckle wasn't going to be where she called home one way or the other.

She'd told him that she would go with him back to Dupray after it was all over, and she'd meant it. Of course, calling the FBI in would mean that she wouldn't be able to see it 'til the end, but she'd seen it far enough, at least.

She sat on the couch with the light on, practically giving up on thinking she could just drift off. She was exhausted, but her mind was running a mile a minute. On what? Well, everything and nothing at the same time. She was far too tired to make any sense of it, but she was far too worried to put it to rest.

A knock came on the door at Benson's trailer, a welcome interruption. She had no idea what time it was, and she didn't think

Benson got visitors like this, but she was happy to check for him. She peered through the window, taking a look before opening the door.

It was Cora McCreary, and she was holding what looked like a casserole dish covered in foil. Two potholders were in each hand on the sides, so it must have been hot. Cora smiled at Madds through the window.

Madds opened the door and let the woman in. Madds moved a heavy iron pan from the counter to the table next to Cora so she had room to put the casserole down.

"Thank you," Cora said. "Sorry, this thing is fresh, and my potholders need a little reinforcing. Hadn't realized that until I carried it all this way. From the oven to the counter, I suppose, was fine, and I'd never noticed it before."

She pulled one of the potholders up, and Madds could see the worn areas she was speaking about.

"It's pretty late to be making casseroles," Madds said, but she truly didn't mind. The company coming by was better than being left alone with her worried thoughts.

"Oh, I know it," Cora said. "But I got to thinking about all of this. Benson's had a hard go of it lately. He's a good kid, you know?"

Madds nodded. "I do," she said. "He might be my best friend at this point." She chuckled when she said it. He'd been one of the first people in Old Knuckle to warm to the fact that she was there.

"I gotta be honest," Cora said. "Part of me is a little nosy, or maybe concerned, I should say. After what happened to Quentin, I figured that would be the end of it. That you'd find Lila, and Old Knuckle could put this whole thing to bed." She looked at the state of the trailer, with the trash and dirty dishes everywhere, and shook her head. "But since nobody is celebrating, I'm guessing you didn't find her."

Madds shook her head. "No, we haven't found her yet."

"But it *was* Quentin, right?" she asked. "I don't think I could take it if you told me otherwise. I felt awful telling Bear about the dress, but the whole thing didn't feel right, you know?"

"You saved a lot of people with that information," Madds said. "You did the right thing. I only wish that it ended differently. That we could have gotten information from him."

"Me too," Cora said. "Was hoping that Benson could get some relief from all of this. He's had a hard life in general, not just now. Say, what is it you're doing here, anyway?"

"Didn't feel like he should be alone tonight," Madds said. "Like you said, a rough go of it."

Cora smiled warmly. She seemed like the kind of woman who was perfect in a small community like this. Someone the people could rely on. Madds was glad to be getting to know her better.

"I gotta say, I really came around on you. You've been amazing for Benson. A real angel through this tough time," Cora said. "I'm glad you're a part of Old Knuckle now." She chuckled. "Would you have guessed that? I think it might be the first time people have started to accept an outsider. We can be some old curmudgeons sometimes, that's for sure."

Madds smiled, but it quickly turned to a frown. "Thanks, that means a lot. But I think I'm leaving tomorrow."

"Leaving?" Cora asked. "Why? What about Lila? What about Benson?"

"It's not really my choice," she said. "It's something I have to do. I'll be heading out with Elven in the morning. Probably just enough time to say goodbye."

"Oh, dear," Cora said. "I don't know if Benson's poor heart can take that."

Madds didn't need a guilt trip right now, but she didn't disagree with Cora, either. "I know," she said. Now she was hoping to have her alone time again. The conversation had flipped to a subject that she didn't want to talk about any longer, and she turned around. "Should I put this casserole in the fridge? I don't even know if—"

Madds's words were quickly cut off. She lay on the floor, her head throbbing for a few seconds as she looked up at Cora, holding the heavy pan in her hand Madds had moved moments earlier. Madds couldn't make any sense of it, no matter how hard she tried.

But she didn't have long to attempt it, because she passed out only a few seconds later.

CHAPTER SIXTY

"Cora!" the man shouted. "Cora!"

"I'm here, Daddy!" she yelled back, though she still lay her head on Dina's chest. It was comforting in some ways, like her daddy, The Keeper, had told her. She'd done his job, making Dina stay in Old Knuckle forever. Angels never left, and Cora—Auriel—had made sure of it.

She looked up as the footsteps grew closer. Her father shoved his arms through the bushes until he made his way to the small clearing Dina and Cora lay in.

"Oh my God," he said. "I thought something had happened to you. I couldn't bear it if—if, well, if she'd have done something."

The look on his face told her that he really was concerned. She'd never seen him this worried before.

"Don't worry," she said. "I'm still here. And look." She stood up over Dina. "I took care of it so you didn't have to." She was still upset about what she'd done, but more than that, she was happy that she was making her father proud.

The Keeper looked down at Dina's body, a small smile growing on his face. "You sure did," he said.

"I'm sorry," she said. "I didn't mean to worry you. I didn't mean to run with her. I just got confused. I thought she was my friend."

He knelt down beside Cora so he was her height. "I know it," he said. "Sometimes they can be scared and trick us. But that's alright because it all worked out, didn't it?"

She nodded. "I didn't want to do this," she admitted. "I had to, though. Right?"

"You did," he agreed. "You did so, so good, my girl. My sweet angel." He ran his hand over her head, then to her face, over the scratch from Dina's ring when she slapped her. He wiped at it with a finger, and she could see the blood on his fingertip. "Angels never leave, and now Dina won't, either. And I knew that you wouldn't leave, either."

He scooped Cora up into his arms and lifted her into the air. She felt safe in his arms, safe against his chest. "I'll never leave you, Daddy."

He stroked her hair as they walked back to the cabin. "That's good, sweetie," he said. "And it's okay that we used our regular names for now. But only this time, okay? We save them for the town, but here, we use our angel names, right?"

"Right," she said.

"That's good, Auriel," he said. His voice was smooth and calm. "I'm so proud of you. I know you'll make a great Keeper when you're older and I can't continue doing it. But there's still so much to learn."

"And you'll teach me?" she asked.

"Of course, my angel," he said. "I'll teach you everything."

CHAPTER SIXTY-ONE

CORA HAD BEEN THINKING A LOT ABOUT WHEN SHE WAS younger. About Dina and the other girls. It was the defining moment of her life. It was when she had made the full decision that she was going to follow in her father's footsteps.

For a while, she didn't think she had a choice. But when Dina grabbed her and ran her through those woods, she knew she always had a choice. And it was clear what that choice should be.

Dina was confused and scared, but in the end, she was trying to leave. To get out. To not be a part of Old Knuckle. And angels were never supposed to leave Old Knuckle.

She drove Benson's ATV through the woods with Madds draped over it. She'd tied her up and injected her with the medicine her father had taught her to make. It was similar to what Jessa would make for people when they needed to calm down, but ten times as potent.

It always did the trick to keep the angels calm, and mostly asleep. There were a few hiccups with waking up, but they never did anything other than watch. She was sure the angels just saw it all happening, like a movie of sorts. And she never gave them anything to worry about.

She wasn't cruel, after all. This was her job, passed down from her father, and her father's father, and so on. She wasn't sure when it had all started, but she just knew she had to carry it on. She may not hear the voices like her father, but she knew it was the right thing to do.

She wasn't worried about being caught, either. She knew that God would protect her, and she knew exactly how. Because she had already thought it through.

The rumor mill was rampant in Old Knuckle, and word had gotten out that Madds was in Old Knuckle for a reason. It made sense because who would pick a place nobody wanted to come to, just to be met with hatred for being an outsider? Madds was running from something, and the law was a big part of that.

And with Madds telling Cora that it wasn't her choice to leave, and that she would be leaving with Elven? The whole thing added up to Madds going to jail.

And nobody wanted to go to jail. So why wouldn't they think that Madds took Benson's ATV and ran off to save herself? She was already on the run as it was, after all.

The plan was fast and loose, but Cora was pretty certain it would work. And the only person she truly had to convince was Elven. Everyone else would just go along with the story of the outsider leaving town. And once Cora was done with her work, she would make sure that nobody ever found her body.

Cora pulled the ATV up to the cabin after the long ride through the night. The darkness made for great cover, and she was certain nobody had seen her pull her out the back of Benson's trailer. Benson had slept through the whole thing. Poor kid was exhausted from everything that had been happening. She hated to see it, but it was also necessary for Lila to stay put. Sometimes, God put people through hard trials to test their will and faith. Maybe Benson was like

Job in some ways. At the end of all this, he would be much stronger for it.

She left Madds, still out of it, on the ATV and headed to the small hunting cabin that she had known her whole life. There was a wheelbarrow sitting along the side. It's what she used to bring the bodies, dead or alive, inside and outside. And this was no different. Madds had fit right into Old Knuckle, and she was an angel like the rest of them.

It was almost never that an angel like Madds came into Old Knuckle. There was no way in hell Cora was going to let that one leave, either.

She loaded Madds into the wheelbarrow, sliding her in carefully so she didn't bang her head. She wasn't a large girl, but she was heavier than she looked. Cora had rarely had to deal with angels who weren't in their early twenties or late teens. But Madds would be the one who was different than the rest.

She wheeled her inside, closing the door behind her. The warmth of the stove was fading, and she opened it up to check. The coals had all burned out. She grabbed a couple of logs she chopped last week and put them inside, following it with some kindling. She lit a match. It caught fire quick enough, and she shut the door. She didn't want to let the cabin get cold, especially not with the girl downstairs, and now with bringing Madds in.

She wasn't going to let them freeze to death. They had to be bled. That was the only way. The way that her father had shown her. She was lucky that it was also the way that Dina had gone out. The knife Auriel had used as a little girl had turned into her rite of passage.

She hoisted Madds up, using all the strength from her knees and not her back, and carried her downstairs. She brought her down into the hallway, the very one she had been in all those years ago, throughout her whole life.

The biggest difference between now and then, though, was that the rooms had no doors. The hinges had long rusted off. That was okay, though. When she was a girl, she'd gotten into a lot of trouble opening up the doors and letting out the girls. So she made an upgrade when she took over as The Keeper. She'd bolted metal loops to the walls and strung chains through them. This way, the girls would stay put in their rooms, and there was no risk of someone else letting them out. Cora was the only holder of the key.

She went to the left, the same room Dina had been inside all those years ago, and walked Madds in. It was no different other than the chains. A clear, basic, open room where an angel would stay while she worked.

Cora gently set down Madds on the floor. Madds rolled her head and opened her eyes like she was coming out of a dream.

"What... what is this?" she asked.

"Shhh," Cora said softly. "It's okay. Just rest."

Madds didn't respond again, but Cora knew she would slowly be waking up fully. But it didn't matter, because Cora had locked the chains around her wrists. There was plenty of room to move and to lie down, but Madds wasn't getting out.

"Hey!" someone screamed. "Wake up! Don't let her do that!"

Cora shook her head and turned around to see Lila. Cora had considered giving her a new name, one that was angelic in nature, but Lila was such a beautiful name as it was, similar to Delilah or Lilia, that she continued to call her Lila. God never spoke to her to tell her otherwise, so she thought it was a fine decision.

"Lila," Cora said. "It's too late. And you should be sleeping. We have a big day tomorrow."

"Fuck you!" Lila screamed. "Why are you doing this? I was always nice to you. I didn't do anything. I thought you liked me and my brother."

Cora smiled softly at her. "I do," she said. "That's why I have to do this. So you don't leave."

"You don't make any sense!" Lila cried, her screams turning into sobs.

Cora shook her head. "It will all make sense when we're done," she said, sighing as she turned back to look at Madds. Her eyes were open, and she'd watched the whole thing.

"This has gotten so out of hand now," Cora said to herself regretfully. "If I would have just buried Shayla properly, but I was in a rush and couldn't find soft enough ground. My father would have been disappointed."

But now, after telling Bear that Quentin had the dresses, and Roy doing what Roy always did and making it worse, she knew that she had covered her tracks enough. All that was left was Lila still missing. But it was a plausible explanation that Quentin had buried her somewhere in the vast forest around Old Knuckle.

They could try all they wanted, but they would never find her.

CHAPTER SIXTY-TWO

Elven woke up with an unsettling feeling in his stomach. It wasn't from the lack of sleep, or anything he ate. It was something pulling at his mind, like he was missing something. He'd been far too tired to realize it yesterday, but now that he was awake and more clear, he knew exactly what it was.

He got ready quickly, grabbed a biscuit, and headed out on the ATV to Benson's trailer, where he knew Madds had slept. He knew she would be on board once he filled her in.

They'd missed a big piece of the puzzle at Quentin's, and he needed to tell them all. They weren't just looking for Lila some-where; he knew they were going to be looking for something more. But he had to get back to Quentin's place first to double-check. After that, they could go to the FBI.

But when he pulled up to Benson's trailer, the very first thing he noticed was that his ATV was gone. Elven hoped they weren't out and about, already starting on the search. But where would they go? And Madds knew that Elven would be right back here to meet them, so why no message?

Maybe Benson had to run an errand, and Madds was still here.

He parked the ATV and ran up the stairs, knocking on the door to make sure he hadn't missed them.

"Madds, you in there?" he asked through the door.

"Hold on, I'm coming," Benson called back. At least he was there to fill him in, Elven thought.

The door opened, and Benson let out a long yawn. His hair was disheveled, sticking up on the right side from where he'd slept on it weird. He still wore the clothes he had on last night. It was early, but they'd been up far earlier since Elven came to town. The kid must have been that exhausted to have slept that long.

"Is Madds here?" Elven asked, expecting Benson to say she was in the bathroom or that she'd run out with his ATV for a moment.

But instead, he shook his head, confused. "Here? No, she didn't come by. I figured she'd have been coming with you."

"She stayed the night here last night," Elven said.

"She did?" Benson asked. "I barely even remember getting in last night." He looked down at himself, still in the same clothes as yesterday, sans boots. "At least I got my boots off."

Elven nodded. "Sure did," he said, not bothering to tell him that it was Madds who did that for him. "So you didn't see her at all? This morning, last night?"

Benson shook his head, then frowned as he looked over Elven's shoulder. "Where's my ride?" He pushed past Elven, still barefoot, and walked out onto the porch. He looked around, trying to find it.

Instead, he saw Bear riding up on his own ATV, parking it right next to Elven's. "Looks like everyone's here about the same time," Bear said, hopping off.

"Everyone except for Madds," Elven said, trying to keep the concern out of his voice.

"She alright?" Bear asked. "Stay behind at Ginny's for something?"

Elven shook his head. "Last I saw her was right here last night," Elven said, gesturing to the trailer. "She didn't want to leave Benson alone. Said she was gonna stay the night."

"I never seen her, though," Benson said. "And now my fucking ride is gone."

Bear twisted his brows like he was trying to make sense of it. "Think she would have gone to the cabin on her own?"

"Doesn't seem likely, does it?" Elven asked. "Take Benson's ATV and leave him stranded. Especially knowing we were all gonna meet here first thing." Elven groaned, thinking about the night before. "I told her we would head to town."

"To town?" Bear asked.

Elven nodded. "Back to Dupray," he said. "I wasn't sure what else we could do here, so I said we might be heading back."

"And going back meant she would get arrested, right?" Bear asked. "After doing what she did, and you getting shot?"

"You knew about all that?" Elven asked in surprise.

Bear nodded. "Trying to kill Hollis Starcher goes a long way for me. Don't matter who her blood is."

"Yeah, well, now I wonder if she wasn't too keen on our deal anymore," Elven said.

Bear chewed the side of his cheek for a moment, mulling it over. Benson shook his head. "I don't know about that," Benson said. "I don't take her as a liar."

"You're a good kid, Benson," Bear said. "But even a good person with their back against the wall can make some desperate choices. Sounds like she already has in her past."

Elven nodded. "I guess so," he said, but he couldn't hide his disappointment. It wasn't not getting the arrest that upset him; it was that Madds had gone back on her word. Again.

"Well, what the fuck am I supposed to do now without my ATV?" Benson complained.

"You can ride with me," Elven said. "I want to go back to Quentin's and check on something. I don't want to start theories without seeing the evidence, but it might be worth a look."

Benson went to the fridge and opened it. "Damn, looks like Cora came by and made me some food," he said. "I've eaten from that casserole dish probably twenty times now." He grinned, pulling it out of the fridge. He grabbed a fork and took a big bite of it, though it was completely cold.

"Speaking of," Bear said. "I want to run by her place and see how she's doing. She gave us the tip about Quentin and the dress. Guilty or not, having the man shot dead in the middle of town might be wearing her down today. Want to make sure she's alright with all of it."

"Hey, tell her thanks for the casserole," Benson said.

"You can come with me and tell her yourself if you want."

Benson considered it, but shook his head. "Not with Lila still out there. If Elven's on to something, I want to be there with him."

"Fair enough," Bear said. "I'll let her know for you."

"Get your shoes on if you're coming with me," Elven said. "It's a long ride."

Benson nodded, taking one last bite of the casserole and leaving it on the counter before grabbing his shoes and heading back out the door.

CHAPTER SIXTY-THREE

The ride went a lot faster, now that Elven was used to the route to Quentin's. Benson sat behind him on the ATV, which wasn't the best situation for Elven's nose. The kid desperately needed a shower and a change of clothes, but Elven had been in such a rush to get him out of there, he had no one to blame but himself. Once they got back to town, he would encourage Benson to wash up before they had another outing.

The house was in the same condition they had left it. That was a good thing; otherwise, they were in for a big scare if someone popped out at them. And Madds wasn't there, either. One more step to confirming the theory that she had left town completely.

But there was no time to worry about that now. Elven made a beeline straight for the evidence he was looking for. The thing that had woken him up so early, convincing him they had missed something.

"What all are you looking for?" Benson asked from behind Elven once he entered Quentin's bedroom.

Elven went to the bed, where the notebook had been left. "This right here," he said. "There were only two places written down, right?"

Benson nodded. "Yeah. That's why we need to look for Lila, 'cause she's probably still alive, right?" He stood beside Elven, looking down at the notebook.

Elven sighed. Benson was already bringing up his sister. If Elven's theory was right, then it made the theory about Lila still being alive a little less solid. For now, Elven opted to ignore the question.

"We were so tired that we hadn't been thinking straight," Elven said. "That, and excited to think that we closed the case on the killer. We were being sloppy."

"What do you mean? You don't think it's Quentin now?"

Elven shrugged. "I just mean that this doesn't prove anything other than he found these items." He picked up the shoebox with the two trinkets and makeshift wings. "He's got the location written down, and these in the box. But these should be in the trees, right? That's where we found the one with Shayla."

"So what? Couldn't he have pulled them down or something?" Benson asked.

"Then what's the theory?" Elven asked. "That he hangs them over a burial site, then goes back later and pulls them down and writes the coordinates down? He should be writing them down first so he doesn't lose them if that's the case. Why wouldn't he have written down Shayla's spot, or Sadie's spot?"

Benson shook his head. "I don't really know." But then he paused. "Because he didn't really know it?"

Elven nodded. "Exactly," he said, proud that Benson was following along. "Because he didn't know where they were. I think he found these items in the tree, thought they were interesting, and wrote the coordinates down. I don't think he had anything to do with the bodies in the ground. I don't think he even knew they were there."

"But what about the dresses?" Benson asked, pointing to the

closet. "Cora said she made them for Quentin, and that Sadie was found in a dress she'd made."

Elven went to the closet and looked at the dresses. There were a few, but not a ton of them. He pulled them out one by one. They were mostly all floral, just different prints. But he noticed one thing about them: they were large. Bigger than Elven, even.

"These don't look like they'd fit any of the girls, do they? How big is Lila?" Elven asked.

Benson scoffed. "Ain't that big. She's smaller than you, that's for sure."

"So who were these made for? Bear said he brought all his mother's clothing in to donate or sell when she died, right?"

"And she was a small little lady," Benson said. "No way she'd be wearing that."

"How big was Quentin, would you say?" Elven asked, holding one of the dresses up.

"He was big. Almost as big as Bear."

"About the size of this dress?"

Benson nodded, but then twisted his face like Elven was crazy. "You saying he was wearing these dresses?"

Elven shrugged. "I don't have any evidence to prove it," he said. "But he kept to himself, right? Everyone thought he was peculiar? Maybe he just didn't feel like he belonged here. Maybe he missed his mama, so he put these on. I don't know, I'm just throwing stuff on the wall and seeing if it sticks at this point." Elven didn't care what Quentin was doing with the dresses, as long as he wasn't dressing up dead girls in them. "But I do know that none of those girls would be wearing these, don't you think?"

"Yeah, Lila would have a small size," Benson agreed. "Is a small one in there?"

Elven filtered through the rest of the dresses, but came up empty on small sizes. "I don't see one," he said.

"Cora said she made them for Quentin, and all these other ones, too. So we ought to ask her," Benson said.

That's when it clicked with Elven. "Cora said she made the dress for Quentin," he said. "Cora made that casserole for you."

"You think there was something wrong with the casserole?" Benson asked, eyes widening.

"No," Elven said, shaking his head. "But if she brought it last night, that's when Madds would have been there, too."

"Bear said he was heading over there when we left," Benson recalled.

"You got a radio on you?"

"Left it on your ATV."

"Good," Elven said. "We need to go right now."

CHAPTER SIXTY-FOUR

There was no answer when Bear knocked on the door. He walked around to the side to look at the small dirt driveway. Cora's ATV was still parked there, so she had to be home. That, or she'd gone on a walk somewhere.

He went back to the door and gave the handle a try. The door opened right up with a creak at the hinges. He made a note to oil them up for her later. She had her hands full with her ailing father and helping the town out. She'd never married, so it was all up to her. The small chores were the least he could do with everything she had on her hands. And he was happy to help out.

"Cora?" Bear called out into the house, not wanting to just barge in. "Cora?"

There was still no answer. He thought about coming back, not wanting to invade her privacy. But then he spotted Howard in his wheelchair, facing the television, but it was completely turned off.

"Howard, are you all alone?" Bear asked.

Howard moved at the mention of his name, but he didn't say anything to Bear, nor did he crane his neck to the door. He must have been having one of his moments, which Cora said were far more frequent these days.

Bear decided to walk in, closing the door behind him. "I'm just gonna come in and check on you," he said. "Don't worry, I'm just here to help, though."

He knew Howard had mostly bad days, so he wanted to try to reassure the man as best as he could. He had known the man all his life. He hadn't always been like this, and Bear hoped that maybe he could remember those times when he was all there in the head.

"She can't be long if she left you here, right?" Bear asked, knowing he was pretty much talking to himself at this point.

He walked over to Howard, finding that he was fine in the chair. Howard met his eyes this time, and Bear smiled. "Hey Howard, glad to see you."

Howard smiled wide, and Bear wondered if he remembered him. "Bear," Howard said.

Bear laughed out loud. "That's right," he said. "Cora around?"

This time, Howard didn't answer, just looked to the blank TV behind him. He lifted a finger and pointed to it.

"Let me help you out there," Bear said. He turned around and grabbed the remote, clicking the television on. He flipped through a few channels until he landed on one that made Howard let out a mumble. "Guess that's the one."

Howard nodded and watched the TV, no longer paying Bear any attention. He figured the man was alright if he could remember Bear for that brief moment. And Cora was his keeper, so she would know better than him.

Bear walked quietly back around the couch and stopped at the bedroom door. He took a glance inside, noticing a picture on the dresser. He thought better of it, but his curiosity won out, and he went into the bedroom.

It was Cora's room, not Howard's. Unless, of course, Howard liked frilly decorations and pink curtains with flowers on them. The queen-sized bed was raised, which would have been too difficult for Howard to get into. The dresser led ear to believe it to be Cora's with the jewelry on top and the pile of women's clothes in the hamper next to it.

But what had caught his eye was the picture on the nightstand. Bear picked it up and studied it. It was Howard in his better days, even younger than Bear remembered him. He held a little girl in his arms, both of them flashing wide, matching smiles. The girl had to be Cora, from the blond hair and the similar features she still had, though now weathered from the years. They stood in front of an old hunting cabin.

Bear had never seen the cabin before. Wasn't even aware that they had one. Howard being a hunter didn't surprise him, but he wondered if Cora hunted at all. If she did, he doubted she did much anymore, having to take care of her father. But it was a shame for the small cabin to go to waste. She had never once mentioned it in all the years he'd known her.

He set the picture down in the same spot where he'd lifted it, and then he noticed the drawer was open a couple of inches. Inside it was a notebook with handwriting. Once again letting his curiosity take over, he started paging through it.

There was a big list, completely handwritten. And the list was made up of coordinates, just like they'd seen yesterday. But there were far more coordinates than just the two they'd seen on Quentin's list. Bear ran his finger over them, his heart picking up its pace.

He didn't want to let his mind go to a bad place, but he couldn't help but wonder if he was holding what he thought he was holding.

Cora was the one who had pointed him to Quentin, after all.

And then his finger landed on familiar numbers, the same ones he saw last night. The ones that had led them to Rebecca Ellison and the other skeletal remains. He let his eyes go down the list and saw that the handwriting changed as he got closer to the end of it.

There were so many coordinates.

"I can't believe it," Bear whispered to himself. It was a list of bodies, and he knew it deep in his soul.

Cora was the one responsible.

His radio clicked on, static blaring from his belt. "Bear," Elven said. "Bear, get out of there. It's Cora."

Bear picked up the radio and turned around, already on the same page as Elven. He wasn't sure how the man had figured it out. Maybe he wasn't such a bad cop after all.

When he turned around, he never got a word out to tell Elven that he already knew. Because right in front of him, Howard stood. The old man's eyes were wide open, and he grinned, revealing a mouth of yellowed teeth. He looked like he was completely lucid.

There was a flash of movement, and Bear felt odd. Suddenly cold, and at the same time, like he couldn't talk. He couldn't even swallow. Looking down, he saw Howard's arm extended toward him. In his hand was a knife, and that knife had been plunged straight into Bear's throat.

"You shouldn't have that! You shouldn't have that!" Howard yelled. "I'm the keeper of those angels. I'm the keeper of them all!"

Howard pulled his arm back, the blade sliding out of Bear's throat, causing blood to bubble from the wound.

Bear couldn't say a word. He dropped the radio and grabbed at his throat. Howard plunged the knife forward again, digging the blade deep into the other side of Bear's throat. Bear stumbled backward, feeling lightheaded as blood poured from his throat. No matter how tight he grabbed his throat, he couldn't stop it.

With his free hand, Bear pulled his revolver. His head was spinning now, and he felt like he was falling. Then it stopped—he was suddenly on the floor. His pistol was raised, and he squeezed the trigger as many times as he could. The gunshots sounded muffled and far away, but he saw the flashes right in front of him.

The whole thing felt like a dream. It was like he was being given anesthesia before surgery, and nothing felt real. A bullet hit the wall. Another went into the ceiling. And then two of them found Howard, and he was suddenly on the floor, crying out about something that Bear couldn't make any sense of.

Bear pulled the trigger until only clicks were left. The gun suddenly felt heavy, and he let his hand fall to the floor with it. He tried to stand up, but couldn't. He just sat there, his back against the wall, feeling like he just needed to right himself up somehow so he would be more comfortable.

He brought his hand down from his throat, finding the notebook on the floor, but he didn't grab it. He just put his hand on it.

And then he let himself drift off, the blood continuing to drench his shirt.

Bear Colter was no more.

CHAPTER SIXTY-FIVE

Madds opened her eyes, her memory hazy. She had the feeling something had gone terribly wrong, and when she saw the unfamiliar room, it started making sense. She remembered Cora coming by Benson's, then being hit on the head. There were some other things she wasn't sure about, but then Cora's voice telling her that she was an angel came back to her. The fragments were all there in some capacity, but connecting them together was proving tricky.

One thing she was sure about, however, was that Cora was the one responsible, and Madds was in serious trouble.

"You okay?" someone asked.

Madds sat up, finding that her hands were locked up with chains. It reminded her of medieval times, the shackles they used back then. Or at least what she thought they'd used. She'd only ever paid attention when she went to a Renaissance Faire once, and she couldn't be sure if it was historically accurate or not.

She tried to focus and find whoever had spoken to her, letting her eyes wander everywhere. Then she saw the girl. She was in the other room, right across the hall.

It was Lila, Benson's sister. Madds recognized her right away, because she'd spent time with Lila in Old Knuckle before she went missing.

"Lila," Madds said.

Lila nodded. "I've been here the whole time," she said. "That is, if anyone is even looking for me."

"We are," Madds said. "Everyone has been. The whole town."

Lila smiled, but it looked pathetic, like she didn't want to let herself hope any longer. "Well, that's nice, I guess," she said.

Lila was chained up the same way Madds was. Madds tried to mess with her chains, seeing if she could break free or test how much slack she had at least.

"Don't bother," Lila said, noticing what Madds was attempting. "I've tried it all. So did Sadie. So did Shayla. Nothing is going to break us free from here but that key."

"How'd you get here?" Madds asked, though at this point, she didn't think it was that important. But keeping Lila talking might help them somehow. She could learn if there was anything that could help them get out.

"We'd been talking about leaving," Lila said. "Apparently, that's all it was. Why we were chosen. Cora invited us over to try on dresses, and then we woke up here. I can remember some of it. She had a trailer that she strapped us to. I think, anyway. It's all kind of fuzzy."

"She must have drugged you," Madds said. "I feel the same way right now."

Lila nodded. "She gave us all some tea," she recalled. "You're probably right. Not that it matters anymore."

Lila wasn't animated when she talked. She just sounded defeated. Like the will to live had been beaten out of her.

"So you wanted out of here?" Madds asked. "Old Knuckle, I mean."

"We were just talking," she said. "Sadie and Shayla definitely wanted to get out. I was on the fence."

"Because of Benson?" Madds guessed.

Lila nodded. "Because of Benson. I was gonna ask him to come with if I got real serious about it. I hoped he would have said yes. Guess it don't matter now, though. I'm never leaving Old Knuckle."

Lila started to sob, tears running down her face. Madds just wanted to hold her and tell her it would be okay, but she was still locked to the wall. And she didn't know if she'd be lying to the girl by saying it.

"If it takes staying here for the rest of my life if I can just see him again, then that's what I'll do," Lila said between sobs.

"We will get out of this," Madds said, deciding that some hope was better than none. "People are out there looking for us still."

Lila shook her head. "No, we won't. First Shayla. Then Sadie. I'm next." She locked eyes with Madds. "And then it's you. Once you passed out, Cora told me that nobody was gonna be looking for you. Said you were on the run, and that someone she called Elven would think so, too. So I know it'll be me, and then it'll be you."

"You don't know that," Madds said. But after hearing Lila's words, she had to admit that she wasn't so sure that they would be getting out of there.

CHAPTER SIXTY-SIX

A crowd gathered at Cora's house. Nobody said a word to Elven or Benson as they both rushed past them and went to the door. Roy Leven and a few others stood in the living room. Elven wasn't sure what to make of the whole thing, but he knew that it had to be bad.

The television played in the background, but nobody seemed bothered by it. Roy turned to Elven and Benson. "We heard gunshots and came to check it out," he said.

The look on his face told Elven everything. But he still had to see it for himself.

"Let me in," Elven said. He put his hand on his gun for added emphasis, not wanting to argue about it. Roy, however, was accommodating and gave a nod, scooting to the side so Elven could walk past them and into the bedroom.

That's where he saw Howard, dead on the floor. He'd taken a gunshot to the chest, and another one to the throat. He saw there was blood on his hands as well, but they were spread out to his sides. And that's when Elven looked further into the bedroom.

Bear Colter lay against the wall, his legs straight out. His chin was tucked against his chest, which looked uncomfortable. But it didn't matter, because Bear was dead. His eyes were wide open, staring at the floor. He had gone pale, most likely from all the blood that had gushed out of his throat. He still had a knife sticking out of his left side.

"What happened?" Roy asked.

Elven shook his head. "Your guess is as good as mine," he said grimly. He was done giving any information to Roy after what had happened to Quentin. He didn't need the man messing up anything else. But Elven had to admit, it was already pretty messed up right now.

Elven looked at the floor where Bear's hands lay. One held his gun, and the other rested on top of something. Elven carefully stepped around Howard's body and around the puddle of blood that surrounded Bear. He lifted the notebook from underneath Bear's hand, knowing that no crime scene investigation was needed at this point. Not that there would have been one, anyway, up here in Old Knuckle.

He looked down at the notebook, seeing the same thing Bear must have noticed earlier. Bear knew the truth, too. Elven may not have reached him on the radio in time, but he was pretty sure he'd figured it out himself. And it had cost him his life.

The notebook was filled with coordinates. Not just the two that Quentin had written down at his home, but a full page of them. The handwriting changed the further Elven went down the list, and the penmanship faded away the further up he went. He took a look at Howard again, figuring that he had been a part of it. He probably was the one who had put those two in the ground that they'd found last night.

But it didn't tell Elven anything about where Cora was. And now he was absolutely sure that Madds hadn't run off. She had to be with Cora.

"Did Cora or Howard have a cabin out there in the woods?" Elven asked. "Maybe a place they went to get away, or something like that? Maybe Howard went hunting?"

Roy shook his head. "I'm sure he hunted back in the day when he was able, but I don't know about a cabin."

Then Elven spotted the picture on the nightstand. It had fallen over, which must have happened during the struggle between the two men. In the picture was a young Howard and what looked like Cora as a child. Behind them was a cabin.

Elven lifted the picture. "Here," he said. "Where is this?"

Roy shook his head. "I don't know if I've ever seen it. But it's hard to say. Just looks like a hunting cabin."

For as much as the people of Old Knuckle knew about each other, Cora and Howard were really good at keeping a secret. Not just about killing folks, but about a lot of things, it seemed. They weren't going to be any help.

Elven turned to Benson, who looked more serious than he'd ever looked before. He motioned with his eyes to go outside. Elven nodded, following him out there.

"I'm gonna see if I can check out back for anything," Elven said.

Thankfully, Roy didn't seem to pick up on the lie. The pair walked outside and around the building, outside of any prying ears.

"I didn't want Roy hearing, after what happened with Quentin," Benson said.

Elven held back a smile, feeling another sense of pride for the kid. That was smart thinking. Looping Roy in on this was a horrible idea. "Good thinking," Elven said.

"I know it, though. The place." Benson said. He pointed to the cabin, right where a small wheelbarrow sat along the wall on the picture in Elven's hand. "I've seen it before. Kind of rusted out now, though. But I remember running around with Davin once. We went pretty far out there where we didn't usually venture. But we spotted that place. Nobody was there, but as soon as we drove up to it, the whole place just gave a weird vibe. Like, I don't even know how to describe it. Just like when someone walks over your grave or some-thin'. You know?"

Elven nodded. "You remember how to get there?"

"I think I can get us there."

"Good, 'cause we're leaving now," Elven said.

CHAPTER SIXTY-SEVEN

Madds and Lila had stopped talking for a long while. Madds had tried, but Lila had pretty much given up. The poor girl had been here for weeks, almost a couple of months at this point. She'd been through a lot, and the fact that she was still alive was amazing. Generally, once someone had been kidnapped, it wasn't long for them until they were killed.

But Cora was a different kind of killer. One Madds surely had never dealt with. She could see the similarities when she'd been kidnapped and taken to Monacan, but that was still something different. Targeted more toward one person, while Cora targeted multiple. She saw herself as a *keeper*. Whatever that meant.

Madds, however, wasn't done trying. She checked every single link on the chain, testing its strength. Then she opted to try the bolt in the wall. But no matter what she tried, it was no use. Every single place she could think of was a dead end. The chains were too strong, the bolt far too embedded.

Lila had been right about it all, but Madds still didn't see it as a waste of time. She wasn't going to give up.

The only place Madds could think of that she hadn't tried was her wrists. Not the shackles around them, but her actual wrists.

It scared her to think of it, but it might be her only option. She'd never broken something on purpose, and she wasn't even sure where to begin. Maybe it was better to start with her thumb and slide her hand out that way. The chain was looped through the eyehole in the bolt, and it looked like she could slip out the shackle if one of her hands were free. She'd just have to carry the chain around with her, but that would be okay, wouldn't it?

If she did that, she would definitely be hobbling herself. And then would she be able to fight her way out? If she got the jump on Cora, she thought she could. But if Cora had a gun, all her efforts might be fruitless.

It was an idea, but she wasn't sure it was a good one. She would save that for the very last, desperate moment if it came to it.

The door opened upstairs, and she could hear someone coming down. "Are you two angels getting along?" Cora asked.

Her voice was sweet, like a mother asking if two girls were playing well together. It made Madds sick to her stomach to hear it.

Cora appeared in the hallway, standing between both of the open rooms. She looked at Lila, then shook her head. "You've seemed to have lost your will, my sweet angel," Cora said. She then turned to Madds. "And you, I just realized we haven't named you yet."

Madds didn't know what the hell she meant by that. "You know my name."

Cora shook her head. "Not your angel name."

"Jesus tits, you are crazy," Madds said. "What the fuck are you talking about?"

Cora looked stunned, staring her down a moment. "I don't appreciate those kind of words here," she said.

"But you're okay with killing girls?" Madds snapped. "Okay, sure. That makes sense. Killing is okay, but cussing isn't. Gotcha. Priorities, right?" She was scared, but she wasn't going to let Cora see that. So, she opted for defiant sarcasm.

Cora shook her head. "You might think I'm killing, but it's not that. I'm making sure these angels stay in Old Knuckle. Forever."

"Whatever you say," Madds said.

Cora smiled. "You'll see, soon enough. But it's not your time yet," she said. "Try not to get scared."

"I think we're past that part," Madds said.

Cora didn't respond. Instead, she turned to Lila and headed into her room. "My angel, it is time," she said.

Lila sat up, shaking.

"Hey! Get away from her!" Madds yelled.

"Please, don't," Lila whimpered.

Cora shushed. "It's alright," she said. She pulled a syringe out.

Lila quickly scrambled away, but only got so far when the chains stopped her. "Please, I'll just go. Don't give me any of that again. I don't like it," Lila said, her voice desperate.

Cora considered it and let out a sigh. "If you are lying to me, I'll give you that and more."

Lila nodded, and Madds believed that she was going to cooperate. Cora had broken the girl down to a shell of herself.

"Okay," Lila said, a few tears running down her face.

"That's a good angel," Cora said. She pulled a key out of her pocket and unlocked one of the chains around her wrist. She threaded the chain through the eyebolt, just like Madds had thought she could do, and then locked it around Lila's wrist again. She was no longer bolted to the wall.

"Lila, fight!" Madds yelled.

But Lila only looked at Madds, her eyes telling her she was sorry. No words needed to be said.

"See?" Cora said to Madds. "Maybe you'll be this good for me, too, when it's your time." She pulled at Lila. "Come on."

Lila went with Cora up the stairs, out of sight from Madds. Madds knew the fight had left Lila, but it didn't mean she needed to die because of it. She looked at her wrist, deciding if now was the time to make a move.

She didn't have to decide long. Because when Lila started screaming, the choice had been made for her.

That's when she bit as much of her shirt as she could and started stomping on her hand.

CHAPTER SIXTY-EIGHT

Benson was right. The trek out to the hunting cabin he had recognized in the picture was far, which was no surprise to Elven. That was the way it was in Old Knuckle. Elven was impressed that Benson remembered the way. He let the kid take the handlebars on the ATV, and Elven sat behind him. It was faster that way, and Elven had to admit, Benson knew how to drive.

He took the twists and turns in the forest like a pro. There were times that Elven thought they were going to tip over, times Benson had to drive along a ridge and didn't seem to worry about how close they got, and other times that they zipped through the trees without a care about being knocked from the seat. Well, Benson didn't have a care. Elven felt his cheeks pucker on more than one occasion.

But Benson got them there, and as soon as Elven saw the cabin come into view, he knew exactly what Benson meant when he described it to Elven. The whole vibe of the place, the air, the way the wind blew, it just felt... evil. It was a place that had seen a lot of death.

This place wasn't anywhere Elven wanted to be, but it was also the place he had to be.

And he knew it was where Lila and Madds were.

"This is it," Benson finally said. If they had any remaining questions about it, Benson's ATV sitting right out front put those ideas to rest.

"We need to be cautious walking in," Elven said. "We don't know if Cora has a weapon, or if there's any sort of traps set in case someone comes in. So let's take it slow, and let me take the lead, okay?"

"I can do that," Benson said, nodding.

"I know your sister could be here and be in trouble, so I don't need you getting yourself hurt," Elven said. "I'm gonna stress it again —let me lead, and don't go in there guns blazing because you're bound to get hurt, alright?"

"I get it," Benson said. "Don't worry about me. I'll follow you."

"Good, now—"

A scream erupted so loud from inside the cabin, it felt like it was right in Elven's ear. He'd heard pain before, but this was deep. He didn't recognize who it belonged to, either.

But Benson did.

"That's Lila!" Benson cried. "I'm coming, Lila!"

He continued yelling at the cabin, blowing any sort of advantage they may have had. He immediately jumped off the ATV and ran toward the small cabin.

"Benson!" Elven yelled, trying to keep the kid out of harm's way. But it was too late. Benson had let his emotions get the better of him.

Benson had made it four whole steps from the ATV and through the tall weeds that surrounded the cabin before a loud snap came. Benson let out a scream to match that of his sister's, and he fell to the ground.

"Fuck!" Benson yelled. "My fucking leg!"

Elven got off the ATV and followed carefully where Benson had gone. He checked the ground as he did, making sure to not get stuck in whatever Benson had walked into.

Once he reached the kid, he saw the pain on his face. And then he saw Benson's leg. It had been caught in a bear trap, very similar to the one that Elven had stopped Bear from stepping into when tracking down Shamus.

Benson reached for his leg, but he didn't want to touch it. "Oh my God, how bad is it?" he groaned.

It was pretty darn bad from what Elven could see. The teeth of the contraption had sunk straight through the kid's pants and into the meat of his leg. He could see the blood soaked into his pants, and the exposed white fat where it had torn the fabric and his skin.

"Okay," Elven said, "I can get this off of you. You just gotta hold still."

"Fuck, I think my leg's broke."

Elven didn't doubt it. The teeth clamping together had made a hard sound, and that amount of pressure was bound to break bones. Elven put his hands on the metal and tried to pry the teeth apart.

Benson let out a scream as he did so.

"Come on!" Elven yelled. "Come on!" He had moved it just enough where Benson could slide his leg out, and he did.

"It's bad, ain't it?" Benson asked. Blood poured out of his wound, and his leg flopped sideways into an unnatural position.

Elven pulled his belt off and wrapped it around Benson's leg, just in case there was too much bleeding. He tightened it, and Benson yelled again.

And then Lila screamed again.

"You have to go," Benson said. "Leave me here and go get her." He grabbed Elven and shoved him back before he could clasp the belt down. "I can do that—just go."

Elven had never seen a more determined look on someone's face, but he knew why. Benson wouldn't be able to help him now.

Elven drew his pistol from its holster and ran to the cabin, watching every single place his foot could land.

CHAPTER SIXTY-NINE

Elven rushed straight into the door, turning the handle, putting all his weight into it at full speed. It wasn't locked, and he barreled straight into the open room.

Lila was strapped to a table in the middle of the room with chains around her wrists and ankles. Her arms and legs were pulled taut at all corners. Her shirt was lifted up, and he saw why she had been screaming. Her flesh had been carved into. A large flap of skin was peeled back, still connected at one point, like turning the pages of a book. There was another cut of skin on the other side of her belly. A bowl sat on the floor with bloody rags and the knife that had done the carving.

Elven assumed Cora was preparing the wings for whatever trinket or scene she had imagined in her head.

But Elven knew he'd been too reckless with his entry and that Cora had heard them outside. She was no longer standing at the table, doing the carving. She stood on the other end of the room beside a door, pointing a double-barreled shotgun right at him. And he was still stumbling on his feet from rushing in too fast.

He didn't have time to think, and Cora clearly wasn't going to let him. Instead, she steadied herself, a determined look on her face much like the one Benson had. He knew the trigger would be pulled before he could even think about diving out of the way.

Before she pulled the trigger, though, the door next to her opened up. Cora clearly didn't expect it, because she turned her head, the gun angling away from Elven as she did.

And then Elven saw the face he'd been hoping to see.

Madds lunged out of the door with a yell, tackling Cora to the ground. The gun went off, blasting into the wall away from anyone, sending splinters of wood raining down through the air.

Elven finally grabbed the table to steady himself, his gun dropping from his hands as he did, nearly toppling the whole thing over with Lila still strapped to it. She had completely passed out, either from being drugged or from the shock and pain she'd been through. He figured the latter, from the way her screams had pierced the air.

Madds used one hand to wrap a chain around Cora's neck. It was shackled to her right wrist. She pulled as tight as she could, but he noticed that she kept her left hand out of it. He saw her thumb dangle to the side, the skin bruised and cut open. It was completely broken, and he knew that she'd done it to herself to get out of the shackles.

Cora fired again, this time getting a lot closer to Elven and Lila. His heart skipped a beat as a few bits of the scatter hit the table that Lila was on. He dropped to the floor as soon as it went off, hoping he wasn't in the line of fire. Luckily, none of it hit Lila or Elven, but another shower of wood splinters rained down on them.

Madds pulled tighter. "Give it up," she said through grit teeth. But she wasn't strong enough to finish the job.

Cora grabbed at Madds's broken hand and hit it as hard as she could, smashing right on her broken thumb. Madds let out a scream, and the chain went slack. Cora pulled out of the chain and got on top of Madds. She started swinging down on her, hitting her across the face once, twice, and a third time.

Elven made it to his feet and rushed to Cora. He wrapped his arms around Cora's throat and yanked her off of Madds. She beat against him with her hands behind her, searching for anything that could help her. But Elven was too strong. He flung her backward toward the wall, and she hit her face hard against it. Her body slumped to the floor, no longer moving.

He bent over, wrapping a hand around Madds's good arm and hoisting her up. She was bleeding out of her nose now from the punches that Cora had dealt her, but she was okay.

"Watch the thumb," she groaned.

"I noticed," Elven said, helping her to the bed that was against the wall. "Sit down. Do you know where the key to that is?"

Madds pointed to Cora on the floor. He walked to her and flipped her body over. She was out cold, but still breathing. He saw the key poking out of a side pocket on her pants and pulled it out. He unlocked Madds's right wrist, and she dropped the chain to the floor.

"We should lock her up with these and bring her to town," Madds said. "And by 'town,' I mean Dupray."

Elven couldn't agree more. "Let's get Lila out of here," Elven said. "She's in bad shape. Benson's outside, not doing much better."

"Alright," Madds said, standing up. She cradled her left hand against her chest.

Elven went to Lila and started to unlock her. He wasn't even sure what to do about her wounds at this point. Madds grabbed the blanket off the bed and handed it to him with her good hand. "Best I can think of," she said.

Elven nodded and wrapped it around her wounds. Luckily, she was still out cold. But soon, she would be awake and in a lot of pain. He then unlocked her wrists and then her feet.

"Elven!" Madds yelled.

Cora had come to. And she wasn't done fighting. She had grabbed the knife off the floor that she'd used to carve up Lila and plunged it straight at Elven's midsection.

Madds ran right between them, the blade never touching Elven. But instead, it sunk straight into Madds's stomach. Madds reared back and decked Cora in the face, sending her sprawling against the wall. She hit the back of her head hard against it. Just after, Madds dropped to the floor, grabbing at the handle as the blade stayed in her stomach.

Cora fell to the ground, once again seemingly knocked out cold like before. This time, though, he wasn't going to make the same mistake. He quickly got the shackles off of Lila and wrapped them around Cora's arms. After wrapping her body up, he locked her legs next. There was no way she could get out.

"Elven," Madds whimpered.

She looked at him, half sitting up, still holding the blade that was sunk into her belly. Blood had soaked through her shirt where the knife had entered. She pulled it out, and they both watched the blood seep out.

He grabbed the pillow off the bed, pulling the pillowcase off of it and pressing it against her wound.

"We're gonna get you out of here," he said.

CHAPTER SEVENTY

It was still daylight out, with plenty of it left so the pathways were easy enough to navigate. Elven drove as fast as he could, Madds behind him, her arms wrapped around him as tight as she could get them. It was difficult with her thumb being broken, but she managed. Though, the closer to town they got, the more he could feel her grip slipping. Her hand was no longer clenched, but going slack a little more with each passing minute.

"You okay back there?" Elven yelled, making his voice louder than the engine.

He felt her chin bob up and down on his back in a nod, but she didn't say much. He needed to get her some medical attention as soon as possible. The knife wound may not have been fatal on the initial stab, but left too long, it surely would be.

He hoped her wound was something that Jessa could handle, because if they had to drive to the hospital, there was no way they'd make it in time. He hoped, too, it was just the bleeding that needed to be stopped, not any vital organs that needed surgical attention.

Benson and Lila rode behind him somewhere. He didn't bother to check to make sure they were close. Benson knew the way even better than Elven, but he had to take it a lot slower due to Lila's condition. She wasn't at risk of dying from her injuries. She'd woken up and been coherent enough to tell him she'd be alright. Just in a ton of pain, which accounted for why Benson had to drive slow. On top of his own broken foot.

Elven had to give the kid credit, though. He didn't complain one bit, and when Elven hooked up the trailer to Benson's ATV, with Cora bound to it, he said he could handle the load and the ride. Nobody protested at bringing Cora, and Elven couldn't just leave her out there alone. He didn't think she'd get out, but he also wasn't sure if anyone would come back for her.

He was no murderer. If she was put to death for her crimes, then so be it. But she deserved justice, and he was going to take her back to see that through. He wasn't going to take that upon himself unless pressed to do so. He'd been down roads like that before, and he wasn't about to test that path again.

Finally, after what felt like forever, Elven made it to some trailers, the first evidence that he was nearing the town center. He didn't bother stopping, instead speeding past them. There was not going to be any help there. He was gunning for the town center, and then he could get to someone who could help him. He hoped that Jessa was around.

The rest of the way flew by, and he pulled into the very spot where he'd had to talk the mob down, and then where Quentin had been killed by Ronnie. It seemed to be the place where one went if they wanted the most attention from the town.

And right now, Elven needed all of it.

He had considered driving straight to Jessa's place, but with everything that had happened in town with Bear and Howard, he worried she would have her hands full elsewhere instead of being at home. He had to drive through the center of town to get to her place, anyway, so he figured it was best to stop first. If they told him to drive on to her place, he'd do that. But if he found out she wasn't home, then someone could fetch her and have her meet him there.

Just as he had hoped, as soon as he stopped, people started to gather, already discussing what had happened earlier with Bear and Howard and now wanting to see what the commotion was.

"I need some help," Elven said, sliding off his ATV. He looked to Madds, who was pale and faring much worse than he had thought. But she was still hanging on. "You okay here?"

Madds nodded weakly. "I'll be fine," she managed to say.

Roy Leven was the first to approach, seemingly the only one who could represent the town now that Bear was gone. "What's going on?" Roy asked, a worried expression on his face.

"I need Jessa. Is she here?" Elven asked.

Benson drove up next to them. He had shifted his weight in favor of his unbroken foot, keeping almost no pressure on the wounded one. Lila clung to him Madds had clung to Elven.

Roy saw Benson with Lila, and his face paled. "You found her?" he asked. "My God."

"Roy, is Jessa here?" Elven asked, clapping his hands to pull his attention back.

Roy nodded, looking to Elven. "She was at Cora's house, dealing with the bodies," Roy said. "But she's already headed back now."

"Good," Elven said, turning around.

"It was Cora," Roy said. "All of this. It was her." He saw Cora on the trailer and ran to the back of Benson's ATV, quickly disconnecting it.

The crowd gathered, and Elven heard people shouting in favor of Roy. This wasn't going to end well, especially after what had happened with Quentin.

"Stop that," Elven barked, running up to Roy and getting between him and Cora. "I'm taking her to Dupray, where she'll be arrested."

Cora screamed, and Elven turned to see people on the other side of the trailer. It was practically surrounded at this point. She was being pulled at while people messed with the chains, yanking her off of the trailer bed.

Elven's hand found his gun, his fingers wrapping around the grip. He was going to pull it out, stick it in the air, and fire off a shot. But Roy put a hand on his shoulder. It wasn't forceful, and it wasn't threatening. Instead, it was almost as if a friend was reassuring him.

"Elven," he said. "Old Knuckle knows how to take care of their problems. You pull that gun, and you might become one of them."

Elven grit his teeth. "This ain't justice."

"Right now, you've got bigger problems to deal with," Roy said, his eyes darting to Madds.

Her eyes had closed, and she had slumped forward, on the verge of letting herself give into the fatigue. She needed to get help right now.

"Elven, he's right," Benson urged. "We gotta go."

Elven swallowed hard, closing his eyes for a brief second. He didn't like it, but if he was going to save Madds, then worrying about what the town was going to do to Cora was the last thing that needed to be on his mind.

He turned around and hopped on the ATV, driving off. Getting Madds and the others help was the only thing on his mind.

CHAPTER SEVENTY-ONE

Jessa was already at her house by the time Elven and the others reached it. She took one look at the four of them and didn't need any explanation, going straight into help mode. Elven had wondered how much help she could be, but he ended up being surprised by her thoroughness.

She assessed the three injured people and established a hierarchy of who would receive help. Madds came first because of her deep stab wound. Elven helped, but he was sure that Jessa only wanted to keep him occupied so he didn't get in the way.

He held Madds down while Jessa cleaned her wound and stitched her up. He figured she'd thrash against him when Jessa had to dig her fingers deep into her to make sure nothing important had been cut open, but Madds only writhed slightly as if she were uncomfortable instead of in pain. The herbs Jessa had given her had done some real wonders, and Elven wondered what was actually in them that could be so potent. But he was too busy to ask questions.

Once Jessa had decided that Madds only needed surface-level stitching, she went to it and was quick with it. The knife wound was wider than it was deep, and Madds rested once it was all taken care of, her injured thumb in a brace that Jessa had put together.

Lila and Benson were next, and she helped them just as she had Madds. Lila's wounds were far less drastic than he had first assumed they were. Most of it was just blood from the cuts. Once that was washed away, he saw that the flap of skin that Cora had cut away wasn't as large as he'd thought. Cora was apparently only going to make small wings instead of the large ones that Sadie had worn. So she needed less skin.

But some gauze, stitching, and a lot of those herbs put Lila back together. There would be some nasty scarring, but she would live.

Benson needed the most help. He held the kid down while they reset his leg. He let out a yell, squeezing down onto Elven's arm as hard as he could. But he took it like a champ, and Jessa had a boot to put his foot in, ready to go.

It was like a well-oiled machine at Jessa's, and Elven was impressed. He wasn't even sure that Driscoll back in Dupray could have handled these injuries as efficiently as she had. He had half a mind to invite her down to Dupray with him, but he was sure she would decline. Besides, they had a hospital nearby. The way nobody here wanted anything to do with something outside of Old Knuckle, it would be a death sentence for them to lose her.

Once everyone was fixed up, they spent the day resting at Jessa's where she could keep an eye on them. Of course, she'd done such a good job that there was nothing left for her to do. Benson sat in a room with Lila while she slept. He didn't let his broken leg bother him at all, now that his sister was safe with him again.

Elven spent the rest of the day in the same room as Madds, watching her sleep. He tried to sleep himself, but he could barely get any of it. The thought of almost losing Madds all over again ate away at him, and the wall he had built toward her was starting to crumble. Knowing that she was safe was all he needed now.

After some time, she woke up and stared back at him as he sat at the end of her bed. "What are you doing?" she asked.

He shook his head. "Just making sure you weren't going to disappear again."

She smiled and sat up, wincing as she did. She was close to him, and he could feel the warmth of her face approaching his. He leaned in, and their lips brushed together. They shared a kiss, and he remembered everything he had lost when he discovered her betrayal. The memories and the feelings of who she was to him flooded back.

She pulled away and rested her head against his. "We need to leave," she said. "This place isn't right. After what they did to Cora, or what I assume they did to her, it's just not a place we should be in anymore."

Elven nodded. "I agree," he said.

When he was alive, Bear might have been holding the place together as best he could, keeping the people from harming themselves, but even he couldn't have stopped it altogether. And now that he was dead, Old Knuckle was probably going to get even darker.

"We can leave in the morning," Elven added.

She shook her head. "I'm not going to spend another moment here. This place is tainted for me."

She stood up, steadying herself. She seemed good enough to travel. Elven just hadn't expected to be leaving so soon. But he wasn't going to argue the point, either. He'd been wanting out since before he even got here.

Elven and Madds left the room, stopping by Benson and Lila's room. Both of them looked at them from the open doorway.

"We're heading out," Elven said. "If you want to come, we can take you to the hospital. Not sure Old Knuckle is the place you want to be."

Benson nodded. "I understand."

Lila, however, shook her head. "This is our home," she said.

Elven looked her over and saw the trauma all over her face. He didn't know her before all of this, but he had a feeling she was a completely different person from before she'd been taken. And she would likely never be back to her old self.

"This is where my friends are, and I want to stay," Lila said.

Elven didn't protest. Neither did Madds.

"Thank you for everything," Benson said, starting to stand, but Elven held a hand up to stop him. He went into the room and shook the kid's hand. Madds followed, wrapping her arms around him for a hug.

"Give this to Ginny," Elven said, slipping Benson some cash that would more than cover the cost of their stay. "If you change your mind, I could use someone like you in Dupray."

Benson smiled, a look of appreciation on his face. One that Elven wasn't sure he could grasp fully. The kid had lost a lot, and been through even more. Elven just hoped Old Knuckle had taken its pound of flesh from him.

Madds and Elven left, not wanting to make any other announcements to anyone else in the town. Nobody else deserved it, and Old Knuckle was going to handle things however they wanted. There was no point.

On the way to the ATV, Madds let out a long sigh.

"What's wrong?" Elven asked.

"Lila deserves better. This town is toxic," she said. "Apparently, Cora was right."

"Angels never leave?" Elven asked, repeating what he'd heard from Madds and Lila.

Madds scoffed. "Maybe not about that," she said. "Because this angel is getting the hell out of here."

CHAPTER SEVENTY-TWO

THE DRIVE TO DUPRAY WAS A QUIET ONE. FOR THE FIRST HALF of it, not a single word was spoken between the two. Elven wasn't sure if it was because of how tired they were, or what they had experienced in Old Knuckle. There were some good people up in that town, but the poison of what Cora had done had infected everything she'd touched.

He wasn't sure there was any saving it, and he felt like Benson and Lila didn't stand a chance. But it was their home, their choice, and there was nothing he could have done to convince them otherwise.

If he were being honest, he thought if both he and Madds could forget about Old Knuckle altogether, it would be for the best. The only thing that he'd learned up there was what was truly important to him.

And she was sitting right next to him.

They'd taken one of the vehicles back in the lot right outside the small post office. Elven didn't recognize it, but he didn't question it when Madds picked it and tossed him the keys to drive. She seemed to know which one to go for, and he trusted her.

Trusted her.

That was something he didn't think he would ever feel toward her again. It felt good, and at the same time, it made him sad. Because he knew what he still had to do.

But he didn't have to do it yet. Not tonight, anyway.

About halfway on the drive down from Old Knuckle toward Dupray, Madds decided to break the silence. "I'm sorry," she said, her voice shaking with emotion. "I'm so, so sorry."

Elven looked over at her, and that's when he realized she had been crying. For how long? He wasn't sure. But she sure had the floodworks going now.

Elven pulled the truck over to the side of the road, nestling it between some trees.

"Hey," he said, looking her in the eye. "You didn't cause any of that. What happened up there wasn't your fault."

She shook her head. "No, I'm sorry for everything I did to you," she said. "I was scared. I didn't think I had a choice. And then Hollis said that he'd make sure I was safe."

"Madds," Elven said.

"And then I met you, and everything went to shit. I didn't know what to do anymore, and—"

"Madds," he said again, his voice rising. This time, he took her good hand into his, pulling her attention to him. "I know."

She looked confused. "You know?"

He nodded his head. "I know why you did it," he said. "I've always known. It was obvious with your ex and the cartel. It doesn't matter now."

"I know," she said. "Because in the end, I hurt you. And that's the last thing I ever wanted to do."

He shook his head. "No, it doesn't matter because I forgive you," he said. "I forgive you, you hear me?"

She sniffled. "You can't do that."

"I sure as heck can forgive you," he said. "And I forgive you for whatever you have done to me, or whatever you think caused me harm. I forgive you for everything that I'm able to forgive you for."

She stared at him like he was crazy. "But what about how I betrayed you? I *lied* to you. I fed Hollis information that caused cases to hit dead ends and not be solved."

He sighed. "I can't do anything legally about that," he said. "But being forgiven has nothing to do with legalities. In my heart, that's what I know."

She looked like she was about to cry again, but he reached over and wiped the tears before they had a chance to form fully. "It doesn't make sense," she said.

"Madds, all I know is that I was being too stubborn to see straight. I was angry, and I was hurt. But when I thought I was gonna lose you up there, I stopped my head from taking the lead and let this take over." He tapped his heart. "I love you, Madds. And I know that you're not the person Hollis wanted you to be. I saw the person you are up in that town."

She smiled. "I love you, too, Elven," she said. Her smile faded, dropping completely from her face. "But you still have your duty to do."

He swallowed, knowing that she wasn't wrong. "What if there was another way?"

"What do you mean?"

"I mean, what if you made a deal? You could flip on Hollis. You could get immunity."

She shook her head. "I can't do that. As much as he might deserve it, he's family. And I don't want to be looking over my shoulder all the time, thinking he might be sending someone for me. Besides, they've already got that idiot cousin of his to fill that role. They might not even bite."

He nodded. She wasn't wrong. Being the first to sing was usually the best. Everyone else just got sentenced, and Madds was part of the everyone else.

Another idea crossed his mind. One straight from his heart, not his head. But it felt like it could be right.

"Then I don't," he said.

"Don't what?"

"Turn you in," he said. "We run away together."

Madds's eyes widened. "Elven, you can't—"

"Why not?" he asked. "I'm not the sheriff anymore. I've got all the money we need. We just leave Dupray and don't come back. We can be together."

"You'd be okay with that?" she asked. "Leaving your whole life behind?"

"Madds, watching you rot in a prison cell when I feel this way about you, and knowing that it was me that put you there... well, I think that just might kill me," he admitted. "My heart can't take that."

Madds smiled and leaned in, kissing him. He held on for a bit longer, holding her right there in the truck. And then they pulled away.

"Okay," she said. "I'm in."

Madds woke up in the middle of the night. She looked over to Elven, who was still sound asleep. His steady, rhythmic breathing told her he wasn't going to wake up any time soon.

They'd gone back to the motel where he'd been staying since his home had burned down. There, they'd cleaned up, reconnected, and spent the rest of the night talking about what their life would look like when they left Dupray.

Eventually, they had grown tired and went to bed.

Madds had a wonderful night with Elven. All the different versions of their future life together were amazing to dream about. And he had the money to take them wherever they wanted to go. She had to admit, it sounded like the perfect life.

She watched him sleep. He looked peaceful, but she knew that leaving Dupray wasn't what he truly wanted or needed. He might be saying one thing, but there would always be a little part of him that would regret it.

Madds knew that, because she knew him.

Moving quietly, she got up and got dressed, determined that she wouldn't be the cause for Elven to change who he was. He was a good man and deserved better than that.

She slipped out the door without him ever knowing.

CHAPTER SEVENTY-THREE

ELVEN OPENED HIS EYES AS THE SUNLIGHT SHONE THROUGH THE window. He was immediately met with a sinking feeling in his gut. It might have been because of what he was talking about doing with Madds. But he meant what he said last night. He couldn't turn her in, knowing that she would be going to prison.

But running away also didn't feel right.

Part of him knew that last night's dreaming together was just that. A dream.

The right choice was the one that was going to break his heart. The one that he felt would kill him inside.

He couldn't run away with her.

He turned his head and saw that Madds wasn't there. He propped himself up on his elbows and looked around the room. "Madds?" he called. "You in the bathroom?"

There was no answer. The shower wasn't running. And the door was open with the light off inside the bathroom.

Madds wasn't in the room.

Elven shot up from the bed. Throwing his pants on, he ran to the door, ready to check to see if she was still outside or if she'd taken the truck somewhere. But then he saw the piece of paper that was on the floor. It must have fallen from the bed when he stirred awake.

He bent over, picked it up, and unfolded it.

Elven,

I loved dreaming about our life together, but I knew it wasn't going to happen. I think you knew it, too, deep down. But thank you for indulging me last night.

The truth is, you're a good man. And I've hurt you enough. For as much as you say that your heart can't take turning me in, well, my heart can't take knowing that I've compromised you.

You would have regretted it every day, and it would have torn you apart from the inside. You'd always wonder if you should have just handed me over. It's what would have been right, and it's what you should absolutely do.

Even though you might not be sheriff anymore, you can still do so much good here. They may not deserve you, but Dupray still needs you.

Besides, I'd still be running. That's how I got into this mess. Running from my ex, from the cartel, from you and the law. I'm done running.

So I'm taking the weight of the decision for you.

I love you, Elven Hallie. But I need to do what's right for both of us.

Love,
Madds

Elven folded the letter back up and sat on the edge of the bed. He wiped at his eyes where the tears welled up, knowing what she had done for him. She had taken the agonizing decision away from him, and she had saved him by doing it.

Madds took a deep breath as she opened the door to the station. The smell of the old carpet and coffee brewing brought all the memories back to her. She walked straight toward the desk, where Meredith sat typing away at something. The older woman didn't even bother to look up. Not until Madds said something, that is.

"Hi, Meredith," Madds said.

Meredith looked up and over her reading glasses. Her face dropped as soon as she recognized her. "Dear Lord," Meredith whispered.

"I'm here to turn myself in," Madds said, the weight from her chest lifting.

Be one of the first to know when the next book in the Sheriff Elven Hallie Mysteries is out by signing up here!

AFTERWORD

Thanks for reading Forsaken in the Forest, the eighth book in the Sheriff Elven Hallie mysteries.

This felt like a big book for me. Madds and Elven needed to have their story told in a way that made sense and was true to the characters. I feel like this did just that, and I hope you do, too!

There are so many more stories that are going to be told in the world of Dupray and with Elven at the helm, they just may look a little different. Hollis is in prison, Madds turned herself in, and he's not the sheriff anymore. I can't wait to explore the next chapters in Elven's world!

As always, thanks to my wife Sara, my two boys, my editor Chelsey Heller, Lisa Lee for proofreading, my sprinting buddy Doug Pratt for keeping me on task, and of course, all of you for reading and allowing me to continue with writing this series and do this full-time!

As I've said before, being an independent author, I don't have a huge publisher's budget, so reviews are very important. If you have the time, please consider popping over to Amazon, or your favorite place to leave reviews, and post one!

To keep up to date and get some fun freebies, join my reader's list:
http://drewstricklandbooks.com/readers-list/
-Drew Strickland
May 26, 2025

ALSO BY DREW STRICKLAND

Standalone Thrillers

Last Minute Guest

A Secret Worth Keeping

The Carolina McKay Series

Her Deadly Homecoming (Book 1)

Her Killer Confession (Book 2)

Her Deadly Double Life (Book 3)

Poaching Grounds (Book 4)

Winter's Obsession (Book 5)

The Nameless Graves (Book 6)

Bury Her Twice (Book 7)

The Sheriff Elven Hallie Mysteries

Buried in the Backwater (Book 1)

Murder in the Mountains (Book 2)

Hunted in the Holler (Book 3)

Abducted in Appalachia (Book 4)

Secrets in the Squalor (Book 5)

Vendetta in the Valley (Book 6)

Carnage in the County (Book 7)

Forsaken in the Forest (Book 8)

The Cannibal Country Series

The Land Darkened (Book 1)

Flesh of the Sons (Book 2)

Valley of Dying Stars (Book 3)

The Soulless Wanderers Series

Tribulation (Book 0)

Soulless Wanderers (Book 1)

Patriarch (Book 2)

Exodus (Book 3)

Resurrection (Book 4)

Coming Soon! (Book 5)

ABOUT THE AUTHOR

Drew Strickland is the author of the Sheriff Elven Hallie Mystery series, Soulless Wanderers: a post-apocalyptic zombie thriller series, and the co-author of the Carolina McKay thriller series and the Cannibal Country series, both written with Tony Urban. When he isn't writing, he enjoys reading, watching horror movies and spending time with his wife and children.

www.drewstricklandbooks.com